RAYLEIGH MANN IN THE COMPANY OF MONSTERS

RAYLEIGH MANN
IN THE COMPANY OF
MONSTERS

CIANNON SMART

HARPER

An Imprint of HarperCollinsPublishers

Library of Congress Control Number: 2022049067
ISBN 978-0-06-308125-3 (trade bdg.) — ISBN 978-0-06-337421-8
(special edition)

Typography by Chris Kwon
23 24 25 26 27 LBC 5 4 3 2 1

First Edition

Marley & Raphael,
I wrote this adventure for you

One's word is their bond, Dear Reader, and you must promise this—
Should the urge to look o'erwhelm you, resist, resist, resist.

Avoid wicker baskets and underneath beds,
For those be places they love to tread.
Those who hide so they might seek
A searching hand or unsuspecting feet.

For there monsters lurk, Dear Reader, we know this much is true.
If you find that you must look, for what you think is took, then I'm afraid so do you.

—Preface, *The Book of Night Things*

ONE

ALL TRICKS, NO TREATS

It wasn't yet five o'clock when the city began turning blue.

The bell on his bike's handlebar was a trigger beneath Rayleigh Mann's thumb, one he flicked in warning as he skidded around blind corners; he weaved between puddles from an earlier rainfall, dodging clusters of London's harried commuters. Beneath the indigo glow from streetlamps, their pinched brows were illuminated. People were concerned, no doubt, by nightfall's stealthy arrival. With autumn's early sunsets came the increased risk of missing curfew. It only took one delayed train. A missed bus. That friend or colleague who rambled a little too long. For everyone else, at least.

Rayleigh gritted his teeth, feet pumping at the existence of a far greater threat.

He had a phone call to intercept.

There were no fouler words a teacher could say to a student than *I'm phoning home.* They came second only to *I'll be assigning homework over the half-term break.* Rayleigh's teacher had in fact said both statements, after school. However, it was the first that galvanized him out of his seat as soon as detention ended and sent him running past his friends with a shouted promise to try and meet by the designated trick-or-treating spot later that All Hallows' Eve. Overhead, thunder rumbled through gray clouds; Rayleigh, clearing a zebra crossing at record speed, chanced a look upward. Across the city, lightning flashed.

Hold on. He willed the storm. Hold on.

It was a relief when Brutely Estate reared out of the fog. The highrise was a dull-gray blight against the darkening skyline, but it was home, which forgave it most of its sins. Rayleigh endured the short elevator ride to his family's top-floor flat with a snoring Clyde. The suited man was possibly a resident in the block (though perhaps not). This afternoon, Rayleigh didn't spare his company so much as a second look. Anticipation flooded his limbs when the doors pinged open, but he was no fumbling novice. Hopping over Clyde's prone limbs, Rayleigh took his keys out before he reached his family's corner flat. He took care not to jingle them as he opened the front door. His bike and bag he abandoned in the hallway with nary a whisper. A red light flickered in warning on the answering machine his mama had installed for moments such as this. Rayleigh bet Mr. Glower had delighted in leaving a message—almost as much as Rayleigh would delight in deleting it.

"Too late, boy."

Rayleigh flinched around with a yelp of surprise.

Erect in her mobility scooter at the end of the short entrance hall, Nana fixed Rayleigh with the Look, the one responsible for her notorious reputation around the estate for not giving a hoot about whose feet, or other wayward limbs, she ran over in her scooter. "I already heard the message."

"Let's not do anything hasty, now," said Rayleigh, his voice smooth and sure, having recovered from her ambush. "We both know I'm your favorite grandchild."

"By default, seeing as you're my only grandchild."

"I'll take it."

Something like a smile twitched on her mouth. "Did you really break a window?"

"It was an accident. I was participating in a class assignment." There may have been some screaming, and furious stop-this-right-now hand waving from his history teacher, before Rayleigh's monstrous papier-mâché boulder was fired from a rather brilliant catapult—but that was neither here nor there in the context of the conversation. "Medieval weaponry. Apparently it's dangerous stuff."

"Is that so?" The golden color of Nana's eyes had faded to a watery blue over time, but a fierce heat still blazed there regardless. One that raked across her grandson's features, probing for cracks in his well-tried armor.

"That's so." He wasn't lying, exactly. He didn't do that with his family.

Loopholes, though, he did those—*specialized* in those.

"What about the supergluing incident in science class?"

Rayleigh's confidence slipped. Dr. Ramsey called too?

"Well, that, Nana, wasn't my fault."

Not entirely, anyway. While he might have spilled something on his teacher's seat, Ramsey's trousers seemed to like it. Enough, in any case, that they parted ways with his legs in somewhat of a hurry, Rayleigh recalled. He suppressed a grin under Nana's scouring scrutiny.

"No? Then I think we can spare your mama the screams of an irate, and rather cold, from what I gathered, miser." Nana leaned over and hit the delete button, erasing the message. "I know I could have done without hearing about his exposed cheeks."

Rayleigh's sigh turned into a groan of deep disgust. "Where is Mama?"

"She called earlier." Nana paused as thunder rolled outside. "The conference is running late."

Last year Rayleigh might have whined, Again? But Mama had been working longer hours, he knew, for him. For the life she wanted him to have, in the future—away from their estate, free of elevators occupied by strange men perfumed with the stale tang of body odor and urine. Brutely had a strong community of wonderful people, but more often of late, the bad seemed to outweigh the good.

So he merely said, "Okay."

Nana withdrew a large square envelope from the pocket of her fleecy housedress and waved it at Rayleigh until he approached her to take it. "Your mama wanted to make sure you got that." With one touch of its gearstick, Nana turned her chair around. "And read it."

"Thanks," he called after her.

She paused to rotate her chair back around and repeated, "Read the card."

An amused Rayleigh shook his head. The envelope was unremarkable. White, plain. His name was written in Mama's neat cursive on the front, along with their address. He already knew what the card inside would say: I'll be home soon. Be good. Keep an eye on Nana—both eyes, in fact. And the one warning Mama always included: do not go out after curfew. Rayleigh weighed the envelope in his hand. It seemed a little heavier than usual. Mama likely included a list of chores for him to complete too.

Retiring to his bedroom, Rayleigh chucked the envelope on his bed and swiped up a sponge basketball. If he didn't open it now, technically, he wouldn't know not to meet up with his friends later, would he? Those chores would also go by unacknowledged.

He killed time practicing shots in the basket hanging behind his door. The netting whispered his victory again and again. Bowing for an imaginary audience, he considered it a good omen for the evening's trick-or-treating plans—something his phone's clock informed him it was about time for. He shot a quick message to the friends to confirm their meeting time and location. A couple minutes passed without replies. Not even from Phoebe. Small and loud, to make up for the former, she was unofficially in charge. The others usually waited until she added a message to their group chat before sending their own. No news from her must have meant everything was on as planned. Cool.

After changing into jeans and a hoodie—plus a heavier jacket, when more thunder boomed outside—Rayleigh slipped from his room with a practiced lightness of foot to check on Nana. In the living room, Nana was stationed in front of the television; a news show droned on, but her head was slumped down on her chest; soft snores rumbled through her nose. He bent his body this way and that, testing to see if she was faking it. He could never be too sure with her. But she didn't stir.

"Remember, Lights Out to Help Out is more important than ever this All Hallows' Eve," a reporter droned. "Despite the holiday, the government's initiative to combat climate change needs you indoors after six p.m.; stay off the roads and streets to keep our energy the happy kind of blue."

The clock that sat on the mantel beside a framed photo of his dad showed an hour till lockdown. Rayleigh had plenty of time to leave and return, sweets in hand.

"The true fright this Halloween," the reporter continued, "is that the discovery of the alternative energy source we rely on today, known as Volence, was meant to slow climate change. But in the thirty years since its development, it has proven unreliable, leaving our city in complete darkness by six p.m." He finished, "Keep a strong vigil out there tonight, folks. And now to Pete, with the weather."

Nana snorted. Rayleigh froze. Waited. She didn't wake. He backed away. Successful in his clandestine exit, he fished out the pillowcase and mask he'd stashed in his school bag last night. The stretched scarlet mouth of the clown leered up at him in triumph.

Happy All Hallows' Eve indeed.

Before the broad face of the setting sun, the estate's high-rises lifted from the ground like the stiff gray fingers of a giant zombie hand reaching for freedom. Fallen leaves in a spectrum of autumnal colors whispered past on a stinging breeze; with them came the loud chorus of jubilation as Brutely's residents gathered to celebrate before the storm broke. Or the first peal from the claxons stationed around the estate could warn of the approaching curfew.

Fidgeting from one foot to the other as trick-or-treaters blustered past with fat sacks of spoils, Rayleigh scanned the costumed crowd for his friends. He'd made the meeting time, a quick check of his phone confirmed. Perhaps they'd gone on without him. They planned an elaborate prank every Hallows' Eve. He'd never been part of it before, with Mama typically home. This was his first All Hallows' Eve out on his own; perhaps they forgot to invite him along tonight. Or they didn't want him there. Rayleigh had an itching suspicion that he might end up being on the receiving end of said prank. Not for the first time, he considered that *friends* might have been too strong a term for the regulars he met in detention.

The choice to set off alone became less difficult to make.

Despite the scare tactics in the news, there was never a safer time to venture out. Residents were more vigilant, given the holiday. The government liked to believe it was the extra police officers they stationed around the city to ensure trick-or-treaters made it home before curfew. They weren't new to Brutely. Passing a trio of gossiping officers, bright headlamps strapped across their brows, Rayleigh walked a little faster. While they stood as reminders of the folly of missing curfew, there were also the times he'd seen them hauling one person or another off in the back of their cars on the estate. Naturally his mind combined both scenarios—him being hauled off *and* missing curfew.

Fighting a shudder, he headed to the part of the estate that had houses, rather than high-rises. They were mostly occupied by older people, who took pity on him when they saw he was alone, giving him an extra dip in their bowls of spoils. Others, he reckoned, felt sorry for his lack of inventive costume.

It was, admittedly, among the weakest of efforts when a variety of monsters plagued the estate.

Sporting manes of spikes or grinning with mouths of crooked fangs, they were joined by wizards with spells flying out of homemade wands and warrior princesses with tiaras, who also carried bows and arrows; several ghosts had even illuminated the underside of their sheets with white fairy lights. The best costume, though, belonged to one of the adults.

Rayleigh came to a dead stop when he spotted the Volence-Corp engineer tinkering inside a lamppost's cavity. The man's black uniform, including a thick utility belt slung across his hips, looked like company standard issue. The large gunmetal-gray horns jutting from his wide brow and curling over his bald pate did not. Lightning flashed. In the violet light, there was something about the man that made goose bumps rise on Rayleigh's arms.

It wasn't just that he was as wide as the communal bins beside the lamppost, and tall enough to jump up and touch its rectangular bulb; coupled with the brown of his skin, as dark and rich as Rayleigh's, he looked like he'd decided to dress up as a particular Caribbean monster straight from Nana's collection of nightmarish tales, *The Book of Night Things*—a Rolling Calf. A terrible omen, in Nana's stories.

A ridiculous thought, of course.

Yet Nana's insistence that monsters were real, that she'd seen them growing up across various islands in the Caribbean, came to mind. Many of the monsters looked human, she would say. To better trick their prey. But the V-Corp employee was just a man in costume—a freakishly tall man, with a freakishly good costume. And Rayleigh was a Londoner: tough, pragmatic, in possession of very talented elbows, should he encounter something nefarious hiding in the dark. So with a defiant resolve not to listen to anything his nana said about monsters again, he moved on.

By now he was ready to rub his candy bounty in the faces of his friends—maybe not-friends, if they were planning to prank him. Either way, Rayleigh kept an eye out for them as he took the long way back to his tower block.

"Watch it!"

A body plowed into Rayleigh's with a force that stole his breath. Hands braced against his arms, but they didn't save him from slipping off the curb with a startled *oof*. And they certainly didn't save

one of his limited-edition trainers from plunging into a freezing puddle of murky water.

"You should be more careful," the voice admonished.

"You're telling me that?" Anguished, he tore his mask from his
face and gaped at the small, warm-brown-skinned girl who'd crashed
into him. "Who has the wet foot here?"

Almond-shaped eyes dipped; she winced. "Let me make it up to
you." Her accent was distinctly north of London. She was a tourist.

They were known far and wide to be a tricksy sort.

"I'm good," said Rayleigh. And he was. If good meant about to
combust. "I need to get home." If he had a hope of rescuing his
trainer, he had to leave ASAP.

Limping away from the girl, he freed his afro pick from his jacket
pocket, and restored the height to his hair the mask crushed. If only
fixing his trainer was so easy. Dogged by an uncomfortable awareness of the warming puddle water now oozing between his toes, he
hurried toward the alley that would take him home fastest. Wedged
between a line of garages and the windowless side of the first Brutely
high-rise, the solitary streetlamp didn't do much against the darkness. Or sudden influx of fog. Mama hated him walking there. Her
words of warning rang clear in his head when footfalls sounded
behind him, echoing off the cracked concrete, graffitied wall, and
corrugated metal that gave Brutely its reputation as one of the ugliest
estates this side of the Thames.

"Thought I'd walk back with you!"

Surprised, Rayleigh spun, wet sock squelching in his sodden
trainer. It was that girl. Again.

She jogged toward him with all the subtlety of a traveling percussion section, layered against the season's bite in her oversized leather

jacket and stomping combat boots.

"It's close to curfew, and you seem to know where you're going." She panted.

"Home." He shoved his afro pick back into his side pocket. "My home."

"That's fine." Hitching up beside him, she continued with, "I don't know anywhere around here. I'm visiting."

Rayleigh couldn't help snorting. "Why?" Regardless of the evening's high spirits, the estate housed more than a few individuals who did worse things than ruin a hot pair of trainers like this girl. There was a gang notorious for pinning people down to steal the kicks right off their feet.

"Well . . ." Her grin was sudden. A real jack-o'-lantern leer that curled the corners of her mouth up. "I came here—"

A patrol helicopter chose that moment to whirr overhead; its bright spotlight doused the estate in a happy blue light.

"What did you say?" Rayleigh hollered over the din.

"I said—" The girl whipped a length of rope out of her pocket and looped it around Rayleigh's left wrist. "I came here for you."

TWO

THE MONSTER UNDER THE SOFA BED

Rayleigh's first instinct, much to the girl's surprise, was to start laughing. Thunder followed in a riotous echo. "Which one of the crew put you up to this, then? Phoebe?"

"Nope. None of them." She said, wicked smile still in place, "Last I checked, they were all a little . . . tied up. Especially that Phoebe. She had a right gob on her."

The evening, heavy under a mantle of fog and the threat of more rain, became weightier still.

Phoebe's cheek was the best and worst part about her. Everyone on the estate knew that. But this girl said she was visiting. How would she know?

"Since you're wondering, yes," the tourist continued. "I meant tied up literally."

"I wasn't," Rayleigh said. But he was now. There was something about the look in the girl's eye, a glint of confidence Rayleigh knew he often bore himself, that left no room for disbelief, but plenty for confusion. "Who are you?"

"I'll be asking the questions tonight."

"Is that so." He kept his voice light, but disquiet squatted on his chest. She clearly wasn't after his trainers, having ruined one earlier. Maybe it was his candy she'd set her sights on. There was always a gang of kids roaming the estate on All Hallows' Eve, determined to steal spoils from unwitting trick-or-treaters. Either this girl was one of them or she was lying about Phoebe. She might be his friends' big prank. "How about you get on with it, then, North? I have places to be."

"Glad to," the girl said. "Where's your dad?"

Rayleigh blinked, confused. She'd have had more success asking him to name the international dish of Switzerland.

"No clue. Haven't seen him in ages."

"Liar-liar." The girl snatched at the rope, making him wince. "Tell me the truth."

"I swear." Rayleigh was actually being honest. And with a stranger he could have lied to, no less.

Aside from the yearly birthday and holiday cards from Robert Mann, Rayleigh had nothing to do with his father, and hadn't since he was a baby. Mama and Nana said his work for V-Corp kept him away. He was a big-shot manager for the various energy factories that powered London—soon the world, its founder, Luther Volence, promised.

Volence was as secretive as it was dangerous. Rayleigh had tried asking, begging even, to see his dad, but no luck. Eventually, he'd accepted that he had his mama and Nana. They were more than enough.

"Why d'you want to know?" he asked the strange girl, North, his brows lowering. Parents weren't something he discussed with his detention crew.

"You can't answer a question with a question," she hit back.

"I think you'll find you can't tie strangers up either."

"Look." She rolled her shoulders, gearing up for a fight, by the looks of things. Rayleigh reared back, wary of this off girl. "We can do this the easy way, or—" She opened the right side of her jacket, revealing a bum bag.

And just like that, Rayleigh's wariness was replaced by loud laughter. It condensed in the evening air like a mocking specter, a third participant in their odd little party.

"Or what? You'll lob your *fanny pack* at me?" Kids around the world knew the difference between being branded Fashionable or Parent on Holiday was the placement of a bum bag. Across the body was clearly the right way to carry one. Around the waist it became a fanny pack, and who wanted to be known for carrying one of those?

Being a tourist wasn't the worst of it. No doubt the girl was deranged too. He'd feel bad for her, if his left wrist wasn't beginning to chafe beneath her rope. While North harped on about whatever she had stuffed in that bag around her waist, Rayleigh took a surreptitious assessment of his surroundings. Finding Phoebe would put an end to her rubbish prank. Alas, he didn't see anywhere she might have hidden to watch her prank unfold. In fact, shadows thick enough to dim the reach of the alley's lone streetlamp loomed with menace. It was difficult to see much at all—until one pulled away from the others, twanged like a soundless piece of elastic, mammoth horns first.

"Wotcher."

The cockney hello echoed down the alley. The accent was that of a typical East End geezer, full of charm and swagger, and entirely no-nonsense. The girl stopped midsentence and whirled toward it. Her long dark curls whipped Rayleigh in the face.

"All right there?" It was the engineer from earlier, striding toward the duo with a seesawing gait that was all elbows and shoulders. "I've been looking for you."

"Let me guess, he's here because you probably pushed him into a puddle too," Rayleigh said tetchily. His left eye was sore and watering from the girl's hair. Though that pain was soon eclipsed by the sudden wail of the estate's claxons.

Boy, girl, and horned stranger stilled.

Brutely's curfew notification wasn't the quick peal of an emergency vehicle's siren, or even the annoying trill of a fire alarm. It was the deep throb of a funeral dirge, the insidious plod of something heavy making its way through the approaching dark.

In half an hour, another warning would sound.

After that, there would be no more.

"He's not here for me." North's voice was hoarse.

"Well, he's not here for me either. But I'll do the talking," Rayleigh decided, the warning ringing in his ears. The engineer was between him and his flat. Him and safety—him and *sanity*. "I'll make him leave."

"You won't go with your Snatcher?" the girl asked.

Rayleigh gasped at her. "I know you're not from here, North, but in this city, we don't go off with anyone we don't know. Especially not Snatchers. We run. Sometimes we run and yell. Loudly."

"My name's Marley, not North." Her frank appraisal turned to surprise, as though she was seeing him for the first time. "You don't know anything, do you?"

An indignant Rayleigh was waylaid from telling her how much he did in fact know by the weighty tread of the horned man. Wind puffed through the mouth of the alley, knighting the stranger with an eerie cloak of brume. Something that wasn't helping to contest his monster-like appearance, it had to be noted. Especially since he wore a pair of mirrored aviator sunglasses. Anyone sporting those at night was begging to be treated with suspicion.

Facing him, Rayleigh squared his shoulders. "You're the bloke from the bins."

The engineer stopped short. "That's . . . not how I'm often remembered, I must say."

"Well, I'm pretty sure I've never seen you anywhere else."

"Pretty!" He clapped two massive hands. "That's more like it. Though I tend to prefer handsome, dashing."

"Speaking of dashing," muttered Marley, giving the length of rope a tug.

The stranger's focus shifted to her. "And who are you?"

"I'm a friend."

"Not one of mine," Rayleigh said.

Marley cut a look his way. "I could have been," she muttered.

"And since we're not friends either, little one—" The stranger's manner transformed from loose and cordial to tight and watchful as he addressed Marley. He unclipped a long metal cylinder from his belt. "I think it's time you make like a leaf."

"I wouldn't, Snatcher," Marley singsonged, a hand on that fanny pack and the threat of insurgence emblazoned across her brow. "I'm not going anywhere without what I came here for."

Somewhere between being impressed and baffled, Rayleigh

assessed his odd companion anew. She didn't seem older than his twelve years. Though she did have a sort of rough and ready look about her that he was without. Country versus city. Perhaps it was the beat-up old jacket. It made her look like a girl who'd lived and wasn't afraid of what the world had in store. Where had his friends found her? But, more importantly, what did he have to do to lose her?

"This is the only time I'll ask." A streak of brilliant white energy erupted from inside the stranger's canister. It sparked and crackled like a bolt of the lightning that zigzagged through the fog at his back; its tip was honed into a merciless point, like—like a *sword*. "Step away from the boy."

Rayleigh flung his tied wrists over his eyes to combat the weapon's dazzle—an honest to goodness sword. In East London. Hang on. Did the man say "the boy"? Him? He wanted to help *him*? Help him into the back of a van, Rayleigh would bet.

Instead of doing as ordered, Marley sprang forward and launched a small vial from her right hand. With a lazy grace, the sword rose to meet it. Whatever was thrown burned away in an explosion of purple smoke, the kind seen in movies or wafting from cars filled with teenagers parked up in one of Brutely Estate's lots.

"You missed." The man took a step forward, and—stopped, froze, like someone had hit a remote and paused him.

Rayleigh understood why people rubbed their eyes when faced with something unbelievable. It didn't help, though. Not the first time, or the second.

Marley dusted off her hands. "They never think to look at their feet."

Shattered glass sparkled around the stranger's boots from a

second vial; a soft gray smoke slinked up his legs, his torso. It twined itself around his arms, neck, head, and horns. Denser than the fog, it moved with the predatory elegance of a python, and seemed to have trapped him in his immovable state. Eyes rubbed raw by now, Rayleigh blinked, stupefied. He had to admit this was way too elaborate a prank for the crew from detention to pull off. They couldn't be trusted to hold a pencil the correct way up, if one end didn't have an eraser.

Who were these people?

"We need to leave before he can—" Marley halted in surprise when she clearly didn't find the rope in hand—or Rayleigh, whose legs, as it so happened, were just as talented as his elbows.

Much as the engineer hadn't watched his feet, she too had been distracted enough to let something important slip from her hands. Rayleigh.

Devouring the last twenty meters or so to his high-rise door, he whipped his keys out and slammed the fob against the sensor. Throwing his body through, he flung it shut behind him.

Moments later, Marley grabbed the handle and gave it a vicious tug. "I saved you!" She banged her fists against the glass. "Let me in!"

"That was cool, whatever it was—" It was also weird. "But I'd go now if I were you." He pointed over her shoulder; his pillowcase of treats swung in his grip. The girl looked back at the stranger, who was stirring—thawing like a prehistoric relic warmed by a ray of sunlight.

Landing a look at Rayleigh that promised a continuance, she bolted into the night.

Before the horned man spotted him, Rayleigh split too. By the time he made it to the door of his flat, adrenaline had given way to the shakes. He opened and closed his left fist. It was slightly numb. What happened had to be a case of mistaken identity, a Halloween prank meant for someone else, orchestrated by someone with far more talent than Phoebe and the others. Elaborate, and rather cool, it almost made him wish he paid more attention to Dr. Ramsey during science class.

In the flat's hallway, Rayleigh paused before the sideboard. Mama's envelope, the one he'd left on his bed, was now propped up against the overflowing basket of mail. Frowning, he took it up and proceeded to the front room—where he found something else amiss. Nana was gone; in her place before the television, a hulking stranger was seated.

Forget Halloween being affiliated with night of the living dead. Rayleigh was experiencing a night of never-ending strangers. Had he forgotten they were having guests over? He glanced back down the hallway. Nana's umbrella, the one she used to knock objects down from shelves in shops, was gone. She disliked guests as much as he did. But to leave him alone with them? They had an unspoken pact when it came to friends and family who stayed far too long, ate way too much, and never seemed to take the hint when it was time to go. Stick together. Always.

Quietly, so as not to give himself away to the stranger, he slipped a finger beneath the envelope's seal. Perhaps Mama wrote to tell him about their guest. Two slips of thick paper fell out of a folded card. The first looked like an invitation to some sort of ceremony during his half-term break. He skipped over that, allergic to anything vaguely institutional while on holiday. The second slip was a diagram of a kid who looked a lot like Rayleigh falling down a dark chute. He paused on that, his bottom lip between his teeth as he tried to work out what it meant. Giving up (any activity that required serious brain power was also to be ignored until half-term break was over), Rayleigh opened the card; it was as plain as the envelope. Inside it read:

> My darling boy,
> My treat to you, this *All Hallows' Eve*, has been twelve years in the making.
> I love you.
> Behave.
> —Mama

Frown deepening, Rayleigh's eyes shifted to the question mark in the leather jacket seated in the front room. Suspicion felt as uncomfortable as the dirty water in his trainer.

Were they being burgled?

Albeit by a thief who preferred streaming over ransacking the place in search of nonexistent family jewels. What a night. Trouble: it was like Rayleigh couldn't help attracting it in waves. Shoving the contents of Mama's envelope in his pocket, he retreated into the hall for the landline, his focus never straying from the stranger, who was laughing at something on the TV. And not quietly either, the brazen swindler. When Rayleigh's back hit the wall, it was with a certain amount of relish that he hit the speed dial for one of their downstairs neighbors. Big Paul was a minor celebrity in the lucha libre world, and a personal friend of Nana's. With his wrestling skills, he'd have this thief sorted in a—

A hairy hand seized the phone from over his shoulder. "What's this, then?"

Rayleigh wheeled around, a shout trapped in his throat.

What he'd assumed to be a wall was, in fact, a second burglar. The lurcher turned the phone over in their large hands. They were coated in hair that was twin in color to the first burglar's—*he* was coated in it—but unlike his counterpart in front of the television, he was wearing nothing else. Was he supposed to be a yeti? Bigfoot? Small, dark eyes narrowed behind a mask so realistic, it was creepy.

"Do you know," breathed Rayleigh, "I think they were calling for you."

The burglar's eyes dipped to the phone; Rayleigh made a break for the door.

"Not so fast."

Rayleigh choked as his hoodie cut into his neck. His fingers scrabbled to separate fabric from skin, but the burglar reeled him in by his hood with quick, sharp tugs that cut off his air.

"Hey, Wrong! Get off your lazy butt, I've got him."

The television clicked off; thudding footsteps made their way to the hall. Spots danced across Rayleigh's vision as his eyes bounced between the thieves, widening. They were twins. Identically costumed Bigfoots—Bigfeet?

Rayleigh reared back as they both leaned in and sniffed him. "Hey!"

The one without the jacket nodded, confident. "This is the kid Marley's been following."

North.

Rayleigh might have snarled.

"She's carried his scent home. Trust me, I'm Right."

"Yes, you are."

Laughing like a pair of jack-in-the-boxes, they slapped a high five. Before Rayleigh could make it clear he had nothing to do with tourists, his front door opened. Marley stepped inside.

Flashing him a quick censoring look, she addressed his captors. "He's not the one you're looking for."

Rayleigh's face went slack. So she was in on whatever this was with whoever these people were. But not with the stranger outside. The horned man who also wanted him, for some reason. Rayleigh's head was beginning to spin.

"What's going on?" he demanded.

"You sure?" Wrong asked Marley, ignoring Rayleigh.

"Nah," his twin returned. "Sure's our cousin. This is Marley, our little sis. And as our little sis, sis, we know when you're lying."

There was a moment of tense stillness. Rayleigh eyed the Bigfeet and Marley, their sister, apparently. Her hand crept toward her fanny pack, but the twins were faster. One lunged forward and grabbed her by the scruff of her leather jacket.

"Especially since we already know you're a *thief*. This is mine!" The twin tried for the fanny pack around her waist; Marley kicked out and caught him on the elbow with one of her boots. He roared in pain. "I say we bring them both in!"

"And I say, you're not Wrong."

"No, I'm Right."

Rayleigh bared his teeth at Marley while her brothers fell about laughing, again. This madness was her fault. Some odd family affair he, for reasons beyond his understanding, had been drawn into.

"What is going on?" he bellowed.

"We were getting to that, little Mann," said the leather-jacket-wearing twin. "Tell us, where's your dad?"

There was a grinding clash of metal against metal; the sofa bed in the front room opened upward like a yawning mouth. From the new opening, the horned man from the alley stepped out and into view, peeling a stray sock from one of his horns as casually as one might remove a piece of lint.

"Why don't you raspberry tarts try picking on someone your own . . . ah." His impressive height was rendered almost normal before the Bigfoot burglars. "No matter. It's not the size that counts, it's how you use it." And with that, he pointed his metal canister at the twins and fired two fizzing orbs of light.

THREE

DON'T SCREAM

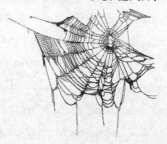

Right dived with a yelp. Freed, Rayleigh threw himself onto the runner and shielded his head with his arms. The orbs smashed through the wall overhead. Plaster and paint rained down like shrapnel. Number thirty's dog started barking down the hall; it was fast joined by flat twenty-eight's.

"You all right, Nephew-mine?"

"Nephew what?" coughed Rayleigh, looking up.

The horned man charged through the dust haze. "Wasn't there some kind of card that explained who I am?"

"Never mind that now. Hurry up and *move*." Marley hoisted Rayleigh up and away from her brothers as they untangled their long limbs and clambered onto hairy feet.

"You made a mistake coming here, Grandpa," one of them jeered. Possibly Right, though their decision making was decidedly wrong, before the stranger with the weapon.

"Grandpa?" The man chuckled. "Clearly I did make a mistake. I was ready for a real fight, not a pitiful attempt at bruising my ego."

In the same casual manner that he seemed to do everything else, he fired a single ball of light from his weapon. It caught Right in the stomach. He flew back down the hall and crashed through the front door in an explosion of wood. "Pillock," the man muttered.

"Hey!" Rayleigh shouted. "You're ruining my flat!"

The man winced. "Everything is under control. Mostly."

"Oh, yeah?" Still standing, Wrong reached into a fanny pack like Marley's around his waist and unleashed a slim vial. He popped the cork, and aubergine smoke oozed out. Slinking down the container's sides, it coalesced into something spindly and sharp that stood on two feet—a creature of smoke and nightmares. Emerald eyes glinted in its cheap impression of a face, one that swirled and eddied like a storm cloud as it advanced with slow, careful steps.

Rayleigh's instinct, hardened by city living though it was, told him to make a run for it. Something weird was going on, and he wanted no part of it.

"Nephew-mine," said the horned man, tossing his canister from his left to right hand. "Do you recognize this beast?"

"Please don't call me that."

"Well, do you?"

Nana's *Book of Night Things* might have had a similar illustration, he thought. So what?

"You expect me to believe that thing's a monster?"

"As much of a monster as I am." The man cocked his head to the side, sunglasses flashing. "But then, you already knew that, didn't you?"

Gooseflesh pimpled across Rayleigh's skin.

He thought back to the lamppost outside; how eerie the engineer had looked in the fog. His feeling of unease took on a new significance in his flat that was currently filled with strangers wielding things he could only explain as . . . unexplainable. He was beginning to think, however wild, however mad, that they weren't wearing costumes.

"We're out of time for reading, gov." The lightning sword from the alley snarled its way into existence from the man's canister. In the Mann family's humble flat, it seemed even bigger and more threatening, as otherworldly as the beast on clawed feet before them. "These interlopers shouldn't be here. Me on the other hand, I'm here on behalf of your old man."

Rayleigh felt the blood drain from his face. That made three mentions of Robert Mann in one night.

"He wants to see you."

"He does?"

"Sorry. I think there's been a mistake," the twin still standing said, with no small amount of awkwardness. "This is a Snatching?"

"What did you think it was?" the man asked.

"Not that. Let me just—I'll recork the thing. Yeah. We have a few more seconds before it attacks. I didn't mean to get in the way of your work, man."

"I'll get to you and your pet in a moment," the horned stranger said, with no small amount of irritation, before turning back to Rayleigh. "Will you trust me, Nephew-mine?"

"Trust you?" His voice was hoarse with disbelief. "I don't even know who you are. Who any of you are!"

"Get down!"

At Marley's shout, Rayleigh ducked. A clawed hand sank into the wall where his head had been with a hollow thud. He twisted away and surged to his feet. Growling, the creature from the vial had finally come fully alive, snapping a jaw filled with sharp little teeth as it fought to free itself from Sheetrock.

"Oh—that's not supposed to happen." The twin fumbled with the bottle, the cork.

"Because it's not a genie! For fright's sake. Clear out of it!" Lethal as a tank, the horned man drove in. The smoky monster lashed out with its free hand. It caught him in the face. His head snapped to the side so fast his glasses flew off and clattered against the floor, breaking with a crunch of glass and metal. He rallied with a chuckle. Dodging another swipe, the man moved in low. Swinging his weapon up in a powerful arc, he sliced through the creature; light defeated darkness too fast for the monster to scream. If indeed it was a monster. Rayleigh didn't know which way was up anymore.

"Definitely made a mistake." Wrong winced. "I think I'll—I'll see myself out." He took one look at the slain beast, twitching its way to a silent death, and hightailed it down the hallway.

"That's your first sensible decision of the evening!" the man called after him.

"You coming, Marley?" the twin asked, framed by the wreckage that was the front door.

"Not with you two idiots."

Shrugging, he tucked his arms under his comatose brother's armpits and dragged him down the hall. "We were only trying to help," he explained, dark eyes flickering between Rayleigh and the horned man, whose weapon was still aloft, before he disappeared from view.

"Help with what?"

In answer to Rayleigh's question, Marley rolled her eyes over to the horned man, who scoffed.

"My question exactly," he said. "What do you get with two pillocks?" With the click of a button, his sword withdrew. "Nothing but a headache. Honestly, Hallows' Eve brings all kinds of weirdos to the fore," he stated, as though he wasn't one of many weirdos Rayleigh had encountered this evening. "Now then, you wondered who I am, Nephew-mine?"

Rayleigh sucked in a sharp lungful of air as the man looked his way. His eyes were a deep gold, a brown touched by perpetual sunlight—just like Rayleigh's own.

Like the fierce eyes of his father in the photo on the mantel.

"Thelonious Tickle, at your service." He bowed his head. "Ick to my enemies and exes, but to my admirers, Chief of the Terrors, Second-Class Eldritch Honors, and Patron to the One-Horned League of Creatures and Critters. Pleased to meet you, kid, at long last."

Rayleigh could only stare at those eyes, at the thick eyebrows above them that he too sported; at the quirk of a mouth so like Nana's—his paternal grandparent. This man was so close to the picture of Robert Mann on the mantel, Rayleigh might have been convinced it was him, had he not introduced himself as someone else. His uncle. Rayleigh's heart was thumping in his chest, hard enough that he wondered if the man could hear it along with the thunder outside.

"Was it the titles?" Thelonious took another pair of mirrored aviators from one of his pockets and put them on. "They can be a bit of a mouthful." He scratched the tip of his left horn. "Though I suppose they might have been in your mama's card."

"They weren't."

"No? Thought Drea might have mentioned me at least. Nothing about the horns?"

"Where is Mama? Nana? And my dad, you said—you said he wants to see me?"

"Whoa." Thelonious raised his hands. "The first two are safe. A Snatching's easier without the human guardians around. Not to mention without *my* mother being around. And your dad—"

"I'm sorry. A what?"

"Told you he was a Snatcher," muttered Marley.

Thelonious cringed. "I suppose this isn't a good time to circle back to that question about trust?"

"Hate to break up the family reunion." Marley leveled a finger down the hallway. "They're not supposed to do that, are they?"

The quivering halves of the creature had graduated to violent jerks. An arm shot free from its wounded side with a squelch, pungent bodily fluids splashing. Rayleigh and Marley recoiled. The monster was growing out of its halves, regenerating.

"No clue." Thelonious frowned. "Come this way." The children were ushered further down the hall off the front room, which led to the bedrooms. "Mind giving us a bit of space?" Thelonious asked Marley. Looking from him to the monsters, she scowled, took a small step away, and turned her back. "All right, Nephew-mine, this might sound strange, even unbelievable—actually, it's probably not that hard to catch on to after the night you've been having. Look, as long as there have been humans—"

"There have been monsters?" Dazed, Rayleigh shook his head. "That's from Nana's *Book of Night Things*."

"It is. If the old bird's been reading that with you, then you'll know all cultures have their own creatures of the moon, monsters of the night, beasties of the shadows. What you won't know is that most of them call subterranean cities in the Confederation of Lightless Places home—most of us, that is." He bowed his head. "You buying what I'm selling?"

"No."

"No?"

"Monsters don't exist." Though his words were stated with a calm surety, Rayleigh couldn't help looking sideways in the direction of the regenerating creatures in the hall. "They can't. If they did—"

"Rulers around the world would make up excuses to introduce curfews? Ones that keep people inside at night? They'd put out special bobbies on the beat, headlamps strapped across their brows, to keep watch in the dark?"

"The patrols and curfews are to preserve energy and keep us safe from darkness," insisted Rayleigh. "They keep us safe from the idiots taking advantage of the darkness. That's what the prime minister said."

"Which?"

"What?"

"Which one did he say? Are you keeping out of the darkness, or are you avoiding criminals?"

"Both? I don't know. I'm *twelve*."

"Twelve or not, I thought you'd know better," Thelonious mused. "Criminals are the least of London's worries once the sun goes down. I thought, if the old bird's been reading you the stories, you wouldn't rely on what you're being told. You'd trust what's in there." He touched Rayleigh's forehead. "Because I know you've wondered about that itch. The one satisfied by mischief and mayhem. By the supersized catapults and superglue. Didn't you ever want to know where that monstrous urge to create chaos came from? It isn't the sort of thing born from light, Nephew-mine. *Thems that do know what it means to walk in the dark.*"

Further arguments staled on Rayleigh's tongue.

What was it Mr. Glower said when he told him off earlier? *Wrong will always be wrong.* Mama was formidable, there was no doubt about it, but she exuded warmth and smiled in a way that made others reciprocate. Most teachers frowned when Rayleigh came around. A few even cried when they faced the entirety of his detention crew. Rayleigh knew long ago that whatever miscreant bone he had that attracted trouble, craved it sometimes, wasn't from Mama.

"If you're a monster, a monster," he said, the words heavy and awkward between his lips, "is Nana?" Thelonious nodded with an encouraging smile. "And my dad?"

"He is too."

Rayleigh's stomach twisted itself into knots a sailor would have been proud of. In *The Book of Night Things*, monsters, no matter whether they were from the Caribbean, or elsewhere, were agents of shadow and misery who enjoyed tormenting their enemies. If his dad's side of the family were all monsters . . . well, it certainly gave new meaning to Nana's dark cackle at being known as that demon on wheels around the estate.

It also stood to pattern that Rayleigh was a monster too.

He couldn't bring himself to say it out loud.

"Why so glum, gov?" Thelonious asked. "Is it the whole 'monsters are evil' thing? Listen, we aren't all the wicked beings stories present us as."

"He's not lying," Marley pitched in over her shoulder. "They scare kids straight, so they don't grow up to become real-life monsters, like murderers or grown-ups who wear sandals with socks. Might not look like it with those horns," she said, sending a disparaging look Thelonious's way. "But they're the good guys."

"And your old man?" added Thelonious. "He's *the* good guy."

A discordant assault of snarls drew their attention back to the severed monsters.

The monsters held themselves aloft on spindly arms, jaws snapping. A tiny stubby leg stretched itself into being from both halves, oozing something foul over the runner.

"Oh, yeah," murmured Rayleigh. "Regular heroes they are."

"Not them. Your old man is, though. And I can prove it to you, but we're kind of against the wire here, Nephew-mine. There'll be plenty of time for stories once we get below pavement. Will you trust me on that?"

Rayleigh took a long, hard look at the man—his uncle. "You're serious about all this?"

"As a Knickerbocker Glory with two cherries on top."

Rayleigh gave himself permission to think about that bridge. The one he always imagined between him and his dad. Something like happiness bloomed in his chest. His dad hadn't avoided him his entire life. He was a good guy, a hero.

People who looked like Rayleigh and his family weren't seen as heroes, traditionally. And kids like him definitely weren't heroes. The word hummed, pulsating with possibility—with promise. It sparked through Rayleigh's skin, his bones, crackling in his fingertips like something he could shape and hold.

"Nephew-mine?"

Meeting his dad must have been what Mama's strange bundle

of cards alluded to. The man whose absence she'd always explained away; the man he'd wondered about from time to time; enough that, now he had the chance, he wanted to see. Very much. While he didn't want to leave Mama and Nana, they had practically given him permission to go. And he'd be back. Right?

"I'll be back, right?" he checked.

"Whenever you want. You can see your mama, the old bird. Your friends too," Thelonious added.

His friends. "Hey, did you really tie them up?" he asked Marley.

"The rope isn't tight," she said over her shoulder. "They can get free. They might be already."

They hadn't stood Rayleigh up after all. But that didn't change the fact that he wouldn't have been surprised if they had. He'd never wanted a fresh start away from them, but now it was here and, with it, a chance to see his dad—it was time to cross the bridge.

"I'll come," he told Thelonious. "But only if I get the full story as soon as we get below . . . pavement?"

"Below-London. And yes, of course. Tip top!" Thelonious clapped his hands. "Now, do you have a washing hamper, or an underbed space?"

"Hello!" Marley turned, arms splayed. "What about me?"

That was a good point. "Why are you still here?" Rayleigh asked.

"Yeah. Didn't you hear me earlier?" Thelonious waved goodbye. "Hit the road, kid."

"I just helped you out, Mr. Tickle, and I saved you from my brothers, Rayleigh."

"You brought them to me," Rayleigh corrected her. "Get home safe now."

Exasperated, Marley turned to Thelonious. "With all due respect, you can't leave those monsters here."

Almost entirely whole, the monsters watched them with wicked eyes from down the hallway, as if weighing up the best course of attack after the failed first round.

"And you can't let Rayleigh travel to Below-London alone. It's his first time. He could end up anywhere."

"I'm sure I'll be fine," Rayleigh defended himself. "I've taken the tube before."

Thelonious sighed. "Actually, she's got a point there, gov."

An incandescent triumph blazed across Marley's heart-shaped face.

"London's transport system only spans the city," Thelonious went on to say. "The system you'll be taking is the Vol-way. It connects countries around the world. You two go on ahead. I'll meet you both as soon as I'm done here. You got that, girl?" Thelonious's expression grew stern. "Don't make me come looking for you." Blanching, Marley nodded. "Take the West Begetter Vol-way." He dug a hand in his jacket pocket and tossed a coin to each child. "You'll need these."

Rayleigh turned it over in his palm. Hexagonal, its silver center was bordered with rose gold. *Vol-trix Token—Admission 1* was incised across its middle. A profile of a bald man—who might also be the cousin of a walrus, considering the gigantic tusks—graced its back.

"Get on with you, now." Thelonious took up position in the center of the hallway, facing down the monsters. The sword barreled out of the canister once more. Lowering his horns, he dragged a booted foot back once, twice.

The last thing Rayleigh saw before slamming his bedroom door shut was his new uncle breaking into a run. Thelonious's sword spun before him in a sparking cyclone. Strangest of all, he wore a half smile on his face.

"Let's get out of here," Marley breathed, with an air of relief.

"Give me a minute." Reaching for the afro pick he kept on his bedside table, Rayleigh sank down on his bed and ran through his hair with slow, measured movements. It was how he thought best. Something slid into his thigh—*The Book of Night Things*. Pausing the comb, he picked it up; the weighted ends of its ribbon book-marks clacked rhythmically against one another. When his dad was a boy, its cover might have been a rich indigo, the letters gold foil. Over the years the grandeur had peeled and faded, replaced by the worn look of something that was well loved—or often consulted.

The stories and legends were scribed by hand, different hands, making it more of a record than a book of fairy tales. More than one person had captured stories; some even added illustrations. He'd never considered that some of them could have been written by his dad. Nana must have left the book in his room, knowing what the evening would bring for him. But then . . . why hadn't he?

Why hadn't he known about his dad, his monstrous heritage, any of it?

In fact, where was his dad? Why wasn't he the one picking Rayleigh up?

"You don't need to pack anything," said Marley as she rooted through the junk on a dresser. "None of this stuff will be any good Below."

Approaching a stage of thinking that required him to be on his feet, mobile, Rayleigh sprang up. "So are you a monster too?" he asked, making sure his phone was secured in his back pocket.

"Mostly," was her answer. "Does that freak you out?"

"I'd say it fits."

Marley's forehead wrinkled, like she couldn't tell if he was insulting her or not.

Rayleigh wasn't sure either. Still ticking things over, he changed into his lucky leopard-print socks and stuffed his feet into his second-favorite pair of trainers. The pair he wore tonight would be left to ruin. A shame. No, a crime. One that couldn't be helped.

Despite what Marley said about his Above-London stuff, he grabbed a small backpack and threw *The Book of Night Things* inside; he also packed his pillowcase of treats and a couple picks for his hair.

He glanced around his room one last time. He'd never traveled away from home before. Outside he could hear the clash and crash of furniture, suggesting there wouldn't be much left of it when he returned—because he would. He was only going to meet his dad, the good guy. So good, in fact, that he'd sent his brother to collect the son he hadn't seen in twelve years instead of going himself.

"It's best not to think." Marley waved a contemplative Rayleigh over to the hamper. "You have your token? Toss it inside."

A second after it landed in the basket, the clothing began to swirl around the coin, slowly at first and then faster until they twisted their way into a vortex of shadows. A warm breeze blustered up and out of the wicker basket. The air in the room crackled with a stormlike energy. Rayleigh clenched his shaking fists, willed his heart to calm its drum solo.

"West Begetter Vol-way," instructed Marley, in a clear voice. "Right, keep your arms folded across your chest in an X; jumping from one place to another via Vol-ways tends to produce a velocity that will rip any wayward limbs from their sockets."

"What?"

"Arms!"

Rayleigh gripped both shoulders. "Just—hang on!"

"Don't worry. Vol-way commuters hardly break bones anymore. They fixed the gravitational pull."

"We'll come back to that," Rayleigh remarked, eyes darting to the clothing hamper. "Look, is it weird that my dad wants to see me but isn't here?"

Edging around the hamper, Marley didn't say anything.

"You came to London looking for him, so did your brothers." His mind, a marvel to few and a menace to most, built a puzzle that was a few pieces short. "If everyone's looking for him . . . where is he?" He turned to look at where Marley now stood at his back, twisting her mouth like she was chewing on a secret. "Was he meant to be picking me up? Hey—is that man, Thelonious, really my uncle?"

"Yes."

"Yes to which?" His eyes narrowed. "What do you know?"

"Only that you shouldn't scream," she said. "You never know what you might wake."

And with that, she shoved him squarely in his side.

With his arms folded, Rayleigh was unable to steady himself. Startled, he toppled sideways too fast to yell as the washing basket gaped open and swallowed him whole.

FOUR

WHO'S YOUR DADDY?

Traveling via washing basket was like skydiving, at night, without a parachute.

In short, Rayleigh wouldn't recommend it.

He never quite managed to yell, not with the screeching winds sucking all moisture from his mouth as he hurtled through darkness, buffeted and tumbled like a loose sock in a dryer. But that wasn't to say he didn't want to. He couldn't believe Marley had pushed him headfirst into, well, something he didn't fully understand. She'd been right about one thing, though: inside his hamper was nothing like the tube. The tube used trains; the Vol-way seemed to consist of air alone; that was all he could glean in the dark. Half of him worried he'd never feel solid ground beneath his feet again, and the other half was concerned about impact. He didn't want to break a bone. Or, worse still, ruin another trainer.

As it turned out, he needn't have worried. Unbidden, the winds slowed from a tumult to a light breeze; he found himself cradled safely to the ground—at which point his legs collapsed beneath him. The crackle of something breaking made Rayleigh roll onto his side in a panic. Brazier flames roared to life in brilliant flares of light. The nearest wall sconce illuminated his destroyed mobile phone as he pulled it out of his back pocket. In pieces. With a half-hearted effort, Rayleigh tried to turn it on. No dice.

As far as first impressions went, Below-London wasn't winning any awards. Not any notable ones, anyway. He'd landed in what seemed to be a vast disused tunnel. Its stone walls arched up around him like, he noted with some annoyance, a train tunnel. Darkness loomed before him, endless and deep, just like the tube stations back home. Admittedly, there was no platform, no tracks. What it did have, unfortunately, was the musty tang of the charity shop near Brutely. A potent cocktail of old clothes, vacant despair, and dead things. It was, without a doubt, a dump. A never-ending dump that stretched into unknown shadowy depths to the left and right.

Did Marley give the wrong instructions back at the flat? And speaking of the tourist—where was she? Thunder rumbled overhead; Rayleigh looked to his left and right for the source of the sound, ready to run at the appearance of a train. Noise echoed once more, but from above. He looked up. Shadows met in the center of the ceiling like a living net of dark cobwebs. It was not unlike the roiling inside of his hamper before Rayleigh was shoved inside. He threw an arm over his eyes as dust clouded, squinting up as something drifted out of the Vol-way—someone.

Thelonious landed on his feet, coattails flapping behind him, kicking up dirt that squalled around his boots. He nodded at his nephew. "Made it in one piece, then."

"Of course. Piece of cake." Mostly. Rayleigh cleared his throat. "Where's Marley?"

"Gave her a dud token." Thelonious chuckled. "I have some friends on their way over to your flat now for cleanup. They'll make sure she gets home safely. I wouldn't worry. Now." He puffed his chest out. "Rayleigh Jude Mann," he said, his voice weighted with meaning. "On this night, your twelfth All Hallows' Eve, when the veil between worlds is thin, you've been Snatched via proxy to meet your monstrous parent and begin—"

"About that," Rayleigh interrupted. "You're my real uncle."

"Is that a question?"

"Can you take your sunglasses off again?"

Chuckling, Thelonious dipped his shades, exposing those bright eyes before raising the lenses once again. "Of course I'm your real uncle. How many strangers do you have telling you they're family?"

"Well, you're the first. Why didn't my dad come and get me himself?"

Thelonious flattened a large hand over his heart. "You wound me."

"The horns are great and all, it's just . . ." Like the city he hailed from, Rayleigh was used to the grit in life. Something had to be wrong. It always was. And he liked his bad news up front. "Marley asked about him, her brothers too, and he's not here. Should he be?"

"Don't concern yourself with the Liu family. There are these treasure hunts Below-London, a set of them. They were created by this bloke who clearly had too much time on his hands. Anyway, none of the hunts have been completed, and some of the participants can get a bit more fanatical about winning the financial prizes than others. Finding Bogey tends to play a big role in them. He's badgered for photos, chunks of hair, and other items I can't bring myself to mention, so hunters can progress to the next level."

Rayleigh frowned. "What?"

"Don't say I didn't warn you, Nephew-mine, but if you really want to know—"

"Not that. Did you say Bogey? Bogey . . . Mann?"

Thelonious's smile was slow, catlike. "That I did."

"You call my dad Bogey here, not Robert?"

"Yup."

"That's kind of nasty."

Thelonious laughed. "Bogey *Mann*. They go together like peanut butter and jelly. Marmite and pickles. Jam and clotted cream. It's a title, Nephew-mine, recognized globally. In the Confederation, we bestow it on the most fearsome monster in the world. It's only carried by one at any given time. And right now, your old man is the Bogey Mann, Supreme Scarer for the entire Confederation of Lightless Places."

An army of goose bumps rose across Rayleigh's body, with the kind of rapidity that burned away his lingering doubt faster than igniting the head of a struck match. He didn't understand every title, but he understood what they signified.

He understood it was time to say out loud that which he couldn't before.

"I'm a monster too, aren't I." He managed to avoid touching his forehead to check for horns.

Thelonious tipped his head to the side. "You don't sound best pleased about it. Nephew-mine, this is the start of the rest of your life. Well, not this place. This Vol-way is a sort of between place, a stopgap. The equivalent of an out-of-service station in your tube system. Were it not for Stupid, and Even More So, back at the flat, we could have had this conversation over a cup of tea. Instead, I'd advise you don't attempt to drink any liquid you find in this tunnel."

Rayleigh didn't feel like laughing quite yet.

"Tough crowd. I'll get to the root of it then, shall I?" Thelonious's tone assumed its earlier formality. "Like thousands of other monsterlings around the world—"

"Monster what?"

"Monsterling. A kid monster. Just—do me a favor and hold the questions a moment, will you? Cheers. Right, you've been offered a place to induct in your designated Confederation city, Below-London, a monstrous twin of Above-London. There should have been an invitation?"

Ah. The fancy thing inside Mama's folded card he'd ignored earlier.

"I got it. Didn't read it, though."

"It would have informed you that you'll be partaking in a fortnight of trials to see how the monster thing fits. It might not."

"I might not be a monster?"

Thelonious nodded.

Rayleigh wasn't sure how he felt either way just yet. Everything happened so fast. He was still catching up.

"How will I know?"

"That question I will allow. If the trials help you manifest your monstrous identity within three weeks, you become a citizen of the old Feddy. There'll be a new home, a new school for you—the best school in Below-London, in fact, if your old man and I have anything to say about it. After you graduate in five years, you get to decide which role you'll play in our vast machine. Pukka." He exhaled, and rolled his shoulders. "Now you can hit me with the rest of your queries."

"Wait. I'd be moving here for at least five years?" Rayleigh thought this was a visit. In and out. Or up and down. Whatever. "For school and—what?"

"A home." Thelonious's rough grumble softened. "A life where you'll never have to apologize for being yourself again, where things will feel so right, you'll never wonder if you're the wrong one. We're in the business of trouble down here. Actually, no. We're in the business of goodness. It just so happens that the best way to be good is to be bad. You follow?"

"No."

"No again?" Thelonious sighed. "I'm botching this, hey. It's my first time, you know. Meeting you, the Snatching. It's a lot harder than you'd think it would be."

"Right." Rayleigh elongated the word. "I can help, maybe."

"Yeah?"

"Yeah. The whole five-year thing? I don't know about that."

Thelonious's face fell. "You don't?"

"No. And three weeks for a transformation, is that guaranteed? At the end, I'll be different? If I change at all, I guess."

"Sort of. For most monsterlings, there will be a transformation in twenty-one days, but it will continue to develop as they stay in their Confederation city, go to school, all that good stuff. You've lived in the human world; it will take longer to stoke that monstrous side of your parentage. Sort of."

"Okay, but look, I don't want to have more than two legs."

"O-kay. I don't actually have any control over what you may turn into."

"Do I?"

"Let's circle back to that one."

"Why?"

"It's tricky. And I'm tired. We can tackle it when we're fresh. Yeah?"

"I—guess."

"Pukka! Are we done?"

"No. You said you're in the business of trouble. What exactly is that?"

Thelonious snapped his fingers. "Volence! Of course. I should have started with Volence. You know about that, don't you?"

Pleased to be anchored in a conversation that had previously set him adrift in a sea of confusion, Rayleigh nodded. Who didn't know about the energy powering a large percentage of the world?

"Our business is in Volence production," Thelonious continued with a big grin.

It would seem that apparently Rayleigh didn't know about the energy powering a large percentage of the world.

"But Luther—"

"Volence? That energy magnate is just a figurehead," his uncle cut in. "We keep him around as a liaison to communicate with humans. Volence is our gig. Some monsters, like your old man, scare naughty children in order to make them better people."

"How does fear make them better?"

"It makes them confront that which prevents them from being better. Monsters act as mirrors. It's why we exist. We reflect the worst versions of people, physically, to humans. When they see that, they want the opposite. They want—"

"Better," Rayleigh finished.

"Exactly. And when those field monsters succeed in their mission, rehabilitated children emit a faint energy vapor when they sleep, a goodness we harvest—it's totally pain free." He waved a dismissive hand. "I think. It's not my area of expertise. I mainly deal with other monsters these days—and that's the kicker, Nephew-mine. Below functions just like Above. There are many jobs and roles; each is important. A mate of mine works in a bank. A banshee. She's always employee of the month, since no one wants to visit her to withdraw any cash. All she does is scream at them. Her bosses are right pleased. But Volence is our bread and butter. Without it, the entire world— Above and Below—will fall into darkness. Both the literal kind, and that other one."

"Other one?"

"Oh, you know," Thelonious said, vague.

Rayleigh didn't know. He recalled the brevity of the note Mama left him, the illustration he now recognized as instructions for traveling by washing hamper, and whatever good feelings his uncle's earlier promises instilled curdled. "Why didn't my family tell me about any of this?"

"Well, monsters have to be a secret in order for our work to succeed. Because we have to be so careful, we require complete ignorance until any monsterlings living Above turn twelve. And that's not all of you. We bring the hopeful to the Confed after you're informed about matters. Even then, sometimes the monstrous half of a child's heritage doesn't manifest. It's a little like eye color. There are strong genes, but there are always exceptions. That isn't anything to dwell on, though. I want you excited about the possibility of life in Below-London. I should have made that clear."

A possibility was different to the promise Thelonious shared, in Rayleigh's flat. This felt weaker, more ephemeral, like a strong gust of wind could sweep it away. Never mind a strong wind, actually. A sigh would do the job.

"It's a choice?" Rayleigh didn't understand.

"It's a choice," Thelonious confirmed. "Your choice. I'm not dragging you away from Above-London. Though, the old bird and your mama aside, I couldn't tell what you liked about that place so much. There was no me, for one thing. No Vol-ways. No—other great stuff I can show you once we leave this musty old dump."

Rayleigh cleared his throat. "Why isn't my dad giving me this information?"

"Your old man's on a research trip," admitted Thelonious. "He wouldn't have stayed away if it wasn't important work. But it's high time that he came home, and I think the knowledge that you're here will work like the bucket of cold water he needs. No pressure," continued Thelonious. "But I am kind of counting on you to help me pull your old man out of his work. I'm even desperate for your help, you might say. Without hope, if you turn me down. Lost in a sea of eternal—"

"Okay!" Rayleigh had a feeling his uncle could talk enough nonsense for Above- and Below-London, if given free rein. "I don't know about moving here." He cast uncertain eyes around the tunnel once more. "But I'll wait a little longer, you know, since I'm needed and everything." Rayleigh's tone was casual, breezy, but he couldn't deny that his dad choosing work over picking him up stung, just as he couldn't deny his curiosity about him. "No promises about those five years, though. No offense."

"None taken." Thelonious paused. "Okay, some taken."

Rayleigh laughed; his uncle's responding grin was blinding.

"You might change your mind once you've seen the real view." He strode across the platform to the curved wall and pulled open two doors Rayleigh hadn't noticed before; someone came flying in through them.

"I was worried after we saw the flat!" The speaker's voice, while musical, warm, was fraught with anxiety and magnified by the tunnel's acoustics. "Please don't tell me he's been hurt."

"Looks like you'll get to meet one of the Terrors early, Nephew-mine."

"The Terrors?" Rayleigh didn't quite manage to hide the uncertainty in his voice.

"The friends of mine I mentioned earlier," explained Thelonious.

"You have nothing to fear from me, Mr. Mann." The speaker stepped into the flickering light of one of the braziers; unable to help himself, Rayleigh gasped. It wasn't the sheer quantity of tweed encasing the speaker's colossal frame. Nor was it the bottom incisors thrusting upward like two daggers from a monstrous underbite that prompted such an uncharacteristic reaction on his part; it was the fact that the speaker appeared to be some kind of troll.

"Apologies for that little episode. I'm so glad to see you're well." The monster's voice was courteous and softly accented. "I'm Gasp of Hule, North Cape, Below-Norway." He ran a hand through a shocking quiff of white-blond curls that clashed brilliantly against his deep green skin and sparkling blue eyes. "I've been waiting for this meeting for twelve years." He seized Rayleigh's hand in one of his own mammoth paws and pumped it, shaking his entire torso while Rayleigh did his best to remain on his feet. "My, you look like your father."

Something warm spread through Rayleigh's chest.

"I do?"

"Why, yes. And your uncle."

The warmth grew.

"If you're quite done ruining my line, Gasp?" Thelonious asked impatiently. "There's something for my nephew to see."

Releasing Rayleigh, Gasp stepped back, letting the boy be the first to pass through the tunnel walls—where everything he had assumed about subterranean worlds was swept away by a biting gust of autumnal air.

FIVE

TERROR TOWER

Beyond the doors, the dimness of the Vol-way station was gone. Instead, stone and earth arched hundreds of feet in the air, like the bowed legs of old men, over a nocturnal *city*. Cobbled streets and tall, rickety brick houses were alive with the din of celebration; All Hallows' Eve festivities rang through the night. Rayleigh's eyes were wide as he traced the flight of large creatures circling narrow, tall buildings in the distance, vast wings fanned against a dark sky.

Thelonious should have led with this.

"You have stars down here?" Rayleigh marveled, his chin tipped upward.

"Not quite. The light comes from window pockets in the lid," Gasp explained. "It's like a flap between Below and Above."

"Where do the clouds come from, then?"

They were gathering overhead in a swirling force that looked very real.

"Water vapor from witches' cauldrons stationed across the city. There's a challenge, actually, to visit all several hundred and receive stamps from each witch in a little passport." Gasp shook his head.

"Living down here, you'll soon find that most monsters have a flair for the dramatic."

"Witches are monsters?" Rayleigh asked. The number of questions he was asking was even starting to annoy him, at this point.

"'Monster' is a label our world is trying to edge out," Gasp said. "'Creatures of the night' is better. More inclusive, considering the variety of inhabitants in the Confederation. Though even that's misleading. Many inhabitants of our magical world don't need the cover of night to walk the human one."

"I like 'inhabitants of a magical world,'" Rayleigh said.

"Me too," Thelonious agreed. "It really is magical. Quick geography lesson for you, Nephew-mine." Striding across the rooftop, he threw his arms out wide. "The easiest way to imagine the Confederation is to picture your average globe. Each of our Below-insert-the-place-of-your-choosing is attached to its twin major city in the Above world."

"So there's a Below-Cardiff, a Below-Dublin?" Rayleigh checked.

"Exactly." Gasp beamed down at him. "Now, some cities in the Confederation are also home to Cabinets. Above, in the UK, just as there is one government that operates with a prime minister, there is one government Below. That's the pattern around the world. As Above, so Below. Mostly."

"When it comes to monsterlings and the Induction," Thelonious cut in, "each Confederation city will host its own. For England, it happens here, in Below-London. In Wales, it's—"

"Below-Cardiff," Rayleigh concluded.

"Exactly. Lesson done and dusted."

Inhaling the sweet scent of caramelized apples and pumpkin pie perfuming the city beneath them, it became almost too easy for Rayleigh to imagine what it would be like to live in a place where the sky was false and witches controlled the weather. His home Above had some upsides, such as Mama and Nana, but Brutely couldn't quite compete with this vista.

A low rumble of thunder echoed in the lid.

Thelonious looked upward. "We'd better get a move on," he said. "Our witches love to celebrate the holiday with a storm."

As they descended into the city, Gasp regaled Rayleigh with tales of his favorite All Hallows' Eve parties of years past. Ahead, leading them through the labyrinth of raucous streets with tall, thin red-brick houses, Thelonious chipped in with corrections, and an outright denial whenever karaoke came up. Friends and neighbors spilled out onto the tree-lined residential streets, merry with food and drink as they celebrated a holiday made for monsters. Seemingly avoiding them, Thelonious kept their party to dimmer side streets. A few sharp turns, and Thelonious halted Rayleigh with a hand to his shoulder in a shadowed alleyway sheltered between two white villas.

"Where are we?"

"Making one last check to ensure we weren't followed," Thelonious murmured to Rayleigh.

"More treasure hunters?"

He nodded, grim-faced. A bolt of violet lightning split the night; Rayleigh saw himself in concerned miniature, reflected in Thelonious's sunglasses. "We had a break-in several weeks back at our offices, a first, and it was a bad one."

"We're still not entirely sure how they found us." Gasp shivered. "Or the nerve to break in. Whoever it was, they must have been following us awhile."

Rayleigh fought the urge to look over his shoulder. Right and Wrong said Marley had been following him too. He'd have to be more observant. All three could decide to look for him again, if it meant getting close to his dad. He told Thelonious as much.

"Never fear, Nephew-mine. This is the simplest of several precautions we've installed to make sure Terror Tower doesn't get pawed at by the same sticky fingers." Thelonious nodded across the street.

"Terror Tower" sounded like it should have turrets and iron spires; its front would be an uninviting Victorian grimace, fit with a crotchety butler who'd yell at kids who dared ride their bikes too close to the riot of weeds he'd call a garden.

It was none of those things.

Taller than the other sprawling houses on the street, it was a well-presented whitewashed home. Embraced on both sides by trees ablaze with an autumnal gamut of leaves, it was more of a self-satisfied smile.

"Indeed" was Thelonious's response when Rayleigh pointed this out. "The name looks mighty impressive on our business cards, though."

Gasp shook his head. "What did I say about monsters and dramatics earlier?"

Thelonious gave the all clear, and the trio crossed the quiet curve of the road to climb up the broad stone steps to the cherry-red front doors; they swung open at Gasp's touch.

A generous hallway stretched to a dark wooden staircase that angled up and out of sight. At its base sat a cluster of pumpkins. Their warm orange interiors glowed, lending a cozy warmth that made the grand surroundings less intimidating. Movement drew Rayleigh's attention to the walls. Their upper halves were papered with sleek black panthers in jungle-green rushes. Rubbing tired eyes, he looked closer. They were *moving*. Cats stalked through grass;

others basked in imaginary sunlight; across the wall, cubs pranced on top of one another. It was as though the walls contained a living world of their own.

"Shoes off please, Nephew-mine." Having hung his long coat on the stand beside the front doors, Thelonious had already exchanged his heavy boots for a fluffy pair of slippers. "These should do nicely for you." He nudged a pair of sliders Rayleigh's way.

"Bit disappointed there aren't any more fluffy ones."

"You have to earn those, kid. Right, the library is through the sliding doors to your left, and the office through the doors on your other side. Feel free to use the library. Stay out of the office." Thelonious took off down the hallway runner, coveted slippers slapping against his soles. He pointed toward an alcove next to the staircase. "That door leads to the chef's kitchen; that one to the basement." He nodded at the door beneath the stairs. "There's a pool down there, but I think we're having a problem with a couple of squatters." He glanced at Gasp, who flushed crimson. The hue was a tad unfortunate against the green of his skin.

"The clubhouse should have more than enough amusements for you to distract yourself with," continued Thelonious. "And all without the unfortunate risk of drowning. Now, these stairs will take you from the hall to the clubhouse and nowhere in between." His eyes were still concealed behind sunglasses, but he managed to convey an expression of the utmost seriousness. "To gain access to one of our floors, ask me, Gasp, or one of the other Terrors I'll introduce you to tomorrow. You see, you'll need an invitation, imagination, and in some cases an empty stomach. If we're not around the clubhouse, or down here in the library or office, use an intercom. They're stationed around the gaff. It's very important that you don't try to access any other floor by yourself—not even your dad's—without permission."

"He lives here too?"

"Of course. It's his home. Now, the tower has been known to be a bit temperamental, to say the least." Thelonious lowered his voice, as if worried about being overheard. "The last guest who went looking for things they weren't invited to see, well, we still don't know where they are."

"The tower, what, ate them?"

"Pretty much."

Rayleigh swallowed. He'd been joking.

"So, I have your word, then?"

"You can have seven," he vowed. "I won't go where I'm not invited."

"Pukka! Come on, then." Thelonious bounded up the staircase, dodging draped cobwebs and hanging ghost lanterns.

The clubhouse was like one of the photos Mr. Glower had framed in his history classroom. It bore the historic feeling of an era of wood-paneled walls filled with books, shiny parquet floors, and lofty ceilings where glitzy chandeliers hung. All it was missing was women in bejeweled finery; men in suits lounging in the wingback chairs, tumblers of drink held in hands crowned with pinkie rings. Rayleigh couldn't quite believe this was to be home. For the rest of his Above school break, at least.

What about the next five years? a small voice asked.

"Let's take a look at your room, Nephew-mine."

Suddenly aware of how heavy his bones felt after the events of the evening, Rayleigh waved farewell to Gasp. Thelonious steered him into the adjoining dining room, through a games room complete with bowling alley and arcade, and out into a wide hallway adorned with large gilded frames; at its end was a single stately door.

"It's not decorated yet, but in time the room will reflect who you are."

Rayleigh'd expected paint cans and plastic, but the space on the other side of the door was furnished with a vast bed. Its wood was stained dark; so were its accompanying furnishings. If there were any shortcomings to be found, they'd be a lack of windows, and plain walls decorated only by the warm silvery glow from the bedside lamps. But they were hardly things to complain about, especially given the purity of the glow cast in his room.

"I can't remember the last time I saw a bulb that wasn't blue," Rayleigh remarked, stunned. "How is it like this? I thought Volence was blue."

"It is, when there's trouble about," said Thelonious. "This light means you're in a safe place, Nephew-mine. But we can talk about this more later. You look bushed. Get some rest. I'll see you in the morning."

Thelonious was gone before Rayleigh realized he didn't have any pajamas. He opened the armoire doors and pulled out each drawer in the bureau—everything was empty. The clothes he'd worn all evening, however dirty, would have to suffice. A small en suite bathroom was discovered behind a second door before he spotted a neatly folded pair of pajamas atop the pillows on his bed. Had he been more alert, he would have recalled that they hadn't been there when he'd first entered the room.

The moment his head touched the pillows, he sank into a deep, dream-filled sleep—one that felt so right, it wouldn't have surprised him to learn that, aside from a few sticky-fingered swindlers, he'd have been hard-pressed to find anything wrong with Below-London at all.

SIX

THE PROVINCE OF DREAMERS

I f there was anything that would rouse a notoriously late sleeper out of bed before sunrise—a new alarm clock on Rayleigh's bed-side table revealed—a house filled with monsters would do it.

Sprawled across the largest bed he'd ever slept in—the softest too—Rayleigh revisited the events of the previous evening. He'd traveled a magical tube line without trains, accessed from his washing hamper, to a city beneath London. An entire world that had existed below his feet this entire time. Now he was in a house where his dad lived—who happened to be the best of all the monsters—with the promise of a future as a creature of the night at his fingertips. Not only was he somewhere trouble was expected; it was celebrated. And he had the chance to induct for a permanent place in a matter of hours.

Rayleigh near vibrated with equal parts excitement and curiosity. He slipped out of bed and padded over to his backpack to retrieve Mama's envelope. He shook the contents out onto his bed and stud-ied them as he styled his high fade for the day. In addition to Mama's mysterious cards, he'd missed a shining silver Vol-trix token. It was identical to the one Thelonious had given him. Dropping Mama's card beside the clock, Rayleigh focused on the invitation he'd avoided yesterday.

The Monsters Cabinet
Bureau of Monster Regulation

Master Rayleigh Mann,

Following the commencement of your twelfth All Hallows' Eve, you are cordially invited to meet the monstrous half of your family and attend your Monstrous 101 Induction, Below-London.

You will undergo three trials that will take place over a fortnight in your designated city: Below-London. The Monstrous 101 Induction determines your monstrous heritage, and whether or not you will have a permanent home in the Confederation of Lightless Places—ultimately, however, the decision is yours. Either you will thrive or you will decide that life in the Above world is more to your liking.

On November 1 you are to assemble in the Monsters Cabinet's main atrium no later than 9:15 a.m. You are encouraged to dress appropriately. Your first trial, the Trial of the Creator, will be held following a tour. If you are successful, you will participate in a luncheon tea party at which you will meet your potential classmates.

We look forward to seeing you for the first day of your Induction.

Yours sincerely,
Octavia Brand
The Office of Inductions, Welcomes, and Warnings, Below-London

Thelonious had mentioned most of what the invitation alluded to, except the office it came from. Inductions, Welcomes, and

Warnings? What was the *warning* part? Perhaps what would happen if a monsterling was unsuccessful in passing their first trial.

The letter withholding that tidbit seemed like a bad sign.

And while it was true that five years Below still felt like a lifetime, if Rayleigh met his dad, they got along, and he didn't pass the trials, he'd regret not trying. Trials, not tests, he rationalized. His last trial had been for the basketball team at his school, which he'd aced.

Following a rushed shower, the effects of which were slightly undone by the fact that he had nothing but yesterday's clothing to dress in, Rayleigh ventured out into the hallway beyond his room. It was rather distinguished, with its rich emerald carpet. The dark, tall walls were stacked with individually lit oil paintings. A plaque beneath the first read Sir Vulpine Machiavelli, First-Class Eldritch Honors, Chief of the Terrors, Year of the Flood. The monster wore black tails. His entire body was coated in short red fur; his muzzle was quirked in a rakish grin. The neighboring frame was empty. Its golden plaque read Bashful Bruiser, Early Years Terror. Rayleigh wondered what had gone wrong there. Or was it right?

On and on the paintings stretched, each depicting Terror alumni. The crew Thelonious mentioned seemed far bigger than Rayleigh thought—it took unbearably long before he stood before the painting that mattered the most.

Bogey Mann's sense of style was somewhere between an East London geezer and a lord from the Victorian era. Stiff white ruffles peeked through the neckline of his black coat, which bore a high collar that peaked sharply on either side of Bogey's strong chin. A stylish flat cap was tilted jauntily to the side and pulled low over his golden eyes—the Mann eyes; they glinted with arrogance, as did his shifty grin.

Rayleigh stepped closer, staring hard enough to discern paint strokes. He'd hoped for a sense of knowing when he saw his dad. A kind of "oh there you are, I've been looking for you." But were it not for the nameplate, Bogey Mann, First-Class Eldritch Honors, Chief of the Terrors, Decade of Light, he could have been looking at a stranger whose eyes happened to match his own. A stranger with dark skin, like his, a strong jawline shadowed with stubble, not unlike the photo of Robert Mann on the mantel in Rayleigh's flat. But a stranger nonetheless. Their in-person meeting would be better—it had to be. And it could happen as early as this morning if his dad's work trip had finally come to an end.

Ignoring the remaining frames, Rayleigh hurried after the scent of breakfast until he alighted upon a scene not out of place in an average household, but somewhat unexpected in one of monsters. Pots and pans hung from a rail along the ceiling. Dried bunches of herbs tied with thin strips of ribbon lent a traditional, cozy air. Were it not for the winged creatures banking in the—not sky. Gasp called it something else last night. . . . The lid! Yes, were it not for the winged monsters outside the windows on the east wall—and a pile of laundry folding itself into neat piles on a large wooden table—Terror Tower could have been in Above-London.

In a hearth tall enough for Rayleigh to walk inside, a large pot of porridge floated above a fire. It bubbled and popped like something more magical than an average breakfast meal. A humming Gasp oversaw multiple sizzling pans of bacon and eggs atop a hob. In contrast, a silent Thelonious sat at a mammoth kitchen island Rayleigh vaguely remembered from the previous night. Fondness for the two Terrors kept Rayleigh in the doorway a moment longer. His uncle wore striped pajamas and nursed a large mug of something steaming and dark. Gasp wore a matching trouser and shirt set too; he'd tied a frilly apron over his.

"Morning," Rayleigh finally said, shifting away from the doorframe.

"Ah, Rayleigh!" Gasp turned with a smile; thin wire glasses were balanced on his bulbous nose. "I'll put a plate together for you."

"Thanks."

"Morning, Nephew-mine." Thelonious's voice was gruff. "I was just about to come for you. How'd you sleep?"

Rayleigh slid atop a stool at the island. "Well, thank you. Is Dad home yet?"

"Not yet, but I'm sure he will be soon. And if not, then he'll be at the Cabinet later."

"When are we leaving?" Rayleigh patted his pockets for his phone, redundantly. "Oh yeah, my phone broke last night."

"You have time to eat. Sorry about your tech. It wouldn't have worked down here anyway. I can sort you out with something new. Fair warning, our stuff is a little different."

"Everything is different. I saw the paintings of the Terrors in the hall outside my room, instead of the photos we have. It's hard to believe you're the good guys. No offense."

Thelonious scratched his left horn. "None taken. Mostly."

"I bet you generate loads of Volence—though, you said you work with monsters?"

"That's right. We operate as agents for our world's equivalent of an Above city's secret crime branch."

"You're police?" Rayleigh asked with a little anxiety.

"No." Thelonious shook his head. "Law enforcement officers have a different name here. Our crew are more like spies."

"Oh, cool." Thelonious might have been the best uncle he'd ever met; far better than the one who chased Rayleigh and his cousins around at family get-togethers, asking them to pull his finger.

"Four or five of us operate officially at any one time," Thelonious went on to explain. "We were named by all the criminal monsters we've caught and imprisoned throughout the decades."

"So monsters aren't all good guys?" Rayleigh pointed out.

"You get bad apples everywhere."

Just then a woman drifted into the kitchen.

"Except Terror Tower. Meet the infamous Bloody Mary." Thelonious gestured to his crew member with the hand not nursing a vat of coffee. "Scourge of London since before the twentieth century. Though I know she doesn't look a day over a hundred."

She'd have looked almost ordinary, if not for her skin. Both pale and fragile, like butterfly wings, it was a delicate, deathly blue. Her long dark braid only made her look all the more translucent.

"Good morning, Mr. Mann." Her accent was clipped, rich. "Welcome, on all counts."

"I've heard of you," Rayleigh said, somewhat taken aback.

"I worked the Scare Duty circuit before I joined the Terrors." Sitting beside Thelonious, she reached for a teapot. A faint smile lingered in one corner of her rust-colored lips.

There was something about her; Rayleigh was uncertain if it was her beauty or haunting air that put him most out of sorts. It was an impressive feat, given the fact that she was wrapped in a silk pajama robe and not, as Phoebe had sworn, crying blood in the reflection of the mirror as she predicted a horrible fate for her, the summoner.

He'd dismissed the story as typical Phoebe nonsense. Sure, he hadn't tried saying Bloody Mary three times into any mirror in his house, as Phoebe dared him to. But that was neither here nor there.

"So people Above can know about you? Last night you said we couldn't, Thelonious."

"They don't know," Mary answered. "Not for certain. Thelonious was right. There are rules for Scare Duty, and indeed all monsters in the Confed. Being seen by adults breaks every one. Children grow up, hopefully, into decent people once we're done with them; their night scares are forgotten. Adults with children might be more open to believing something is terrorizing their progeny at night, but largely the mystery, the dread, only helps fuel a child's fear, which helps us in the long run."

"With Volence," Rayleigh said, the pieces from Thelonious's explanation in the tunnel coming together to form a clear picture.

"Exactly." His uncle briefly lifted his mug and cheersed in Rayleigh's direction.

There was another matter Rayleigh meant to raise with Thelonious, but he couldn't put his finger on it. And when Gasp deposited a plate heaving with bacon, eggs, and toast down before him with a smile, he forgot completely.

"Looks great, thanks!" Not able to recall the last time he'd eaten, Rayleigh dived in with gusto. When he came up for air, his uncle and Mary were watching him. The former looked amused, the latter mildly disgusted. "So," he said, a little sheepish. "Can I ask what sort of monster you are?" He had a brief flashback to someone asking where he was from. London hadn't been a suitable enough answer, even though that was where he'd been born. "It feels weird, like asking where you're from."

"I get that, Nephew-mine. And sensitivity toward others is a brilliant trait to have. During the Induction, I imagine you'll all be asking one another what monsters you are. It's not like asking where someone is from, but it can feel just as personal to some. Others will be happy to tell you; some will prefer keeping that to themselves."

"Sensitivity," Rayleigh repeated.

"Sensitivity." Thelonious nodded. "If they don't broach it—"

"Don't ask."

"Right. We're all citizens of the Confederation, at the end of the day. That's what truly matters."

"Me, I'm all too happy to discuss myself." Mary waved an elegant hand at him; fizzing balls of sparks danced between her fingers.

"Yes, yes, you're a witch." Gasp shoveled some hash browns onto Rayleigh's plate. "Now put those out before you set something alight."

She smiled. Rayleigh thought he saw something lurking beneath her skin. Something sinister that might explain why Phoebe's account of meeting Bloody Mary was almost convincing.

"Asking about powers is the same deal, right?" he asked his uncle.

"You've got it, kiddo. Though, for the record, we steer away from terms like 'powers.' A monster's talents are known as bents."

"They're particular abilities that help us bend a child's reality," Mary added. "Scaring them senseless, or whatever the law demands."

Rayleigh gave Mary a suspicious sidelong look. Phoebe had never behaved better than that week she'd sworn she saw a woman in her mirror. . . .

"Some bents aren't terribly useful during Scare Duty," said Gasp.

"Mine, for instance, is control of earthly matter. Plants, dirt, that sort of thing. I'm strong too, but that comes with being a troll. We're no longer allowed to smash things for dramatic effect out in the field. Too traumatic for the kids we scare. But working with the Terrors? I do so enjoy knocking together the recalcitrant heads of rogue monsters. The earthly, a literal green thumb you might say," he chuckled, "comes in handy with my allotment."

There really was a place for all kinds of trouble Below. Rayleigh glanced at his uncle. Sipping at his coffee, Thelonious didn't offer any insight as to what his bent was. Rayleigh's curiosity reared its head. Witches and trolls were simple, magic and strength. But his uncle was from Jamaica, a land rich with monstrous tales. In the stories, some of the magical creatures lived in the water, others on land; there were some who flew through the night to suck blood from the chests of their victims. . . . Not Thelonious, though. His horns were sharper than his teeth. His bent could be anything—Rayleigh's bent could be anything.

"What about—" *Me?* Rayleigh had been about to ask when, in the corner, the washing basket's lid toppled off. Shadows spooled from within the wicker cylinder. Oozing over the rim, the amorphous mass grew into a column that sharpened into a tall, thin man in a trench coat and a battered old top hat.

"This is Bogey's son?" He tilted his chin up, revealing a long face and a pair of suspicious brown eyes beneath the hat's brim. "Shade Ornery. Penumbra."

Rayleigh gaped. "You're made of *shadows*? So cool."

"Unless the kid he's scaring turns the lights on." Thelonious yawned. "Then he's so gone."

"I'll have you know." Shade's tone was tetchy. "That for all your derision, in the Order of Corner Creepers, Ceilings, et al., I'm considered a Supreme Cobweb."

"Yeah, yeah. You keep pushing that so-called Order, and yet I've never heard of it."

"It's invitation only. Terribly exclusive." Shade sniffed. "Not to mention, you're far too bulky to creep in any corners."

"When do I figure out my bent and monstrous identity?" Rayleigh cut in, before his uncle could retaliate.

"Haven't you told him anything?" chastised Mary.

"He knows things," Thelonious said defensively. "Plenty of things. And I'm about to tell him more. Before we head over to the Induction, Nephew-mine, we need to see about kitting you out. New communication device and all. What sort of uncle, nay, frightparent, would I be if I didn't make sure you're turned out smartly for your first foray into monstrous society?" He angled his mug at the other Terrors. "What, nothing to say?"

"What are the chances the boy knows what a frightparent is?" Shade drawled.

"Nil," said Mary.

"Zip," Gasp chimed in.

The handle of the mug snapped off in Thelonious's hand.

"Frightparents, child of Bogey, are the monster equivalent to god-parents," droned Shade. "After you were born, your father asked us to take on the responsibility." He shook his head, a puzzled expression on his face. "No idea why. If it comes down to saving you or myself, I plan on making the smart choice." He paused. "That would be res-cuing myself, in case you're not so smart. That gormless expression you're sporting doesn't fill me with much hope."

"Wait—what?"

Shade drifted across the kitchen without another word.

"Your father asked us," Gasp said, shaking his head at his team-mate, "because he wanted to make sure that when you came to the Confederation, you had a family who'd protect you."

"We are the tough act he knew needed to follow Drea and Helene," said Thelonious. "Quite the team you've got there."

Rayleigh hoped they were telling the truth. He wanted to believe his dad thought about him, though he was currently putting work before him. And had done so his entire life. He wanted it more than he cared to admit.

"About Mama and Nana, can I talk with them?"

"How about we give them a bell after the Induction? You can tell them all about it." He pushed back from the counter. "Now, Gasp's taking you out this morning. The tailor's a personal acquaintance of his." Gasp flushed a bright red and busied himself with loading a dishwasher that may, or may not, have licked a plate clean with a giant pink tongue. "I'll meet you there, and we can travel to your Induction together." He mussed Rayleigh's afro in passing—even harder when Rayleigh tried to duck away, lamenting the comb he'd left in his room. "For now, try that enjoying-yourself thing. I hear it's good for digestion."

A few streets and a couple of corners away from Terror Tower, Rayleigh heard threads of music cascading out of a fenced-in square of garden. It was filled with bright flowers, a pond, and the sweeping arms of trees withholding the last of their leaves. Nestled atop its stage, beneath an ivory covering, an orchestra captivated monstrous commuters.

"The Morning Aria is my favorite way to start the day." Lost in the melody, Gasp wore an expression of rapture.

It wasn't the sort of thing Rayleigh would turn up on the radio. But with the day dawning bright and cold, the delicate combination of strings and percussion, accompanied by the mournful yet hopeful solo of a clarinet, filled him with the sense that anything was possible.

Rayleigh shoved his hands into his borrowed jacket's pockets. He brushed against the comms device his uncle had given him; he had several spares around Terror Tower, being prone to breaking them frequently. Round like a disc, it fit snugly in Rayleigh's palm.

Following one last soulful peal from the soloist, the orchestra bowed to riotous applause. Gasp and Rayleigh made a move. The duo passed artists painting behind easels, dancers leaping, ribbons twirling like spun silver in their hands. There was actual birdsong.

No one had scowled at him yet, or crossed the street to avoid him, dubiously eyeing the hoodie beneath his jacket, his afro. People—no, monsters—tipped their hats at him and Gasp, waved menacing paws of sharp nails, or smiled with mouths that oozed perniciously colored slime. There was no doubt that many were fearsome, but it was equally undoubtable that all were kind.

"This place is kind of brilliant," said Rayleigh, relaxing into their walk.

"Isn't it? The Province of Dreamers is known for its creators. It's the reason I suggested it as our second base within the city. I once fancied myself as a bit of a painter."

Gasp hailed a cab that was black and shiny like a beetle. He gave the cyclops driver the tailor's address. Winking at Rayleigh with one large brown eye, the monster swapped his cigar to the other side of his mouth and floored it.

"Where was I?" Gasp sank back in his seat, unbothered by the way the cab was careening through traffic. The driver whipped through impossible gaps between sleek town cars and carriages alike. "Right, artist. It didn't last long. Like all cave trolls, I was born a historian. My only love has ever been the richness of stories, their roots."

"Uh-huh." Half focused on Gasp and half on the road, Rayleigh winced at a near crash between their cab and a rider sitting atop a unicorn.

"Listen to me, boring you with my babble when you probably have more questions."

Rayleigh had many questions, about the Monsters Cabinet, and why the office his invitation came from contained *Warnings* in its name, among them, but he couldn't think about anything except his imminent death in the back of the cab. There was traffic ahead—a sea of brake lights with no room to maneuver. "Hey," he couldn't help calling. "There's traffic ahead. Maybe we should slow down."

"You think I can't see because I only have the one eye?"

"What? No!"

"I'm pulling your leg, kid." The cyclops released the steering wheel and turned to Rayleigh. "First time Below?"

"Yeah, and if you don't mind, I don't want it to be my last! Watch the road!"

Everything played out in slow motion.

The cab was approaching at a speed that would make stopping

impossible. Sure they were going to crash, Rayleigh cringed back into his seat. Then the unexpected happened. With one smooth bounce, the car shot up in the air and leapt over the traffic to land with a squeal of wheel spin on the other side. He sucked in a startled breath as another cab landed before them in a similar manner, sprouting six thin metallic legs.

Rayleigh grinned at his frightfather and the concerned eye of the cyclops watching him through the rearview mirror.

"You still with us, kid?"

His grin grew. "Can we do that again?"

The driver winked—or blinked, it was impossible to tell. "Just you wait."

SEVEN

WHAT'S IN A NAME?

With one final stupendous bounce, the B-Cab landed alongside a busy bystreet. Within seconds it became clear that traveling in such a buoyant manner with a full stomach wasn't the best of ideas. After a pitstop to a café for a soothing ginger tea—Rayleigh's—and something with a lot of cream and marshmallows for Gasp, the pair ventured onto the quiet cobblestoned thoroughfare.

"I read my Induction invitation," Rayleigh began, once his stomach had calmed. "It came from the Monsters Cabinet. Which monster's?"

"A government of them." Gasp laughed. Raising a hand to his trilby hat, he ducked beneath a low-hanging string of fairy lights looping between the parallel buildings. Their bulbs were abnormally large, like footballs. "Honestly, rather than asking what Thelonious did tell you, I should have checked what he didn't." He shook his head. "You'll learn all about our government at the Induction. Are you looking forward to today's events, the rest of your time Below?"

"Do I stay after, if I pass, or go home?" The world above was already becoming a less attractive option. Not least because the Induction coincided with his half-term break. Or that, once the three weeks were over, Dr. Ramsey and Mr. Glower would be waiting, detention letters in hand.

"We can cross that road when we come to it."

"I'd rather know what happens if I don't pass, if that's all right?"

"I understand. You—well, you wouldn't forget about your monstrous parent, about Bogey." Gasp drew a deep breath. "But you wouldn't remember he's not human. Or that you came Below. Met any of us. It's necessary to protect what we do, but it is cruel. For us."

Rayleigh's heartbeat ratcheted, like he was back in the B-Cab. He wasn't sure he wanted to stay, but he knew he didn't want to forget anything he'd experienced so far. "How many kids don't pass the first trial?"

"Around a third of the monsterlings you'll induct with will remain at the end of the Induction period. Some children who grew up in the Confederation won't pass either. They're permitted to stay Below, though, since it's their home. It's unfair, really."

Rayleigh was more concerned with the number. "A third?" In the thousands of monsterlings Thelonious said induct, that was insane.

One of Gasp's frying-pan-sized hands engulfed his shoulder—both of them, in fact, and Rayleigh's back, it was so vast. "I don't want you to think about the numbers. Think about what got you here—that propensity for trouble, as they call it Above. I have no doubts that you'll shine."

At least if he didn't, he wouldn't remember it for long.

"And what exactly are the trials?"

"Now, that I can't say." Gasp was firm. "But as I have said, you will do just fine."

"Because I control whether I pass or not?"

"Exactly." Gasp came to a stop before a shop front simply labeled Modiste. "I think we know who we're going to be early on, even if it sometimes takes us a while to realise that."

"Thelonious said monstrous identities can be like eye color. There are strong genes, but there are always exceptions. I didn't choose to have brown eyes," said Rayleigh.

"That's true," Gasp mused. "But you choose how they look upon the world."

That gave Rayleigh something to think about.

Gasp rapped the brass knocker on the bright yellow door with two large fingers, despite the sign in the window reading CLOSED. "It's early, which is why I didn't call, but the tailor won't be pleased." He banged the knocker again, cringing at the hollow thud of wood that rang down the bystreet. "You'd better stand right here." He moved Rayleigh closer to the door. "She always liked your dad. Her family has been creating ensembles for the Terrors since the Battle of the Sky and Earth. You know, that was—"

The door opened a sliver; a bespectacled eye peered through the gap.

"Whatever it is, come back in two hours."

The door would have closed were it not for the foot Gasp wedged against it. He looked meaningfully at Rayleigh.

Catching on, he gave his most winning smile. "Morning. I'm Rayleigh Mann."

"Bogey's son," added Gasp.

Rayleigh wouldn't have thought it possible, but the eye widened.

The door opened, and the voice, disappearing with its owner down a hall, called, "Make yourself comfortable, Mr. Mann. I'll be right with you."

"Told you," murmured Gasp. "Nice work."

The interior of the shop was a picture of neatness. An array of fabrics and patterns were folded away in alcoves; everything was color coded and militant in its presentation. Mannequins were presented in various states of dress. Several had multiple arms, a few had additional legs—one even had wings and wore dull metal armor.

"Is my hair all right?" Removing his trilby, Gasp raked fingers through his thick curls.

"What was wrong with the hat?"

"Manners, Rayleigh," Gasp said, pocketing his hat.

And not a moment too soon, for the tailor materialized from behind a pair of red velvet curtains, providing Rayleigh with his first good look at her. With the six tentacles in place of arms and legs, she could have made any child behave if she appeared in their room under the cover of darkness. But beyond the obvious, her skin was light pink, and she wore a cardigan; it was buttoned up— incorrectly—over a high-collared shirt, and the thin-rimmed glasses balanced on a pert nose were slightly askew. With larger than average eyes blinking owlishly behind their lenses, she seemed kind of sweet.

"What can I do for you?" she asked; her voice was carefully detached, like she was preparing to intercept an awful request.

"We need some clothing for Rayleigh, if you'd be so kind." Speaking of strange voices, Gasp's had become an octave higher than usual. "He's being inducted later today. I do believe there are clothing requirements."

With a curt nod, the tailor turned to Rayleigh. "Good morning. I'm Taylor Modiste."

"That's lucky."

Her brows rose to the messy bun of dark hair atop her head; it was skewered by several sets of scissors. "Luck has nothing to do with it. Why do you think he's called Gasp? Or your uncle Thelonious Tickle? Please, come through."

Swathed in dark velvet paisley wallpaper, the spacious workshop was cozy yet grand. Light flooded in through a pair of skylights, but Taylor flicked on several high-wattage lamps. Rayleigh stepped onto a circular podium surrounded by mirrors. Facing multiple versions of himself, he couldn't help reflecting on his potential transformative process once more—and whether his dad would be there to see it.

"Can you tell me a little more about the name thing, Ms. Modiste?"

The tailor peered up at him; her tentacles moved in various stages of measurement, with several different spools of numbered tape. "Look at your father's title, the Bogey Mann. Above, it's recognized as something to fear. In the Confederation, it's revered. When creatures hear my name, they understand that I slice and dice." A set of scissors clasped in a tentacle snipped a little too close to one of Rayleigh's ears, making him flinch. "Clothing, that is. Then there are those who opt to choose different names. Should you decide to do that, think carefully." Her tone took on a sharp edge of warning, similar to the scissors gliding through fabric draped over his torso. "Many a name's meaning has been distorted by a monster."

Despite the warmth from the lights, Rayleigh felt a chill brush against the back of his neck. "What do you mean?"

"I would have thought Gasp, with his interest in history, would have told you about the Confederation's greatest stain, the Illustrious Society?" The scissors cut a vicious chunk out of what Rayleigh thought was becoming a long-sleeved top.

A mottled flush made its way up Gasp's neck.

Rayleigh looked from his frightfather to the tailor and back again. "So, the Illustrious Society?"

"You'll at least know, I hope," said Ms. Modiste, shooting another reproachful look at Gasp, "that not all monsters work to benefit the symbiotic relationship between the Confederation of Lightless Places and Above. For some, their chosen plight is the exact opposite. The Illustrious Society believed monsters should be terrifying for no reason other than that's who we are. They started a war to make their dream a reality, the Battle of Caelum et Terra—"

"I mentioned that earlier, the Sky and Earth," Gasp offered.

"Lift your arm a bit, Mr. Mann, that's perfect—all that's to say: *Illustrious* once meant 'distinguished, prestigious, important.' But now the Society's become a warning about the short distance between power and madness. They lost the battle, of course, and most of them were imprisoned."

"So no one worries about them?"

"They," Taylor said, "are out of sight, and therefore far out of the minds of most feddies."

A bell rang out in the shop front.

Ms. Modiste rested the scissors on her equipment tray. "I have a pair of trousers that will fit you, Rayleigh. They won't be bespoke, but they'll do you right today. As for the rest of your wardrobe, I can have a complete wardrobe put together and messengered over to the tower within the next few days or so."

"I don't mind popping back?" Gasp said hopefully.

Either too focused on leaving to answer the door or simply flat out ignoring Gasp, the tailor handed Rayleigh a pair of black cargo trousers before she flounced through the curtains without a response. Unfortunately for his frightfather, Rayleigh was convinced it was the latter. Eager to avoid being drawn into whatever was going on there, he surveyed his new smart black T-shirt. In the time it would have taken Rayleigh to dress, she'd sewn a top with removable sleeves. Gasp, sniffing a little, turned his back so Rayleigh could slide out of his bottoms, and into his new pair. The cargos possessed more pockets than he knew what to do with. The fabric was like liquid swaths of night, light but durable, just like his top. Over his heart, a tiny blue logo had been sewn. A face. Its chin was pointed, and it had horns.

Rayleigh traced over it with his fingers. "What is this?"

"An emblem of ours, in the Confederation. A gargoyle. We consider them guardians, of a kind. The inductees must be required to wear clothing with them featured. I lost the uniform document, but Taylor has likely been making up clothes for half the city."

It was a shame to cover her creations with his hoodie and then his jacket, but it was a nippy November 1. Seemed unfair of the witches who controlled the weather not to keep Below in a state of perpetual summer.

Having tidied his hair with his pick, Rayleigh was sliding his feet into his trainers when a set of horns poked through the gap in the curtains.

"Wotcher." Thelonious winked. "All suited and booted?"

The trio bid Ms. Modiste farewell, leaving her shop to pile into a waiting B-Cab on the livelier avenue outside.

True to form, Rayleigh had plenty more questions, but the bouncing travel made it difficult to hold a conversation. It was a relief when a Volentic sign featuring a B-Cab with an angry red cross through it flashed; the jumping was exchanged for the slightly less nauseating, but semi-illegal, road maneuvers.

"Look!" said Gasp. "You can see the Monsters Cabinet roof from here!"

The cab sped through streets that resembled the glass and steel of central London Above; it even had buildings shaped like items found in a cook's pantry.

"Can you see the dome?"

It rose above the traffic. Flagged by steeples, spires, and columns, the Monsters Cabinet looked like the ivory decoration atop a fine cake. Throngs of vehicles and animals gathered on the steps before its elegant façade. They flooded out into the street; cameras flashed; crowds shouted.

Hope was like a lightbulb in Rayleigh's head. "Are they here to see my dad?"

Thelonious twisted in his seat to look through the windscreen. "Probably just journalists hoping to snap shots of inducting monsterlings. Speaking of, Nephew-mine, might be better to keep your surname to yourself for a while, to avoid accruing a swarm of adoring fans like the Liu girl and her brothers."

Rayleigh frowned. Though he hadn't known Thelonious for long, his uncle had a habit of deflecting. He was beginning to suspect that there was something he wasn't sharing.

"Look, if my dad's not coming, you can tell me." He did his best to sound unbothered. "I'd rather know."

"Nephew-mine, where's this coming from?"

Rayleigh was used to bad news—detentions, groundings, and the like—his gut was fine-tuned for detecting when something wasn't right. "It seems like you're hiding something."

Gasp became terribly interested in an invisible stain on his left trouser leg. But Thelonious leaned across the cab. Rayleigh could only see his reflection in his uncle's sunglasses, but he had the distinct impression Thelonious was taking a good, long look at him.

"Is it a feeling you're getting, or do you think you can hear it in my voice?"

Rayleigh blinked. "What?"

"Some monsterlings' bents manifest earlier than the Induction. So, feeling, or are you hearing something?"

Rayleigh leaned in too. "Is there something to hear?" He wouldn't allow himself to be distracted by the chance of figuring out his bent, his monstrous form, early. Even though, on the inside, he was freaking out at the possibility. "Or feel?"

A slow smile broke on Thelonious's mouth. "If I knew your old man wouldn't be there, I'd tell you. Promise."

Honesty. Rayleigh both heard and felt it. Not magically or whatever. At least he didn't think so. He wouldn't give Thelonious the satisfaction of asking. Yet.

"Why do I have to conceal my surname if my dad's going to be there?"

"A salient point—though I'd rather we not test the reactions you're bound to receive in front of the press. Might be better off taking another entrance, actually." Thelonious rapped the glass partition. "Take the next turn please, cabbie."

The driver veered the cab left, over a curb with a bump, and down a dingy side street, where Thelonious and Rayleigh alone egressed before an audience of several pigeons. Gasp remained seated.

"You're not coming?" asked Rayleigh.

"I happen to love having my photo taken." Gasp tweaked a magenta bow tie; it was paired with a buttercup kerchief in his blazer's top pocket. "You'll do brilliantly, Rayleigh. I'll see you later—perhaps the monstrous you. Can't wait either way!"

With the B-Cab rambling back out to the main road, Thelonious marched up to a metal door at the side of the grand building, thumped twice, waited, and then thumped three times.

"Not the most covert of signals, I know," he said, beckoning his nephew toward him.

But it did the job. The door whined open.

"Chief of Surveillance, and you still haven't oiled those hinges?"

A rasp of laughter cut through the shadows. "What can I do for you, Thel?" The riot of ginger hair beneath the man's hat was a sight to behold. With its hue and volume, it was hard to believe he did his job well when, surely, the point of surveillance was to avoid being seen. "And you must be Rayleigh Mann, with the bounty of gold in that gaze." He seized his hand. Round blue eyes shone with kindness. Rayleigh couldn't help but smile back. "Your uncle's done nothing but tell me how excited he was to welcome you Below. And I understand I'm one of a select few who knows you're here. Consider me flattered."

"You can release my nephew's hand, Lowell. He'll need it for the Induction."

"Apologies, it's just—Do you think this counts as shaking the Supreme's hand?"

"Let me guess, treasure hunt?" Thelonious glanced down at Rayleigh, who was sure his uncle was rolling his eyes under his sunglasses. "I won't tell if you don't mind us slipping in this way. The front's a bit of a media circus."

"It's a deal."

Thelonious ushered Rayleigh into a vast, dimly lit basement space filled with bleeping machines, and up a metal flight of stairs. "Lowell, I almost forgot, did you manage to collate the footage from the other break-ins that happened around the same time as Terror Tower's?"

"Not yet." At the top of the stairs, the chief of surveillance tapped a security pass on the pad beside the sole door. "You know how it is around here. I'll get on it as soon as I can."

"We appreciate it. And thanks for this too."

"Hey, I'm only a few finds away from my platinum hunter badge. Thank *you*. And you, young Master Mann."

"Have a good one, Lowell. Come on, Nephew-mine, we're just through here."

Rayleigh blinked as the dim confines of the basement were replaced by a bright, cavernous space—one that was nothing like a cabinet, small and stuffed with useless junk, the odd spider. It was a palatial rotunda, the lost cousin of a cathedral.

And it was positively heaving with monsters.

EIGHT

THE MONSTERS CABINET

"**W**elcome to the Sphere of Doors, gov." Thelonious strode at the fore, head, shoulders—and horns—above many of the transient throng. "Our hub of sorts, here in the Monsters Cabinet. It hasn't warmed up yet, but it'll get there. Monsters will be popping in from all corners of the world, not just Below-London. Keep up. I don't want to lose you."

The Sphere functioned as a vast reception area, with a large circular desk at its center. Tall screens, like those in train stations, displayed messages too small for Rayleigh to see at his distance—but there were plenty of other distractions that caught his eye. In an uncanny way to Londoners Above, monsters wended their way across the black and white checkerboard flooring with the merciless focus of a chef's blade. Similarly dressed in suits and flowing coats, some of them looked almost human. Others adopted different shapes, species. Something ephemeral swirled past Rayleigh; a living storm cloud. Winds tugged at his clothes like fingers.

"Sorry," they said, with no discernible mouth to be seen. "I'm in a rush."

"No worries," breathed Rayleigh, unable to fully understand who he was talking to, even in the bright morning light streaming in through the glass dome overhead.

Halls speared off around its circular hub, like the spokes of a wheel. Light streamed down one such hall. Windows ran the length of the tall corridor; Rayleigh glimpsed a sparkling ribbon of dark water that reminded him of the Thames.

"When you said Below-London was a mirror," he called ahead to his uncle. "You really meant it's just like Above."

"Oh yes. Though this government office is prettier than that house they have up there," Thelonious said over his shoulder. "It has the same junk, though, like the geezer who oversees it."

"Not my dad?" Rayleigh asked, hopping over a slime trail left behind by a monster that was at least half slug.

"Not my dear big brother, no. He's as much an underling as the rest of us. The monster with that honor is called the Chancellor."

Rayleigh was sidetracked by movement on part of the Sphere's wall. It bore all manner of doors: red ones, tall Gothic monstrosities, doors crafted from leaves and vines, minuscule fairy doors; they were arranged in no particular order. It didn't matter that some were upside down, or incredibly high. Creatures passed through those with elegant sweeps of their wings. Something vast and serpentine, on many legs, slunk out of a lime-green door; immediately, it disappeared into the epic battles of creatures painted in the dome above. Rayleigh didn't realize his mouth was open until it became uncomfortable to swallow.

"Quick sharp, Nephew-mine. I'm running a little late."

Rayleigh, though tall himself, had to hurry to keep up with his uncle's strides. Thelonious was cutting a channel toward three bold words, BONO MALUM SUPERATE, carved above one of seven giant archways the dome squatted upon like a spider. On either side of the dictum, golden gargoyles grimaced down. Rayleigh started when one abandoned its perch, taking off above the throng with a sweep of wings. It was madness. Functional chaos. He loved it.

The intensity of the emotion took him by surprise—and then there was another, deeper resonation. How would it feel to belong somewhere so perfectly fitting for who he was? Five years Below could be a vacation from the dull realities of life Above, not to mention the struggles. If Rayleigh wanted it to be.

"Can people—no," Rayleigh corrected himself. "Monsters—"

"Try feddies. As in, those of us who live in the Confederation. Or people."

"People?"

"Yeah. Not like you're callin' us human, is it?"

"Er, I'll take your word for it. So, can feddies, people, watch the trial or—"

"No, it's private." Thelonious stopped a ways from a cordoned zone labeled Induction—Meet Here. "We're a little early." No one was waiting yet. "But I'm afraid I can't stay and meet your potential peers, Nephew-mine." Distracted, he glanced down at his watch. "There's somewhere I need to be, but I know you'll pass, and I'll find you at the welcome tea."

"With my dad?"

"Hopefully, yes."

"Hopefully?" Rayleigh's eyebrows lowered. There it was again. Thelonious and his diversions. "I thought you said he'd be here."

"Bogey's always loved making an entrance, so we won't discount him yet."

"Fine. For now." According to the invitation, the day was going to be long. There was a tour before the first trial, the main event, and then the tea party afterward. If he passed. "Any last-minute advice?"

Thelonious glanced at his watch again and winced. "Use your natural gifts, your instincts, that inclination for trouble, and you will be fine. Also, try not to get eaten."

A record scratched in Rayleigh's head.

"Eaten?"

"Mmm, yeah. Your mama would never forgive me, and my ma would skin me alive. Horns and all." With a parting shudder, Thelonious took off, coattails cracking like a mighty sail warring with the wind and sea.

"Wait!"

"You'll be great!" he shouted over his left shoulder, not slowing.

A dumbfounded Rayleigh stared after him. His uncle paused at a screen, turned on his heel, and hurried toward one of the halls.

Exhaling, Rayleigh turned away from the vast openness of the Sphere. Desperate for a distraction, a roadblock to spring up between him and the rising desire to run after his uncle for those answers, Rayleigh looked beyond the cordoned space. In an alcove set deep into the curved wall, a large bronze bust of a noble-faced monster was lit from below by a handful of spotlights. He sported impressive tusks, kind eyes for a statue, and a hideous curled wig that was stiff with importance. He also looked somewhat familiar.

The plaque beneath the effigy read:

WALLY RUSS ESQUIRE. FOUNDING CHANCELLOR OF THE
CONFEDERATION OF LIGHTLESS PLACES. FIRST-CLASS
SCARE MASTER. SUPREMELY HAIRY. CONDUCTOR OF
MONSTER PURPOSE AND POSITION
⸺ ALWAYS OVERCOME EVIL WITH GOOD ⸺

Rayleigh fished the Vol-trix token included in his invitation pack out of his pocket. He turned the silver coin over in his fingers. The monster before him was the same as the one on the token—the one Mama gave him because she believed he would figure things out. Nana too. He wanted to believe he could do it, but there was so much he didn't know. So much he was sure Thelonious was keeping from him. Rayleigh looked across the sphere, at the screen his uncle read before hurrying away.

He edged around the rope. No one pointed or shouted at him. No one looked his way at all for too long. He took several more casual steps. When no one challenged him, he made a beeline for the screen. Winged creatures, no larger than pigeons, flitted across the large rectangle. With spindly arms, they arranged letters to form bulletins. Rayleigh scanned the words from left to right. Times, meeting rooms—no, courtrooms, and . . . there. His father's name. 9:15, COURTROOM NO. 3, BOGEY MANN HEARING.

The sensation of having an egg cracked atop his head sent a chill down Rayleigh's spine.

So his dad *was* at the Cabinet. And it seemed as though Thelonious had rushed off to meet him. Why not explain that to Rayleigh?

"Forget whatever it is you're thinking. Here's what should be going through your head," said a familiar voice to his right. "She's found me again. How brilliant. I should let her in on whatever I'm planning."

Surprised, Rayleigh glanced down to find Marley, who, smirk aside, looked much as he'd left her yesterday.

"You again?"

"It's what I do." She shrugged. "I'm more interested in what you're doing."

"Leaving. Don't follow."

"Stay."

"I'm not a dog."

"Must be why you're not that great at listening."

Amused, Rayleigh shook his head. "Why are you here?"

"Matching all black clothing not enough for you?" Marley gestured at the top she wore under her leather jacket; the same gargoyle insignia was sewn on her chest too. "Same as you. Duh. The Induction."

More kids had arrived since Rayleigh had snuck away and were waiting behind the cordon. All sported black cargos, durable jumpers, and jackets. A few stretched, limbering up.

"Your uncle thought he was rid of me, but here I am. And here you are." Marley looked up at the screen. "Standing by this message board instead of with the others—oh. Your dad's here."

"You know who I am." It wasn't a question. It was a reminder of who she was. "You're after the treasure—right?—in that stupid city-wide hunt. Look, you can shake my hand but then you need to go. I'm a little busy."

"What? No," she said, sounding most aggrieved. "I'm not a crazed game player."

"You're not?"

"Absolutely not." Marley's dark eyes became loaded with sympathy. "I came looking for you because, well, I didn't expect your dad to be so easily found." She gestured toward the board.

"I don't understand."

"I thought he was missing."

Rayleigh's stomach lurched like the Monsters Cabinet had just plummeted several stories beneath his feet.

"So did my brothers. That's why they followed me." She rolled her eyes. "I found out about you purely by chance. Well, not chance. A lot of reading about your dad. You were buried in there pretty deeply, but I found the family tree. It was surprising. I always thought Bogey had a daughter."

"Hold on." Rayleigh put his hands up to slow the tide of information Marley was launching his way. "Why did you think my dad was missing?"

"No one's seen him in weeks. There was some speculation. Nothing official. Your uncle didn't say? I guess he wouldn't. He's probably seen him. They're probably in on it together."

Doubt niggled at Rayleigh's confidence in that sentiment.

"That's so cool, by the way, that Thelonious Tickle is your family. Everyone knows about the Terrors, of course. But no one really sees them, because they're, like, spies, right? My brothers are so embarrassed. They thought they were saving you from someone who not only turned out to be your Snatcher, but your family too. Your famous family." Marley laughed, but stopped abruptly and peered up at Rayleigh. "Are you okay?"

Rayleigh felt as far from okay as the earth from the moon. He'd known somehow that Thelonious was keeping something about his dad from him. The Terrors too. But his dad couldn't be missing, not when his name was on the board above. He was here.

He was here, and Rayleigh would see that for himself.

"You don't look okay," Marley answered for him. "Do you need to call someone? I can lend you a comms. I carry spares." She proffered several slim, dark circular objects.

"I'm not making any calls," Rayleigh decided. He wanted to look into Thelonious's eyes, sans sunglasses, when he asked him what was going on.

"What are you going to do, then?" Marley glanced over at the kids waiting by the sign.

Rayleigh did too. They'd been joined by what looked like a tree—a monstrous tree holding a clipboard. They were fascinating, to be sure, but he couldn't go back now. His brain was already whirring with the makings of the kind of plan he was renowned for—or renounced, depending on who was asked.

"I'm going to make a quick visit to see my family. I'd appreciate it if you didn't tell anyone where I was going."

"On one condition," Marley said. "I get to come too."

"It's nothing serious."

"Yeah, okay. Tell that to your face. It's looked all scrunched up and hopeless ever since you read this board. If something's going down, I want to be there for it. For you," she was quick to correct.

Rayleigh snorted. "Yeah, right."

"Either I come with you—" Marley's face tightened with stubbornness. "Or I happen to mention where I saw the son of the Bogey Mann heading off to."

"You'd snitch?"

"No way! But if I mention it to myself, and someone overhears me . . ." Marley shrugged.

"That's as bad as snitching."

"Fine. You want to charge through the Cabinet on your own, be my guest. But you looked like you could use a friend. And I could be that, you know." She scuffed her booted toe against the floor. "It's the least I could do, after I was sort of the one who made you think something was wrong with your dad."

Rayleigh considered Marley; swamped in her leather jacket, she was small despite the platform boots on her feet—and experienced. He could do with a guide who was used to the monster stuff. Not to mention that, of all the new feddies Rayleigh had met, Marley had been the most honest. The most annoying too. But without her tenacity, he'd still be in the dark. Well, more in the dark. "You can come."

"Good choice. I would have made the same. So, plan?"

Rayleigh checked on the treelike feddie with the clipboard; distracted by the growing number of monsterlings, they looked like they were sweating needles. Perfect.

"We run. Now," he decided, beckoning Marley to follow him into the same hall Thelonious disappeared down earlier.

NINE

INDUCTIONS, WELCOMES, AND WARNINGS

The duo followed golden signposts for the courtrooms, advertised as being "a giant's hop and skip away," at a sprint. Rayleigh was confused, but it wasn't the time for questions. The first hall spawned an entire litter of halls that fed into one another. Rayleigh and Marley ran until both breathed heavily. Light stone was exchanged for an austere gray slate that reminded Rayleigh, for the first time, he truly was underground; braziers appeared on the walls, cupping flickering cool blue flames. They cast shadows that seemed to chase the pair.

Slowing before the doors of courtroom no. 3, Rayleigh and Marley found them hanging by their hinges like something had rammed into them. Two somethings. Maybe a pair of horns sprouting from the pate of an audacious monster. Panting and sweaty, a dubious look passed between Rayleigh and Marley.

"Maybe we wait out here," she breathed.

"No. I'm doing this."

"*We're* doing this. In a second. I swear. But—" Marley eyed the ruined door once again. "What is this exactly? Other than interrupting an official government hearing."

Rayleigh paused. "Er, interrupting an official government hearing."

"Thanks for clearing that up. I feel so much better knowing all the details."

"I thought you'd have done something like this before."

"Surprisingly, no."

"Not sure if that makes me feel better or worse."

"Suppose I can add and scratch it off my list in one go, which is kind of cool."

Rayleigh looked her over, oddly relaxed by her company. She had a way of taking things in stride. He was the same, Above. "You're . . . not as bad as I thought you were."

Marley shrugged. "I get that all the time."

"Because you regularly go around tying up strangers?"

"Now, that I have done before, and more often than you might think." She smiled.

Rayleigh would have laughed, if he wasn't so nervous. He never thought he'd appreciate a tourist so much. "Let's do this."

Pushing a door each, they entered the courtroom. Like the halls outside, the lack of windows made its vast interior dim: a central aisle that stretched between two shadowed seating areas and a low wooden partition that separated the rows of chairs from an open floor space before a broad pulpit. It was there Thelonious stood with someone else, a man. They both turned to the open doorway.

"I asked for a closed hearing. No gallery." Thelonious's voice carried with ease; he didn't sound as though he saw who had entered. Indeed, it was unlikely that he saw anything at all; the back of the courtroom was wreathed in shadows and darkness.

"You don't make the decisions here," said the second man; he was pale, with a wheedling Irish brogue.

Pleased he'd gone unidentified, possibly forgotten, given the distracted argument taking place, Rayleigh started down the aisle while his uncle and the man bickered. Marley moved alongside him.

"Look for my dad," he whispered to her.

Rayleigh squinted at the shadowed gallery for a man dressed in all black with golden eyes and a cunning smile. Thick candles dripped wax down lofty perches. Despite their quantity, they were an ineffectual light source against the slate and dark wood—even with the help from the muted glow of several bobbing lanterns. Not lanterns, Rayleigh realized, doing a double take. Stationed around the edge of the room were a number of uniformed ghosts giving off strange light of their own. Rayleigh stopped short; Marley crashed into his back with a cry.

"What—is someone there?" the second man snapped. "Parcter!"

Previously unnoticed, strange given his size, a monster that rivalled a mountain for intimidation rose to block the aisle in front of the children. He was a monumental feat of sinew and pale green skin. Beneath narrowed eyes, shadows lingered; yellow bruising flowered across one cheekbone, and scars peppered his skin, ugly intersecting lines. Regardless of the smart suit and the shirt buttoned high on his thick neck, the monster looked the sort to crush first and ask questions later. He gave an unnerving twitch.

Rayleigh and Marley took a simultaneous step backward.

"What's happening?" Thelonious called.

"Rayleigh?" Gasp stood up in the right side of the gallery, clearing the low shadows that concealed the brightness of his blazer. "It's Rayleigh, Thelonious! And another child."

"Nephew-mine?"

"Nephew?" the other man repeated, stunned. "What the devil?"

"Not the devil, Seamus, Rayleigh," Thelonious corrected him. "Now do me a favor and call off your lackey."

"Absolutely not. The boy shouldn't be in here. Neither should anyone else—there's another, your man said? There are rules, protocols for these things. You yourself said this was to be a closed hearing."

"Rules, huh. Then let the records show," said Thelonious, his voice undercut with menace, "that I gave Seamus and his mindless buffoon the courtesy of asking first."

"Enough."

The interruption was both in the room and Rayleigh's mind, slithering around like slime laced with grit. He cringed; beside him, Marley's hands flew to her head.

"Marley Clementine Liu, wait in the gallery. Rayleigh Jude Mann, come forward."

"I—Your Excellencies," said Thelonious, in a different voice altogether. "While my nephew is remarkable, a chip off this old block, you might even say, there's nothing—"

"Come forward!"

The collection of voices surged down the aisle in a torrent. Marley's curls took flight. Rayleigh squinted. Wind plumed outward from the dark pulpit, extinguishing candles. Though they reignited within a few seconds, the effect wasn't lost on Rayleigh. He wished he'd taken a little longer to think his interruption through.

"Captain Scáthach," that hive of voices murmured. "Tell your man to stand down."

"As you wish, Your Excellencies. Parcter. Step aside."

The monster turned stiffly and edged back into one of the gallery rows, opening up the front of the courtroom.

"Son of Bogey Mann, if you will."

Two of the ghost guards drifted over to flank Rayleigh, leaving him with no choice but to forge ahead without Marley. She gave him an encouraging nod. Alongside, the ghosts' faces were concealed by towering visors, like knights' helmets. Their uniforms were sort of stately too, like some sort of silent, fluid armor. Combined with the candles, their light just managed to illuminate a row of cobwebbed lumps seated behind the pulpit high at the head of the room. At first glance, anyone would have been forgiven for assuming someone had abandoned a mammoth pile of dirty laundry up there. But as Rayleigh drew nearer and his eyes adjusted to the gloom, he could see that there were bodies shrouded in those filthy robes.

Thelonious's face was tight as he stood before the pulpit; his eyes, as always, were concealed behind a pair of mirrored sunglasses. A slight man in a billowing coat peered around him. His expression would have been near comical in its surprise, if Rayleigh had been in the mood for humor. There was no sign of his dad.

"Quorum of Elders," Thelonious said, "allow me to introduce my nephew." In an under-the-breath aside to Rayleigh, Thelonious added, "The Quorum are Below-London judges. Let me do all the talking." He cleared his throat. "As I was saying, my nephew. He was blessed with all the looks, as you can see."

See? Rayleigh eyed the thick cobwebbed fabric shrouding the three judges in doubt.

"Yes, see."

He flinched.

"We are both in your mind and beyond it, Rayleigh Jude Mann."

He resisted the urge to rub his forehead. He didn't want monsters he couldn't see digging around his thoughts.

"You wish to know where your father is," they continued. "As do we."

"The boy doesn't know where his father is either?" Seamus's eyes, green and flat as a stagnant pond, lit with triumph. "Ho! Ho! This is further evidence that the Terrors have no idea where their former teammate is. I move for the immediate dismissal of Robert Mann as Supreme Scarer."

Rayleigh's mouth popped open. Whatever he and Marley had walked in on felt as unpleasant as his trainer filled with puddle water. Something was very, very wrong. If his dad wasn't present, wasn't a participant in the hearing, that made him the subject?

Could Marley have been right, Bogey Mann was missing?

"Slow your roll, Seamus," rumbled Thelonious. "We know exactly where Bogey is."

Hopeful, Rayleigh looked up at his uncle.

"You know what they say about making assumptions, old boy, so I won't bother elaborating. But you be careful." Thelonious's expression was without its customary humor; when he spoke, his tone bore an edge of danger.

"*You* be careful!" Seamus retaliated. Though the threat was made less effective by the steps he took backward, away from Thelonious. "And that's Captain to you, Ick." His weak chest puffed out. "Captain of the Cabinet's Guard."

The ghosts around the room drifted in a little closer, roused by the name—their name. The Cabinet's Guard.

Thelonious was unperturbed. Only the bottom of his long coat moved, stirring in the ghostly wind. "You say that like it means something. You, me, everyone but my nephew—though he'll soon find out—knows that your reach doesn't extend beyond this building.

You are a small fish, Seamus. While I'm happy to remind you of that fact, you should try to remember and save me the trouble. What's happening here doesn't concern you, or the guards you send to rustle up shoplifters and retirees who forget they're in the Cabinet gift shop, never mind that they have to pay for things." Thelonious appealed to the lumps of material behind the pulpit. "It doesn't concern him, Your Most Esteemed Ones."

"I do not speak for me. I speak for the Confederation," Seamus said with great pomp and circumstance. "If our Supreme doesn't care enough to turn up to work, it's time to instate a new one. And this isn't a conversation for progeny to hear." He looked down his narrow nose at Rayleigh. His threat was lukewarm; Seamus, bless him, bore an expression of one constantly in a state of worrying about an appliance he may have forgotten to turn off. "If you are indeed Bogey's son. I, for one, have never heard of you."

"Oi—" Thelonious took a menacing step forward.

"It's okay." Rayleigh shrugged off the slight. "I've never heard of the Captain either."

Seamus's expression soured.

Rayleigh had met plenty of kids like him—spiteful rule followers who couldn't abide people who thought differently from them. Buttoned up in an oddly hairy coat, Seamus looked like he'd never veered off the set path in his life. It was no wonder he couldn't stand Thelonious, and by extension, Rayleigh. But he wouldn't be intimidated.

"If you're talking about sacking my dad, I'm staying." He had to; it was his mind the Quorum read. His fault discussions of firings were taking place. "I'm staying right here."

"There needn't be any talk of firings if, as you say, Thelonious, you know where our Supreme is?" the Quorum said.

"I do." Thelonious cleared his throat. "Bogey has been on a trip researching new Scare Duty practices."

"Yes, but in the request he filed for this sabbatical, he said he wouldn't be gone for longer than ten days," Seamus was quick to cut in. "Yet it has been almost four weeks."

"We're expecting his return momentarily."

Rayleigh's Thelonious Detector whirred. That was as vague a line as he'd been issuing since they met. He was becoming rather dizzy from his uncle's many brush-offs.

"On balance we find that Captain Scáthach speaks much sense," the Quorum said.

At the compliment, the Captain refocused with a simpering grin.

"Who are we to monsterkind if we do not uphold the rules we ourselves established? Not the leaders they entrust our judiciary system to, that much is certain. So." They paused before delivering their verdict: "While we have made allowances for Bogey's son, given the time they have spent apart, he cannot remain in this hearing."

"And not just this hearing, in Below-London at all. Should he wish to remain here," Seamus said, "he must first prove his monstrous heritage. He must prove he is who you say he is."

"Well, he was already here to do the Induction's first trial. And you don't get to deliver ultimatums to me, mate. Not in that jacket." Thelonious paused. "But I can be sporting. By all means, take it off and try again."

"Oh, very mature—"

"Enough!" the Quorum intoned. "Rayleigh Jude Mann will rejoin his Induction party."

"And if he doesn't agree, or fails to transform," Seamus chimed in, "he stays here, under guard, until Bogey makes a reappearance to account for abandoning his duties for so long. For his own safety, of course."

"You'll lock me up?"

"Now, hang on a moment," started Thelonious, hands raised.

"Approved." Gavel hit pulpit with a ringing finality. "Now, what says the monsterling? Will he accept the terms of his stay?"

Thelonious ground his teeth and clenched his fists, but didn't say anything else—couldn't. The decision was Rayleigh's, and it wasn't one he wanted to make. Passing the trial before this hearing was one thing; passing it now he knew the alternative was being stuck with Seamus Scáthach for company? That brought an entirely new type of pressure.

"Rayleigh Jude Mann, if you accept the terms Captain Scáthach established, you and Marley Clementine Liu will rejoin your fellow monsterlings in the Hall of Waiting, where you will prepare to face the Trial of the Creator. Your decision, please."

"Marley, oh yes." Seamus turned around to peer into the dark gallery. "That child has also heard too much this morning."

"She's with me," Rayleigh said.

"She is?" came from a surprised Thelonious.

"Yes," Marley was happy to state from beside Gasp. "I am."

Rayleigh looked back at her—well, in her general direction, given the darkness in the gallery. "It's true, Thelonious."

"Then she can be trusted along with my nephew," his uncle said.

"Leave it now, Captain Scáthach. Marley Clementine Liu is not a cause for concern."

"Exactly," Rayleigh directed Seamus's way. "I'm trying to make an important decision." One that no longer felt as bracing as it had yesterday evening, in the tunnel with Thelonious.

For if mischief and mayhem were the order of the day in the Confederation, he stood a great chance of succeeding in his Induction. He had both in spades, after all.

"After I've inducted," Rayleigh called to the Quorum, "I'll know if you're firing my dad?"

"You'll know" was their reply.

"I won't let that happen," Thelonious murmured. "You hear, Nephew-mine? I'm going to fight so that doesn't happen."

And Rayleigh would fight to ensure the Captain didn't succeed in steering him and his dad away from one another.

"Then I accept." Rayleigh directed his answer to Seamus. He could bring it on. So could the Creator. Not being eaten was no longer a matter of survival; it was a matter of pride.

"Glad to hear it. It's time to escort you back to the Hall of Waiting." Seamus clicked his fingers. "Guards, corral him."

The uniformed ghosts around the edge of the courtroom drifted closer. Their movement stoked a cool wind; it was stronger than earlier. Unlike that from the Quorum, theirs was stale, a reminder that these monsters weren't quite living. Maybe.

"Hang on, Seamus, I want a word with my nephew," insisted Thelonious.

"Not possible, and not happening. Guards!"

In the recesses of the courtroom, Marley shouted at the ghosts, warning them not to touch her. Rayleigh understood what she meant—recoiling from their chill, he found himself unable to escape or even to struggle without the risk of what he was sure would be an icy sting.

"Don't make this difficult." Thelonious jabbed a finger in

Seamus's direction, then to Gasp. "Help Rayleigh!"

The Terror rose; imposing and vividly green, in the surrounding dimness, he shunted aside benches in a bid to get to the front of the courtroom. But before he could, Seamus's muscle Parcter shot out of his seat to intercept him, as though programmed to step in at the first sign of conflict. The Quorum of Elders remained unmoved, but a gavel clashed with wood again and again to silence the noise. It was pandemonium—a different sort to the one Rayleigh had witnessed in the Sphere of Doors. That had been a musical build to an exciting crescendo, like the aria in the Province of Dreamers. This felt like the drum dirge announcing war.

"Use your wits, Nephew-mine!" Thelonious had bounded over to Rayleigh and was striding alongside his ghost escort. "What's in there might look different, but inside, it's something you face every day in Above-London."

"Not another word," Seamus howled. "Not another word! Family and friends aren't part of the Induction for a reason. Influencing outcome is forbidden! Protocol!"

"He missed the tour," Thelonious said. "And the talk. I'm not telling him anything he wouldn't know."

"He'll learn it all when his guide receives him! Any further cheating, and I'll lock him up!"

Thelonious reared around. Seamus took a step back, wide-eyed and somehow even paler.

A set of doors appeared in the wall to the left of the pulpit. Opened by invisible hands, they revealed a stately hall through which children were funneling toward a doorway.

"I'll be fine, Thelonious," Rayleigh called, pleased his voice didn't reveal his worry. Because he was worrying, now the high from sticking it to Seamus was fading. What if he turned into something like the half-slug creature he'd seen in the Sphere of Doors? What if this was the last time he had hair?

"You will be fine," Thelonious confirmed. "Great, even. Do you hear me, Nephew-mine?"

In the doorway, despite the guard closing in, forcing him out of the courtroom, Rayleigh looked back. His uncle stood with a hand raised in solemn farewell, while a struggling Gasp was kept back by Parcter at the head of the aisle, arms outstretched. Seamus looked on, pinched and irritated. Marley, entombed in her own cyclone of ghostly guards, had a hand on her fanny pack and another outstretched in defense.

"Good luck, monsterlings," the Quorum intoned. "Farewell."

Rayleigh was forced out into the Cabinet Hall, Marley stumbling beside him. He steadied her as the doorway circled out of existence, as though hoovered up by an invisible nozzle.

They'd been deposited in what seemed to be a different hall to the one they'd run down, what felt like hours earlier. The walls and floor were made of light-colored stone, and the windows in the ceiling revealed soft blue slices of the lid. Rayleigh reached out to touch the wall where the doorway had been.

"I want to ask if you're okay," Marley broached. "But it feels like a stupid question after all that."

"I think—I think if my dad gets fired, it'll be my fault for crashing the hearing."

"If it helps, I think the hearing was to decide if he deserved to be fired anyway."

Then, Rayleigh thought, he'd all but tipped the scales in Seamus Scáthach's favor.

"Yeah, that doesn't help," he said.

"Ah, our two stragglers!"

The tree with the clipboard from earlier hurried down a broad stone hall, needles whispering. At their back, a half a dozen or so children stopped filtering into a room to watch.

"I'm Conny," the smiling face in the trunk of the tree said, stopping before Rayleigh and Marley. "Though perhaps it's best you call me Ms. Fir. I'm not quite sure. This is my first time leading an Induction." She waved a slender bough, scattering softly scented needles everywhere. "I received a message from the Quorum." Conny exhaled, reaching them. "Rayleigh Mann. Mann. Wow. The son of our—I'm fussing. Sorry. And, oh!" Turning to Marley, she started; her face, somehow both solid wood yet soft and expressive. "Miss Liu, I have to say, I am a huge admirer of your mother. Wow, the pair of you are little celebrities."

Rayleigh looked Marley over in surprise. "Celebrity?" he murmured. Red-cheeked, she didn't answer him.

"You've missed the tour, I'm afraid." A tiny blue bird peeked out of a hole in her throat and chirped.

Rayleigh's mouth popped open.

"But I'm sure someone can take you around later if you wish. I'd be happy to. Hey, maybe your dad can, Rayleigh!"

Not quite able to smile, he grimaced instead. The bird chirped sharply in response.

"Don't mind Belle. Terribly jealous, I'm sure." She beamed with straight, but undoubtedly wooden, teeth. "There was also a prerecorded message from Octavia Brand, who works for the Office of Inductions, Welcomes, and Warnings. Again, you can pop into a later session to watch, if you like, but I can give you the gist of what was said now." Conny beamed at them as Belle dive-bombed into the hole in her throat. "The Confederation understands how jarring it can be to live one life for twelve years before you're expected to accept another reality in a matter of days. It can seem frightening, or exciting, initially. But rest assured, monsterlings have more control over this change than they think. Come with me." Conny spun around and headed back down the hall. "Inside, inside, monsterlings!" she called, waving at the inductees who'd lingered to listen in on the exchange.

"Celebrity?" Rayleigh whispered again to Marley, as the pair followed Conny.

"I don't want to talk about it" was her response.

It was a shame, because, poised between the first trial ahead of him and the hearing going ahead without him, Rayleigh could have done with a way to take the edge off what was turning into the most important day of his life. Two colossal decisions would be made by its end. He'd do his best to ensure he'd be happy with both of them.

TEN

THE TRIAL OF THE CREATOR

Beyond the doorway, beneath a glass ceiling that revealed the bright morning lid, a group of fifty or so monsterlings stood clustered together in the middle of a broad aisle. A storm of curious looks was launched their way, whispers; some of the inductees had heard them called by their first and last names. So much for anonymity. Rayleigh lifted his chin, met every eye. He would not be daunted.

"Oops, sorry there!" Conny called, bobbing and weaving between them. A stocky boy took a face of needles; the girl beside him too. "Welcome, monsterlings, to the Hall of Waiting! Ow. Watch the roots, please."

It seemed like more of a chapel. Two rows of long wooden pews sat beneath its peaked ceiling. At the head of the central aisle, a plain altar held a pulpit. Tall, thin clear glass panel walls revealed a lush garden outside. It was replete with vast leafy trees and bright plate-sized flowers. Had he not seen the Cabinet outside the doors, Rayleigh could have been convinced they'd traveled somewhere else in Below-London entirely. Somewhere that calmed his breathing and quieted his thoughts. Beside him, Marley stopped patting her fanny pack. Her hands relaxed by her sides.

"And welcome—" Conny squeezed her way out of the crowd and into the aisle ahead of them. "To the Trial of the Creator."

"Psst," one of the monsterlings hissed. "Outside, are those what I think they are?" They leveled a finger toward the garden.

Nestled among the waist-high blades of grass were white stones—teeth, in the wild jaw of the garden.

"Are those headstones?" the monsterling asked, their voice quivering.

"They are headstones!" another kid shouted. "We're all going to die!"

"Die?" another asked. "We're dying?"

Murmurs became frenzied; bodies packed together. Marley was jostled into Rayleigh.

"Oi!" He called. "Watch it."

Sweet music cut above the panicked chatter. Heads turned to locate the source of the sound. Belle the blue bird sat in one of Conny's uppermost branches, emitting the calming song. Delicate but mighty, it washed over the crowd, until they stilled. Rayleigh couldn't have run if he'd wanted to. Was that Conny's bent? Bodily control through music?

"Okay," she called. Belle stopped singing. "I understand some of you are frightened by the presence of the headstones. Rest assured, those have nothing to do with your trial. They're simply resting places for Cabinet workers who wished to forever remain here."

"That," Marley whispered, "might be scarier than us dying here."

"Sadder, for sure," Rayleigh murmured back. Who loved their job so much they wanted to be laid to rest there? None of his teachers.

At least it wasn't an omen for the path ahead. This relief was dispersed through the crowd. The buzz-headed boy who kickstarted the hysteria fainted.

"Um, Ms. Fir?" someone called. "Rex has fainted."

"Probably for the best," Conny said. "We'll let him have a short nap—which I encourage any of you to have, should you need it."

Monsterlings jumped back as a sea of roots slithered between their feet and ran underneath Rex. Lifting him several inches off the ground, they retreated back through the crowd—to Conny. She raised Rex up onto a pew, turning him on his side. The silence that followed was stunned, awed. Rayleigh looked upon her, impressed.

"The Hall of Waiting is indeed a space for you to become comfortable with the idea of accepting what the Trial of the Creator means: saying goodbye. For some of you it will be to your past selves as you embark on a new path. In less pleasant circumstances, some of you will say goodbye to the friendships you may already be making. To the dreams you had of staying Below. Life as a monster is, ultimately, a higher calling. As excited as you all are to transform and discover your bents, our work in the Confederation is a responsibility not all can bear. And so, monsterlings, you are encouraged to use this time, the serenity of your surroundings, wisely; to truly think before you take the steps to the trial." Conny gestured to the front of the hall. Murmurs rose from those close enough to see what she was pointing at.

"What's happening?" Marley jumped beside Rayleigh. "I can't make it out."

"She's pointing at a dark square on the floor," Rayleigh said.

"It's the staircase opening," a girl, significantly taller than Rayleigh, explained. "We walk into that darkness, and the rest of our lives change forever. Or not, if we're duds."

"Right?" another girl furiously whispered. "I don't care what Conny said. If I don't get my mum's bent of communicating with hammerhead sharks, my family will disown me."

"What if we don't want to go today?" another kid called.

"It's true the Cabinet has a magic of its own when it comes to time and space," Conny answered, "otherwise we wouldn't be able to accommodate the thousands of you Inducting. But the trials have a set time period. If, by the end of your two hours here, you don't take the steps to complete your trial, you will have another opportunity after everyone else has had their time. Keep in mind, however, all monsterlings must complete the first trial before they're told about the second, and so on. If you wait until the night before the second to complete the first, you will miss out on ample study time. Just— think wisely. Belle and I will be here, should you need anything. Your time, monsterlings," Conny called, "starts now."

"My dad says I have to go today," said a boy as he looked out at the graveyard with wide, panic-filled eyes. "I don't think I can. I don't want to turn into something scary."

"You can control what you turn into," another inductee responded. "When we face the Creator, we just have to wish really hard on the monster we want to become. It takes that into consideration."

"The Creator is a person?"

"My mum told me it's—"

"Come on." Marley took Rayleigh by the arm and pushed her way through the crowd of kids. "Best not to listen to rumors. Let's sit."

"Or," Rayleigh decided, stopping her a short distance from their peers, "I can just head for the square, the stairs, and get started."

"I know you're worried about your dad." Marley lowered her voice. "But he's not missing. You don't have to rush this."

"That's just it. He might be," Rayleigh admitted. He now knew that Thelonious had a habit of telling half-truths, and in some cases, withholding the truth entirely. He hadn't, for instance, mentioned that Bogey had been away longer than intended. He hadn't mentioned the hearing either. "When you came looking for me in Above-London, why did you think my dad was missing?"

Marley winced. "I thought I heard Ma say the Supreme was missing."

"She didn't actually tell you, then?"

"I might have got a bit carried away reading between the lines, but I was only trying to be helpful," Marley said defensively.

"I know." Rayleigh sighed. "I'm just not sure why."

"Why what?"

"Why all of it? Coming to my flat, finding me at the Induction. Joining me in the courtroom."

Marley fidgeted. "Suppose it's only fair. . . . Look, my ma thinks I need to go to school, rather than working with her in the field. We have a sort of family business, like the Terrors. We don't hunt rogue monsters, though. We find people Above who hunt monsters."

Rayleigh untangled the differences.

"Ma got a tip your dad was missing and put out some feelers to see why. In the Above world, you have all sorts who believe in monsters. Our family friend Nessie has had so many close calls in Scotland.

Ma's had to free her from fishing nets, delete footage from satellites. The works."

"And because she does that, she's famous?"

"I guess." Marley sighed. "She's saved lots of monsters. I want to work with her to do the same. Locating your dad would have showed her I'm ready, but now he's maybe not missing—hey, you could tell her for me?" she said, in a different sort of voice. Less confident, it was almost shy.

Rayleigh paused to think. "Can we go in pairs?"

"What?" Marley was surprised by the question.

"In pairs," Rayleigh continued. "Can we do this trial together, you and me?"

Marley's cheeks grew red, but she shrugged, as though unbothered. "I didn't hear that we couldn't. Monsters love a good loophole, so I think we could?"

"In that case, if you help me, I'll tell your mum whatever you want."

"Deal."

"Between your fanny pack and my brains, we'll ace it." He willed it so.

Marley laughed. "That's not what my bag is called."

"It is if you keep wearing it like that." Rayleigh grinned back. "Either way, Seamus can take a running leap."

"Hopefully he'll trip over his ugly coat. Always hated that ghost."

"That's what he is?"

"I mean, technically he's a poltergeist. Troublesome, they are. Though you gave as good as you got." Marley looked Rayleigh over with approval. "You know, you're not as uptight as I thought you were, Above."

"You tied me up!"

"How'd you slip my hold, actually? I thought I'd secured you good and proper."

"Have any more rope? I'll show you."

"So it's true."

Rayleigh and Marley turned at the soft, high voice behind them. The crowd of monsterlings they'd escaped were fanned out at their backs. In the fore stood two slight, pale kids. Twins, if their similar dark, slick hair and haughty, pointed features were any indication. Nothing against them, but mentally Rayleigh groaned. He wasn't quite over his encounter with the last set of twins he'd met.

"There's a Mann and a Liu in our Induction party," the girl continued. "Add our family, and, well." She shrugged a broad shoulder beneath her sweeping midnight-blue coat. "You know what they say about the best things."

"They come in threes," the boy drawled; his voice, soft like his sister's, was like a brush of icy wind against the back of the neck.

Marley's eyebrows lifted. "There's two of you."

"So?" the twins said in unison.

"There's two of us. That makes four." Marley gestured to their audience. "Not to mention everyone else here."

A few of the onlookers laughed. It was without malice, but the girl and boy seemed to darken. It was something in their manner. Something unused to being shown up.

"I'm Verena," the girl announced. "And this is Victor. We're famous too."

"We didn't call ourselves famous," Marley said. "Nor would we."

Rayleigh looked on, unsure whether or not he should step

between Verena and Marley before they stared holes through one another.

"It's fine," the boy, Victor, said. "You're not wrong. Your mum is famous, Marley, is it? And, Rayleigh—" His focus shifted. "Your dad is famous. So is ours."

It was like they were pushing to be asked who their dad was. Rayleigh wouldn't give them the satisfaction. Further proving she was a good friend, Marley didn't either. The same couldn't be said for their peers—someone asked the question.

"Well, Marley's mum is a famous monster guardian in the Above world. And Rayleigh," Verena paused, her dark eyes narrowed with pleasure. "He's the son of our Supreme Scarer."

Whispers ignited with alacrity. Rayleigh's cheeks grew hot under the surveillance.

"And our dad—"

"Would love to hear more," Marley interrupted. "But we've got a trial to ace."

"You're going first?" Victor's eyes widened with shock. "Interesting strategy."

"Why's that?" Rayleigh asked.

"We're waiting until the last possible minute," Verena said.

"We're manifesting our monstrous forms," Victor finished.

"Cool." Rayleigh nodded. "We'll leave you to it, then."

The twins' smiles faltered. "You mean, you don't want to team up?"

"Er." Rayleigh was growing uncomfortable. "Our strategy is just for us two, sorry."

"Of course," Victor said, in that soft way of his.

Rayleigh wished he'd shouted his answer. It would have been less . . . unsettling.

"Good luck," the twins said together.

It had been Rayleigh's choice to undergo the Trial of the Creator immediately. But under the watchful gaze of the twins and the rest of their Induction group, it didn't feel like his decision. Every step he and Marley took down the aisle, toward the dark square in the floor, felt forced—driven—as the crowd at their backs edged after them.

Marley glanced back and sighed. "I was hoping to keep my name quiet until at least the second trial."

"Me too." Rayleigh didn't look over his shoulder. He wanted to, but he wanted to give the twins satisfaction even less. "How high is the chance that Seamus is Victor and Verena's dad?"

Marley shuddered. "I don't like those odds."

"Oh, wait! Wait!" Conny hurried up the side of the hall and cut down one of the aisles to reach the duo. She was holding a metal plank in the shape of a cricket bat with white lights running along its edges. "Our first trial participants. Of course, it would be the two of you. I just need to check for any contraband. You can't use anything to help with the first trial." She ran it over Rayleigh first. Nothing happened. When it hit Marley's midriff, the lights changed to red.

Marley reluctantly handed over her pack. Rayleigh groaned internally.

"Okay," Conny breathed, once she'd completed a final check of Marley to ensure there were no other hidden surprises. "Best of luck. Not that you two need any."

"Can you imagine," Marley whispered, as she and Rayleigh

resumed their march, "if nothing happens? We do this trial, fail, and get sent home?"

He could, actually, especially without the fanny pack; he didn't need the reminder. Not while they closed the distance between them and the square in the floor; not when they were close enough and he saw that the base was in darkness, and not when he paused to look back at the hall and found inductees had climbed onto benches to watch them.

"Fancy going down first?" he asked Marley.

"Um, no."

"Right." Drawing a bracing breath, and then another, Rayleigh took the first stone step down in the darkness.

The second was no easier.

In fact, his limbs protested the entire way down.

"You still alive?" Marley called.

"I think so." Rayleigh searched for the next step with his foot and didn't find it. "I've reached the bottom." Cautious, he edged forward.

Lights sparked to life on the walls around him.

His heart thudded. What was it about Below-London and their use of braziers to scare people out of their wits?

"Why is it still dark?" Marley called.

Rayleigh turned; instead of the stairs behind him, he was surrounded by the cavernous reaches of a real tunnel—not a Vol-trix.

"Marley?" he called. His voice rang around him in a mocking echo. "Marley!"

"I'm right here."

Rayleigh started. She stood behind him.

"But you—" He twisted around, gestured at the high stone ceilings, the stalactite and stalagmite. "I thought—the stairs—"

"They disappeared, huh? Yeah. Space magic."

"Space magic?"

"Helps the Confederation to expand, exist in general, really. Super confusing, and we have enough to think about." Marley kicked a crate brimming with sinister weapons, alerting Rayleigh to its foreboding presence. "Look at these."

"We won't need them, will we?" Rayleigh bent to retrieve the handle of an ancient mace. His arms shook beneath its weight. He was disturbed to find its spikes were stained with something dark. He tossed it back with a grimace, scrubbing his hands on his trouser legs.

Marley frowned down at the weapons. "These aren't monster friendly."

"Not sure we'll meet many friendly monsters down here." Unearthing a slingshot, Rayleigh pocketed it. Among the wedges of metal and spiked things, it was all he felt comfortable using. "So, we just walk until something happens?"

"I guess so. My brothers didn't tell me anything about this. Idiots."

Rayleigh was happy to agree.

Falling side by side, they forged ahead, following the light from the braziers. Their footsteps echoed, loud as artillery fire and equally jarring to Rayleigh's nerves. Monstrous stalactites and stalagmites grew from the darkness, squatting in the tunnel like calcified beasts of a time long forgotten. Each appearance drew Rayleigh and Marley closer together, until their shadows became conjoined.

Who with any sense wasn't a little afraid of the dark?

Marley sucked in a breath and grabbed Rayleigh's wrist. "Something moved ahead."

A hushed argument about who would investigate ensued. After a tense game of Rock Paper Scissors, which Rayleigh won, Marley should have led the charge. But she insisted they share birthdays, which led to the discovery that she was several months older than Rayleigh. And that, she said, was reason enough for him to be the one to go first.

Disgruntled, because while she was older, he was taller, and that should have counted for something, Rayleigh nevertheless padded toward the noise. Marley was close behind. Their approach was nothing more than a whisper against rock. The duo paused behind monoliths of stone, peering out to ensure the way ahead was clear as they edged toward the sound.

Close and closer still they crept. A mental image rose from Rayleigh's fear, a wild monster using one of Rayleigh's legs as a toothpick between its jagged teeth, his mouth wide in a silent wail. . . . Mama always said he'd regret jumping headfirst into things. She might have been on to something.

Steeling nerves fit to burst through his skin, Rayleigh emerged from the cover of a rockslide and found himself standing before, well, himself. He laughed with relief. They'd been playing a game of chicken with their reflections in a monstrously sized mirror.

The cave opened up to showcase the sheer scope and height of the looking glass. Growing from a raised platform of stone, its oval shape was both futuristic and classic. So startling was its clarity against the dull brown of its frame, it didn't matter that Rayleigh and Marley had to scramble up ledges of stone to reach it. No one would have been blamed for thinking there was more tunnel ahead, instead of a picture of what was behind.

"Is this the trial?" he asked. "We just look at ourselves?"

"Well, monsters act as mirrors. Did you know that?"

"Thelonious said, yeah." Scare Duty works because monsters

show kids who they're at risk of becoming if they don't correct their paths, he remembered. "Maybe we touch it and change?"

"Go on, then." Marley stood some distance away.

Rolling his eyes, Rayleigh ventured closer to the mirror. "Are you going to come and stand with me or what?"

"My lace," Marley muttered, kneeling down. "It needs tying."

Her voice bore a slight tremor, and Rayleigh suspected she was nervous. But for the first time since he'd learned about the trial, he wasn't. This was easier than he'd thought it would be.

Eager to speed up his transformation and rejoin his uncle and Gasp and maybe find his father at last, he touched the mirror.

"Ow!"

"You okay?"

"Electric shock." Rayleigh shook his fingers.

Aside from the surprising sting, the mirror's surface had been cool beneath his fingertips. In the wake of his touch, its surface undulated outward like the top of a pond disturbed by the nose of a fish. Rayleigh traced its length with his eyes. A large winged gargoyle perched at the very top of the frame. Skinny arms stretched possessively around the mirror's curve, like it was claiming ownership; it leered down with a horrific wrinkled face and long snout. Rayleigh reached for his slingshot, half certain the creature had winked at him in the flickering firelight.

"Now, I'm not sure," Marley said. "But I don't think the trial involves standing there and admiring yourself."

Before Rayleigh could get a rebuttal in, a screech shredded the air.

A giant fist punched through the surface of the mirror. It was followed by another meaty hand; both sets of fingers were tipped with blackened nails long and curved like the hooked beaks of vultures.

They dug into the earth; veins burst through sludge-colored skin, tough with calluses and scars.

"Is this where you tell me not to worry?" Rayleigh breathed over his shoulder. If those hands had come out several more inches to the right, he would have been knocked across the cavern and into the wall. "That everything will be fine?"

"No way." Marley shook her head firmly. "We should run."

Before the creature could be birthed from the mirror in its entirety, the duo darted behind a lanky stalagmite. Rayleigh moved so fast he was sure he'd left something behind. Maybe it was his courage. He did feel lighter, and decidedly less brave. The tunnel quaked around them as the monster released another eardrum-bursting scream; pebbles fell like hail; dust was a veil of rain.

"What *is* that thing?"

"Judging by the thickness of its nails and the size of its hands, an ogre." Marley swallowed, grimaced. "They're known for always having their mouths full."

"Full of what?"

"What do you think?"

Eaten. Thelonious had warned Rayleigh not to get *eaten*.

"They've really trapped us down here with something that can digest us?" Incredulous, he stared at her.

"Not all ogres are bad. I know a few, and they're great. But—" Marley rambled. "I don't think they'd put something nice in here to test us. Anyway, once we've transformed, we might be able to inflict the same damage."

Rayleigh didn't have time to dwell on the thought of becoming something that could spar with an ogre. The hairs on the back of his neck jerked from his skin. He froze. It was like the shift in an atmosphere before the skies opened beneath the weight of rain. Rayleigh knew—somehow he knew that the ogre was out of the mirror, in the tunnel, watching them. Nearby.

"Scramble!" he yelled, just as the creature made a vicious swipe at them from above with one of its weaponized hands.

Marley rolled one way; Rayleigh went the other.

Flattened against a boulder, safely out of range, breathless and weak at the knees, he hoped Marley hadn't been crushed by the ogre. A real, honest-to-goodness ogre.

The tunnel thundered with its heavy footfall.

Rayleigh edged his face around his hiding place. A hideous hairy bottom greeted him as the ogre scratched himself beneath a filthy shift. Blech. He looked up at its astronomical-sized head and remembered an incident in PE involving one of his peers and a wayward rounders ball. Thelonious said Rayleigh needed to use what he knew. To rely on instinct, what was familiar. To Rayleigh, that was elaborate schemes, which landed him in trouble—just the ticket for Below-London.

Before he lost his nerve, Rayleigh darted out and freed his slingshot. Bending to pick up a stone, his hands shook around the fork. Catching the elastic, he drew it back and found himself the focus of the ogre's rheumy eyes. It had moved and was close enough that when it lashed out with a filthy hand the size of a small car and caught Rayleigh in the stomach, he was launched across the tunnel.

"That better not have been plan A," Marley called.

Splayed like a discarded rag doll in the dirt, Rayleigh patted his legs, his arms, his face. Nothing appeared to be broken. Or bleeding. But everything ached, including his spleen, and he wasn't even sure where that was.

"You'll be fine." Marley appeared over him and stuck out a hand. Rayleigh took it and let her help him up. "You stood before the mirror, and its magic called to your monstrous genes. They'll provide you with more strength than regular kids. The bravery, though, that's all you. I didn't know, in that alley."

"Know what?"

"That you're not entirely hopeless." Her half smile softened the insult. "Aim for the belly button."

"No way." Rayleigh was emphatic. "A head shot might knock him off balance, and then gravity can do the rest." Simple science.

Marley gripped his wrist. "Trust me."

Rayleigh considered her. There was no denying the experience her jacket foretold.

"Fine." Closing his right eye, he took a deep breath. "Hey!"

The ogre lumbered around; its tiny eyes narrowed when it beheld them. Time seemed to slow, and with it Rayleigh's heartbeat. The latter echoed in his ears. *Boom boom.* He took another breath. And then time caught up. With a roar, the ogre charged. Its hairy gut wasn't much better than its bottom. It jiggled about with each of its steps, but Rayleigh kept his eye on the dark smudge in the center of his belly and waited until—

He missed.

"Go again!" shouted Marley, hysteria making her louder than the thudding steps of the advancing ogre.

Rayleigh fumbled for a stone at their feet, hands shaking. Seizing one, it took several tries to place it in the center of the elastic. Marley's orders were a frenzied scream at this point. Rayleigh stood and looked up. Avarice gleamed in the ogre's eyes. Fleshy lips were drawn back in a smile that exposed broken teeth. As its arms stretched out to grab them, Rayleigh dipped the slingshot, drew the elastic back, and fired straight between the monster's hands.

The rock whistled through the air, and planted itself in the ogre's belly button. There was a beat in which it looked down in shock and then back at them before vomit exploded all over the tunnel— and all over Rayleigh and Marley. He was sure the hard knot that bounced off his nose was a piece of bone.

"I think I'm going to be sick." Soaked in steaming, violent-yellow vomit, Marley looked how Rayleigh felt.

"There's enough of that already. Come on!"

With the ogre busy emptying its large gut, the two hauled themselves to the mirror, skidding across a lake of regurgitated things neither was willing to look at with much consideration.

"Reckon we have to pass through it to leave?" Marley asked.

"I'm not sure."

"Well, I don't see any other way out, and the cave dead-ends. If this trial was about facing our monstrous selves, then isn't this part of it too?"

Rayleigh looked himself over; the ogre's vomit was warm; steam wafted from his clothing in gentle waves. He hadn't changed. Marley wasn't standing very close to him or the mirror, though Rayleigh could see her reflected in it beside his own reflection, completely unchanged too. Rayleigh was more than a little uneasy about their appearances, but maybe Marley was right. The only way out was through.

The only way to learn the hearing's outcome was through.

"In that case," Rayleigh began, "I'll see you on the other side." With only a moment's hesitation as to what he'd find, Rayleigh charged through the Creator's cool surface.

ELEVEN

BAD OMENS

Passing through the mirror felt like getting caught in the rain during midwinter. Slowing from a fast run to a slow jog, Rayleigh shivered in the almost dark; it was speckled with silver, but beyond that, there was nothing but the chill; he looked forward to the celebratory tea, when he passed through to the other side. Hopefully there was actual tea. And hot crumpets.

A pinhole of light appeared ahead; it grew brighter and larger, swelling like a cool-blue star. Rayleigh sped up, sprinting toward it. The surrounding air was heavy, like gravity was working against him. Still, he pushed. He fought against wind that felt like treacle, eyes on the blue light until it hurt. Until it was all he saw—until, suddenly, it was gone. As was the feeling of being caught in the rain.

Rayleigh blinked, waited for his eyes to clear, and found himself . . . back in the cave?

Frowning, he turned on the spot. The stone landing the mirror sat upon was the same—the mirror was the same: oval, as tall as a house and just as wide. Unease crept up alongside him. There was no

Marley to be found, no vomiting ogre. In fact . . . Rayleigh patted his clothes, his high fade. His clothes were clean, dry. The Creator's magic had cleaned the vomit away as he'd passed through—because he had passed through, he thought. Then why didn't the weight lift from his shoulders?

The hairs on his arms stood erect. As did those on the back of his neck. He inspected the mirror with his eyes only. The spindly gargoyle still clung protectively to its top. Bony legs pressed against the mirror and the stone at the curved oval edges. Was it alive? Rayleigh wondered, staring hard at the stone face as it flickered in the blue light from the braziers. Did the gargoyle determine if he passed the trial? Was the gargoyle the Creator? He hadn't felt his limited size before it with Marley. Alone, he wasn't a Mann before a magical mirror; he was a boy from East London.

Just a boy.

Understanding eased its way in, past his questions. It stemmed them like a dam. Rayleigh was back at the mirror, alone, because he'd failed the Trial of the Creator. It struck an even bigger blow than he would have predicted before the trial. His heart began to race; his palms turned slick. He was . . . *afraid*. And the thing that frightened him most?

How completely and utterly *un*frightening he was.

Rayleigh couldn't have been more crushed if the rocks above had fallen down on top of him.

Concerns about being slug-like aside, changing into a feddie would have made him part of a world where he'd have been free to engage in as much mischief and mayhem as his heart desired. For twelve glorious hours, he'd believed he would be able to pick a different trajectory than the one he'd been on. But things had righted themselves, and he was exactly as he'd been Above, out of place and in trouble.

"That's for the best."

Starting, Rayleigh looked up at the gargoyle. Did it speak? He patted himself down for the slingshot, but he didn't have it with him.

"Now, this is just embarrassing."

Stilling, Rayleigh dropped his chin.

"Shall we forget you didn't look at us first?" his reflection said.

Rayleigh—both the real boy and the reflection—took backward steps.

"I'm insulted." The reflection's voice—Rayleigh's voice—echoed in the heights of the cave. "Who can you trust if not yourself? Come on, doesn't that sound like something we'd say?"

Ill at ease, Rayleigh took another step back. Unwilling to look away from the reflection for too long, he made quick darting glances around the cave. No Marley, still.

"She's passed the trial, genius. Now, will you talk like you know who we are?"

"Stop that."

"Stop what?"

"If we're us, shouldn't you know what?" Rayleigh asked, unable to believe he was talking with himself.

"Since I'm you, I know I would only ask that question to catch me out."

The reflection had a point.

"Okay." Rayleigh shrugged. "If you're me, how do you know where Marley is and I don't?"

"I can see the celebratory tea from here. You could too, if you come back in." The reflection held out a hand. "Conny said they had a way to comfort the losers—this is it. Before the memory wiping. Though, what's so great about seeing your friends get something you wanted but didn't get, I don't know."

"Right?" Rayleigh couldn't believe that was meant to make him feel better. He was sure he'd feel happy for Marley eventually, but not yet. Not while he was talking to himself about how he'd lost. "Hey, what did I do wrong? How come I didn't pass?"

"You just didn't want it enough, I guess."

Rayleigh chewed his lower lip. "I didn't?" It was true he hadn't wanted to stay Below initially, but he'd wanted to hear the outcome of the hearing. He'd wanted to see if he would transform. He still did. It was a stunned sort of ache, at the moment. Like when he slipped down the stairs or fell off his bike. The full pain didn't sink in until after he acknowledged that he'd been hurt. If he let himself feel the extent of his jealousy about Marley, that pain might come in waves great enough to submerge him.

"Are you coming to see Marley?"

"I don't think so." Rayleigh sighed. "Hey, can you help me get out of here? Seamus wants to lock me up—us up. Do you know a way out?"

"Sure." The reflection held out a hand again. "Come with me."

"Thanks, man." Rayleigh started for himself and then—stopped. Something inside, some sense of awareness, of natural suspicion, told him not to move. Just as surely as he knew Thelonious had been keeping something from him, he had the suspicion that his mirror self was too. "How are you going to get me out if I step in?" he asked.

His reflection smiled with a mouth just like his, only less something. Less . . . less human, Rayleigh realized. This thing . . . it didn't feel like he was looking at himself.

"What's up?" it asked.

Rayleigh had a question of his own. "What are you?"

"I'm you." The reflection's smile stretched from ear to ear; its face distorted, like Rayleigh was looking into a fun house mirror.

"No." He refused to lose any more ground to whatever was in the mirror. You're not me."

The reflection laughed; hollow, it rang in the cave, pealing like a warning bell around Rayleigh. "Who else would I be?"

"Part of the trial." Rayleigh would have bet money on it. Marley said monsters acted as mirrors; they reflected who kids had the potential to be. This first one was meant to show how Rayleigh saw himself. But this smiling performance delivered by his reflection wasn't one he recognized. He didn't want to be a person who watched from the sidelines. He wanted to celebrate with his friends. He wanted to pass this trial with Marley. "You're not my reflection," Rayleigh mused. "Not now, anyway. You're not who I want to be. You're not how I want to see myself." His tone grew more confident. "You're who I'm leaving behind. I don't choose this, and I don't choose *you*."

A crack spliced through the reflection's face. A violent purple, bright and bold, fractured outward in a series of sharp screeches, like cries from gulls.

Rayleigh started, but did not shift back. This time, he ran toward the mirror—sprinted toward what he hoped was the promise of life in the Confederation on the other side. Arms up over his face, he burst into the glass—only, it wasn't glass. Soft, malleable, it turned into air, and he landed on something springy. Lowering his arms, Rayleigh straightened to riotous applause.

A small party stood before him, beneath the domed roof held aloft by a collection of strong pillars. Monsters, citizens of the Feddy, clapped and cheered for Rayleigh before a backdrop of Below-London's cityscape. In their fore were Thelonious, Gasp, Bloody Mary, and Shade. The first three bore large smiles. The latter, well, the latter was there. And bunting was also present, garlanding the pillars alongside more of the same giant fairy lights Rayleigh had spotted while shopping earlier; there were tables of food and drink—including warm tea. All in all, it was a cracking celebration. And one, Rayleigh realized, was set in the gazebo-like topper of the Monsters Cabinet.

"I passed?" he breathed.

The applause faded as all turned to Rayleigh's left.

"Congratulations, Rayleigh Jude Mann." A woman sat in a large fishbowl on wheels. No, not a woman. Rayleigh stared; at least, not entirely a woman. Her lower half twisted and curled in the water, suction cups and all. "You have passed the Trial of the Creator."

Applause struck up once more. It was loud, impassioned.

"That really was extraordinary timing, young man." The monster in the fishbowl propelled herself toward Rayleigh. "Octavia Brand, Office of Inductions, Welcomes, and Warnings. I know your father, of course. I'm sure he'll be proud when he hears how quickly you worked through the trial."

"Thanks. Has my friend come through yet?"

"You weren't alone? Well, no one else has appeared yet, but we'll give them time." Octavia offered Rayleigh a sympathetic smile. "It's a trial in three parts, you see. We have an affinity with that number, in the Confederation. First you had to prove your bravery by taking the stairs. Then you needed to show imagination in facing the Creator's guardian. Lastly, the hardest part, facing your own reflection; confronting who you were and deciding who you wanted to be. Can I ask, how did you determine it wasn't who you wanted to be so quickly?" She watched him intently, like he was keeping a pivotal secret.

"I'm not sure. I think maybe my bent helps me tell when feddies are being honest. My reflection didn't seem like me."

Octavia nodded. "Well, we'll have to keep an eye on you, Mr. Mann. Though I see you have four sets looking out for you already. Five, when your father returns. Before I leave, this is for you." She handed Rayleigh a plain envelope, much like the one Nana gave him from Mama. "I will pop in throughout the week, but even with the time magic we use to fit the thousands of inductees into one day, I can't wait for everyone. I did, however, want to make sure I met you." She bowed her head. "Good day."

A cluster of monsters, including a faun in scarlet robes, lingered to take Octavia's place; Thelonious edged ahead of them. The rest of the Terrors followed suit.

"Congratulations, Nephew-mine!" Thelonious swept Rayleigh up in a headlock. "Never doubted you for a second. Do I feel a pair of horns coming through?"

Rayleigh wrestled himself free from his uncle. Bending double, Gasp drew him into a gentle embrace. Rayleigh had to stretch to reach his waist; his arms could not meet at the troll's back.

"Bravo, Rayleigh." Mary planted a kiss on his cheek; he warmed right through, no longer needing that cup of tea to do the job.

Before Shade, he raised an expectant brow.

"If you think I'm going to kiss you," the penumbra drawled, "prepare to be disappointed."

Rayleigh laughed.

Thelonious squeezed Rayleigh's shoulders. "You're a monster, kid. I'm so proud. I would have been proud either way. But welcome to the rabble."

"I'm a monster," Rayleigh repeated, testing the shape and taste of the statement. Saying it out loud didn't feel strange or ridiculous—didn't feel wrong. It felt like a title he was born to carry; it tasted like a life he was made to live. But there was a cloud in his otherwise bright future.

"What was the outcome from the hearing?"

"We can talk about that at home, Nephew-mine," Thelonious breezed. "Did I hear you tell Brandy you did the trial with a friend? That Liu girl?"

"Yeah. I'd like to see her finish."

"That we can do. B?"

"Be?" Rayleigh asked. "Be what?"

"Bloody." Mary smirked. "It's a nickname. Shade and I can return home, yes," she told Thelonious. "Well done, Rayleigh. We're all so proud of you."

"Why aren't you staying?"

"Work." Mary glanced at Thelonious. "See you soon."

"Come on, Rayleigh." Thelonious slung an arm around Rayleigh's shoulder, near buckling his legs. "I see a few school scouts lingering to talk with you. There's really only one school worth its salt, in Below-London. It has the best range of subject specialists eager to impart knowledge to little monsterlings. It'll shape you to be whatever monster you want."

"Because I'm going to be one, even though I don't look like one?"

"Oh yes," Gasp answered. "You missed the talk, I keep forgetting. The Trial of the Creator is the hardest. You have to accept in yourself that you are a monster. That's the majority of the hard work accomplished. Now we get to sit back and wait to see how your bent manifests, and whether or not there will be physical change. Personally, I think you'd look smashing in green."

"There are no trolls in our family, Gasp," Thelonious argued.

"Then let Rayleigh be the first."

"If he's going to take after any of us, it'll be his old man, or me."

"Will you two ever tire of bickering?" A suited person stepped into their path. "Perhaps you can stop for long enough to introduce me to your charming nephew, Thelonious." Kind green eyes smiled down at Rayleigh from a face that didn't suggest any monstrous heritage at all. His features, though handsome, distinguished, were cold. Like he was hewn from a glacier. Perhaps he was.

"Undersecretary Duplicious, it would be an honor. Rayleigh, this feddie is someone we've been trying to convince to join the Terrors for decades. Aside from his terrible taste, as he keeps refusing us—" The Undersecretary laughed. "Meet Ian Duplicious, Undersecretary to the Chancellor of Below-London."

"Those titles mean he's rather important," Gasp whispered in a false aside.

"Or so they tell me." The Undersecretary's smile created deep lines around his eyes, his mouth. "It's a pleasure to meet you, Rayleigh. I'm a huge supporter of your father. And now you, after today's performance."

"Thanks."

Gasp nudged Rayleigh's shoulder with his hand.

"Er, sir. Thanks, sir."

"It's quite all right. I see why Bogey filed so many requests to see you, Above."

"He did?"

"Oh yes. Terribly fond of you, he was. And you are proving to be as skilled a monster as he is."

"Thanks. Sir. Thank you, sir." Rayleigh rolled his shoulder; Gasp's knock felt more like a thump, with his large hands.

"I'll leave you to your adoring fans." The Undersecretary winked. "Thelonious, we'll talk about the hearing at a later date?"

"Sounds good, sir. Take care now."

"You all too."

"He was kind of cool," Rayleigh observed. "Seamus should hang out with him."

"Not if Ian's here. They hate one another. There's a running joke that you'll never find them in the same room." Thelonious flagged down a waiter with a platter of drinks and handed a teacup to Rayleigh. "For your mouth. I suspect it's about to get rather dry. I know we said we'd keep your surname out of things, but we roll with the waves in our crew."

Rayleigh, as it happened, could barely keep his head above water. After the Undersecretary, there were more Cabinet workers who wanted to meet Rayleigh. Many of the latter served with his dad and couldn't believe he'd kept Rayleigh a secret for so long. Others understood why. Though Thelonious or Gasp would cut them off whenever they'd attempt to disclose specifics.

"Is my dad in some kind of danger, as Bogey Mann?" Rayleigh asked during a lull in visitors.

"Nothing he can't handle" was Thelonious's diplomatic, and vague, answer. Turning to deposit his large mug of tea on one of the banquet tables, he caught his horns in the tangle of lights strung between the pillars. "Bloody fairy lights."

Rayleigh reached to help, but his uncle was too tall—even more so with the horns.

"Watch it!" a muffled voice called. "You'll tangle us up."

With the lid brighter than it was when they'd first arrived on the shopping street, it was easier to see inside the bulbs. Rayleigh found they weren't lights at all. Inside each large glass bauble, opaque wings wafting lazily, were creatures he'd heard of without the aid of *The Book of Night Things*.

"Hey, there are fairies in there."

"Oh yes," said Gasp, reaching over Rayleigh to help free Thelonious. "Imprisonment in those bulbs is a lifelong sentence decreed by the Bureau of Monster Regulation. It's a shame. They're only Category Fours."

"Category Fours?"

"It's a ranking system for sentenced monsters—Categories One through Three are meant to be the worst. They're kept in a special prison. But Category Fours have to do their time in community service. The fairy rebellion decided that. Tired of 'hiding their light,' their words, fairies fled Above and allowed themselves to be seen. There were photos, newspaper articles—a movie." Gasp shook his head. "It was a catastrophe."

"I've never heard of fairies existing Above."

"Oh, the Bureau cleaned up their mess. With a rather flimsy excuse, if you ask me, but one that worked all the same. They had to.

The power of monsterkind is in our anonymity. There is no greater danger to our existence than exposure. Monsters teach children what to fear, but we also teach them how to overcome their fears. Fairies, nasty little nips, became sweet to bovers—er, humans," Gasp clarified. "Those who live Above. Irreparably so. To that end, the Bureau gave them what they craved, a mandatory number of hours serving the community they almost exposed, in the spotlight."

Rayleigh glanced up at the fairies again. "What if I turn into one?"

Free, Thelonious waved off one of the winged creatures, who gestured rudely at him. "Don't commit treason against the Confederation, or we'll have to install you in a lamp at home."

Gasp tutted. "He's kidding, Rayleigh."

"Of course I am." Thelonious looked down at his watch, and winced. "Kid, I know you wanted to wait for your pal, but we have to make a move."

A couple of hours had passed since Rayleigh successfully completed the first trial. None of the other inductees had appeared yet.

"She helped me."

"You'll see her soon for the second trial," Thelonious reasoned.

"And you can have her over, if you like?" Gasp suggested.

Rayleigh didn't want to leave. "We can't stay a little longer?"

"Afraid not, kiddo. Sorry. Duty calls."

Rayleigh patted his pocket; at least he had his comms. When he was back at Terror Tower, he'd figure out how to call her.

"Okay."

"You'll perk up once you see how we're getting home." Thelonious patted the side of his nose. "A little treat for how well you did today. And a sorry from me."

"For not telling me about the hearing?"

"Yeah. That. Come on!"

Someone had told the press Bogey Mann's son was present in the building; the noise outside the Cabinet had tripled in volume from when they'd arrived in the morning.

Thelonious frowned. "Okay, so we'll take the back way."

Rain had fallen at some point, while Rayleigh was in the Cabinet; it turned the light grey pavements and stone buildings of the city dark and moody. Thelonious led the way through the maze of side streets littered with bins and rubbish, past sporadic splashes of graffiti and posters advertising something to do with horns and running.

Before a garage door, Gasp unlocked the chain with a small key and slid the door open with a grind of rust. Inside was a junkyard of abandoned relics. They wove around hulking contraptions cloaked in sheets and shadows, heading deep into the belly of a warehouse to board an ancient metal lift.

Watching him wind an ancient-looking lever, Rayleigh had to ask, "Is this safe?"

Death by elevator seemed quite mundane after everything he'd been through.

"It's sufficient," puffed Gasp.

The elevator lurched to life, chugging its way up and up. Passage through a series of doors put the trio on the rooftop; the air felt heavy with an electricity that foreshadowed more rain. Fitting in, a giant aviary crested the clouds like a Gothic castle; inside were three of the largest birds Rayleigh'd ever seen.

"You're not afraid of heights, are you?" Thelonious checked. "Or birds?"

"How could he be afraid of birds with you clucking like a mother hen?" Gasp tossed at him.

Feeling closer to fearless than frightened after the trial, Rayleigh approached the ground floor of the cage. The lone bird there, smaller than the other two but still as large as a B-Cab, stared back at him; intelligence glinted in its eyes as it cocked its head.

"They're called Bad Omens." Gasp reached through the bars, something shiny between his fingers—a coin. The omen hopped over and nuzzled into his hand, making a keening noise in the back of its throat. "They have a malicious reputation, but give them something shiny, and they'll love you forever. They used to fly before plagues, or in times of tribulation when bovers needed an extra incentive to change."

"Bothers?"

"*Bover,*" Thelonious corrected. "As in, person who dwells Above. Though, some monsters do think humans can be a bit of a bother."

"I get that." Rayleigh grinned before turning back to the omens. "Do we get to fly them?"

"Not quite." Thelonious opened the cage door and hoisted himself onto the second floor. He offered the omens coins too, tossing them into their nest. "See here, beneath Kedara's wing is a feather that's longer, stronger, and thicker than the others." Teal and purple shimmered in the plume, blending into pearly white tips. "We use these to direct the omens while they hold us against their chests in their talons. It's a great honor that these magnificent creatures permit even that."

Rayleigh nodded. He couldn't help but notice there were three omens.

"Am I gliding on my own?"

"One day, if you're lucky," Thelonious said. "Tonight you're with me."

Using a complicated knot of belts, he strapped Rayleigh to his chest like a giant baby. At least his feet still touched the ground, otherwise he'd have to rethink how cool gliding was going to be. As it was, he was already having second thoughts.

They'd moved to the edge of the roof to watch the Bad Omens stretch their wings in preparation for their flight. The third would fly alongside them to an aviary close to Terror Tower. Winds battled and roared, tearing past the exposed skin on Rayleigh's face. The threat of the surrounding darkness made the fall from the roof seem both infinite and short. Behind the gathering clouds, jagged streaks of lightning were realistic enough that one could forget witches were in control of the weather.

"You ready?" Thelonious asked.

"What do I do?" Rayleigh murmured. "Other than not scream?"

A caw sounded behind them, followed by the drumbeat of wings.

"You walk with courage." His uncle's voice rumbled up his spine. "And then you enjoy yourself, of course." And without further warning, Thelonious stepped off the roof.

TWELVE

MANN DOWN

Rayleigh's stomach shot to his throat as he at once regretted any trust he'd placed in his bonkers uncle. At his back, Thelonious's laughter was wild. Unlike Rayleigh, he was unbothered by the fact that the street—where several unwitting pedestrians strolled—rose to meet them with startling speed.

But then Kedara was there, plucking them from their freefall. Drawing the duo in close, she dropped like a lightning bolt before releasing her wings with a crack of thunder. They tunneled up through the clouds with the speed of a fast train. The lid wasn't the sky, which meant it had a roof, a ceiling. Cringing against Thelonious in his harness, Rayleigh could have sworn that each of his organs was splayed across the bottom of his stomach. It would be just his luck to survive the Trial of the Creator only to splatter against the top of a false sky. His eyes closed.

"Are you looking, Nephew-mine?" Thelonious yelled in his ear. "This is my favorite part!"

Rayleigh couldn't bring himself to. Instead he felt the point when

Kedara's wings fanned outward. The stop was abrupt, and the anticipation of the fall—the drop—paralyzed him with fear. But it never came. Cautious, Rayleigh opened his eyes.

Kedara drifted back through the clouds, as light as a floating leaf. Rayleigh's pounding heart calmed in his chest. He stretched out a hand as the clouds dissipated around them. Fake, of course, they weren't wet and cold. Soft to the touch, they caressed his fingers like fine silk. With death less imminent, clasped to the omen's chest, there was a thrill of weightlessness, freedom.

"This," Rayleigh said, "is amazing."

"Maybe you'll grow wings." Thelonious's arm came into view as he gave one gentle pull of the omen's steering feather. In response, she curved around the trunks of earth and stone, wings shimmering like they were lined with her gifted coins.

Being in the lid felt apropos. Rayleigh wasn't sure if he'd ever come down from what had started as a questionable day, before it ended as one of the best in his life. And though that didn't mean he was ready to say goodbye to his life Above, inside he knew that if he didn't have a life in the Confederation too, he'd forever feel like his world was the wrong way round.

Much too soon for his liking, Gasp called, "Terror Tower in a giant's tumble!" before he spiraled away in a mint humbug of feathers.

Kedara dipped like a raindrop sluicing down a window, low, lower, through a gossamer isle of cloud until Rayleigh was provided with an unobscured view of the Province of Dreamers. If Brutely was a sepia wash of brick and concrete, his current pocket of Below-London was a feat of Technicolor. A kaleidoscope of sounds and smells, it unfurled and rolled, abounded and zigzagged.

"Prepare for landing!"

Thelonious pulled on both steering feathers. Kedara banked, wings arching high on either side as they approached a rooftop where an aviary perched like a crown.

Gasp swooped in beside them. His curls were a snowstorm atop his head. "And how was that?"

"My bike is ruined for me." Above, the closest he'd come to flying had been flying down the tall hill behind his school on his way home. It would never be the same. If he chose to return home.

After the third omen landed, all three were watered, fed, and secured in the aviary. Thelonious, Gasp, and Rayleigh took an elevator just as rickety as the first to the bottom of another warehouse. Once the door was secured behind them with a thick chain, Thelonious strolled through the province into Terror Tower's close like he didn't have a care in the world. Something Rayleigh couldn't help finding a little strange, given the measures he'd taken the night before.

"Aren't you worried about being spotted by more thieves?" Rayleigh queried.

"The omens prevented that." Gasp ushered Rayleigh across the street. "Now, I fancy a large slice of cake and something hot with lots of whipped cream, don't you?"

Inside, Terror Tower was warm and brightly lit. Peeling off his layers, Rayleigh broke out in a broad smile. The house, with its living wallpaper and secret floors, would be his home for at least the next few days. Longer, once he passed the second trial—Seamus was likely having a tantrum. And speaking of the Captain—

"Now we're home," he said, turning on Gasp and Thelonious, "what did the Quorum say?"

Footsteps echoed at the top of the stairs. Mary peered down at them from the lower landing.

"There's something you need to see," she said, forestalling any response from Thelonious and Gasp.

At the top of the stairs, the clubhouse floor was a sea of balloons; a large banner was strung from left to right, congratulating Rayleigh. Thelonious and Gasp paused, but Rayleigh charged after Mary. Celebrations could wait. She and Shade waited in a room Rayleigh'd yet to enter. Windowless, with dark walls and several rows of cinema-style red seating, a lone object drew the eye. A pearlescent orb, about the size of a bowling ball, sat atop a table. From its inside, a nimbus of light projected a news broadcast onto the wall opposite.

"And for those who missed the troubling segment earlier," said the reporter, twisting his mouth in a frown that still managed to show his large white teeth. "We have received reports from a trusted source inside the Cabinet that the Terrors, a band of decorated special forces operatives within the Cabinet's Shadow Guild, have been charged with tracking down the Bogey Mann. That's right, citizens of the Confederation, we have it on very good authority that our Supreme Scarer is missing."

Rayleigh's stomach jolted like he'd missed a step, though he stood quite still. Missing? He looked around the room in disbelief. None of the Terrors looked surprised. Thelonious was downright livid.

"Seamus *Bloody* Scáthach," he hissed.

"The Cabinet's official stance is that our Supreme Scarer is on assignment; they repeated this when approached for a comment about the news, which we here at *The Vulture Culture* find troubling. The fact of the matter is this: Who has seen the Bogey Mann recently?" The reporter shuffled his cards. "There is one source who may know where our Supreme has gone. He calls our Bogey Mann *Daddy*."

Rayleigh started as an image of himself appeared beside the reporter.

"That's right, citizens of Below-London, our Supreme Scarer's son is undergoing his Induction to life in the Confederation. From reports we heard, he underperformed during his first trial, and—"

"I did not!" It wasn't enough that the image they used of Rayleigh looked as though it had been captured in the lowest resolution, using whatever Below-London's camera equivalent was. He'd been caught mid-blink too, which changed his perpetually sleepy look to straight-up dopey. "Where are they getting this from?"

"I think the bigger problem, Nephew-mine, is that they have it at all." Thelonious's knuckles cracked as he squeezed his scarred fingers into fists. "I am going ghost hunting at the FIRST opportunity."

"I don't think it was the Captain." Mary winced. "Aren't those little monsterlings the children of—"

"No way," Rayleigh said slowly, as the camera cut to an interview with the twins from his Induction.

"Terribly conceited and terribly undertalented," Verena said. "We offered to help, but that Mann boy was terribly cruel."

"I was not!" Outrage warmed Rayleigh's cheeks. "They're lying!"

"False news," Shade mused, as though experienced in the matter.

"Thank you to our illustrious monsterlings. The future of tomorrow. At least, some of them are." A blue cross appeared over the image of Rayleigh beside the reporter. "Perhaps Bogey is on the run to avoid an unwanted family reunion."

A strained sort of silence took over the snug, like everyone was restraining themselves from sharing a few choice words.

Gasp huffed. "I will write a letter. Two!"

"Don't bother." Rayleigh's hands shook. "I'll just beat the twins, again, at the next trial."

"And maybe I'll pay that reporter a visit," Thelonious said, menacingly. "Make sure he really digests the meaning of your missive, Gasp—two, you said? I vote for more."

"In other news, we here at *The Vulture Culture* encourage all citizens to check their windows and doors regularly, especially in light of the ongoing burglaries. If—"

The projection rescinded into the orb; an overhead pendant filled the snug with dim light.

"Okay," Rayleigh began. "That news show is clearly rubbish. It lied about me, so it has to be lying about my dad. Right?"

"I need some time with my nephew," said Thelonious.

Shade glided out with a knowing sniff. Gasp squeezed Rayleigh's shoulder in passing.

Mary, regal in a long robe, looked between Thelonious and Rayleigh. "Tea will be waiting, when you're done." The door closed softly behind her.

Rayleigh folded his arms over his chest. "Thelonious—"

"I know, Nephew-mine," he sighed. "What I have to tell you is something we would have discussed yesterday, if I wasn't hoping to be proved wrong this entire time." He dragged a hand down a face stripped of its usual joviality. "But given the lengths to which Seamus is going to undermine us, it's now imperative that you understand what's happening."

Both uncle and nephew braced.

"The Terrors have a wireless frequency we use to transmit code to one another, off the grid," began Thelonious. "We used it to reach out to Bogey again this morning to notify him that you were heading to your Induction, should he want to finally make an appearance. But as you know—"

"He didn't come," murmured Rayleigh.

"Bogey's absence isn't a reflection on you, Nephew-mine. Do you hear me? Not returning our correspondence for the past month was one thing. But if he didn't show up to see the son he looked forward to knowing more than anything across the four realms, we could no longer assume that he was in control of his circumstances."

Rayleigh wet his lips. "What does that mean?"

"We thought he was distracted with his work. It happens often. Now we're considering something more nefarious, another reason as to why he wasn't here for the Confederation. For you."

Rayleigh's body ran cold and then hot, in quick succession. "He's in trouble."

Thelonious's great shoulders slumped.

Rayleigh sank onto the chair, his anger leaving him, turning stiff limbs soft.

"I hope you can forgive this old sport for keeping it from you. I didn't want to deceive you, Nephew-mine, only to spare you from what I hoped—from what I hoped would be unnecessary worry."

"Why didn't you tell the Quorum? Or Seamus? They could help. We need to find him, Thelonious—" He began to blur around the edges as Rayleigh's eyes began to fill with water. Furious, he blinked it away.

"Hey, hey." Thelonious eased onto the chair beside Rayleigh. "We don't know if he's been taken, or if he's hiding or what. Just that he's in trouble—and it might be a trouble we can fix without ringing a bell that cannot be unrung. It's complicated, Nephew-mine. Bogey isn't just our family, he's a symbol—a light across all four realms. The Supreme generates the most Volence during Scare Duty, easily five times as much as the average monster. If there's not enough being created, eventually demand will outweigh supply; Above and Below would both be in trouble. If we announce that light has been extinguished, it sends messages to everyone. Including those bad apples we discussed at breakfast this morning. Are you with me?"

Breakfast had only been this morning. For Rayleigh it felt like it happened days ago.

"Nephew-mine? I need to know if this is too much for you."

Rayleigh met his reflections in Thelonious's sunglasses. "I can handle it."

"Okay."

"No more lying."

"Technically I used a loophole, but—"

"You said Marley was a fanatic, like that guard from the Cabinet, your ginger friend," Rayleigh pointed out. "But she was searching for my dad same as you."

Thelonious bowed his head, nodded. "No more untruths."

"What now?"

"I'm hoping this will help."

The overhead light dimmed as smoke and light expanded inside the orb, stretching against the glass until Rayleigh was sure it would explode. Instead, light beamed outward and projected another image onto the wall—a familiar, and instantly much missed, image.

"Mama," he breathed. "How?"

"This is a Seer's Eye. You can see anything, anyone, if you think hard enough about them." Thelonious paused. "As long as they're not in the bathroom, on the toilet, that sort of thing. There are privacy blockers."

Mama sat behind her desk at work. Beneath her blouse, a flimsy necklace was just visible. Rayleigh'd made it for her at the local community center during a summer break. She'd accepted it with a wry grin and never worn it, though it took pride of place in her jewelry box. And yet there it was around her neck in all its ugly, mismatched glory. Humming, she touched it every now and again. Whenever she did, she'd smile.

"She's happy."

Rayleigh'd forgotten how she wore joy. How it seemed to shine through her dark skin like she was filled with it; how it rested on her brow like a glistening crown. As more detention letters had made it home, too many for him to destroy, she'd started to look more like an executioner than a queen.

Realization was a heavy weight around Rayleigh's shoulders. "She doesn't know my dad's missing."

"No."

"And I can't tell her."

"Drea believes you and Bogey are bonding and that she'll see you, monstrous you, in three weeks. Nephew-mine, I'm sorry."

"I won't say anything." He near wished he didn't know himself.

When he thought back to Mama, to the way she smiled when she touched the necklace he made, he couldn't be the one to ruin that. He wouldn't. "What did the Quorum say about him?"

"To avoid a public panic, it's in the Quorum's best interest not to doubt his return until they can't any longer. They've given him, and by extension us, three weeks. We think for you. So you can meet him."

Not *for* him, Rayleigh thought. *Because* of him. Because he'd interrupted. If he hadn't, his uncle might have had more time.

"They know we'll be looking for him. They will be too." Thelonious clasped Rayleigh's knee. "I am going to take care of this, Nephew-mine. And you. Do you hear me? Can you hear the truth in my voice?"

Rayleigh's stomach knitted together painfully. "I hear it."

"Okay. What do you need?"

"Can you make the Eye show me Nana?"

"I've always found the old bird a bit of a battle-ax, but I can do you one better." Thelonious retrieved a comms from his pocket. He flipped it open, raised it to his mouth, and said, "Old bird." A second, maybe two passed, before something in a shimmering pale blue rose from the device in Thelonious's palm. A head, followed by a neck, shoulders, the upper handles of a mobility scooter.

Rayleigh sat up straight. "Nana?"

"Rayleigh," the projection said lovingly.

Thelonious raised a finger to his lips and passed the device over to his nephew.

"Is my second-born there?" she asked with a frown.

"Er—"

"Get away with you," Nana aimed at Thelonious, neck craning as she tried to find him. "I don't need you around while I fix your mess." Suddenly quite small for a mammoth horned man, he schlepped out of the room. "Close your mouth, boy," Nana said to her grandson. "There are far bigger things down there that could zoom inside than flies."

He did as advised with a snap, before opening it again. "Do you know?"

"About your father? I know." Sitting back in her chair, she cast a disapproving look around the dark room, lit only by the undulating glow of the Seer's Eye. "Don't try that opener on your mama."

"I wouldn't." Rayleigh was defensive. "I'll speak to her when Thelonious finds Dad." He knew that if he did so sooner, she'd hear the worry in his voice. "I only said that because you're like me—I'm like you. A monster."

"You are. This isn't the life I hoped you'd find when I let you sneak out on All Hallows' Eve." She gave him a sardonic look. "Yes. *Let* you."

Rayleigh's cheeks warmed. "Don't suppose you could have slipped me a quick word about all this Confederation stuff before you disappeared."

Watery eyes cut him to the quick. "You're the son of the world's most fearsome creature of the night. You are my grandson. You didn't need a forewarning." Her voice softened. "This life is something I've been preparing you for since the first time you sat at my feet and I read from *The Book of Night Things* the same way I read to your father and uncle. Bogey came to see me shortly before all this started." She waved a hand. "Told me to make sure you brought it with you, Below, so you'd have something familiar."

"Why didn't he talk to me?"

"To keep you safe. It's why I moved in with you and Drea. So you both would never come under any harm from those who wish to hurt your father. He has a lot of enemies."

Enemies. The word didn't feel silly and exaggerated, as it did on the playground when friends fell out. It felt foreboding. Thelonious suspected the Bogey Mann of the Confederation of Lightless Places was in trouble. And back at the Cabinet, during the tea, monsters Rayleigh met had alluded to the danger Bogey was in, as Supreme Scarer.

"He wanted to be a part of your life more than anything. But there are beasts of legend and nightmare who'd stop at nothing to get rid of him, including going after you when you were at your most vulnerable, Above."

It was weird to hear about his dad wanting to protect him. Rayleigh never would have guessed he thought about him at all. It made a similar desire rear in Rayleigh—a fire, a furious blaze reserved for whoever took him.

"I'll make them pay for this."

"No. You won't. You won't defeat darkness with more of it. That's not what your dad does. That's not what we do. The measure of a Mann is in our legacy. It's in who we decide to be, especially when things get difficult. You keep yourself safe. I'm keeping an eye on things up here." Nana smiled; her teeth retracted, and twin rows of spiky ones took their place.

Rayleigh flinched. "Er, Nana, what kind of monster are you?"

"Still got it." Nana looked pleased with herself. "If they'd allowed female bogey men in my day, your dad wouldn't be the first in the family to carry that title. For now, make sure you *take care of yourself,*" she repeated. "I already have two foolish sons. My heart won't take a foolish grandson too. Not that you've proven yourself to be anything but the very best, so far—congratulations on a successful first trial, by the way."

Rayleigh'd forgotten about defeating the Creator, his own mirror self.

"Continue to be your supergluing, catapult-making self and do me proud." Nana sank back into the comms device. Rayleigh saw the pride blazing in her eyes long after they disappeared.

He sat a moment, fists clenched and face tight, before he strode across the snug and opened the door. The Terrors were all seated in the clubhouse.

"Done with the old bird?"

There was another question concealed in Thelonious's tone. Did Rayleigh forgive him?

It wasn't the best of times he'd had, being the last to know some pretty big details—missing Dad, monstrous Nana, enemies who would go after Rayleigh to get to his dad—but he understood that his uncle had been trying to balance several spinning plates. Along with his own hope his brother would return safely.

"Yes."

Thelonious gave Rayleigh a grateful nod. "Good. Now, Gasp is staying back this time, but don't feel like you need to keep him company. That being said, I don't want you staying up to all hours as a habit, okay? I'm trusting you to get yourself to bed in a timely fashion, as I'll be gone most nights."

"You say that like I'm not an excellent companion," the troll protested.

"I mean, I've spent time with worse," Thelonious countered.

"Is that so—"

"Hang on." Bewildered, Rayleigh looked from his uncle, to Gasp, to Shade, to Mary. "I thought my dad was in trouble. I thought we'd do something about it."

"We are, Nephew-mine." Thelonious's gruff rumble was soft. "You understand?"

"I don't get to help find him?"

Suddenly all four Terrors found it difficult to meet his eye.

"No." Rayleigh shook his head. "You needed me. You told me you needed me to help bring my dad back."

"Kid, I still do." Thelonious approached Rayleigh. "I need you to focus on your next trials right here, at Terror Tower. Your identity will have stirred a lot of interest outside the Cabinet; inside, your trial successes will be popular conversational fodder too. The good news is that Terror Tower was built to entertain. And on the chance you don't have something you need, ask. It's very obliging. Study. Relax. We've got this."

"Wait—What if something happens to you guys too?"

"We're no strangers to a bit of the old Barney Rubble."

Trouble, Rayleigh understood. His uncle expected trouble, and for that reason he was to be left behind. Without further debate. He stood, stunned, as the Terrors took their leave from the clubhouse. Gasp promised to return for cake and hot chocolate as soon as he'd seen his teammates off.

When it became clear they weren't going to yell "surprise" and return apologizing and inviting him to join them, a mortified Rayleigh slunk off to his bedroom. He paced back and forth past the plain walls. How could they expect him to relax with his dad missing? Then there was his photo that was broadcast on the news, and a second trial. The hollow in Rayleigh's stomach was a familiar ache; it was like being left out by Phoebe and the crew Above. Like being underestimated by his teachers. Sure, his uncle wanted to keep him safe, but Rayleigh could take care of himself.

He was *that* Londoner. Not every inhabitant of the capital had the guts to cycle its chaotic streets. And he did so in fresh kicks, knowing he was skilled enough to avoid puddles that would dirty them. The Terrors might have watched him, checked in on him, Above. But not closely enough. And he'd prove it during the second trial. They'd let him help then.

Unfolding the envelope Octavia Brand had given him earlier, he tore through it to reveal another gold-pressed invitation.

The Monsters Cabinet
Bureau of Monster Regulation

Master Rayleigh Mann,
Your first trial was a success, congratulations.
Now begins the real work; for although you have accepted yourself, Below, our Confederation city needs to accept you. To that end, you are invited to undergo the Trial of the Architect.
On November 7 you are to assemble outside the Arcadia Hippodrome Vol-rail station no later than 6:15 p.m. You are encouraged to dress appropriately.
We look forward to seeing you then.

Yours sincerely,
Octavia Brand
The Office of Inductions, Welcomes, and Warnings, Below-London

Shorter than the last, the invitation was just as vague. If the Creator was the mirror, what would the Architect be? Rayleigh didn't want to sit idly, alone, contemplating the nature of the second trial. And he didn't need to. Not when he had a friend, Below.

Marley would understand his determination to perform just as well during his second trial as he had at his first.

Taking the comms from his pocket, he tapped both faces inside the device. "Er, Marley?" he said into the screens, just as he'd seen Thelonious do in the snug. The left screen lit up in his hand, casting a soft blue glow, and the device began to ring.

And ring.

Marley didn't pick up, and the option to leave a message never presented itself.

That earlier loneliness returned with a vengeance; worry chased it, like a thing on four legs, both for his missing dad and his uncle. He'd told Thelonious he could handle this. And like Nana said, he was a Mann. With the world watching him, waiting for his dad, he'd make sure that stood for something.

THIRTEEN

YOU WIN SOME, YOU LOSE SOME

The next morning, light sliced through the blinds in Rayleigh's bedroom like sharp, hot fingers. Groggy disorientation had him grabbing blindly for the curtains, but his fingers only met air.

Hang on, light?

He squinted, and then sat up fast enough to make his head spin.

His *room.*

Instead of the four windowless walls, clouds dappled with buttery sunlight migrated as though stirred by a morning breeze. Were it not for his bed and the room's furnishings, he could have been gliding beneath the lid in the clutches of a Bad Omen. He swiveled to touch the wall behind his bed; his fingers met only air, like his bed had grown wings and taken to the actual sky at some point during the night. It was only the sugary scent of pancakes that told Rayleigh he was still in Terror Tower. This transformation meant his room had accepted him. He smiled sleepily. He wouldn't change a thing about his new room. Indeed, he wouldn't change anything about the house. As for the circumstances affecting his stay . . . as if his room too remembered that his dad was missing, the warm yellow light gilding the clouds faded.

Rayleigh tried Marley again. Like last night, the call rang out. A slight worry set in for her too. Way too many people in his life were missing these days.

Frustrated, Rayleigh sank back against his pillows; the clouds on the walls darkened. He was half convinced a full gale would break out. Instead, a single shaft of light pierced through the clouds. It fell across a gift at the end of his bed. Rayleigh cast his eyes around his room, like the tower was watching him. In case it was, he offered up his gratitude.

"Thanks." Though he wasn't sure what for. Towers couldn't wrap gifts.

Could they?

The square box was red and topped with a giant black bow. Curious, he tugged at the ribbon and took off the lid.

"It's about time you opened me up!"

He flinched from the snide voice inside.

"I thought I was going to run out of air," it continued. "That witch made the box soundproof. I've been shouting for the past hour!"

With caution, Rayleigh leaned over the box. Nestled within was a delicate glass bulb resting on a bed of dark velvet, inside which was a slip of a creature, who, though fragile as a crystal figurine, snarled up at him with uncensored hatred.

"You're a fairy," he needlessly pointed out.

"I hope stating the obvious isn't a habit of yours," she said through the glass orb, running lavender eyes over him in a scathing manner. "Or this will become tedious very quickly. As it stands, you are in the presence of an elite fairy, close enough to royal blood that I may as well be a queen."

"So a princess?"

"No."

The fairy's haughty face told him she wouldn't elaborate.

"Is that disappointment I see? You should be grateful." She ran those condemning eyes over him again. "My kind are renowned for our knowledge. To be in the presence of a fairy—a recipient of a private audience with one, no less," she said, with such diction the inside of the bulb was flecked with saliva, "is a privilege many monsters barter over in lesser-known channels. That witch bestowed a pretty penny to purchase yours truly, and it's clear from your unkempt appearance that you're in desperate need of my brilliance."

Yeah. Rayleigh decided he didn't want a fairy in a lightbulb.

At home he could shove things he had no need for in a box under his bed or pass them off to his cousin, who had a good thing going in their school's black market. What did he do with this gobby sprite? His eyes landed on the lid.

Under its shadow, she raised her arms. "No, wait! I can be useful. In fact, I have some things the witch and the others asked me to tell you."

Rayleigh sat back on his heels, making sure she could see the lid. "What things?"

"I have to show you. You'll need to install the bulb."

Curious, against his better judgment, he dragged his chair to the center of the room, where a single socket was suspended. "Are all fairies as"—*spiky, rude, disdainful, annoying*—"knowledgeable as you?"

"Not at all. Many are foolish, and it's because of them that I'm in this position."

When Rayleigh returned to his bed to pick her up, she was pacing back and forth across her football-sized bulb. Her feet were bare, and she wore a dress in a softer purple than her eyes; it resembled spun sugar.

"Do you have a name?"

"Careful," she chastised, her tiny hands pressed against the side of the bulb. "And don't turn the bulb too fast, I don't like feeling dizzy. My name? It's Winsome. Though I suppose you may call me Win."

Rayleigh tried not to snort. She felt more like a loss.

Ensuring the bulb was secure, he returned his chair to its corner and looked up at her. "What's the message?"

She clenched her fists, her brow wrinkling in concentration as a pair of gossamer wings unfurled on her back. Patterned in a delicate latticework, they glowed brighter and brighter, filling the bulb with an iridescent white light that projected on the pale blue sky above Rayleigh's armoire in shimmering letters.

'Lo Mr. Mann, do we Terrors have a story to tell.
It's one of several parts, so be sure to listen well.

"You can do magic?" He was, admittedly, impressed.

"Hm." Her head tipped to one side. "I thought you were pretending, earlier, but you really don't know anything, do you?"

And with that, he was back to feeling irritated.

"I know it annoys me that people keep saying that."

She heaved a sigh. "Monsters' gifts are called bents."

"I knew that."

"With the sentencing, a fairy's bent has been reduced to more of a trick of light." Win shrugged, dismissive, but Rayleigh could see she was impressed he'd noticed. "The bulb limits my reach, makes it difficult for me to do simple things like light cast, as I'm doing now. Speaking of which, there's more. Follow along. Thank goodness you can read. I was beginning to have my doubts."

He opened his mouth, changed his mind, closed it, and waved her on.

Days one, two, and three require you access what's within.
Whether it be by hook, by crook, with a grimace or a grin.

On days four, five, and six, bells will toll.
Will it be round one or two when you defeat the cave-dwelling troll?

Days seven through nine the darkness will reveal who's willing to fight:
A boy who need only know when to turn on the light.
For to battle the night, to overthrow the dim,
One must have more than wood, plastic, or tin.

Last is a note from Thelonious, who abstains from all rhyme.
He simply says, "Kid, be ready for me at any given time."

There was no other way to interpret this than the Terrors were going to help him pass his next two trials. All of them, if Rayleigh was understanding the riddle correctly. It was one of the more generous things anyone had done for him; his bad mood lifted some.

"Are you going to take this down soon?" Win ground out, her body shaking. "I can't hold it forever!"

"Sorry." Rayleigh fished out a pen from his bedside cloud and scribbled his schedule down on several squares of toilet paper. "Right, I'm done!"

The fairy released a relieved sigh.

"Can I bring you anything? Food? Water?"

"My warden takes care of . . . my needs." She yawned. "Everything . . . is . . . provided. I just need . . . rest."

"Cool." Rayleigh clutched the toilet paper, resolving to copy it onto actual paper lest he blew his nose with it by accident. "Any idea what 'access what's within' means, Win? Winsome?" He glanced up to find the fairy slumped against the side of her bulb sleeping, her mouth open and fogging the glass. So much for being a fountain of knowledge.

After showering and dressing, Rayleigh continued muttering the lines for his first training session while styling his hair. The latter parts of the riddle all but named each Terror—Gasp the cave-dwelling troll, Shade the darkness, Thelonious who wouldn't rhyme, but did—that meant the opening had to be about Mary. Bloody Mary, who loved to haunt children through reflective surfaces.

Days one, two, and three require you access what's within,
Whether it be by hook, by crook, with a grimace or a grin.

Rayleigh tucked his pick into his hair. With a swipe of his hand, he cleared the condensation from the mirror above the sink. When he hit the middle, it warped inward. He drew his hand back and met the wide eyes of his reflection.

Could his access point to Mary's floor be through a mirror?

Rinsing his mouth, Rayleigh clambered onto the sink. He pressed both hands against the center of the glass. It was like pushing through toffee, without the stickiness. On the other side, his hands swiped about for a sign of what to expect. They only met air.

Well, walk with courage, and all that.

Taking a deep breath, he leaned into its surface.

FOURTEEN

FRIGHT CLUB

This was Rayleigh's second trip through a mirror, after the Creator. Maybe third. Space magic was confusing. He was unsure where his confrontation with his mirror self had happened. Either way, he'd passed through that mirror. This time, invisible forces tugged his body *down*. Which, he couldn't help noticing when his head popped through the cool surface, was a slight problem. Mary's entrance hall wasn't beneath his feet, it was beneath his head.

He was growing out of the ceiling like his neighbor—a red crystal chandelier fashioned after several falling drops of blood. Refusing to believe it a sign, Rayleigh squirmed against gravity, wriggling backward like a worm that had spotted the circling flight of a bird. It was futile. His body slipped through the portal with a sickening pop. He tensed, expecting the fall.

It didn't come.

He was suspended as if time had been stopped, and his eyes widened in disbelief as the world righted itself. Instead of crashing into the ground, he landed on his feet like he'd merely jumped.

Stumbling, he fought a wicked hit of dizziness.

Space magic had struck again.

The click-clack of heels echoed across the checkerboard floor; Mary appeared, drawing a silk robe tighter around her waist. "You solved Winsome's riddle, then. And early too. I expected you to arrive around lunchtime."

Straightening, Rayleigh cleared his throat. "I can come back?"

"It wasn't a criticism, Mr. Mann. Quite the opposite. You chose your mirror wisely too. Some of them toss you out in the most awkward places."

He kept quiet, doing his best not to look up at the ceiling.

"The tower rights all wrongs, literally, more often than not, but there's only so much it can do to help when you're forced to enter through a toilet's U-bend."

Suddenly the gravity-bending, world-turning ceiling no longer seemed quite so bad.

"Any chance I could get something to eat?" Rayleigh changed the subject. "I didn't stop for breakfast before I came." A circumstance he was happy about, all things considered.

"So long as you promise not to be sick. You'll find the ceiling's effects rather long-lasting." With a knowing look, Mary turned on a heeled foot. "Follow me."

Rayleigh wobbled after her, hoping the floor didn't have any additional surprises up its decadent sleeves—ones that defied all logic given Terror Tower's size. She swept past a grand staircase that was double the height of the one from the entrance hall to the clubhouse. And then there were the lofty ceilings and cavernous halls that would have been more at home in a castle. Or an actual tower.

"Do you control Terror Tower's space magic?" Rayleigh asked.

"Oh no. HQ was brimming with magic long before I joined the Terrors."

Candles burning in wall brackets emitted a warm, slightly smoky scent. Tall, thin windows were set deeply within the walls. Most were concealed behind heavy curtains, but those without the trappings revealed sweeping landscapes. Craggy and verdant, they flailed beneath the lashings of a morning storm. It was moody, and mysterious. Entirely Mary, Rayleigh decided. She glided ahead, shoulders thrown back, her thick braid of dark hair nestled between them, looking very much like the queen of the castle.

"Have you been to my dad's floor?"

"Of course."

"Can you take me?"

Mary hesitated. "It's not letting any of us in. It hasn't since he left for his trip. I suppose it might feel differently about you, since you are his son."

That was another avenue Rayleigh could explore. Thelonious had warned him against it, but his dad's floor might have secrets only he could decipher. Clues from when Bogey watched from afar, Above-London.

Inside a candlelit room rich with rugs and velvet couches, a tea set was laid out before a low fire. It consisted of crumpets and honey, boiled eggs, and thick slices of toast. More trays were perched on a sideboard overflowing with fruits and pastries.

"Looks like the floor has prepared quite the spread for you."

Rayleigh sank into a seat and reached for a crumpet. "You said Dad's floor might feel differently about me. It can do that?"

"The tower senses desire. It's a boon that's taken years to mature and mold to our needs and peculiarities. It's a special haven for the Terrors. And now you too." Her eyes, full of ancient knowing, stared unflinchingly into his own. "It will know what your intentions are and try to help. Where it can."

Rayleigh tried not to fidget. It wasn't often someone succeeded in making him feel uncomfortable. The way Mary held herself reminded him of a predator; she always seemed like she was considering whether he was worth eating straightaway, or toying with first. Rayleigh knew, somehow, that asking her anything more about his dad's floor might make its way back to Thelonious. He cleared his throat, racking his brain for something else to say. Mary beat him to the punch.

"I thought Thelonious should have gone first." She waved elegant hands; her robe's sleeves undulated in silk waves. "This Induction accompaniment was his idea. He also has a way of making people feel comfortable, just as I have a way of making them feel the opposite." Despite her words, Mary looked entirely at ease. It was as if frightening children wasn't just her job, but her calling. "This will be a new experience for you and me," she continued. "But it's one I agree is important. And so, Mr. Mann, we will treat our time together seriously. You never know what skills you'll find useful, down here, that you can use during your second trial."

"Cool."

The silence that fell then, filled with the clatter of spoon against china and the crunch of Rayleigh's crumpets, was the least uncomfortable it had been. There was, however, an itch he needed to scratch. Something Thelonious said that would explain why Mary seemed so . . . omniscient.

"Are you really over one hundred years old?"

She choked on her tea.

"If you learn anything from me today, Mr. Mann," said Mary, a delicate flush on her cheeks. "Let it be to never ask a witch her age. I might not be a wand caster like some of my sisters, but I know how to make even the deadliest of poisons taste like poetry."

Rayleigh eyed his tea.

"As you've officially eaten me out of house and home, run along to the gym. I'll be with you shortly." She delivered simple directions for how to get there before waving him away.

Striding past dripping candles and tapestries, all of which featured women completing amazing feats—fighting dragons, standing before crowds with fists raised to the sky, sitting with children, charging into battle—Rayleigh knew he didn't want glory. He wanted to help find his dad. He wanted to become a monster.

Taking a right, by *The Tapestry of Night Witches*, as Mary directed, he jogged down a dark flight of stairs and found himself in a low-ceilinged room that looked more like a dungeon than a gym. Sconces filled with low fires cast uncertain shadows on the gray walls, and all sorts of medieval-looking weapons winked in the flickering light. Their metallic odor was strong, alongside the deep tang of whatever herbs and oils Mary burned in her sconces. The maces he recognized, and the staffs, but there were also things he didn't expect. How would a set of forks help anyone?

An image of himself waving one at Seamus's witless henchman, Parcter, had Rayleigh wrestling his face still. His reflection in the mirrors lining one of the walls sent him into silent fits again; Mary chose that moment to glide into the gym.

"You're not having a stroke, are you?"

He cleared his throat. "I was thinking about something funny."

Though he suspected the time for amusements was over. Mary had changed into leggings and wore a smart tunic over a long-sleeved top. She moved across the training room as though she was done playing with Rayleigh like he was food. It was time to pounce.

"I'm not going to hit you," he felt a strange need to say.

"No need for that. Today." Her mouth curled slightly in the corners. "We're focusing on aesthetics. It's more than looking like a monster, it's acting like one, regardless of whether you're the most terrifying, or a sweet boy with a comb in his hair. And, for most of us, in one way or another, our bents manifest."

"Winsome showed me her bent. Thanks for her, by the way. She's . . ."

"I know," Mary finished for him. "Reducing the fairies' time is of interest to me. Not everyone thinks they should have received community service as a sentence."

"Community service? She told me you bought her."

"I haven't yet started work on their continued delusions of grandeur. Fairies are not for sale. They donate their time in penance for a crime they, stupidly, committed. It's really quite ridiculous, considering they are among the most erudite of creatures. Now," Mary said, becoming brisk and to the point. "You had a successful first trial, but the second will demand more from you. I think, and Thelonious agrees, that we should try to coax your bent into revealing itself. Either your gut instinct is near infallible or there's something else going on. Do you have any idea?"

"I mean—it could be anything, right?"

"Yes."

"Well, yeah, sometimes I get this feeling, like I know when someone is being untruthful."

"You may have some sort of sensing bent. I worked with several individuals who had similar abilities when I was completing my Scare Duty. I'm not a fortune teller, or truth seeker. I was the magician, the showperson with the flair and the dramatics. Did your little friend who I appeared for tell you I cried blood?"

Rayleigh nodded.

"That was part of my act. My partner, she did the predictions. I do know monsters who can only sense things when they incite a physical change. Maybe for you, we can coax your bent out by seeing if you have another form that's diluting it. This current look, well, it's a little . . ." Eyes darted from the comb Rayleigh hurriedly pulled from his afro, to the egg stain on his jumper, and down further still to his lucky leopard-print sock-clad toes visible in his sliders. "Blunt. Your body is your weapon, and as such should be respected. When they look at you, people will see what they want—it's your job to let them, at first. And that's when the terrifying can truly begin." Her mouth peeled back, widening into a wicked grin; smooth skin wrinkled and rolled until it became rough and ancient, like time hated her and had left every inch of its disdain in the deep grooves of her face.

Rayleigh looked on warily. "You'll be disappointed if you think my mouth can move like that."

"Today's function is to determine what, precisely, it can do."

"Then what's next?"

But no matter how many times Mary told him to do this, or that,

Rayleigh couldn't quite summon that same unsettling air she carried regardless of the face she wore. It was more than terrifying those around her. It was the sense that she knew she made them feel that way. She was in control; she'd told Rayleigh not to copy her, but he wanted to have a similar effect on those he met. He wanted to feel that confidence in his place, Below. And so he tried. Before too long, he did find if he squinted his eyes and grimaced, sort of lifting one eyebrow and thinking about something he disliked, he developed a kind of sneer she didn't hate.

"You're positive you can't make one corner of your brow lift any higher? I thought I saw something."

"No." Rayleigh sighed for what he was sure was the hundredth time. "I don't think my bent is going to change me. I don't think it needs anything other than me as I am."

"We won't give up quite yet." There was a moment's hesitation, and then, "I was a complete lost cause when I met your father. Hopeless, unlike you. He never gave up on me."

"What do you mean?"

"After my Scare Duty tenure ended last year, before I joined the Terrors full time, having helped out with the occasional assignment, I had a brief period as a lone wolf. Witches who aren't wand casters are rare. There aren't a lot of covens. I lived many solitary lives across continents for various Scare Duty assignments in the Above world. Your father tracked me down in Japan. Inducting me into the Terrors permanently, he gave me the coven I never knew I wanted. Family. And family members don't give up on one another, so you will go again. Not with that expression, though." Her head tipped to the side. "It's far too . . . gassy."

Rayleigh pulled faces before the wall of mirrors until Mary's intercom sounded with news of a lead. The interruption was both welcome (his cheeks were hurting) and irritating, as he was no closer to relaxing into his identity as a monster. Nevertheless, she escorted him to the gym door, opening it to reveal the clubhouse.

"Space magic?" he asked.

"Indeed."

Making him promise to practice ahead of their second session, she bid him farewell. The door closed, melted back into the wall, leaving Rayleigh alone. He hadn't heard what Shade said when he called through for Mary via the intercom, but whatever it was had to be important enough to make her drop everything and run.

Rayleigh drifted from the clubhouse toward the kitchen, eyes wide open and ears alert for any clandestine conversations. Alas, upstairs was quiet. The Terrors were no doubt off chasing other leads. Crossing everything with the exception of his eyes, Rayleigh wished to whoever answered his innermost desires that Marley would pick up his next call.

Just because the Terrors couldn't get onto Bogey's floor didn't mean Rayleigh couldn't—wouldn't—try. Thelonious's warnings about the sentient tower weren't to be ignored, but Rayleigh had a plan for that too. He needed Marley. And her fanny pack.

"You've hardly been gone for long," Winsome said when Rayleigh blew back into his room. "Training didn't go well?"

"Or I'm such a fast learner, I finished early." Rayleigh reached for the comms device on the bedside cloud that had replaced his table.

"That's why you're holding the comms upside down, is it? Mr. Fast Learner." The fairy released a snigger. "What are you doing with that, little Mann?"

"Don't call me that." He scowled up at Winsome, who, pressed against the side of her bulb, wasn't attempting to hide the fact that she was watching and would absolutely be listening to Rayleigh's call. He took the comms to the bathroom.

Perched on the edge of his bath, Rayleigh placed a continuous stream of calls to Marley. She didn't pick up until lucky number five.

"Finally!"

Curly hair rose up from the left side of the screen; a forehead preceded large dark eyes narrowed with annoyance. "You're the one who abandoned me at the trial. I don't think you get to be annoyed."

"I waited as long as I could. My uncle—something came up, which is why I'm calling."

"Saw the news. Guess the hearing didn't go well?"

"Can you come over?"

Marley blinked at him. "To the Terrors' house?"

"Yes."

"I would love to!" Annoyance forgotten, she beamed at him. "When?"

It was a long shot but, "Now?"

"Oh. No can do. My ma's making me study for the next trial. Took me a while to beat the mirror version of myself." Her eyes dropped. "Heard you aced it, despite Victor and Verena saying otherwise on the news. Everyone was talking about you at the tea party."

"But you passed?"

"I did."

"Well done."

"Yeah, try telling my ma that." Marley rolled her eyes. "Maybe I can convince her to let me come around in a few days? Wait—I just noticed. You didn't change. Me neither, which you can see too."

"Oh, yeah. Did any of the others?"

"A few did. This boy turned into a spider. All he does is cry. I felt like crying too. Hate anything with that many legs, and his were massive. He was like the size of a B-Cab. Anyway, tell me about the hearing."

Rayleigh leaned against the cool tiles of the wall beside his bath. "The Quorum gave the Terrors our Induction time to find my dad."

"So he's actually missing?"

"You can't tell anyone." Rayleigh lowered his voice and glanced at the shut bathroom door. "He's in trouble."

"Oh, Rayleigh. I'm so sorry."

"The worst part is, my uncle and the others won't let me help find him," he admitted. "And if I hadn't burst into that hearing . . . they might have had more time. I made a mistake, and I want to make it better, but I need help."

"You're not alone in making mistakes." Marley's expression grew pained. "My ma doesn't let me help either, remember? But I'm good. Found you, didn't I?"

"Twice. That's why I need you. And your fanny pack."

"Okay, well, I'll try to convince her to let me come over. She loves your dad, and she admires what the Terrors do. She might try to come along."

"Don't bring her this time. But tell her we'll be studying—which we can. There's a library here. I have time with a fairy light too."

"No way! They're meant to be some of the wisest creatures across the four realms. Though how wise can you be if you end up imprisoned in a bulb?"

"Right? That's what I was thinking."

"Did you open your second invitation?"

"Yeah. Any idea what the trial will be?"

"No clue. I asked my brothers, but they said the trials change every year. I do know Arcadia Hippodrome." She grimaced. "It's touristy. Monsters are always getting ripped off by peddlers and street performers there. It'll be even worse on the seventh. Fireworks night."

"I thought Fireworks night was on the fifth."

"Above. The first holiday after All Hallows' Eve is always delayed. It's our busiest holiday. Takes time to catch up afterward. Anyway, you should study maps for the area. I know it pretty well. Ma has me studying roads. Space magic. They might fold us up inside and force us to find a way to escape. If we participate in Scare Duty, you know, after we've been through school, we'll have to master it. How else do monsters manage to fit under beds?"

"What?"

"Hit the books, Rayleigh. I'll ring when I know I can come. Talk soon." Marley retracted back into the comms.

"You surprise me, little Mann," Winsome said, when he returned to the bedroom.

Rayleigh sighed. "I've told you to stop calling me that."

"Secret phone calls?" the fairy continued. Lying on her back in her bowl, she was filing her nails; where she got the nail file was beyond Rayleigh. "Perhaps I need to revise my earlier assessment. It seems you're a tad more interesting than I thought you'd be."

"And you, dear Winsome, I should have put back in that box."

"You'll be glad you didn't when I tell you everything I know about space magic."

Rayleigh threw his hands up, frustrated. "You heard me?"

"Maybe I'll tell you a few things about fairies too, like our excellent hearing." Winsome rolled onto her stomach to look down at him. "If you tell the witch I helped?"

He thought about it. "Only if your information is helpful."

"Well then, little Mann, prepare to have your small mind blown to smithereens. Check the top drawer in your bureau."

Rayleigh did as instructed; a lined notepad and a smart fountain pen sat as though waiting for him.

"Firstly," Winsome began. "'Space magic' is an ugly colloquialism for one of two ancient and respected foundations of the Confederation of Lightless Places: spatia liminaria. Shall I spell it for you?"

"Please." With the notepad pressed against his chest, Rayleigh could have done with a desk; no sooner had the thought entered his mind than a thump sounded across his room; there, against the walls that were a bright, brilliant orange as though somewhere a sun was setting, sat a new desk. The wood was dark, like the rest of his furnishings, with the exception of his transformed bedside clouds.

"You summoned that?" Winsome asked.

"Uh-huh." Rayleigh settled into the tall wingback chair. Soft, it was like a warm embrace.

"Let's see if I can summon things too. Try opening that drawer. If I can, you should find some snacks inside."

Speaking of snacks . . .

"I had a pillowcase of sweets I brought with me." He hadn't seen it since his first night, in Terror Tower. "I thought I brought it in here."

"The tower probably ate it. You snooze, you lose. Try the drawer."

Irritated, Rayleigh glanced up at Winsome, before doing what she suggested. "Two for two, Win. Terror Tower listens to you too?" He selected one of the packaged chocolate bars—a 'Mallow Mouth—and took a generous bite. "You were saying."

"Yes, I was. But you won't for a while. Not after a 'Mallow Mouth." Winsome cackled.

Rayleigh worked his jaw—to no avail. The soft filling of the chocolate bar, while delicious, was no doubt cement by another name. Try as he might, he couldn't chew enough to free his mouth to speak.

"You did this on purpose!" he meant to yell at Winsome, but all that came out was a muffled series of wasted breaths.

"Now I can deliver my lesson without interruption." Indecently delighted, Winsome stood.

Rayleigh would have thrown something if he hadn't been worried about shattering the bulb. Freeing the troublesome fairy.

"While Volence is our energy, the Confederation is held together with more fibers than that. Including what you'll know from movies and books as traditional magic applied to space and time." Hands clasped behind her back, Winsome paced the distance of her bulb and back again as she lectured. "Most commonly traditional magic is wielded by witches and warlocks. The wielders can help if you have a friend who is always running late—they gift her with a piece of jewelry, or a permanent body tattoo, that will help her keep time. Perhaps your new home is too small, and requires more rooms. Those are easy spells. In rare instances, even older practitioners control spatia liminaria and tempus. Sorcerers. Terror Tower is an example of sorcery. But the Confederation is a better example of what sorcerers can do: build worlds. For the purpose of your trials, they may indeed use spatia liminaria and tempus."

The first trial had used tempus, Rayleigh knew. He would have told Winsome this, if the 'mallow hadn't been holding his jaw hostage.

"Your second trial is all about being accepted by the Confederation, I believe?" Pausing, Winsome looked down at Rayleigh. "Aren't you going to write this down? I thought that was implied, given the fact that you cannot yet speak."

Though he muttered several unsavory—but unintelligible—insults at the fairy, Rayleigh did indeed take up his pen and begin to write. But not what Winsome had already shared. Not yet. His initial note was one for himself.

> Do not accept gifts from fairies.
>
> Ever. Again.

FIFTEEN

SOS, MARLEY

Mary's mysterious lead had kept her away from Terror Tower, and Rayleigh's Induction training, for a day longer than planned. With his second day of training canceled, the Terrors in and out, and Marley still under her mum's lock and key, he had to find ways to pass his unexpected day off mostly alone. Above, his possibilities had been endless; but Below, with awful images of his face circulating on the news, at Thelonious's behest, he was stuck in the tower.

And stuck with Winsome.

It was true that she knew a lot, but he could only spend so much time with the fairy before her tales of grand larceny and jewel heists became far too irritating to sit through.

Rayleigh would have thought that, after the 'Mallow Mouth wore off the morning after her first and last victory over him—and he'd unleashed every thought he'd been unable to the night prior—she'd be less willing to talk with him. But Winsome had enjoyed their lesson on spatia liminaria and tempus so much, it seemed, Rayleigh wished he could sneak her a bite of the jaw-locking chocolate.

There was the arcade, which was useful for avoiding the wily fairy. The dark room was packed with fun games not too dissimilar to those in the Above world—their only flaw was that they required money. A measure, Thelonious explained, to deter Shade from beating too many of his high scores. He'd given his nephew a fat pouch of Below currency to use; at the rate Rayleigh was going to avoid Winsome, he'd use the entire bag up before his first week Below was over. And so, out of ideas, and with no choice but to spend time in her company, he channeled his frustration with the fairy into practicing the expressions Mary taught him while Winsome pontificated from the ceiling. It soon transpired that they came with far more ease, in her company. Who could have predicted it?

There was also the library, he remembered, when his cheeks began to ache. Terror Tower provided ample help in preparing for his trial as far as reading material. There was so much more to being a monster than terrifying naughty bovers. The term wasn't a particularly kind moniker for humans, given that some monsters used it to mean humans were a *bother*, but Rayleigh's intentions were simply to take advantage of the ease it afforded. *Humans Above London* and the *Above-Londoners* and *Humans in the Above World* were all so wordy. *Bover*, however, was efficient. Unlike much else Below. With the second trial's focus shifting to the Confederation, he was trying to learn as much about the monstrous world as possible. Including its bad parts. Thanks to a selection of books left out by Gasp, he discovered the Confederation was one realm in four monstrous worlds that existed alongside the human one. It was considered the main hub, like the capital of the four. Respecting its importance could be tantamount to his success in the second trial.

Like Above-London, Below consisted of thirty-two boroughs. Only they were known as provinces. Rayleigh studied so intently, he even made note of the names of councilors who represented the wards within the provinces. It was all terribly political, which bored him to no end, but he wanted to cover all bases to stay Below. At least until he met his dad.

Considering spatia liminaria played such a huge role in the Confederation, and the previous trial, Rayleigh pulled as many books as he could on the subject. Tempus was simpler to understand. The simpler the magic, the greater the likelihood a witch or warlock was behind it. Given the importance of the trials, Rayleigh bet Octavia Brand's office would use a sorcerer. What the world builders touched was more complex. Rayleigh could find himself sent to the past, with no choice but to work his way out. A space affected by time magic would bear signs. A faulty clock, most often. But the easiest sign was the people—those living in the present can't also walk a past memory, so they appeared without faces. Indeed, they would look like shadows, ghosts, Winsome had shared. Rayleigh's senses hadn't indicated that she'd been lying; it was what Marley said that had him concerned. That the city could fold up like a map and trap them inside. Space magic was altogether harder. Most books advised marking entrance points to use as exits.

Rayleigh had yet to find a passage in one of the books that explained how to find an exit if one hadn't seen the entrance, for either discipline of magic. The last thing he needed was to end up like the poor guests lost in the tower, when he attempted to infiltrate his dad's floor. For that, he returned to his room and, begrudgingly, asked Winsome for help.

"I'm not starting at the end," the fairy told him. "We'll pick up where we left off, last night. Hungry?"

"Not a chance."

"We'll see," the fairy promised, before she began quizzing Rayleigh on his understanding of which places could be altered using spatia liminaria (every single one, apparently—even teapots).

Late in the day, Rayleigh's comms buzzed.

"Aren't you going to answer?" Winsome asked.

"Nosy." Rayleigh tucked a sock into the book he was using in the quiz, so as not to lose his place, and checked the comms. Marley had sent a message. She could come over tomorrow. He called her to sort out the details and the address. It took for a while for her to answer.

"What's wrong with messaging back?" Marley's voice floated out through the comms.

"This is easier." He also had no idea how to send messages. "Why can't I see you?"

"Does it matter?" Her tone was unnaturally cutting.

Rayleigh pressed his lips together but decided not to push it. "I guess not. Terror Tower is in the Province of Dreamers." He didn't have the exact address, so he gave Marley instructions based on the places he'd been. "Think you can find it?"

"Finding things is my speciality."

A click signified the end of the call. Rayleigh sat and frowned at the device.

Winsome whistled. "She doesn't sound pleased with you. I like her already."

"Yeah, yeah. Back to the quiz. Right, I can use spatia liminaria if I have the appropriate spell."

"Charged spell," Winsome corrected him. "We don't know if you're a warlock or a sorcerer yet. A wielder would need to share the magic so you could use it. But you're getting ahead of yourself, without a thorough understanding of the rules. Do you think you can finally name something unaffected by space magic?"

Winsome didn't blink. Neither did Rayleigh.

"People," he stated.

"Incorrect."

"What?" Rayleigh sank back on his heels, disappointed. "So you can make yourself taller?"

"How do you know I'm not already tall?"

". . . I can see you."

The fairy looked down at herself. "Oh. Yes. Next guess."

"Nothing. There's nothing space magic can't affect."

"Actually, it doesn't work on brains. Unfortunately for you."

Rayleigh balled up his second sock (the one thing he'd realized wouldn't break the bulb), and threw it up at the ceiling. A grinning Winsome didn't flinch.

The following day, Mary summoned him into their third and final training session.

"Sorry, Rayleigh," she said, as they hurried through her castle's halls. "We missed a day, and I know you have a friend coming to the tower. Our final session will be more practical than it should, perhaps, but you know what they say about pressure."

"I don't, actually," Rayleigh said, striding alongside her.

"Either it breaks you or it makes you. Let's do this."

Back in the gym, she instructed him to stand still and maintain his practiced expressions as she hurled the forks past him. As it so happened, they were far scarier than a kitchen utensil had the right to be.

"No matter what comes your way," she said, drawing her arm back. "You retain your expression of confidence. You don't let them see you sweat. Understand?"

"Uh-huh," Rayleigh exhaled. "Hey, how come you haven't used your bent?"

Mary wagged a finger; silver sparks crackled at its tip. "We shouldn't rely on our bents. Some monsters can dampen them, preventing us from using them. For monsters who don't have bents they can draw on in conflict, they learn how to get by without them. These forks, for instance. Want to have a go throwing them? Anything can be a weapon, with the right amount of force." Mary paused. "I'm not sure Thelonious would be pleased I told you that."

"Mary?" Gasp's voice rang clearly in the gym from Mary's intercom. "Rayleigh has a visitor."

"Okay," she called. "He'll be right out. And—" She turned to Rayleigh. "You won't say a thing about what I just said."

"I won't." Sweaty, Rayleigh wiped his face on his T-shirt. "How'd your lead work out the other day?"

"Never mind that. How do you feel?"

"Like I wish you guys would clue me in."

She looked at him with sympathy. "About the trial, Rayleigh."

"Yeah, I know. Fine I guess. I think I can give a good face. Convince whatever the Architect is that I'm not afraid of Below-London. That it should accept me. And if it doesn't, I could just grab a fork and—"

"No." Mary's pale cheeks flushed a faint peach. "Don't you say it." She deemed Rayleigh's scowl (the one he saved for Winsome) his best option. She held open the gym door, revealing the clubhouse beyond its threshold.

Rayleigh gave her his best grimace in passing. It was a shock when she flinched.

"It worked?" he asked with eagerness.

"I—It must have been a trick of light. You looked—" She grabbed his chin and tilted his face to the left and right. "Interesting. We may get that transformation of yours sooner rather than later."

"Really?" Rayleigh ran past her out into the clubhouse; he headed for the nearest mirror to inspect his face for himself.

"Um, hello?" Marley called.

"Just a sec." He turned this way and that, but couldn't see what had unsettled Mary. Maybe it had just been his face. A pleasant prospect. "Sorry. I'm doing some training." Rayleigh glanced Marley's way in the reflection. "And I thought—Marley?" He spun away from the mirror. Two piqued ears rose from a corona of long, curly hair. They twitched under his scrutiny. So did the nose at the end of a slightly elongated muzzle. The monster, girl monster, wore a beat-up leather jacket. Combat boots had been exchanged for a pair of slippers but . . . "Marley?" Rayleigh repeated. His eyes roved over the familiar features of her face, beneath all the . . . fur, down to the thick tails, plural, coiling around her legs. "You've transformed!"

The fine whiskers protruding from her cheeks twitched with indignation. "No flies on you."

"When did it happen?"

"I went to sleep that night after the first trial as myself and then woke up hungry. My brothers found me eating my breakfast on the kitchen counter, if you can imagine."

He couldn't. "You're so . . ." How should Rayleigh put it?

"If you say hairy, I'll smack you one." Marley's eyes, unchanged in a face that was indeed furrier than the last time they met, narrowed. "I got enough of that from my brothers. It took a while for them to understand that I'm more vulpine than Bigfoot, so this is fur, not hair. Do you get that?"

Rayleigh nodded. It seemed the smart thing to do, given her agitation. "Vulpine?"

Pulling a face, Marley stood; at her back, multiple furry tales fanned outward, like a peacock's plumage. They were a soft fawn color, like her skin; the tips faded into a milky white. Like a fox's tail. "Because one isn't awkward enough when I want to sleep on my back. I have four."

"Wow," Rayleigh breathed.

"'Wow'? Nuh-uh. You wouldn't believe how hairy my tongue got the first time I tried grooming these things." She turned on the spot; the tails protruded from a large hole cut into her jeans. "I'm using a brush from here on out. I don't care what my wai po says. My gran," she clarified. "She has tails too. But it's so gross. And, get this, my bent is just existing." Marley threw her hands up. "I don't get to fly, or shoot lasers out of my eyes. There's this boy in our Induction group, he has both those bents. Can you believe it?" All talked out, she dropped back onto the sofa and leaned her head against its back. "I'm so uncomfortable," she whimpered.

"You're so *cool*," Rayleigh said, and not without a hint of jealousy. "Marley, you have more extremities than anyone I know. Human or monster. Have you seen kangaroos fight? You might be able to train yours to hold you up, to work like arms or something."

She batted at her fluffy tails. "You think I could?"

"I don't know, but you should ask your wai po."

"Suppose so. She was really pleased when they saw me." She shrugged. "Girls in my family either get tails, this whole fur thing, or they don't. Like my mum."

"So she looks human? Sorry. I know I'm not supposed to ask."

"You can ask me. I don't mind. And yeah, she didn't transform, actually. It happens, sometimes. The Creator reflects who we are inside. My ma is exactly who she wants to be, doing what she loves, helping monsters. Me, I guess this vulpine identity means I'm quick, cunning, agile."

"I'm glad you didn't say foxy."

Marley looked sidelong at him and snorted.

Rayleigh suppressed a smile. "At least I didn't call you hairy."

"You're right. I might have done this." She jumped up and ran over to thump him, though there wasn't any strength behind it. "Anyway, I'm dealing with all this. What about you? How's it been since the trial?"

"No tails, but I have a plan."

"Hang on—can I get a tour first?"

There wasn't much to see, Rayleigh explained, since the tower kept its best parts hidden. He took her into the snug, but she'd seen a Seer's Eye before. Most Confederation households had them, apparently. She was even less amused by the monster being interviewed on *The Vulture Culture*. Not in person. A blank box with her name sat to the left of the projection, beside the reporter. And it was a name Rayleigh knew.

"Mama D'Leau the river witch? She's here too?" D'Leau was one of the first monsters Nana had told him about. She has many names across the islands; narratives of her vary, even in *The Book of Night Things*. But all stories agreed that she was akin to a goddess in the Caribbean, as the ruler of all its rivers and denizens.

"My ma can't stand her. She always said she never knew why she's friends with your dad. Actually, she couldn't believe he's friends with her."

The interview was about Bogey; D'Leau spoke out in defense of his absence in her musical Caribbean lilt.

"She has his back. That's cool. Why doesn't your ma like her?"

"No clue. Tour?"

Rayleigh took Marley to the arcade, into the kitchen to say hello to Gasp, and then down the gallery to his room.

"Can't wait to meet the fairy light."

"Lower your expectations."

But when the duo entered Rayleigh's room, Winsome was missing from her bulb.

"Didn't know she could leave," Rayleigh muttered. "Will have to discuss this with her when she comes back." If she came back. She'd been threatening to escape last night, but he hadn't paid it any mind, thinking it was nothing more than a threat.

Marley found a new distraction, the clouds drifting around Rayleigh's room.

Running her fingers through them, for indeed, they were quite deep, something Rayleigh learned when he leaned against the wall to pull his socks on and kind of just stayed there, being hugged by the soft—totally non-water-vapory—wall of clouds.

"I could stay here all day, but we should start studying. The trial is a few days away." It was November 4. At this time on the seventh, the second trial could already be over.

"There's something else I need to do first. Did you bring your fanny pack?"

"It's a utility belt." Marley swung it round from her back onto her chest, where she now kept it instead of around her waist. Rayleigh gave her an approving nod. "I don't have a bent. I won't be going to the toilet without this pack, at this point."

Rayleigh burst out laughing.

Whiskers bristling in what could only be described as embarrassment, Marley shoved him playfully. "Why do you need it?"

"We're breaking into my dad's floor."

"No. Way."

Rayleigh explained Thelonious's warnings and everything Mary had told him about the Tower's senses. "But I have to try. It might give us a lead."

"Hang on." She held a hand up. "You said visitors were eaten when they went where they weren't supposed to, and you still want to try?"

"He's my dad," Rayleigh said. "He came to see me, Above. He kept me safe from people like the ones who have taken him. Also, I live here. That has to count for something."

"But eaten, Rayleigh? Have you so quickly forgotten about the ogre from the first trial?"

"This is different," he said stubbornly.

"Maybe," Marley mused. "How would Terror Tower even consume us? What would it use to chew?"

That was a good question. Winsome hadn't elaborated when she shared what happened to Rayleigh's Halloween bounty, and it hadn't occurred to him to ask.

A good thing, perhaps.

"I don't want to think about it—I can't." Rayleigh began to pace. "I need to think about the door to my dad's." Like the other Terrors', his dad's floor was concealed. Which meant its access point could appear anywhere.

"So we should look for it?"

"I am." Pausing, Rayleigh shoved his hands in his pockets. "I've only been to one other floor. Mary's."

"Let me guess, she lives somewhere like a castle."

Rayleigh looked sidelong at Marley. "You're a fan."

"I," she began, "have the utility belt. Don't make me leave and take it."

Rayleigh suppressed a grin and returned to thinking. Then he squinted. There was something shimmering amidst the dappled colors on the wall he stood alongside. Two somethings.

Door handles.

SIXTEEN

THUNDER AND LIGHTNING,
OH SO FRIGHTENING

He lunged for them and yanked. Two pieces of wall swung open; the clouds faded into wood. Instead of the houses on Terror Tower's street, behind them was a dense knot of grass, trees, low-hanging vines. It was—

"A jungle!" Marley charged across the room to stand beside Rayleigh.

Something chittered inside; the call echoed through the large banana leaves. They hung low, weighed down by their sheer size and raindrops. Though the sun wasn't visible, it shone with a brightness that made everything vibrant, even the brown of the earth. Something fast skittered through the low bush.

"Animals?" Marley's tails fanned out around her protectively. "Don't alligators live in jungles?"

"I don't know. This reminds me of a picture my nana has of my dad in Jamaica. It was green like this, and wild and full. But the island doesn't have jungles."

"Is this Jamaica?" Marley asked, leaning across the doorway.

"I don't think the tower transports you to literal places. It re-creates them, like memories or safe places. My room is my happiest memory, down here. Mary's is a castle, and she's kind of closed off, mysterious, grand. I can't explain it, but the tower knows us. That's what my uncle said."

"Okay," Marley said, with an understanding softness. "But on the chance the tower has created alligators, we should probably hold this door open with something."

"Maybe my dad went somewhere with a jungle and liked it enough that the tower recreated it for him." Rayleigh grabbed several thick books from his bed. Door wedged, he braved a step inside. Heat was instant against his skin, like a physical thing he could touch. Something buzzed past his ear; remembering what Nana said about large flying bugs and mouths that attracted them, Rayleigh snapped his jaw shut.

"You coming?" he asked through clenched teeth.

Taking a deep breath, Marley stepped through the doorway. "It's humid. Wow. I can't believe this is a floor in a house—look, bananas are growing over there!" Fat and yellow, the bunch of fruit looked good enough to pick, to eat. "Are they edible?"

"I don't know. Wouldn't risk it. Come on. I don't know how many Terrors are in the tower. We need to find my dad's room quickly to look for any clues before anyone comes looking for us." Gasp was always foisting hot chocolate on him. It was only a matter of time before he came around with an offer of refreshment.

The duo ventured through the bush. With a simple thought, Rayleigh asked Terror Tower for a large stick with which to beat back plants and poke vines that looked too similar to snakes. Something fell against his leg. Emitting a high scream, Rayleigh all but leapt into Marley's arms. He was buffeted back by one of her tails, right between the eyes. She'd been laughing already, at his scream, but her sentient tail sent Marley over the edge.

"I thought you couldn't control them?" Rayleigh asked, rubbing his eye.

"That wasn't me," Marley wheezed. "But that scream definitely came from you."

Swiping up the stick, Rayleigh jabbed at her with it. "My eyes are never safe around you."

Tears of laughter streamed down Marley's cheeks. "How do I get one of those?" She shrugged out of her jacket and tied it around her waist.

"You sort of ask the tower by desiring it."

A few seconds passed. Nothing happened.

"Maybe it can't hear you since you don't live here. Take mine." Rayleigh handed it over. "I'll get another." And he did, instantly. He redeemed himself by flinching only slightly when the tower repeated its ploy of dropping a stick against his leg.

"I think it enjoyed your reaction." Marley bore a large grin.

With nothing positive to say about the tower after its behavior, Rayleigh kept his mouth shut. Side by side, he and Marley pushed onward, sticks swinging from left to right to clear a path.

"So the Terrors haven't had any luck finding your dad?" Marley asked softly.

"Not that they've said." And Rayleigh knew they would, if they had something to share.

"You worried?"

He swung his stick at a spiky bush. "I'm here, aren't I?"

Marley knocked her shoulder into his. He knocked back into hers, grateful. Something rustled in the bush ahead of them. They both froze, waiting for whatever had run across the jungle floor earlier to make another mad dash. It didn't. The chittering in the treetops, the clicking of insects faded somewhat.

Rayleigh rubbed a hand up the back of his neck.

Marley's tails shifted from hanging low, like a Victorian skirt, to standing tall over her shoulders.

"Why haven't the Terrors looked for any clues on this floor?" she whispered.

"They said it locked them out."

Marley turned to Rayleigh. "How did we manage to get inside, then?"

He looked at her too. "He's my dad?"

Her ears, high on her head, twitched. "Are you asking me or telling?"

A low growl reverberated in response.

Rayleigh felt it in the earth beneath his feet. In his chest. It was like thunder echoing the wrong way up. Down. Whatever.

"Please tell me that was your stomach?" Marley's ears turned, chasing the sound.

Rayleigh shook his head.

"I think—" Her whiskers twitched. "There's a cat in here."

A terrible feeling oozed down the back of Rayleigh's neck.

"But not a normal cat. It smells bigger. It smells—"

"Like a panther?" Rayleigh finished; his stomach dropped. The ball dropped—one that should have landed the moment he opened the doors. "I don't think this is my dad's floor. I think—" He was about to say, It's a trick by the tower, the tower with living wallpaper that looks a lot like this jungle. But a pair of bright yellow eyes gleamed over Marley's shoulder, close enough that two leaps would close its distance with her. Low in the bush, they could have belonged to a cub. He knew they didn't. He knew, just as he knew when Thelonious was telling half-truths, when his mirror self told half-truths, that was an adult panther. And it was preparing to pounce.

"Rayleigh," Marley whispered. "There's something behind you."

Every hair on his body stood. Up. It was as if he'd been plugged into a socket and charged with pure Volence. A low rumble of thunder sounded overhead, an ominous accompaniment to their precarious situation.

"I'm going to stun it." Marley reached for her pack.

A breath hissed between his teeth. "Don't."

She stilled, save for her ears that turned all the way around. "There's one behind me too, isn't there?"

"Run. Toward the door."

"On my sign." After a beat, she flung both arms outward, releasing a vial from each hand. It would have been an impressive takedown. But the bush was too thick. The glass vials did not travel far enough. Bouncing off leaves, flowers, they hit the jungle floor; cushioned by the fallen leaves, they didn't break. "Uh-oh."

"Just run!" Rayleigh tugged her after him.

They hadn't walked too far into the jungle. One hundred meters at most, but they had only two legs. Panthers had four. Lithe, the great cats were built for speed. Their broad paws were designed to distribute their weight for maximum efficiency. Rayleigh and Marley were never going to reach the door. Overhead, thunder rumbled like drums. It urged them on; Rayleigh felt it in his every step, his every panicked breath.

"Ah!" Marley was tugged back, jerking Rayleigh's arm. "My tails!"

In the seconds they spent wrenching her free from a spiky plant, they were surrounded.

Four panthers, sleek as shadows, padded out of the bush around them. Thunder boomed again, filling Rayleigh's ears, his head, thrumming through his bones until they felt heavy and full.

Marley threw two more vials. This time, they landed by the panthers' paws. The same slinky smoke from All Hallows' Eve was emitted. But unlike then, when the smoke made Thelonious freeze, the panthers didn't react.

"You don't think they'll actually hurt us, do you?" Marley asked.

Rayleigh held his stick before himself and Marley like a sword, switching from panther to panther. "I can't say. The tower has a mind of its own." Below-London had seemed more magical than monstrous, and yet the panthers advanced, muzzles drawn back from large, sharp teeth.

Thunder echoed again, followed by a violet streak of lightning. But not from the sky above them. It charged from the ground, shooting in a sparking path toward one of the panthers. The cat hissed, padded back several steps.

"Did that come out of you?" Marley exclaimed, turning to Rayleigh.

He didn't know until—the panther to his left leapt. Elegant muscle, sharp claws, and an open muzzle flew toward him with the speed and power of a rocket. Purple lightning came in from the crowded dimness of the jungle. Around Rayleigh. It crackled and popped, charging the air with the same electricity he felt in his bones. It was like he was a conductor who pulled that power from inside— no, from the false sky Terror Tower created. Instinctively, it curled around the airborne panther like two clawed hands.

"No!" Rayleigh shouted. He didn't want to hurt the cat.

The panther twisted back, to avoid it. Landing with a thump, it snarled at the purple light. Its pack members hissed, but did not advance. The clawed lightning curled backward to enclose Rayleigh and Marley in its protective, spitting glow.

"It did," Marley breathed. "You made that. This. It's coming from you."

"To the door," Rayleigh said, marveling at their protection. "We're close."

Their cage moved with them. He couldn't see where it came from; there was no tether connecting him to it, yet that fullness that had weighed his bones down earlier was gone. His heart had calmed in his chest. It was like the lightning was his panic, his worry; only the moment it left him, it became a strength.

The panthers did not follow, clearly as stunned as Rayleigh at the lightning. In the doorway, Rayleigh indicated for Marley to go ahead of him. He paused to reach out to touch the lightning—his lightning. It fizzed beneath his fingertips and curled under his hand like a pet.

"I made you," he murmured.

"Er, Rayleigh," Marley called. "You should come in here."

Crossing back into his room, Rayleigh closed the doors. His bent—what he hoped was his bent—faded around him, sparking out like an extinguished blaze.

"My, my, my." Winsome sniffed. "I smell trouble. It reminds me of barbeque."

"Well, I am furious enough to spontaneously combust," Gasp said.

Rayleigh whirled around and found his frightfather standing beside Winsome. He was tall enough that his head was level with the bulb. Marley stood at the foot of the bed, looking very much like she was ready to run. And Winsome oversaw everything; a broad smile dominated her tiny face, as though she was witnessing something highly entertaining.

"Rayleigh Jude Mann," Gasp went on to say, in a voice unlike any he'd used before; it was low, condemning. "Clubhouse. Now."

SEVENTEEN

BENDING REALITY

Sitting side by side on the sofa in the clubhouse, Rayleigh and Marley endured a thorough telling off from Gasp. It was so extensive—their recklessness, irresponsibility, disregard for common sense—he was still on a roll by the time the rest of the Terrors bounded up the stairs. A half hour later. He hadn't even gone hoarse. It was rather impressive.

"Nephew-mine? NEPHEW-MINE," Thelonious bellowed, charging into the clubhouse, huffing and puffing like a furious bull.

Rayleigh cringed into the sofa. "I'm fine."

"*We're* fine," Marley corrected.

Thelonious crossed the room in three steps. Seizing Rayleigh by his shoulders, he looked him over. Reflected in his uncle's sunglasses, his eyes were wide, his face smudged with dirt.

"Miss Liu," Thelonious said, looking down at her once he'd ascertained Rayleigh was all in one piece. "Lovely to meet the monstrous you. Glad the tower didn't chew you up and spit you out. But I think it's time you went home." He sought out Mary. "B, mind doing the honors?"

"Oh." Perched on the armchair by the fire, she shook her head. "I'm not missing this."

"Me neither," Shade said. "So don't ask."

"And I wasn't quite finished with the shouting." Gasp crossed his arms over his chest.

Rayleigh rolled his eyes at Marley. "Look—"

"Don't." Thelonious dropped him back onto the sofa. "You don't get to talk."

Rayleigh wondered how similar to Nana his uncle was, and whether or not he should prepare to duck lest the back of his head met a palm.

"NOT A SCRIBBLE."

Rayleigh flinched at Thelonious's explosion. Marley's fur stood on its ends.

"You didn't leave so much as a SCRIBBLE. It's GOOD MANNERS to notify your family when you're SNEAKING OUT."

"He didn't leave the tower," muttered Gasp.

"SNEAKING IN."

"It is?" Marley whispered to Rayleigh.

He shrugged, just as uncertain.

"Especially when I forbade you from accessing your father's floor. The tower isn't allowing entry—yet you thought it a good idea to swan off without notifying us? What if something had happened to you? What if you became lost, like those other guests?" Thelonious strode over to the fireplace; he gripped the mantel. Its wood groaned as he tried to calm his nerves. "Leaving the tower to venture into the province is one thing, but accessing a floor in the tower without an invitation? You don't do that again. Clear?"

"I—I'm sorry."

"Yeah," Marley added. "Me too."

"Next time I sneak out—in—"

"Anywhere?" Marley offered.

"Right. I'll . . . . leave a note?"

"You'd better. And it won't be to any place I've forbidden you to go."

To say Rayleigh was confused would be an understatement. "But I can sneak out to other places?"

"We're monsters, Mr. Mann," said Mary, suppressing a laugh. "Sneaking is what we do."

"Yes, fine. But not to certain places in this tower," Thelonious added. "Or this city. You know what, I'll write a list."

"That doesn't seem like sneaking to me," Marley muttered.

Thelonious whipped her way. "What was that?"

"Rayleigh has lightning," she said in a rush.

"Lightning?" Thelonious repeated.

"My bent, I think," Rayleigh said, looking sidelong at Marley.

Thelonious looked questioningly at his nephew's hands, curled into fists on his lap.

"It didn't come from my hands," Rayleigh clarified. "It came from around me. I might not have caused it."

"The security floor you accessed was the wallpaper in the hall. A burglar deterrent. They open the door and find themselves in the jungle. It's all—"

"Space magic?" Rayleigh and Marley said in unison.

"Exactly. I've never heard of lightning being a feature."

"How did it feel?" Shade asked.

Everyone turned his way.

"Of all of us, I am the least corporeal," he said, defensively. "If Bogey's son is going to become a live bolt of unrestrained energy, I'm the likeliest to know about it."

Rayleigh described the change from feeling heavy to light, how the lightning had leaned into his touch, like something living.

"It protected us, in there," Marley added. "In the moment we needed it."

Frowning, Shade contemplated Rayleigh. "I don't think your transformation will render you incorporeal, like a living energy bolt. That doesn't sound like it exists in you. It sounds like it exists for you."

"Like my sparks." Mary held up a finger, where a silver ball fizzed and hissed.

"But I'm causing it?" Rayleigh asked. "It's from me?"

"Sounds like it." Mary nodded. "Can you show us?"

Rayleigh looked down at his hands. Marley gave him an encouraging shoulder knock. Cautious, so as not to fry anything, himself included, Rayleigh unfurled his fingers. Nothing happened. He shook them a little. Still nothing. That fullness he'd experienced in the wallpaper, he didn't have it.

"I don't know how to make it come without feeling like my life is being threatened."

"Sounds like a bent to me." Gasp looked to Thelonious. "What do you think, Thel?"

"Thunder," he murmured. "Nephew-mine, was there thunder before the lightning?"

"Light travels faster than sound," Rayleigh said.

"I know, I know, but was there?"

Marley answered. "There was. It was like we were in a storm."

"Brilliant. And, during your first trial, before the Creator, did anything happen?"

Rayleigh hummed a little as he tried to remember. "No thunder. No lightning but—I did get an electric shock from the mirror."

"Oh ho!" A piece of the mantel snapped off in Thelonious's grip. "We have a bent. We have a BENT!" He ran toward Gasp. The two Terrors met; clasping one another's arms, they cheered. Mary launched several balls of silver sparks into the air. Shade rolled his eyes but sat back to take in the show. Sitting on the sofa, Rayleigh and Marley looked at one another; she shrugged.

"Your family are awesome."

"They are." Rayleigh couldn't help the grin spreading across his face.

"Get up here, Nephew-mine!" Thelonious beckoned Rayleigh to join him and Gasp. "You have a bent! You have a bent!" He cheered.

"Even though I can't make it come when I want?"

Thelonious stopped bouncing around and looked at Rayleigh with a warm seriousness. "Sometimes a spark only needs a little kindling to turn into a flame. Your instincts kicked in to protect you. In time we can work on helping you summon that bent whenever you want."

"Because it's mine?"

"It's yours!" Thelonious swept Rayleigh up into a hug that turned into a headlock. "Let me see if those horns are about to come in."

A laughing Rayleigh struggled to free himself; Marley looked on, shouting encouragement.

"But what *am* I?" Rayleigh asked.

"Not sure yet. But with a bent like yours, I don't think it'll be long before we know."

"Could be a warlock," Mary suggested.

Marley groaned. "You get all the luck, Rayleigh. And I got all the tails."

Even Shade cracked a smile at that one.

It wasn't long before Terror Tower got in on the celebration. It materialized all Rayleigh's favorite foods: jellies with whipped cream, sour candy spilling out of bowls, fresh strawberries, mini burgers oozing with cheese. There was even a cake. It was shaped like a lightning bolt. Rayleigh took the spread as an apology in addition to a congratulations. And despite the chaotic events of the day, he allowed himself to soak up everyone's excitement for him.

While he couldn't help wishing his dad had been there to see it—his new bent—he was more determined than ever to help find him. As was Marley. Before Bloody Mary escorted her home, she made Rayleigh promise he wouldn't do any sneaking without her.

"You know what," Thelonious said, from the doorway on the ground floor. Hand in hand, Marley and Mary crossed the road toward the alleyway that would take them out into the province. "That Marley's not half bad."

"That's what I said." Seated on the low wall at the top of the porch stairs, Rayleigh turned as his uncle snorted.

"She might not be half good either, encouraging that creative mind of yours. But I'm glad you're making friends down here, Nephew-mine."

"Me too."

"Now, about your bent." Thelonious gestured for Rayleigh to cross back inside Terror Tower. "We had a quick word upstairs, but is there anything else you're curious about?"

Rayleigh had thoughts aplenty; choosing one was difficult. "Is it really lightning? I know you said we have to give it time, and you haven't seen it but—it didn't come out of me. It came from around me, like I was—"

"Pulling it from the air." Thelonious stopped at the foot of the stairs. "I've heard of a similar bent."

"You have?" Was this the moment Thelonious would share his bent with Rayleigh?

"Oh yes. It had a different name."

"Was it purple, like mine? No, violet. Like, a glowing violet."

Thelonious nodded; his expression was hard to decipher. "They called it levin, the monsters with a bent like yours. But there haven't been any of their kind in a while."

"So I can't be one?"

"Not necessarily. The transformation process is complicated, remember, Nephew-mine." Thelonious slung an arm around Rayleigh's shoulders and led him upstairs. "There's still time for it to manifest before school in January."

"But you don't think I'm anything slimey."

"Definitely not. I'd have to turf you out." Thelonious shuddered.

EIGHTEEN

LIGHTS OUT

Induction training was due to start up again the morning after Rayleigh's bent appeared. Bouncing between his room and the bathroom as he cleaned his teeth and combed his hair, he squinted at the riddle. Winsome had made him copy it down, but at some point it had become wet; more than a few of the words blended into one another.

He could make out "duck" and "cave." That was a toss-up between Shade or Gasp. And there was his uncle, who promised his appearance whenever he felt like it.

"Let's see what's on the cards for you today." Winsome projected an iridescent light from her wings onto the clouds across Rayleigh's room.

> *On days four, five, and six, bells will toll.*
> *Will it be round one or two when you manage to defeat the cave-dwelling troll?*

"You could do that again this entire time?" Rayleigh protested. "Why'd you make me copy it down? And why have you stayed quiet while I've been struggling to read what I wrote down all morning?"

"I told you. I wanted to make sure you could read and write."

Rayleigh shook his head. "Your bent, how did it work when you could use its full reach?"

"Ah, that's a story too long to tell when you have somewhere to go. Chop-chop."

He read the riddle quickly. "Troll. Days four, five, and six will be spent with Gasp."

"We can consider it my gift to you, since I wasn't invited to the party last night." Shaking her wings made the words fade. Straightening, Winsome trailed a finger down her bulb. "Sounded fun."

"You seemed to have no trouble leaving your bulb earlier. I thought you could go where you wanted."

"I go where I'm invited. You should know the rules of the tower."

She wasn't wrong.

"Next time—"

"Don't think of me, little Mann." She sighed. "No one else does. But you could make it up to me. I'd like a box of matches."

"You know what?" Rayleigh grabbed his trainers and socks. "I've got to go."

"But—"

He ran from his room out into the kitchen. Gasp wasn't at his usual spot by the oven, but a bright green protein shake was. Along with a note. *The clue to finding me was in the riddle.* Rayleigh sniffed the drink; his nose wrinkled. He left it on the side.

Mary he found via her preferred method of scaring kids. But as far as he knew, there weren't any bridges in Terror Tower to find Gasp under. None that he could cross, anyway.

But maybe one he could look at.

Rayleigh found Gasp via a painting of a bridge. A combination of factors led him to run his fingers across the soft green color of the rolling hills, the delicate pastels of the flower-strewn meadow. There was the bridge, and the fact that, in the stories, trolls lived underneath them. It was also on display in the kitchen, one of Gasp's favorite places in Terror Tower. But the selling point had to be the fact that Rayleigh'd heard enough about his frightfather's green thumb—in fact, instead of touching the painting with his entire hand, Rayleigh pressed his right thumb in the center of the bridge in the right side of the painting. Within one breath, he found himself standing in the burbling brook beneath the stone arch. Glad he wore his trainers, he stepped with care across the slippery stones in the low brook, heading toward the wide mouth of a cavern in the mountain that overlooked the bridge, the water, and the sweet-scented flowers within the meadow.

Gasp, overhearing Rayleigh's wet steps, met him in the opening with open arms.

"Welcome to my floor."

Their session started pleasantly enough. Gasp showed him around his cozy cavelike abode, pulling books from hewn stone shelves and revealing paintings of his rather distinguished-looking family of bridge trolls.

"You said you're really strong," Rayleigh remembered. "And you can also control plants?"

"Right you are." Gasp led him through the cave and out to its rear, where a copse of trees grew at the base of the mountain range. "I'd hoped you'd become a troll too, but I don't know any of my cousins who can summon lightning—make it in themselves. Whatever you did."

"Do you know any other monsters with lightning?" Rayleigh

had looked at *The Book of Night Things* before bed. There were no recorded monsters with levin or lightning yet. He might be the first in his family—a cool prospect, but one that left him out on a limb. "Thelonious mentioned some creatures with a similar bent. Only, they called it levin."

Gasp started. "He did, did he? Well, while your bent is so nascent, developing as it were, predictions might end up causing more harm than good."

Uh-oh.

There it was again.

A prickling against Rayleigh's skin. Secrets.

"You know, my bent—I think it's my bent, anyway—it lets me know when you guys aren't telling the entire truth."

"Then let me impart my knowledge to you," Gasp said. "It'll be fun."

An hour later, Rayleigh found himself doubting Gasp's assertion that his training was any fun at all. Turned out the peaceful grove of trees housed a wrestling mat. And the moment Gasp tackled Rayleigh and proceeded to run through several complicated wrestling maneuvers on him, he knew for a fact this was the farthest thing from a good time.

"Sometimes you have to be physical," the troll said, legs and arms wrapped around Rayleigh in a hold he'd already forgotten the name of. "You have a bent, but you shouldn't rely on it. Not in life, and not in the second or third trials. I'm strong because I'm a troll. I'm also strong because I train."

Rayleigh struggled to free himself. They'd been at it for ages. He was soaked through with sweat, tired; his limbs felt like stone, but nowhere near as strong.

"Your bent manifested yesterday in response to fear. What we need to work on now is finding a way to summon your bent whenever you need it. Not only when you're frightened." Gasp flipped them both onto their fronts, coiling himself around Rayleigh like a snake. "Start by trying to feel in control, even when you're in situations that might not seem that way."

Rayleigh didn't want to try using his bent with Gasp so close.

"What if I hurt someone I care about?"

Gasp released him. Rolling away, he tossed over a bottle of water. Grateful, Rayleigh gulped it down.

"If you reach for your bent from a place of fear, you won't have that control. Focus on control, not fear. And don't worry about me, I'm pretty thick-skinned. Ready to go again?"

Rayleigh nodded.

He allowed his frightfather to twist him into pretzels. Try as he might to draw his bent from the clear skies above them, it wasn't happening.

Much was the same for his second session, the next day, too. At least if the second challenge was physical in any way, Rayleigh knew a few moves he could use.

"You look terrible" were Winsome's first words when Rayleigh limped into his room that night. "Worse than usual, in fact. Had you showered when I suggested it last night, I imagine your muscles wouldn't be so tight."

Rayleigh glowered at the fairy. She'd kept him up half the night with her "advice."

"If you'd shut up when I suggested it, I would have been able to sleep more."

"Fair enough."

"That can't happen again tonight," he told her. "The second trial is tomorrow evening, and I can't risk being exhausted on top of achy."

"I hear you."

"No talking."

"No talking." Winsome mimed twisting a key in the corner of her mouth and tossing it away. "I got a pair of clogs delivered today. Thought I'd practice my dancing instead."

"We're not doing this tonight. Oh no." Rayleigh clambered up onto his bed and began to unscrew the fairy light.

"Wait—I was joking!"

"You can tell your jokes in the bathroom." Rayleigh propped the bulb up on a pile of towels and closed the door.

"I told Mary that gobby madam would annoy you to no end."

Rayleigh turned to find his uncle in the open doorway to his room.

"She's all right, most of the time. But tonight I need to get my rest."

Thelonious nodded. "I wanted to come and see how you're feeling about the trial, given the events of the week. Your bent and all that."

"I don't know. I haven't been able to summon it, never mind control it."

"Nothing wrong with that. You've had it for all of two days, and you're still figuring it out. There's no rush to decide who you are, Nephew-mine. Not when you've already decided who you aren't. You know that, don't you?"

"I guess."

"You guess?" Thelonious straightened. "Transformation isn't about change alone, it's about *choice*. In the face of challenge, you made the choice to do what was right for you, instead of what was easy. You could have returned to Above-London. You chose to stay.

That's what the Creator reflects, who you choose to be. The moment you stepped before it, it knew you. It saw you. And it wants you to see yourself too—that's what these trials are for. That's what this Induction is for. Trust the process. Trust—"

"You?"

"I was going to say, trust yourself." Thelonious crossed the room, leaned down, and touched his forehead to Rayleigh's. "Those instincts haven't been wrong yet. And they won't fail you tomorrow, either. Come along, I can get the tower to put another bathroom in place for you. Looks like you could do with a long soak. Mary has these oils that'll sort your muscles out a treat."

"Do you have any news for me, about the levin?"

"Hmm? Oh, not yet. As soon as I know, I'll share. Or you might beat me to the punch and transform. Also, I'm sorry to say, there's no further word on your old man." Thelonious rubbed a hand across the wall opposite the gallery in the hall. A doorknob materialized first, and then the frame grew forward, manifesting into something he was able to pull open. "Gasp confirmed what I suspected about your little truth-detecting skills, and I don't want to frighten you, Nephew-mine, but I will be honest. We're trying. We're talking with all our old enemies. We're visiting some in prison, but—"

"You can't find him."

"Not yet." Thelonious entered the generous bathroom.

Everything felt so close and yet out of reach. Rayleigh was in his dad's city, his dad's home, yet he was still missing. His bent had manifested, but he was no closer to understanding what he was. He tried to hear his uncle's earlier words as he fell asleep that night. He hoped they were true, that they'd be enough to guide him in his second trial.

They'd have to be.

NINETEEN

THE TRIAL OF THE ARCHITECT

Marley began sending Rayleigh helpful messages far too early the next morning. Her advice consisted of everything: from what he should or shouldn't eat (for breakfast, lunch, and dinner) to how he should tie the laces on his trainers for this evening's trial. He appreciated her, his friend—his friend with nothing else to do but text him, apparently—but it was difficult to engage in his final training session with Gasp while his comms kept pinging.

Yoga was meant to be relaxing and, according to the zen troll, the perfect way for Rayleigh to connect his mind and body before the trial. But Marley's message alerts had ruined any relaxation. It was just as well that her advice, however irritating in its frequency, wasn't terrible. Marley grew up Below. Here, Rayleigh was the tourist. A turn of events that both concerned and offended him.

Fast enough to make his head spin, the time came to dress for his second trial. Mary had passed by his room with a package from Taylor the tailor earlier; she'd handed it over along with her good wishes. Gasp and Shade popped by too, on their way to do things they were tight-lipped about. Terror Tower would be empty of everyone for the night once Thelonious had escorted Rayleigh to Arcadia Hippodrome. Well, with the exception of Winsome, and the fairy was none too pleased about that.

"You could attach my bulb to a lantern," she argued, as Rayleigh vacated his bathroom in new black cargo trousers and a thermal long-sleeved top. No detachable sleeves this time. "I could be useful. More than that vulpine girl who was here a few days ago. Not only is my intellect superior to most creatures', but I have a built-in light." With a grunt, Winsome filled her bulb with a soft white glow. She rivaled the stars blinking their way into existence on Rayleigh's walls.

"Winsome, you know I can't take you with me."

Taylor's bundle of clothing included a variety of coats. He chose one that was butter-soft and made from a leather-like material. It was identical to the coat his dad was wearing in his portrait in Terror Tower's gallery. They seemed to be the fashion Below, sported in an array of colors and patterns. Taylor had sewn muted leopard-print lining inside Rayleigh's, perhaps in homage to the socks he'd had on when he'd met her. Whatever had happened between her and Gasp, Rayleigh held the latter responsible. She was clearly a gem. Rayleigh shrugged into the coat before the mirror on his armoire and saw, well . . . He saw that he wasn't the kind of kid who could pull off that much leatherlike material.

"Looks like skin you're partway through shedding," Winsome pointed out. "You say you went to a tailor's for that tat? I'd ask for a refund if I were you."

"If you were me, you wouldn't be in that glass."

The fairy went quiet.

Winsome's hurt feelings should have been the least of Rayleigh's worries, but he'd come to accept her cantankerous ways. Sometimes he was even amused by them.

"I'm sorry, Win. Look, I'll fill you in on what happens tonight when I get back, okay?"

"If I'm still awake," she said with a sniff.

There was a knock at Rayleigh's door. "Come on, Nephew-mine," Thelonious called. "We've got to shake a leg!"

"See you," Rayleigh called up to the ceiling light.

"You should bring that purse of coins your uncle gifted," she called, in a pathetic voice. "If you meant what you said about securing me a token of your appreciation. And will you or won't you need keys to come back inside?"

"I didn't think—"

"You didn't, no. But you should."

Rayleigh paused. "Do you know something about my trial?"

"The one question you never asked me." She intoned mysteriously, "Too late now."

"But—"

"Nephew-mine!" Thelonious hollered.

While swiping up the purse of change Thelonious gave him for the arcade was easy enough, procuring a set of keys for Terror Tower couldn't be as simple as desiring them and holding out a hand in anticipation, as Rayleigh was doing, could it?

Turned out it was.

A set of keys appeared in the center of his palm.

"I love this place," murmured Rayleigh, though he wasn't sure he'd need them.

There was a harrumph from the ceiling.

"Look," he said, shoving the keys and money in a trouser pocket. "I really am sorry about what I said." He shrugged up at Winsome. "And, you know, thanks for all the help you've given me."

"Urgh, sentiment." Winsome's mouth twisted with disgust. "Just when I thought you were growing a spine, you go soft on me, little Mann."

Shaking his head, Rayleigh ran for the door to the hallway, forgetting for a moment that he was a kid who couldn't pull off leather and instead looking a lot more like one who could.

Kedara's flight across Below-London was, once again, too brief for Rayleigh's liking. There was nothing like being high above the subterranean city. Not even his bent.

Okay. Maybe his bent.

Still, beneath the star-strewn lid, a thriving Arcadia Hippodrome twinkled with lights from shopping malls, theaters, the steady buzz of road traffic. Ornate rooftops rose and fell like a dark sea. The Bad Omen alighted atop one such stately building overlooking the busiest intersection, according to Thelonious, in the entire city. No less than five zebra crossings, each at least thirty meters in length, enabled hordes of feddies to cross the road at the same time. It was pure chaos—ordered chaos. And overlooking the intersection were tall skyscrapers; screens broadcast a variety of different programs, ads, even the news. A bright red bulletin stretched the length of the largest screen. It would have been hard to miss, wherever anyone stood.

WHERE IS OUR SUPREME SCARER?

"How long has that been running?" Rayleigh pointed it out to Thelonious.

"A while."

Rayleigh flexed his fists. His worry made every word difficult to expel. "There's not much time left to find him."

"About two weeks, yeah. Which is plenty. Seamus is working overtime to impede that. Seamus—" Thelonious tsked and shook his head. "Shameless, more like."

"Why is he doing this?" Back in the Cabinet, during the hearing, Seamus had seemed like a gnat—irritating, to be sure, but small. Insignificant. A plastic bag in the wind. But the news wasn't going away. There it was, before Rayleigh, supersized and unignorable.

"Conviction, Nephew-mine. Everything is dangerous when it comes in extremes. He never thought your dad took his position seriously. He thinks this absence confirms that. We're dealing with it."

"But—"

"We have it." Thelonious's sunglasses flashed. "I will have a word with Seamus as soon as I leave here. Now, where did you say you were meeting the Liu girl again?"

An island-like expanse of pavement jutted out from the main road in Arcadia below. With the exception of the monsters bundled up against the cold, some luminous in the deepening dusk, clever coats catering to their tentacles, wings, and additional heads, Arcadia Hippodrome could have been in Above-London.

They finally spotted Marley seated high up in the peaked ears of a large statue in the center of the island. The bronze creation was as tall as Thelonious and twice as wide. It was big enough to seat at least ten children. How Marley had managed to keep them off, Rayleigh didn't know. He waved to get her attention; two strangers waved back before Marley spotted him. He didn't mind. Their general friendliness was a reminder that, aside from Seamus, Below-London had scored a lot of points on his mental checklist for reasons to stay.

"All right, Nephew-mine. I'm off."

"What, really? But we don't know where the trial is."

"I think you're in it." Thelonious shrugged.

"In what?" Marley panted, joining them.

"The trial, apparently," Rayleigh repeated to her.

"But I haven't seen Conny, or anyone else from the Monsters Cabinet."

With a parting wave, the Terror strode into the crowd.

Marley looked at Rayleigh, flabbergasted.

"He does that." Rayleigh rolled his eyes. "I suppose we should look for some of the other inductees. That boy with the laser eyes should be easy to find, hey? Marley, hello?"

She'd stepped back and was making a show of surveying his clothing. Rayleigh regretted that, in his haste, he hadn't changed the coat.

"Did you borrow that from Captain Scáthach?" she asked with a smirk.

A chill travelled down Rayleigh's spine. "Traitor."

"We should look for some of the other inductees." Marley's smile was sweet. "Do try not to trip."

"Oi!"

"Last one, I swear!" Marley's tails curled around her legs mischievously. "Hey, if you have a wallet, you should hold on to it."

Rayleigh eyed her with suspicion. "Why?"

It soon became apparent, though, as they were stopped by countless peddlers. Trench coats were opened to reveal all manner of items. They were approached by a monster who sold goldfish in bags. They looked ordinary enough, though the beaked haggler swore the fish could grow large enough to transport their owners across the Undersea Channel. Rayleigh was tempted—until Marley caught the monster's tail attempting to slip inside Rayleigh's pocket, groping for his change purse while he was distracted. She stomped on its thin length with her combat boot. The monster howled and slunk away.

"Just as bad as London," Rayleigh grumbled as they headed toward a bright stretch of pavement overlooked by a vast theater. He couldn't believe he'd almost been tricked. Where had all his street smarts gone?

"Below-London is just like any other city." Marley straightened her jacket on her shoulders. "We have bad people too."

"The sooner we figure out this trial, the better. The letter said Below-London has to accept us, right? So it's going to—"

"Hey, you—you're him!" A lithe woman hurried over to Rayleigh; she clasped her webbed fingers to her mouth in excitement. "You're Rayleigh Mann!"

Surprised, Rayleigh could only stare at her.

"He gets that a lot," Marley said, coming to his rescue. "Excuse us."

"No." The creature stepped into their path. "You're him. That's you, up there." She pointed across Arcadia. Broadcast on the largest screen was an image of Rayleigh. A new still of him that again looked like it had been captured by a security camera. A red banner ran along the bottom of the screen.

Can Bogey's Son Provide Insight As To Where His Dad Has Gone?

Rayleigh's stomach dropped. Living in Terror Tower, a thriving ecosystem all on its own, had made him forget that he was of great interest to Below's citizens.

"That's you!" the creature said.

"Does that ugly coat come with a hood?" Marley muttered.

It didn't. And Rayleigh had forgotten a hoodie underneath.

"Hey! It's the Bogey Mann's son." Another feddie stopped before Rayleigh and Marley. He had eyes the size of tennis balls. "Is it true? You know where the Supreme is?"

"Yeah" came from the crowd doubling in size. "Where is your dad?"

"Get away from him!" Marley shouted.

Rayleigh backed up. There wasn't much pavement between him and the building behind, and the crowd blocked him and Marley from the road. More feddies joined the fray. Someone grabbed at the tails of Rayleigh's coat. A tiny insectlike creature waved up at him from the ground. Someone else pinched at his hair.

"Whoa." Rayleigh ducked. "Don't touch me!" In the jungle wallpaper, the lightning came on so fast, he didn't know what was happening until he was in the thick of it. But, facing down the looming crowd, he felt something . . . different. A thrum built under his skin; his bones vibrated. The air around him crackled with electricity. He fought it down; fought down a charge that wasn't just around him. It was in him, part of him. "Get back!" he warned.

Marley threw a concerned look his way. "You're okay. We're okay."

"What you are is busted." Two small monsters pushed their way to the fore of the crowd, though anyone could have been forgiven for thinking them walking light fixtures. Entirely shrouded in shining, metallic discs, while they bore the shape of people, kids, there were no identifiable features to reveal who they were.

"We could have been friends," the one on the left said.

Squinting, Rayleigh recognized the monster's voice—and then her face, as the iridescent skin Verena had been sporting, one that turned her into the dimmer cousin of a disco ball, faded away to reveal her blunt dark hair, bright eyes, and slightly pinched face.

"Instead we're competition," her twin, Victor, finished, shedding his own disco-ball covering like a skin suit. Where it went, Rayleigh didn't know. It sort of withdrew like someone tugged it from behind in a flash.

"Good luck completing this trial tonight, Rayleigh Mann," they said in unison.

"You know him?" one of the crowd asked.

"Yeah. And you're right, he is the Bogey Mann's son. I bet he knows exactly where the Supreme is."

With parting smirks, the twins allowed their places to be taken by others who jabbed claws, fingers at Rayleigh. Without their shining skin, they ceased to be beacons and disappeared.

"Where is your dad?" was shouted in a cyclone of intensity.

"Get ready," Marley instructed. She threw a vial directly at the ground; upon smashing against the pavement, it released a mixture of pure night. Those at the front of the crowd coughed. A hairy paw found Rayleigh's in the dark, then drew back.

"Ah! Electric shock."

"Sorry!"

"It's okay." Marley grabbed his sleeve instead, tugged.

Rayleigh stumbled after her, willing to endure a face full of her furry tails if it meant escape.

The two rounded the corner away from the crowd and flew down the street.

"In here!" Marley darted into a narrow alley; Rayleigh followed.

"That was wild," Marley said, serious.

"It's Seamus's fault as much as those twins'." Rayleigh's hands curled into fists. "He had to know we'd be here tonight. He's messing with me." Unable to stay still, he paced, charged; it was like he'd been plugged into an electrical socket. Only, instead of being shocked, he was absorbing the energy, soaking it up like something porous. He wasn't meant to feel the lightning *inside*. It was meant to stay around him. He could feel it building, rising, like a sea inside verging on something incontrollable. He'd already hurt Marley.

"How's your hand—paw?"

"Hand," she said, firm. "It's fine. It's my fur. It probably conducted your bent."

"Static electricity?" Rayleigh shook his head. "I don't know. I feel different. It feels different, my bent. It's not just around me anymore."

"It's just settling, like having a growing pain or a spurt or something." Marley licked her fingertips and held her hand out. "Let's try again. Coupled with our monstrous genes, the water should act as a barrier."

"That's not water. That's spit. So I'm going to pass." Rayleigh rolled his shoulders and tried to relax. "I can't believe those twins did that."

"They're just jealous." The voice came from the mouth of the alley, but no one stood there.

No one visible, at least.

The voice sighed. "You can't see me, can you?"

"No," Rayleigh and Marley answered simultaneously.

"I'm Mack. Invisible inductee. Can't control it."

"Yikes," Marley supplied.

"Yeah. Sucks for me, but I can help you. I can make whatever I touch invisible too."

"Don't come any closer," warned Rayleigh, firm. "How do we know you're an inductee and not a grown-up weirdo trying to put your hands on us?"

Mack paused. "Gross but fair. Um, I was in the Hall of Waiting when you two went down the stairs. Everyone thought you were so cool. Except the twins. That's how I know they are jealous. I kind of was too."

"Okay." Rayleigh didn't get the feeling that Mack was lying. "So, why would you make us invisible? Will it help us pass the trial?"

"Maybe," they admitted. "I think the twins passed the trial. Being invisible helped me do some spying. After they told that mob who you were, they went over to the statue of the griffin you were sitting on, Marley, and it spat an envelope out for them."

"How did they manage to pass?" Marley's face screwed up in confusion. "Just by ratting Rayleigh out?"

"That's what I couldn't figure out," Mack said.

"Let's break it down." Rayleigh paced past the large metal bin in the alley; it smelled of rotting food. "The Trial of the Creator was for us. We made ourselves into monsters when we defeated our reflections."

Marley ran her fingers through her tails absentmindedly. "Architects are designers, right? And the second trial is about being accepted by the city, having a home here."

"What do we have to do to be accepted here?" Mack asked. "Those twins sold you out."

"No," Rayleigh said slowly. "They used the crowd to stop us from completing the trial before them. They were . . . sneaky. Sneaking is what we do," he said, triumphantly repeating Mary's words from days before. "To complete the trial, we have to be like them!"

"It makes sense, I guess," Mack mused. "Even if I don't like the idea of being like them."

"Not like *them*, like a feddie. The type of feddie we want to be. Not every inductee makes it to the end of the Induction, remember? We make choices that incite our monstrous change, awaken our bents, whatever. What do working monsters down here do?"

"Sneak," Marley said, with a look of understanding. "Okay. So we have to get to that statue in some kind of way that's sneaky."

"Right." Rayleigh rolled his shoulders. "And I have a plan."

It was simple. So simple, all three worried it wouldn't be enough. Well, almost. His idea relied on Mack sharing their invisibility. Through touch.

"I might shock you," Rayleigh warned them.

"You can lick your hand," Marley suggested.

"Gross," Mack replied, as Rayleigh said, "Please don't.

"Maybe you guys go without me," he continued. "I don't want to hurt anyone."

"Then don't," Mack said. "You were right, we're told that these trials are all about choice. It's rich coming from me, since if I could be seen, I would. But maybe I wouldn't, you know? I don't. What I'm saying is, choosing not to hurt us seems like something you *can* do. I don't know you all that well, Rayleigh, but I don't think you'd cause pain on purpose."

"Mack's right." Marley offered her hand. "You won't hurt us."

"But I might not be able to help it."

"Yes, you can," she encouraged him. "You don't want to hurt us. Come on. Take my hand."

"And mine," Mack added. "It's next to Marley's."

Psyching himself up, Rayleigh bounced in his trainers. He wouldn't fry them alive. He wouldn't. He'd take their hands and not hurt them, because he didn't want to cause anyone pain. He didn't want to harm anyone.

Two sets of warm fingers wrapped around his.

"Hey!"

"It's cool!" Marley's disembodied voice soothed. "You're cool. We're cool."

Wide-eyed, Rayleigh looked in her general direction. "You're . . . okay?"

"Yeah." Mack's tone was replete with relief. "Thank goodness for that. Not that I doubted you," they were quick to add. "I just . . . had doubts."

"Misplaced doubts." Marley tightened her hold on Rayleigh's hand. "Come on. Let's finish this thing."

Hand in hand, the trio left the alley. They retraced their steps back to the griffin statue; still concerned Rayleigh's idea wouldn't work, they didn't even laugh when they bumped into feddies, startling them with their invisibleness. The mob had dissipated, but

Rayleigh's image was still broadcast over the intersection, along with a new banner.

SPOTTED IN ARCADIA HIPPODROME THIS EVENING.
THE SON OF OUR BOGEY MANN.

"Okay," Rayleigh whispered, before the large beak of the statue. Its vast head was lowered; lifeless eyes carried a sort of threatening dignity. "Here goes nothing. We snuck here past a broadcast image of me that made a crowd of monsters touch my hair, my clothes, and ask for my dad. They didn't see us this time. We were sneaky. We were monsters."

Nothing happened.

"It was worth a try," Mack said.

Rayleigh felt them shrug, but he wasn't so willing to settle. Not if it meant he didn't pass the trial. Not if it meant he didn't belong. Rayleigh squinted back at the crowd. Was there something he was missing? His plan had been simple, but that was what made it clever. Nana always said the intelligent ones whispered, but people who wished to be seen as smart yelled. How could Rayleigh's skills abandon him here, when he was so close to the third trial?

"Hang on," Marley said. Rayleigh whipped back toward the statue. "Its mouth—something is coming out!"

"Yes!" Rayleigh cheered, startling a passerby. He caught the envelope that slipped from inside the statue's mouth. "This one is for you, Marley. Mack, yours is here too. And mine is coming out as well!"

It had actually worked.

"How *did* the twins know to get the invitation from this?"

"It's a griffin," Mack said, like that explained everything—until it became clear by the silence that it explained absolutely nothing. "Oh, it's just me, and them apparently, who studied the Ancients."

"I know that name," Rayleigh mused. "They live in one of the other realms, right?"

"Yeah. Griffins are part of a group of legends who have retired, more or less. Anyway, they're guardians of priceless things. Griffins. Not the Ancients."

Marley turned her envelope over in her hand. "I feel a bit bad for climbing on top of it earlier. Him?"

"Them?" Mack suggested. "Me too, by the way. I'm them as well."

Rayleigh nodded. "Cool."

"Totally," Marley added.

"All right, I'm going to get on. Thanks for making this the easiest trial yet."

"It's all thanks to you," Rayleigh said.

"Yes, thank you, Mack." Marley appeared as Mack let go of her hand; Rayleigh's too.

"Ah. I'm still invisible," they said.

"I'd say I'll see you around, but we have no idea what you look like." Rayleigh's laugh was gentle.

"Then I guess me saying 'not if I see you first' isn't cheesy. Later."

The soft pad of their footsteps faded away.

"We got lucky with them." Marley did a little jig. "That was so easy! All right, let's head back to yours before you're spotted again."

"Hang on." Rayleigh rapped the envelope against his knuckles. That trial had been easy. Maybe too easy. The first trial had consisted of three sections. They'd only completed one this time around. Maybe two, if working out what the trial was also played a role in winning it.

"Rayleigh, still with me?" Marley asked.

"Let's open this envelope here. I don't think it's over. Mack?" he called.

Marley kicked Rayleigh's trainer. "Stop! We don't want another mob situation."

"I feel bad. I hope they open theirs before heading home. Okay, get into yours. Quickly!" he encouraged.

Rayleigh slid his finger under the strip along the back. The invitation had a single address embossed in its center.

> O'Stensible's Garage
> The Province of Despair

"I knew it," he said. "It's not over."

"Should have known." Marley read her own letter. "Let's head to the Monsters Cabinet. Maybe we'll run into Mack again."

"Wait, the Cabinet? Let me see your invitation." Rayleigh held them side by side. "These are different addresses."

"Is it another trick?" she asked, peering at the two letters.

"I don't know."

"Maybe we're meant to go to both locations?"

"I wish Mack was still here, I'd love to know what address they got."

"We should probably go to the Cabinet last. . . ." Marley was thinking out loud. "That's where Brand and Conny have to be waiting."

"Fine with me. Do you know how to get to—" Rayleigh checked his invitation. "The Province of Despair? Maybe we can take a Vol-rail?"

"You want to risk waiting in line when your image is being projected all over the city?"

Rayleigh had been pleased he understood the Vol-rail must have been a train, and the Vol-way the swirling black holes. "Good point."

"I have another way we can get there to beat those twins." Marley grinned and shouted, "Follow me!"

Rayleigh chased her tails through the crowd; the thrill of an imminent victory all but gave him wings.

TWENTY

THE KEY TO SUCCESS

Rayleigh and Marley crossed the square to Arcadia Hippo-drome's station. An almighty bang echoed throughout the night. Marley flinched, ears erect in her hair; she reached for her fanny pack. Then shimmering lights exploded across the lid, dousing the province in electric blue light. Fireworks.

"I forgot the date," she said, adjusting her jacket.

"Remember, remember," Rayleigh teased, though he'd forgotten too; and as a result, his heart was beating rather fast.

The surprising noises aside, the rockets that whistled through the lid Below, and entire aerial troops of marching toy soldiers, were unlike anything Rayleigh'd seen. Thrilled with the swinging monkeys and waddling penguins, he watched the spectacle as he walked until Arcadia's Vol-rail station rose to block his view. B-Cabs were lined up outside the grand building, lights ablaze on their roofs to advertise availability. The further down the line he and Marley ventured, the greater the unpleasant potency of a foul odor.

"Why does it smell like a farm?" Rayleigh asked.

Marley breathed heavily through her mouth. "Because we might as well be at one."

A procession of ponies and carts was responsible for the stink; even their drivers stood apart from the near mountainous brown piles forming a range of their own across the road.

"You're kidding?"

"B-Cabs are too expensive for where we're going, and we shouldn't risk the Vol-rail." Marley hit the bell hanging on the edge of the first open-topped cart. "With all the drama around your dad, they might start suspending services like last time."

"Like last time?" Rayleigh asked.

"Hang on. Evening." Marley nodded at an approaching driver.

"Where to?" the monster asked, more equine in appearance than his steed.

"The Province of Despair, please. O'Stensible's Garage. Do you know it?"

"I do. That'll be five auxites. Each."

Rayleigh fished out a handful of coins from the purse and counted the required number of the dull golden ones Marley identified. They each handed over their fare before climbing aboard the cart.

"The Cabinet should reimburse us," Marley muttered. "I'll have to get a receipt when we arrive. Maybe they'll cover discomfort too."

The wooden benches were without cushions and rather hard as a result. Both nearly pitched out the back when the pony trotted away from the curb. Launching a scowl at the back of the driver's head, Marley gripped the sides. Rayleigh looked enviously at the B-Cabs in passing.

"You said last time they shut down services." Rayleigh wrapped his coat tighter around himself for more warmth. "What happened last time?"

"Wow. You still don't know everything?" Marley flourished a bobble hat from her jacket pocket. It had special allowances for her ears. "Though, I suppose there was no need for you to know about the curse. Alleged curse. Have you heard about the Illustrious Society, at least?"

Rayleigh nodded. "They wanted all monsters to be monstrous."

"Good. Then you know the Illustrious Three were all bogey men."

The pop and whistle of fireworks faded to white noise.

"They were bogey men?" Rayleigh asked. "Like my dad?"

"Uh-oh." Marley winced. "You didn't know. Again. So I've put my foot in it. Again."

"You've told me the truth. Again," Rayleigh corrected her.

"I'm sure they didn't want to worry you."

"My face is being broadcast on the news across the city."

"Fair enough. Okay, the first three Supremes of the Confederation of Lightless Places all decided to band together for bad, after they each finished their term in charge." Green sparks from the fireworks illuminated Marley's expression of concern. "No one in the Confederation saw the betrayal coming, not even the Seers. Monsters started to wonder if the first member of the Illustrious Three cursed his title, somehow, to corrupt the next Supremes. The first three led the Society, but nearly all the Supremes thereafter became members."

"So when you came for me, in Brutely . . ." Rayleigh spoke slowly, figuring out that which he had wondered about before, what Thelonious had glossed over. "You thought my dad was cursed. You thought he was going the same way as the Supremes before him."

"Yeah, sorry. It was a hunch. A wrong one. I really need to start listening to entire conversations. My brothers told me Supremes don't serve for longer than seventy years now. There's some theory that the longer they serve, the more likely they are to go bad. I should have known your dad wasn't one of the bad ones. He hasn't served for long enough. But I thought your uncle might tell you about the curse, at least. Some things are better coming from family."

But if that was the case, why hadn't the Terrors mentioned it? Suspicion tap-tap-tapped against Rayleigh's bent-enhanced senses. He didn't like how easy it was to believe his dad might have fallen from hero to villain at the hands of a centuries-old curse. But it could explain why the Terrors hadn't made any progress in finding him. . . .

"We need to focus, Rayleigh. Rayleigh?" Marley touched his arm cautiously. Nothing happened. They were both relieved. "Come on. We get through this trial, and you can ask your Terrors whatever you want. Okay?"

He didn't feel okay. Not in the slightest.

"Hey, how far out are we?" Marley asked the driver.

"A giant's leap. So some time yet."

Rayleigh still wasn't sure about the measurements, and, regardless of finally having the time to receive an understanding about them, the driver's attempt to explain how they used giants to measure their distances wasn't any help either. But, as it transpired, he could tell exactly when the Province of Dreamers ended and Despair began.

It started with the air.

It became thicker, heavier on the lungs, as if even the act of breathing was difficult in the province; then there were the buildings. Most were boarded up, abandoned; they sagged, like their foundations never gave them a proper start to their lives and they were doomed from the moment they were created.

"What happened here?"

Overhead fairy lights drooped; sporadic empty bulbs were like missing teeth in a smile. Monsters materialized from shadows in doorways. Without the bright joy instilled by the fireworks they had left behind in the Province of Dreamers, Despair seemed . . . dim, like someone had placed a covering over the top, preventing any light making its way in.

"Your dad planned to help this part of the city, after his sabbatical. It never quite recovered from this big fight that happened with the Illustrious Three."

"Must be why Seamus is so pressed." Looking around, Rayleigh didn't blame the Captain. Though he agreed with Thelonious. What business was this province of Seamus's? What business was anything outside the Cabinet?

The cart slowed beside an expanse of cracked concrete beneath a flickering indigo streetlight. It did little except make shadows seem darker, the night larger.

"Uh-oh." Marley pointed up at the bulb. "My ma always says *indigo means you've got to go.*"

"What?" Rayleigh frowned at her.

"Come on, *the darker the light, the less right?*" Marley blinked at him. "You don't know, okay. So, Volence is all about goodness; the purest form should be a blue so pale, it looks silvery. But it can change in the presence of nefarious company. The deeper the blue of the energy—"

"The worse it is," Rayleigh finished, swallowing at the deep inky depths of the bulb. Thelonious had said the silvery light in Terror Tower made it a safe space; that said everything about Despair. If not for the random fairy lights, the garage would be difficult to see.

"You sure this is where you're meant to be?" the driver called back.

"It's what the invite says," Rayleigh told him. And Marley. And himself.

On a road of boarded-up buildings, only one showed signs of life—and that was generous. A garage. Abandoned cars, carriages, and a sleek train car hulked in the darkness of its yard like agents of its wants. Beasties that crawled from the pages of *The Book of Night Things*.

An internal alarm system was going off in Rayleigh's gut. But when Marley hopped out of the cart, he had no choice but to follow her. Still, he wasn't entirely without the urge to run after the cart as it clunked away and disappeared into the darkness.

"Well, after you," said Rayleigh.

"Don't be such a baby," Marley responded, making no move to enter the lot herself. "Anyway, your invitation instructed us to come here, not mine."

Rayleigh sighed. "Together?"

"If you insist."

So close their shoulders brushed, they crossed the lot with quick steps. Machinery whirred in the open mouth of the garage where a cluster of monsters worked beneath a clunky chandelier of fairy lights. A weasel-faced creature made a beeline for them.

"Here about a vehicle?" He glanced at Rayleigh.

"No. We're inductees?" Rayleigh hedged. "Our invitation instructed us to come here."

"Right. The invitation." The creature backed away, a cunning twist to his mouth. "You must be the Supreme's kid. Little Mann."

Rayleigh was about to say, "Don't call me that." But there was something about the weasel monster's reaction, the twitch of his whiskers, that made his alarm system spread from stomach to skin, coating his body with the inexplicable knowledge that something wasn't right. Seamus had been looping his description on the news. Anyone could have claimed to know him—they might have doctored his invitation, even. After all, why had Marley's told her to go to the Cabinet, but his sent him to this desolate backwater?

"Marley," he muttered through the side of his mouth. The other mechanics were abandoning their tools to stare too. "I think we should go."

"Not until we get what we came here for."

The last time she used similar words, trouble followed.

Before he could drag Marley after him, a monster in overalls emerged from a back office. "Mr. Mann!" he called. "Let me introduce myself, I'm Poltroon."

Portly and greasy, he could have passed as human if not for the four additional arms sprouting from his sides. His face crumpled when he drew closer. "My, you're just a child. I'm so sorry."

Rayleigh took Marley's arm, careful to make sure he didn't touch her fur.

"Hand over the key, and they'll let you go," Poltroon said firmly.

"I–I don't understand." Marley's hand crept to her fanny pack, as though she was, at last, feeling what Rayleigh had been from the moment they arrived.

They'd walked into a trap.

He tightened his grip on Marley's wrist and turned to run, only to find their way out blocked by a phalanx of troll mechanics. Unlike Gasp, they didn't sport checked blazers with elbow pads. Bulbous, with leers exposing broken teeth, they didn't have to thump fists into their open palms to look menacing.

"Leavin' so soon, Master Mann?" a nasally voice crooned.

A cloaked figure emerged from the office, gliding across the grease-slicked ground in a dark cloud of fabric and mystery. They were no taller than Poltroon's waist.

"We've hardly had the chance to get comfortable."

"Not really the setting for comfort," Rayleigh pointed out.

"No? Then let's cut this short. As my dear buddy Poltroon said, we want the Supreme's Key. There's a rumor floating around that he gave it to you, see?"

"No. I don't see. And I don't have it."

"Hoping you won't take offense, Master Mann, but I think you're lyin'." His head tilted up. "Will you allow your friend to be hurt, because you won't hand over the key?"

"The only person getting hurt," Marley said. "Is you." She launched a small vial across the garage.

A yellow-tinged hand emerged from the sleeve of the cloak; its fingers were bony and long, with a sinister addition of joints. A sharp swipe sent the vials crashing into a tall set of tool drawers. Rayleigh raised his coat, shielding himself and Marley from the spray of glass.

"Do you have anything bigger in that pack?" he whispered to her.

"My family doesn't usually hunt monsters, remember?" returned Marley from where she still cowered behind Rayleigh's coat. "What about you, your bent?"

Rayleigh didn't have the time to try and convince himself he was in control of anything about this situation. "I can't risk it."

"Get the girl," the figure ordered. "And grab—"

A cackle rang out from the open mouth of one of the garages.

It echoed off the garage doors and the interior walls, bouncing around until it sounded like multiple women were laughing from the shadows. No, not women—witches.

One in particular. And she wasn't the sort with green skin or warts.

Bloody Mary sashayed out from behind a matte black sedan in leather trousers and a fitted military jacket that kissed the tops of the high-heeled boots climbing her legs. Her hair was drawn back from her face in a severe ponytail, leaving her beauty, and danger, unfiltered.

"Picking on monsterlings, Slydus?" Thick fog, like night itself had dripped down from the sky, roiled around her feet in midnight waves. "And I didn't think you could sink any lower."

"A short joke? Cheap shot."

"I was referring to the depth of your character, I assure you." Blood-red lipstick shone violently against her pale skin as Mary smiled. It widened until her mouth became large enough to swallow a football, her bewitching face wrinkled up like wet bedsheets; she began to appear more like her compatriots with the warts, broomsticks, and uncanny knack of avoiding all flying houses. Rayleigh was impressed to see her technique in action. "Does that complex of yours need a kiss better?"

"I'd rather kiss a brick."

"That," purred Mary, terrible in all her monstrous regalia, "can be arranged."

A shout sounded from across the garage. Rayleigh looked to find the blockade of trolls before the entrance now seemed to be a few short. Tendrils of shadow crawled out of the darkness. They entwined around the remaining trolls, snatching them by their ankles into the night. With several thuds, and a crunch or two, Shade entered the garage.

Readjusting his top hat, he cleared his throat. "As you were."

At that moment, Gasp slipped in from the back and made a beeline toward Rayleigh and Marley, flinging monsters and cars as he went. When the dust had settled, only Poltroon remained of Slydus's party. He quaked like a monster who knew he'd met his maker—the horned monster who strolled out from behind a parked speedboat, mirrored sunglasses glinting, long sleeveless coat swaying, and a charming grin emblazoned on his face.

"Wotcher," said Thelonious. "Fine night." He bore down on the cloaked monster with long, quick steps and seized the scruff of his cloak, hoisting him up. An assortment of improbable goods rained from Slydus's cloak: golf clubs, gloves made for hands as large as small cars, and—oddly—a flock of tropical birds that took off into the night with musical trills. "Now, imp—" Thelonious drove him into the side of a three-wheeled car on a lift, at which point Slydus's hood fell off, revealing a bald head with only a few stray wisps of blond hair, and ears that grew into points. "What are you doing messing with my nephew?"

Slydus issued a few rude insults.

"Ah. My mistake. I thought you were capable of a conversation. Let me put you back where you belong." Bundling Slydus up in his cloak, Thelonious rolled his protesting form across the garage toward the bins, knocking over a mountain of car parts.

Several of the trolls Shade had knocked out began to stir.

"Nephew-mine, let me teach you the second part of our motto," Thelonious said. "There's a time to walk with courage, and there's a time to flee with haste." Lunging for Rayleigh and Marley, he tugged them into a sprint through the shelved cars.

They burst out of a back door and into an alley where a minivan was parked.

"This is the getaway car?" Marley exclaimed.

Thelonious snatched open the sliding door. "What's wrong with Fitzwilliam?"

Without the time to voice how awful it was, Rayleigh jumped inside and found himself at the bottom of an unruly pyramid as everyone piled on top of him. Somewhere above, Shade grumbled about personal space in a loud voice; all the while Rayleigh was pretty certain it was his elbow jabbing him in the forehead.

"Watch it!" he meant to shout, but his voice was muffled by at least three of Marley's tails.

Trapped in an unwelcome game of Twister, Rayleigh angled his neck awkwardly to escape a mouthful of fur. The minivan lurched backward, swinging around to face the entrance to the narrow side street.

"Hold on" was the only warning Thelonious gave before they squealed forward. The strong stink of burning rubber filled the air. There was a thump as they bounced over a pothole. Or a monster. Shade cried out, lamenting his top hat. Someone's foot sank into Rayleigh's stomach. He made his displeasure known with a yell that resulted in inhaling, and subsequently choking on, Marley's tails; Shade screamed, again, and Mary snapped at everyone to *shut up*.

The minivan tilted to the left, cornering on two wheels in rather an impressive manner for a rust bucket, before righting itself and thundering away from the garage. It felt like an age before Thelonious slowed from Breakneck Speed to Tolerably Illegal and gave the all clear. Shade, Mary, and Marley clambered off Rayleigh. The former two Terrors climbed into the back of the van; Shade harped on about the indignity of it all while Mary made unsavory remarks about the size of his bottom.

"That was insane," Marley exclaimed.

Gasp turned in the front seat to inspect her and Rayleigh. "You can say that again."

"How'd you know we were in trouble?" Rayleigh asked.

Thelonious's sunglasses glinted in the rearview mirror. "It's lucky Winsome's mates caught sight of the two of you rattling through Despair."

"She sent you?"

"She's rather fond of you, I think."

That was news to Rayleigh.

"How did you end up over there, anyway? Get lost?"

"No. It's the strangest thing," Rayleigh mused. "We completed the first part of the trial, got our envelopes. Marley's told her to go to the Cabinet. Mine told me to go to that garage. I think it was a trap, but I don't know why."

"What?" Thelonious asked. "Someone gave you an invitation to go there?"

"Yeah. I didn't think anything was weird until the small one started talking about my dad. Obviously, he's an enemy—hey, you should go back! We should see if he has anything to do with Dad! He was after some key of his."

Brakes screaming, the minivan came to an abrupt stop.

Ignoring horns, several deep roars, and an angry unicyclist, Thelonious swiveled around. "What did you say about Slydus, Nephew-mine? The small one."

"The Supreme's Key, whatever that is. He said he heard I had it." The Terrors were silent—contemplatively so. "That's it, isn't it?" A missing puzzle piece sank into place. "Whoever's taken my dad wants this key."

"And," Marley added. "They think you have it."

She didn't say "Uh-oh," but the foreboding exclamation hung in the air as though she had.

TWENTY-ONE

THE MAGIC NUMBER

Rayleigh's revelation about the key triggered a series of expeditious events.

Namely Thelonious's speeding back to Terror Tower; his descent into the underground garage, during which they were airborne for several seconds, thanks to a very steep ramp; and his merciless herding to hurry everyone into the house.

One phone call later, and it turned out the Office of Inductions, Welcomes, and Warnings didn't make a habit of luring monsterlings to rough pockets of Below-London. An investigation was to be opened immediately to discern how, and why, Rayleigh received the invitation that directed him to Despair.

"Did anything strange happen during the first trial, Rayleigh?" Gasp asked, as Thelonious went back and forth with whoever was on the other end of his call.

They were all crowded around the large farm-style table in the kitchen.

"I don't think so." Rayleigh looked to his friend. "Marley, what happened for you during the trial?"

As she accepted a cup of tea from Gasp, her cheeks turned red. "Aside from it taking me a long time? Nothing. I passed through the mirror after you, Rayleigh, and I was in this cave straightaway."

Rayleigh straightened. "Straightaway? You weren't running in the dark for a while?"

She shook her head.

"You were?" Mary asked him.

"Yeah. It was like I couldn't move fast enough, push hard enough. I had to fight to get through to the other side." Rayleigh looked from Mary's tight expression to Gasp's open concern; Shade always looked a little morose, but even he seemed more worried for Rayleigh than himself. "Someone has been trying to get to me since my first trial?"

"It seems like it." Gasp left the table to relay the information to Thelonious.

Whoever orchestrated the note Rayleigh received wanted to isolate him, possibly hurt him, to rob him of a key they believed he had in his possession. A key Rayleigh had never heard of. While Marley presented a strong argument to stay with him at Terror Tower, to plot and strategize, Thelonious thought it best to ring her ma once he'd finished interrogating Octavia Brand.

Whatever Mrs. Liu said to Thelonious was short; what she said to her daughter was even shorter. Marley wasn't happy about leaving, but she didn't argue. Standing beside Thelonious before a swirling Vol-way in a hamper in the utility room off the kitchen, she exchanged a look with Rayleigh. He could practically hear her request that he call her to catch up later.

Once he hopped back out of the hamper, sans Marley, Thelonious looked at his nephew. Rayleigh lifted his chin. Two determined versions of himself were reflected in Thelonious's sunglasses.

"We wouldn't know about the key if it wasn't for me," he asserted. "I don't want to be sent to my room. I want to help."

"Fine."

Rayleigh blinked. "Fine?"

Thelonious nodded. "I don't want you going into another situation like tonight with your eyes closed because we're keeping things from you. You should know what's happening."

"Okay." Rayleigh did his best to stay cool. "Good."

"Let's go through to the clubhouse."

Rayleigh took a seat on a zebra print chaise—not real animal skin, Gasp assured him. Thelonious stood by the fireplace. He'd adopted his favored position, one hand gripping the mantel. The tower had repaired it after he broke it the night Rayleigh's bent manifested. From the tightness in his forehead, the way he kept tapping his left foot, it might need another fix before the night was over.

"So, what's the Supreme's Key?" Rayleigh asked.

"To put it simply," Mary began. "A Vol-trix token. All bogey men are provided with a specific token when they're elected. It's like a symbolic passing of the flame. Theirs differs from regular tokens in that it enables transportation across the four realms without limit. For this reason, it's called the Supreme's Key. It's a necessity, as there's only the one Bogey Mann, and he has an entire world of children Above, and feddies Below, to keep an eye on." Mary shook her head. "It has to be the missing piece that will center this search."

"I guess you guys don't have it?"

"We don't." Mary sighed. "Your father keeps it on his person."

"Not always, though," Gasp said. He turned to where Rayleigh was seated. "For all these weeks, we couldn't decide why Bogey was in trouble. We've been chasing different leads, to no end."

"Now you know about the key," Rayleigh said. "Who do you think would take my dad to get it?"

Thelonious jumped away from the fireplace as though touched by its heat. "Lowell!" he cried, and then promptly strode out of the clubhouse without another word.

Not missing a beat, the Terrors and Rayleigh went after him, down the stairs, and into the office on the first floor. It was a generous double-height room with a mezzanine floor. Thelonious paced before a wall of monitors on its ground floor.

Gasp looked on, concerned. "I haven't seen that look on his face since the runaway Cat Four in Westminster."

"No," mused Shade. "He hasn't shown this sort of mania since the Banshee of Battersea. Care to share with the group, Chief?"

"I think I know," Rayleigh said slowly.

The Terrors turned to him.

"Take it away, Nephew-mine." Thelonious flourished an arm.

"On the day of my Induction, you asked Lowell if he'd had the chance to review the security footage from the break-in at your HQ."

"That I did."

"Since my dad was already gone, you think that whoever broke in was looking for his key."

"That I do."

"Heavens," Gasp breathed. "That was weeks ago."

"If they're looking for it—" Mary stood, shook her head. "Then Bogey doesn't have it."

"He mustn't." Thelonious began pacing once again, back and forth before a large board which displayed many documents. "When we were robbed, the flat was so trashed we couldn't tell what had been taken. And when the insurance company decided they wouldn't cover everything, because we're public figures and undertook the risk of obsessive fans, blah, blah, we decided we wouldn't pay that witch recoupment firm's fee ourselves."

"When I said share, I meant the bits we didn't already know," Shade griped.

"Humor me, Shade. This is for Rayleigh's benefit as much as yours and mine." Thelonious was near giddy, at this point. "We didn't want to pay for the spell to undo the damage, not when the insurer would cover the cleanup charm, so we never really knew what had been taken and what was simply broken. Are you with me, Nephew-mine?"

Rayleigh nodded.

"Now, our burglary fell in with a bunch of additional hits in the city. I kept an eye on them, hoping to discern the thief's pattern to catch them in the act—Mary, there's a list of coordinates I put together. Will you send them up to the map, please?"

"I'm on it." She took a seat at one of the screens, powered it up, and began typing.

"I sent the list to Lowell so he could pull footage, but he's been busy, and I didn't chase him as much as I could have." Thelonious shook his head. "That was my mistake. If I'd looked into it properly, if I *insisted* we all treat it as a priority—"

"The addresses have been sent," announced Mary.

"Pukka." Thelonious rubbed his hands. "No use crying over a

spilt potion, I suppose. Up we go, Terrors."

Up was a spiral staircase to the mezzanine floor, where a vast table, sleek and made from glass, stretched across a thick rug. Thelonious touched its surface, and it came to life. Shimmering 3D buildings grew out of its surface in pairs, like a model city formed from fizzing pale blue lines.

"Volence?" Rayleigh asked.

"Yes," his uncle confirmed. "It's as I suspected," he muttered to himself, near humming with excitement. "There is a pattern. Right, one half of each pair is the broken-into establishment. Next to those buildings were the real targets." Thelonious drew a pair toward them with his fingers. "This bakery, like our flat, was trashed to mask the fact that the burglar wasn't stealing anything. I would bet my horns on them using the connecting wall to take the long way into the building next door."

"The Leviathan Bank," said Gasp. "We have accounts there. And across the map, the building next to the cobblers is Gourmandize Storage, where we have lockers."

Each building beside, or in close proximity to, a business that was burgled was an establishment frequented in some capacity or other by the Terrors.

"Why didn't the Cabinet report the buildings next door were also broken into?" Mary stared at the map. "These aren't local businesses; most of these establishments are chains."

"And it's the chains, I suspect, who wanted their vulnerabilities kept quiet," said Thelonious, his tone one of triumph. "Because they didn't know what we now do, thanks to Rayleigh and Miss Liu. The burglars were searching places Bogey may have left his key. We don't have the video stills to see if we can identify the owner of those sticky fingers, but I bet they left empty-handed every time. I can try Lowell tomorrow, during the day, but I think we can all hazard a guess as to who's behind the bigger picture. Who was searching for the key."

"You mean besides Slydus and Poltroon?" Rayleigh asked.

"It's bigger than them." Mary frowned, in thought. "We've encountered them in our work for the Shadow Guild. They are small players, not the chief."

"That would be the Illustrious Society," Thelonious and Gasp said, simultaneously, just as Mary and Shade offered "That's Mama D'Leau" as their suggestion.

Rayleigh looked between both sets of Terrors. He knew the names they'd said, of course. The Society were the Confederation's greatest stain, but D'Leau—

"I thought the river witch was friends with my dad? She was on *The Vulture Culture* a few days ago defending him."

"D'Leau ran for Supreme Scarer against Bogey, Rayleigh." Mary's beautiful face was drawn with anger. "And they fell out when he won." She turned to Thelonious. "She controls the Undersea Channel in Below-London. In fact, she made a point of assuming control when she arrived decades ago. That's what she has been doing while Bogey maintained our Volentic energy. If anyone was capable of holding him in place while the media discredit him, she is."

"Why would she want his key, though?" Rayleigh asked.

"Exactly!" Gasp slammed a hand on the map; impressively, it didn't flicker. "D'Leau would have been a credible threat, if she and Bogey hadn't settled their differences," he argued. "Unlike the Confederation and the Illustrious Society."

A society filled with former bogey men.

"I thought they were imprisoned," Rayleigh said, his voice tight.

"Its leaders, the Illustrious Three, yes. But not all those harboring a fervent hope that the Society could rise once more." The vivid green of Gasp's skin had paled. "We didn't, couldn't, catch every zealot after the Battle of the Sky and Earth, the Society's first major attempt to dim the Confederation's aim to bring light to Above and Below. And they're the only rogues who have a, er, history with bogey men." Gasp finished with an awkward glance at Rayleigh.

"I know about the curse," he said. "I know, at least, I think I know, that you guys were worried it might have happened to my dad. That's why you didn't tell me about it."

"Oh, Nephew-mine. No," Thelonious said. "Okay, yes. There is a curse. But Bogey hasn't served for long enough to succumb to it.

So it was as Marley had assured him. Rayleigh exhaled. "Why didn't you tell me about it?"

"We didn't want to worry you" was Thelonious's explanation; one Rayleigh didn't get any dishonest vibes from. Good. "Their views are the opposite of your old man's. Their core belief is that monsters should be monstrous. We should be terrifying, not helpful, because it's who they want us to be. Humans should be allowed to devolve to their baser selves. If everyone Above and Below subscribed to their agenda"—Thelonious was grim faced, wary—"there'd be no Volence. No light."

"They never made it out of the Confed with those intentions, though," Gasp added. "Our side's victory in the war sorted that. Of course it means their grand plan—which they called the Dimming—went unachieved. Bogey opposes everything the Dimming stood for.

His formative years of leadership aren't called the Decade of Light for nothing. The Confederation was mostly able to rebuild because of him. If the Society couldn't make him bend—"

"He would never," Thelonious growled.

"Then," Gasp emphasized, "it makes sense that they'd remove him from action as well as send someone to try and steal his key. Benching him would cripple our Volence in the long run, enough to potentially leave us vulnerable. With the key, they could release the Illustrious Three from prison. They could free all Categories, One through Four, to unleash chaos across the four realms and the Above world."

"Knowing all of this, Mary, Shade, how can you think it's D'Leau?" Thelonious asked his teammates. "She has accrued more power over the years, but doesn't have the reach to infiltrate the Monsters Cabinet. She couldn't have ensured Rayleigh was sent to Despair tonight, either. That's someone on the inside. Someone working the Induction. An Illustrious Society plant."

Rayleigh thought about the twins, dismissed them. They were too young, surely.

"Well." Shade shifted in his seat. "When you put it like that."

Mary was silent.

"If the Illustrious Society is doing this," said Rayleigh, who'd been following closely, "can't we report them to the Quorum?" Earlier in the night, when Thelonious spoke with the Office of Inductions, Welcomes, and Warnings; they didn't have a clear suspect. "The Undersecretary is your friend. Can't he do something about it?"

"The Society isn't made up of imprisoned monsters alone," said Gasp. "There are many who've never been caught. In fact, it's rumored that there were kings and queens across the three realms who sided with the Illustrious Three. There are influential families who would have been young then, but will now be old, established. Entrenched in our Society. If we share that we know they're behind your father's absence, this attack on you tonight, Rayleigh, we show our hand too early."

"And we can't have that." Thelonious drew himself to his full height; it was all the more impressive with his horns. "The burglaries tell us Bogey didn't have the token with him, at least. Pity we can't check his floor."

"Hang on," Rayleigh interrupted. "If my dad didn't have the key, why are they still holding him?"

"To stop him from getting it. To stop him from filling both sides of the lid with light." Thelonious's brow was low, tight. "Bogey would fight that with everything he has. Without him . . . darkness."

"The literal kind and that other one?" Rayleigh asked. His uncle had said that before, in one of their earlier conversations.

"Right. Yes, right. But we can walk with courage knowing that since this thief has run out of places to search, they're coming after us. That's what happened tonight. Because, Nephew-mine, you are a member of this team, of this family." Thelonious cracked his knuckles. "And we're going to keep you safe."

"Why would they think I had it?"

"You are the secret son of the most famous monster across the four realms and the human world, Rayleigh." Mary's diction was sharp with pride. "To them you are someone your father sought to protect. I would have looked to you too, when you arrived here. Your affiliation with us hasn't helped matters."

"But it will henceforth." Thelonious's voice, deep and commanding, left no room for doubt, for fear. "Routines change from here on. They have someone on the inside."

"I've been thinking about that," Rayleigh began. "They wouldn't look like a Bad Guy. Monster. Feddie. Whatever." Even if their age wasn't a factor, those qualities ruled the twins out.

"Smarter than I took you for," Shade drawled.

Rayleigh paid him no mind. "We could check out anyone who—" was involved in my trials, Rayleigh had been about to say. But of course . . . "I didn't finish my trial!"

"I've already sent a message, Nephew-mine. Undersecretary Duplicious will take care of matters for you and Miss Liu. We'll also have to discuss your third trial. I don't feel comfortable sending you both out into the city until matters have been taken care of."

"Until we figure out who is a member of the Illustrious Society?"

"Right," his uncle confirmed. "Thought we'd start with its organizers. Octavia Brand's office. They control the invitations."

"There's also a feddie called Conny Fir," Rayleigh added.

"They're all on the list. Though I know Conny. She doesn't have Brand's ambition," Mary said. "That's who I'd put my money on."

"And how will we catch her?" Rayleigh asked.

"I thought we'd attend a party," Thelonious said, much to the surprise of the others. He pulled an envelope out of his pocket; a looping script across its front was difficult to read, but he translated. "Mama D'Leau's masquerade birthday ball, as it so happens, is in four days' time. She's invited us. I thought we could ask for her help in handling the matter with Bogey."

"Really?" Mary asked. "Even after knowing she and Brand share similarities? Octavia is an aquatic monster. She also shares Mama D'Leau's penchant for mobile water receptacles. They call one another sistren. Sisters. What if Brand is helping D'Leau replace Bogey?"

"That's all water in the channel. Come on, now." Thelonious blew a raspberry. "We have under two weeks remaining to find my brother. It was proving hard enough before the Illustrious Society entered the chat. I was merely going to ask for her to add some numbers to our search party. I don't want to call the other Terrors out of retirement unless the situation is dire."

"I'm not entirely convinced," Mary said. "But count me in for the party. Maybe I'll brew a little truth tea and slip it into D'Leau's drink. Octavia might be there too."

Rayleigh got to his feet. "I want to go."

Shade snorted.

"If you don't let me, I'll sneak out after you." He lowered his voice as his uncle did sometimes. "You know what I'm capable of."

"A throat infection, by the sound of things," commented the penumbra dryly.

"Look." Rayleigh pushed in his normal voice, irritation prickling across his skin. "If the Illustrious Society gets into power, the Above world will be in trouble, putting my family up there in danger. I don't want a holiday, or to beat any more of Shade's high scores in the arcade."

"You did what?" the penumbra started.

Rayleigh ignored him. "I choose this, Thelonious."

"Who gave you permission to beat my high scores?"

His uncle held up a hand. Shade squirreled back into the sofa, his bottom lip jutting out. Rayleigh braced for further argument.

"If you complete the rest of your Induction training to my satisfaction, then, and only then," said Thelonious, before Rayleigh could muscle his way in, "will I be on board with you potentially coming along."

Rayleigh thought about the terms and found them almost satisfactory.

"Deal."

"At last!" shouted Winsome when Rayleigh opened his bedroom door. "I thought you'd died!"

"You saved my life tonight, Winsome. And Marley's." Serious, Rayleigh clambered onto his bed so he could look the fairy in her violet eyes. "You're not a criminal to me. Or a huge pain. Mostly."

"Then I'm your hero?"

"Er, not quite."

"Your goddess?"

"I'm . . . going to clean my teeth." Rayleigh hopped down from the bed. "Hey—" He turned back. "What can you tell me about the Illustrious Three?"

The fairy yawned. "I suppose I could share that they went to war and didn't free my kind to fight with them. It's well known that fairies have a history with combat. No doubt that's why the Illustrious Three are in the positions they're in. Three separate prisons that make this"—she gestured around her bulb—"look like a palace. I might have to subject myself to conversing with you, but at least I can. The Three haven't spoken in over a century, and if the Chancellor is to be believed, they won't ever again." She sat down, fabric puffing around her like petals from a flower. "That will teach them, don't you think?"

"Absolutely."

"Leave me be now, monsterling. I tire after saving your life."

Rayleigh felt lighter after what she'd shared. Whatever influence the Illustrious Three had before, they were in no position to take over at present. Now the Terrors knew who to look for, Society followers, he was hopeful it wouldn't take much longer to find his dad. Especially when his third trial would happen within the next week—his last.

When he left the bathroom, the walls in his room were dark with few stars visible behind an abundance of wispy clouds. Shapeless specters, they hung before a pale moon lain on its side. Winsome was curled up at the bottom of her bulb, maybe sleeping. Rayleigh switched on his bedside lamp and rolled to the other side of the bed to retrieve *The Book of Night Things* from the twin bedside cloud.

He winced as the keys he'd pocketed earlier that night bit into his thigh. Freeing them from his pocket, he tossed them across his bed—and immediately scrambled for them.

Keys.

"Thelonious!" Rayleigh army-rolled across his bed, landed on his feet, and ran for the door. "Thelonious!"

Behind him, Winsome yelled a demand to know what was going on.

Sprinting past the gallery, Rayleigh skidded into the kitchen in his socks.

"THELONIOUS!" he bellowed again.

"Rayleigh?"

He spun and nearly lost his balance.

"Fright alive," Gasp said, stepping through a doorway in the kitchen that definitely hadn't been there before. "Are you all right?"

"Yes." Rayleigh breathed. "Where's my uncle?"

"He's gone to the Cabinet with Shade. Are you hurt?"

A second doorway appeared beside Gasp's. It was narrow, as it sat between two standing cupboards. Mary was forced to turn sideways to slip out.

"Is everything all right?" She looked between the two of them. "I heard shouting. And Winsome said you were upset, Rayleigh?"

"Not upset—hey, how did she tell you that?"

Mary, ready for bed, drew her silk robe over her pajamas. "What's the matter?"

Between Winsome's transient habits and the keys in his hand, the latter was by far the most important. Rayleigh held them aloft.

Mary stepped closer to inspect them. "What are those for?"

"Terror Tower. It gave them to me. Are they my dad's?"

She proffered an open palm; Rayleigh passed them over. Was it too farfetched to contemplate that the tower gave him his dad's keys after everything else it had done? Maybe, but Rayleigh thought it was worth a double check. Gasp joined Mary's silent inspection of the keys. She turned slightly in the light. Several circular key rings winked.

"Is it there?" Rayleigh's heart thumped. "The Supreme's Key."

"I'm afraid not." Mary handed the keys back. "These are Shade's keys."

"Yes." Gasp grimaced. "He's been rather put out about losing them."

Rayleigh sighed. Disappointment bore a cruel edge. "I suppose it would have been too easy for the tower to give me my dad's keys."

"I'm afraid so," Gasp said, with a patient softness. "It's made a habit of giving our stuff away over the years. I'm always losing socks."

The key rings clacked as Rayleigh closed his fist. "Sorry to have wasted your time."

"It wasn't a waste. Finding the key without Bogey is like looking for a piece of dandyweed in a field of the plant." Mary turned back toward her doorway, where a sliver of a large four-poster bed was visible. "Don't worry about it, Rayleigh. Good night."

"Fancy a cup of dandyweed tea?" Gasp offered. "It's wonderfully comforting."

"That's okay."

Embarrassment was hot against the back of his neck; Rayleigh escaped to his room without a second look at the Terrors' expressions of pity. Safe in the darkness of the sky, the stars, around his bed, he threw Shade's keys into a dark corner. Overhead, Winsome was missing from her bulb. Rayleigh was glad for a moment's peace. He hadn't told the Terrors about his updated bent, but that could wait until the next day. He wasn't sure it truly had changed; he'd taken a big enough pie to the face for the evening. He took up *The Book of Night Things*; opening its aged pages, he toyed with the weighted ends of the ribbon bookmarks, rubbing his thumb across their surfaces as he flicked through his ancestral map.

He found an entry about Mama D'Leau. Unlike others, her legend didn't contain a single drawing of the witch, only a short poem that opened with the line "Beware the wrath of the mother of the water." She was portrayed as an environmental activist, punishing those who attacked her beloved waters and their denizens. That didn't seem like someone working with a group determined to limit monsters to nothing more than agents of shadows. Unless . . . with the Society's help, she'd have the power she needed to dole out further punishments.

Frankly, Rayleigh had no idea if Mama D'Leau was involved or not. But he was all but a papers-bearing citizen of the Confederation of Lightless Places, with roots Above too. Rest assured, if she was on side with the Society, or working for her own benefit, he'd learn the truth.

Her party was the perfect place for them to find out.

TWENTY-TWO

A MASTER CLASS

"I believe the penumbra is on the agenda for today" was how Winsome greeted Rayleigh the following morning. "With any luck, you'll knock yourself out in the darkness on his floor, guaranteeing a long nap and sparing yourself another day of sore muscles."

"Always thinking of others, Win," Rayleigh called from the bathroom as he dressed. Today's gargoyle emblem on his T-shirt was violet in color. "Mary will be pleased with your progress."

Just as Rayleigh needed to please Thelonious with his, during the next few days of his Induction training. Of all the Terrors, Shade was the hardest to read. But Rayleigh was fairly sure he already knew the perfect entrance for an esteemed member of the Order of Corner Creepers. After a light breakfast, he made his way downstairs to the alcove where the kitchen and basement doors met. There, poised in a nook that was starved of light, an inky web of darkness clung to the ceiling. He dragged one of the accent chairs in the hallway beneath it. When he clambered atop the fancy upholstery, his fingertips only grazed the shadow, but it was enough for the darkness to drop down and slurp him up.

He landed on his feet in what he could only describe as night.

Waving a hand before his face did nothing but catch the tip of his nose. Something that would delight Shade to no end, wherever he was. Mary and Gasp had been there to meet him on their floors; of course the penumbra would be contrary.

As Rayleigh geared up to yell for some light, it shone abruptly down from a cluster of bejeweled lanterns suspended in the center of a highly peaked tent. Its silky fabric rippled beneath fingers of a warm breeze—no. It wasn't fabric. The tent itself was crafted out of shadows. While it was both entrancing and mildly eerie, something else had it beat for shock factor.

"Morning, Nephew-mine," called Thelonious.

Rayleigh picked his form out from the seething shadows around them, barely distinguishing his horns and the flash of his ever-present sunglasses.

"You?"

"I do believe my line in that little riddle instructed you to be ready at any time."

"What about Shade?"

"He's helping by lending us his floor and not sticking around."

Rayleigh closed the distance between them; shadows curled around his feet, lapping and splashing like obsidian water.

"Wotcher." Thelonious's sunglasses were raised by a grin. "I have some good news. Spoke with our good buddy—*our* good buddy, he wanted to make sure I told you that bit—Undersecretary Duplicious. He's taken up for you and Marley with the Office of Inductions, Welcomes, and Warnings. Since you wouldn't have known to go to Despair without first receiving your envelopes, you passed. There was also a kid by the name of Mack who was very complimentary of your problem-solving skills."

Rayleigh perked up at the familiar name. "They were pretty cool."

"Sounds like."

"Any news about who set me up?"

"Not yet. The Undersecretary is running a silent investigation with some of the other members of the Shadow Guild. Octavia and Conny were questioned, of course, along with the rest of their office. We're playing it close to the vest, like we discussed last night. Nothing about the Illustrious Society was mentioned on our end. Which left room for one of the team to admit to maybe making a mistake. No dice. Someone is lying in that office. But we'll be smarter next time—actually, right now. We both agreed, our good buddy the Undersecretary and me, that you and Marley should take your third trials here."

"Here?" Rayleigh gestured at the shadows.

"Not exactly. The tower started working on something else for you last night when I got back. Should be ready in time for you to pass so you can attend the Citizenship Ceremony with the others in your class."

"Wow, Thelonious. I appreciate that."

"Of course. Now—" He clapped his hands together. "How has the training been going?"

"Can't complain."

"Gasp and Mary told me about your time together. Winsome passed along a few thoughts too. Even Shade has popped in to catch up on how you've been doing. Didn't notice any shadows?"

"I did not. So maybe I should complain, then." Rayleigh drew in a deep breath, excuses at the ready, but Thelonious waved him off.

"Your transformation is still in flux. Hence this." He presented a surprised Rayleigh with a gift-wrapped package.

He ripped it open to find . . . "A torch?" And not a new one either, judging by the scratches on the slim chrome handle. "Er, thanks."

"What you hold in your unimpressed little hands is a lumicand." Thelonious patted the silver canister hanging from his hip. "Like mine."

"So, better than a torch."

Thelonious threw his head back and laughed.

Rayleigh knew the gravity of what he held. He turned the weapon over with reverence; as long as his forearm, its base was rough to guarantee a secure grip. The head was wide and flat.

"Steady there." Thelonious edged it away. "Don't want you blinding yourself. It's not entirely like mine, I should clarify."

At his uncle's instruction, Rayleigh stepped back, and Thelonious unhooked his lumicand from his hip. A touch of a button released that shimmering sword of light. In the dark of Shade's floor, it shone like something radioactive.

"Take a look at the handle and tell me what you see."

Rayleigh inspected the length of his lumicand. "Scratches."

"Wise guy. Take another look."

Holding the weapon closer to his face, Rayleigh turned it in his hand. Several of the scratches were clustered together in something that looked like a symbol over the button.

"Are these meant to be beams of light?"

"Meant to be?" Thelonious dragged a hand down his face. "Of course they are!"

A grinning Rayleigh went to press the button.

"Wait! Hang on a sec there. Your button is different to mine. Your weapon is different to mine—but it is a weapon, don't forget. It needs to be handled with care. Now, I had a chat with a few mates who share bents similar to yours. When they were first transforming, they described the sensation as uncontrollable. Gasp mentioned you told him you felt the same way?"

Rayleigh nodded. "It changed during the second trial. It stopped feeling like it was around me and more like it was coming from me."

"One mate said as much. Hence the lumicand. It's for you to channel your bent. You can give it a direction to go in. All that buzzing and fizzing inside—"

"Mine's more like vibrating. Like rumbling on stone."

"Stone. Okay. The lumicand will give that a direction. Those sunbeams on the lumicand button are called a glyph. It's a symbol that your bent will recognize, because magic always finds magic. It worked well for another guy I know. Though his preferred compass for his bent was a hammer."

"Oh, yeah? Is he from Below-London, or elsewhere in the Confed? I could talk to him—"

"He's off realm. And while I'm not certain you're the same, the lumicand is a useful tool."

Rayleigh was desperate to ask what the monster was, but he knew it wasn't appropriate. "Do you use your lumicand to direct your bent too?"

Thelonious's smile wavered somewhat. "No, Nephew-mine."

"Sorry, I shouldn't have asked." He couldn't help himself. His uncle was both exactly who he appeared and someone else. Someone mysterious.

"It's okay. Most lumicands contain Volentic energy. Mine is no exception. This sword is one of the weapons it can manifest."

"You shot balls of light in my flat, in Above-London."

"I did. Seems a lifetime ago, hey? Now—" Thelonious held up the Volentic sword coming out of his lumicand. "This is a virga. Remember, not all monsters joined the Illustrious Society, but not all monsters fought in the war against them either, you understand? Volence, in its purest form, is goodness. Anything that opposes that energy, even briefly, will always feel the burn of a lumicand's touch. I always think that if a monster runs from a virga, they know it will sting." Thelonious's voice was heavy with significance.

"Then it won't harm a good person?"

"Oh, it'll harm anyone who gets on the wrong side of it. So be careful when you turn the lumicand on."

"But what if I can't make the bent come?"

"Magic responds to magic, remember. Look at how I'm holding my lumicand. It's a little like gripping a guitar. Thumb on the large button with the glyph. And then you should feel three additional buttons on the side where your fingers will grip. Can you? Look, if you can't feel."

Rayleigh raised his canister to study the symbols lining the handle. The first was an X. He hit it. All at once his body was filled with the thunderous vibration of his bent; it tunneled down his arm and into the lumicand. A violet circle of sparking light flared from the weapon's inside, spinning around before him.

"Bravo, Nephew-mine! Bravo!"

The canister in Rayleigh's hand thrummed with energy, with power—his power, manifested into a shield before him. He wiggled a bit.

"All right there?" his uncle asked.

"It tickles a little." Rayleigh shook his shoulders. "What should I do with this?"

Thelonious moved one foot before the other and lifted himself onto the balls of his feet before jabbing his virga forward. Instincts engaged, Rayleigh raised the Catherine wheel of light. Sparks flew where offense met defense.

Rayleigh gaped at his uncle. "A little warning might have been nice!"

"I'm sure the next Illustrious Society member will give you a heads-up when you meet."

Thelonious darted in with a slash next. Rayleigh stepped back, unsteady in his trainers. The charge in his hands, his body, began to buzz.

"Put the weight on your back foot and suck in your core. It'll help with balance."

Another blow came down diagonally. It pressed against the shield. Two of himself, teeth gritted, reflected back at Rayleigh in Thelonious's sunglasses. He added a second hand to the lumicand, drew his stomach back to his spine, and sent the weight to his back foot. With a grunt, he pushed against the virga with his shield. It gave an inch. Another.

"Good," Thelonious ground out. "Strong."

"Me or the shield?" Rayleigh spoke with ease; he was half convinced his uncle was having him on.

"The shield comes from you, kid. Second. Symbol."

Rayleigh's eyes dipped to the canister. He pressed the button underneath the solid circle as his uncle tipped his lumicand upward.

An orb of energy shot out, tunneling away into the writhing shadows above. Panting, he stared at his uncle. He could have hit him.

"That was my favorite move to change from defense to offense." Thelonious dragged a hand across his brow. He was sweating. "Close combat isn't necessarily about being the best fighter, it's about meaning every strike you make. The orbs are effective for holding monsters back from several feet away. Though the further away you are, the weaker the aim and accuracy. That's where the next button on your lumicand comes in. Go ahead."

Rayleigh pointed the weapon into the folds of darkness and hit the button beside twin lines. Dual shafts of energy zipped out and blazed through the shadows.

"Lengthier than orbs, bolts are less energy consuming than the virga too. When it comes to battle, strategy is everything. In time you'll know those switches inside and out. For now, we practice. Let's have you try with the virga this time. There's a bunch of classical knowledge about positions and so on, but I find you naturally know when to lunge, when to slash, and when to lop something off. Try to avoid that last one with me, mind."

"Does my father carry one?"

"He doesn't need a lumicand. His bent is powerful enough. But when he's feeling fancy or he's had too much of the old tipple, he's been known to use two for a party trick."

Rayleigh hoped he'd get to see that for himself.

"Thelonious . . ." he removed his thumb from the glyphed power button and turned the lumicand over in his hands, uncertain about whether or not he was making the right decision. "What if D'Leau is the one who's working for the Illustrious Society?"

Thelonious was careful with his words. "The Society's supporters come from all walks of life. But I don't believe D'Leau has anything to do with your old man's current situation."

"You're sure?"

"I said no more untruths." Thelonious lowered his sunglasses and winked at his nephew; the sight of his golden eyes, the Mann family eyes, eased the tension out of Rayleigh's back and shoulders. "Right, now I want you to hit that virga button and ready yourself."

For all his talk of instinct, Thelonious was a stickler for how Rayleigh handled the virga. He had to stand with one foot behind the other, at a slight angle, so as to balance his hits. The tip of his weapon was rarely allowed to point upward, and at random intervals he was encouraged to fire orbs, or bolts, to throw off his opponent.

After two days, Thelonious called Rayleigh a natural.

It was dizzying, fast, and hot on the other side of the Volentic energy. Yet it felt entirely right to have this power in his hands. There was also something cool about learning how to master a sword. Of all the methods of attack the Terrors were teaching him, Rayleigh found he preferred the weight of the lumicand to the possible risk of looking gassy, or the necessity of bodily contact wrestling required. It was an honorable weapon, Thelonious told him on their third day together, right before he shared something else:

"I hope Taylor's pack included dancing shoes, Nephew-mine. We have a party to attend."

TWENTY-THREE

THE UNDERSEA MENAGERIE

The following evening, Rayleigh decided his trainers would be safer than dancing shoes when Thelonious informed him they'd be traveling by Bad Omen the night of D'Leau's party. Shoes without laces were a risk in fast winds, and Kedara had a habit of catching them all. Much to Rayleigh's delight.

The omen drifted to the left, her wide wings fanned against glinting window pockets, as the Terrors—carried by omens themselves—made their descent over a high street with buildings old enough to conceal secrets within their grand walls. Wry-upon-the-Undersea was older than the Province of Dreamers, and more traditional in a stuffy sort of way, with its sleepy lanes, low roofs, and thatched cottages. A towering signpost promised the Wry Bridge and Footpath were a giant's skip away as the party veered past to land before a set of public omen cages.

"We're right on time." Thelonious ensured the floors the omens occupied were locked with an intricate system of ties. Then he added a padlock he fished from inside his suit. The Terrors didn't own any buildings within Wry, as they did in many other locales, to secure their omens. "The party should be passing beneath the bridge in minutes."

And what a bridge it was.

Rising out of the mist-topped Undersea Channel like a great serpent, it was lit by a line of antique streetlamps that stretched away into the fog. Mary's heels and Shade's pointed-toe boots click-clacked as they journeyed to its middle. Across the water, the low hum of music sounded as something large wended its way toward them.

Gasp peered into the night. "We'd better hurry, Terrors."

Shade brandished a slim suitcase, then rested it on the bridge wall. At his touch, the clasp made its T curve into a claw that dug into the stone of the bridge, anchoring itself. The lid flipped back, and from inside unfurled an inflatable tongue—a slide. Thelonious hadn't wanted to risk boarding with the guests at the designated pier. Not after what happened to Rayleigh the night of his second trial. Masquerade ball or not, Thelonious wanted to wait for the guests to imbibe a few rounds of the old tipple first.

The slide flickered once before disappearing. No, not disappearing, blending in with the fog and dark. If Rayleigh hadn't seen it before it vanished, he wouldn't have known where to look for the subtle seam of its edges. He traced the slide through the brume to where the river cruiser finally materialized. A grand mistress of the waters, the ship was festooned in fairy lights. There was an energetic steel-pan band on its upper deck, where monsters twirled and drank, laughed and partied, unaware of the invisible slide settling on the quieter stern.

"Masks on." Thelonious grinned at Rayleigh. "Loved saying that."

"How many masquerade balls have you been to?" he asked his

uncle as he tidied his windswept hair with his afro pick.

"Too many to remember. Always a good sign. Tonight should be fun. Business aside."

"And speaking of business." Mary wore a large, feathered headdress connected to a bejeweled mask. She looked like a dazzling bird of prey. "If Octavia is in there, she's mine."

Gasp shifted his handheld mask away from his face. "Oh, you brewed the truth tea?"

"I did."

"Then I'll keep an eye on D'Leau," Shade said.

Thelonious wore his sunglasses, but from his sigh of exasperation, Rayleigh could tell he was rolling his eyes. "Where's your mask?"

A writhing infinity knot of shadows concentrated on Shade's face.

Rayleigh put his own mask on. Maybe it was the slip of velvet against his face, or perhaps the suit, but the gravity of what they sought to prove, or disprove, about D'Leau and Brand suddenly hit him. Thelonious wasn't worried, but for what must have been the hundredth time, Rayleigh checked his hip for the lumicand.

Gasp and Mary boarded the slide first. They flew above guests who had no idea their party was being invaded by monstrous guests with perfectly legitimate invitations and suspicions. Rayleigh was next on the slide. It was a disconcerting feeling to travel across something he couldn't entirely see. There were few monsters on the stern; their focus was on a shower of sparks in the sky. Mary's fingers danced as she provided the distraction. Thelonious too zipped in unnoticed, followed by Shade.

"Remember," the former said. "We'll meet back here at twelve-oh-one."

"Why such a specific time?" asked Rayleigh.

"Because nothing good tends to happen any later." Mary plucked a drink from a passing tray—floating, with no assist from any creature Rayleigh could see. "See you inside, boys," she said, striding away in a shower of sequins. Gasp and Shade followed her inside the ship through a set of sliding doors.

Thelonious took up a drink himself and knocked it back in one. "Make sure you stick by me, Nephew-mine."

The main party was in a ballroom. A mirrored ceiling above reflected the swarm of monsters spinning and partying to the rhythmic melody of steel pans. Overseeing the revelers from a giant martini glass atop a small plinth was one of the most beautiful women Rayleigh'd ever seen. At least, half of her was. Long dreadlocks tumbled over smooth brown shoulders that were speckled with lighter brown splotches. Her eyes were wide and glistened like onyx in the lights that reflected off the ceiling mirrors.

Her lower half, now? Not so much.

Coiled in the bottom of the glass, and trailing over its rim, was a thick tail like that of a giant serpent. It bopped absentmindedly to the bass thrumming through the floor. The woman's shoulders followed the same beat. She couldn't be anyone but Mama D'Leau. Rayleigh pointed her out to his uncle.

"We'll catch her later," he said. "After Shade's had a chance to prove me right. I smell snacks."

In one of two banquet suites separated by a corridor, Gasp was standing before a buffet, talking to a female troll who sported an impressive beard. The second suite was filled with monsters sitting at tables playing games with cards and chips. The band's music was quieter—enough that Rayleigh picked up a different melody beneath the steel pans. Unlike the joyful notes in the band, this other strain of music was so soft, so hopeless, Rayleigh couldn't imagine any musician who thought that sort of song an appropriate set for a party.

"Can you hear that?" he asked his uncle.

Thelonious shook his head, distracted by a monster at a card table. Indeed, no one else seemed concerned about the haunting melody, even though Rayleigh found himself unable to ignore it. Thelonious proceeded to the table and asked to be dealt in.

"No monsterlings," the card dealer said, one eye on Rayleigh, the other ten on the deck he was whipping out at an alarming speed. "House rules."

Thelonious squeezed Rayleigh's shoulder and muttered for him to find Gasp.

On his way to find his frightfather, Rayleigh heard that melody again, the one that sounded like broken hearts and regrets. What if the singing had something to do with his ability to discern truth? It was easy to forget about that trait in the aftermath of his lightning, but it was the one that had manifested first. That inexplicable knowing he felt when something wasn't quite right. He looked back into the games suite where monsters laughed and jested; Thelonious wouldn't notice if he did a little investigating of his own.

Well versed in the art of sneaking, he tracked the music down past the kitchen, to a spot guests probably weren't supposed to venture. It was shabbier than the splendor he left behind. Rayleigh placed both hands against a paneled wall, leaned in, and almost fell forward when one of them slipped to the side. Behind, a flight of stairs led down into a dimly glowing den in the belly of the ship. It was the perfect hiding place for something Mama D'Leau wouldn't want found.

Maybe his dad.

Freeing his lumicand, Rayleigh checked that the corridor was still empty before he stepped inside. After a little tussling with the secret panel, it slid closed with a muted thump. Careful to keep the virga, bright in the gloom, angled before him, he made his way down the stairs. Each breath he took felt too loud, though he knew he couldn't be heard over the baleful singing still echoing in the belly of the ship. Alighting at the bottom of the narrow stairwell, he saw dozens and dozens of tanks. In all manner of sizes and shapes, they were dotted about as if Mama D'Leau was building a private aquarium. Rayleigh clicked off his lumicand, but didn't return it to his hip.

He crept past tank after oddly shaped, physics-defying tank filled with aquatic creatures. Something in a shell, a cross between a crab and a llama, spat a sticky wad of putrid pink at the glass. Rayleigh recoiled.

"You're fortunate the glass is there."

He fumbled for the virga button on his lumicand as he spun to see who'd addressed him. A girl. She looked to be about his age and might have been the most peculiar creature he'd encountered in the creepy aquarium. For, other than the fact that she rested her elbows atop a vast fishbowl she was half submerged in—fully dressed in a flowing gown of cream silk with a string of pearls around her neck, no less—she seemed human.

"I mean it. The malefeline's saliva is poisonous when it's diluted in water." Cropped and slick against her skull, her hair was as black as the seaweed tendrils swaying around her legs in the cloudy water.

"'Lo, landwalker. Fancy meeting you here." Her words were lightly delivered, but her eyes, a periwinkle blue, glinted with caution.

Rayleigh kept back. "You aren't like the other creatures down here."

"Likewise. Visiting?"

"There's a party upstairs."

"Then why are you down here?"

"I heard singing. . . ." Though he hadn't heard the sorrow-filled melody since he passed a tank of snapping teeth that also happened to be right in the girl's line of sight. "It was you, wasn't it?"

Her brows shot upward. "You heard me?"

"Like I said, there's a party going on. You didn't sound like someone having a good time."

"I'm not." The girl's dress rose around her calves as she kicked her legs out. A cuff was visible around one ankle. It was connected to a thick chain that disappeared into the tangle of seaweed. "I'm a finfrail. Half fish, half girl. Not a mermaid." She rolled her eyes, preempting his question. "No tail. Gills and webbed extremities instead. Usually." She wriggled her feet. They were without webbing. "Mama D'Leau stole the talisman that allows me to transform in all water types. What are you?"

Caught off guard, he blinked. "I—I don't know yet. I also didn't think we were meant to ask."

"We're not. But I'm used to people answering my questions. I forget sometimes. Sorry."

"It's fine."

The girl's wary expression softened. "Whatever you are, I need you to listen. Please." Her brows drew together in a serious manner.

"Sometimes D'Leau's guards come down here. You don't want them to catch you—*I* don't want them to catch you. Not when I need your help escaping. I was minding my own business when I happened to find myself kidnapped. If you can believe it."

"Yeah, hate when that happens."

She laughed.

"Have you seen any other monsters down here?" asked Rayleigh. "Ones with two legs?"

"Landwalkers?"

"I guess so."

"No, I'm sorry. I've been here a long time, but I haven't seen anyone like that. D'Leau's menagerie is filled with aquatic creatures. It's said she's building an army."

"For what?"

"You can't guess?"

"I heard something about her being after power."

The girl scoffed. "You can say that again. She's been giving the Queen of the Undersea a lot of trouble, swimming out of her lane. You think she might have taken a landwalker? I wouldn't be surprised. I don't think there's anything she wouldn't do—" There was a crash above; both looked across the hull, frozen. "We can't let her find you down here," said the girl, her voice lower.

"How about she doesn't find either of us down here?"

"That sounds perfect."

Rayleigh wasn't sure why he agreed to help her. He didn't get the feeling—literally—that she was lying. And the evidence of Mama D'Leau's army was all around him. Even if she didn't have his dad, she was up to something devious. Not to mention the fact that the girl's singing had been so soul-achingly sad he couldn't leave her behind. Not down here.

"You'll need to use your lumicand," she said. "It's one of few instruments that doesn't lose power upon contact with water. When you free me, landwalker, I will owe you two debts. The first for my mother, and the second for me. She'll be relieved to have me back after two months away."

"The thought of D'Leau's face when she finds you gone will be gift enough." Especially since it appeared that she did have a good reason for taking Bogey after all: war. Exactly what happened between the Illustrious Society and the Confederation last time. "Give me a minute."

Rayleigh ran over to where he'd seen some crates and hurried back with them. Stacking them at the sides of the bowl, he climbed up and stood almost level with the girl. Up close he saw the telltale shimmer of patches of scales on her skin, and a line of gills along each side of her neck. They were closed, like slowly healing cuts. She touched a hand to them, as though embarrassed, and winced.

Rayleigh fussed with his lumicand, pretending not to notice. "I don't know your name."

"Nor I yours. Call me Ari."

A wet hand dripped over his lumicand. He took it and pumped once.

"I'm Rayleigh."

Somewhere above, a clock began to chime. Not sure what time it was, but remembering Thelonious's comment about nothing good happening after 12:01, Rayleigh told Ari to submerge herself in the water and swim away from the chain, drawing it as tight as she could without hurting herself. She complied, and he saw bruising on her ankle through the water. A thrill of anger thrummed through him. The clock continued to chime.

Angling his lumicand, Rayleigh fired an orb at the chain; waves rippled in the bowl.

Ari's head bobbed up. "The water makes it hard to get a true reading, so whatever you think you're aiming at, try lower or higher."

He did as she said, but it wasn't until his fifth try that she slung her freed leg over the side of the bowl first. Rayleigh helped her climb down the crates, a tad dismayed to find she stood half a head taller than him. Holding her shoulders in a perfect line, she tipped her chin down.

"Whatever you turn out to be, Rayleigh, don't lose your honor and bravery."

There was something about the way she spoke, formal and sort of old-fashioned, that made him feel as though he should bow.

"Come on," he said, cheeks warming. "I know the way out."

At the top of the stairs, a firm push against the wall opened the panel. Edging out to check all was clear, Rayleigh beckoned Ari after him. Together they snuck through the corridors and out onto the deck. Fortuitously, it was vacant, which made it easy to notice the chiming of the clock had stopped.

"Better be quick," said Rayleigh, helping Ari climb onto the rail. "Good luck getting home."

She made no move to dive into the dark waters below. "I've decided to pay one debt now, despite your protestations—maybe even because of them. D'Leau hasn't thrown this party to celebrate a birthday. Not really. She's thrown it because her comb has been stolen, and she's hoping the thief will use this as an opportunity to approach and blackmail her for its safe return."

Rayleigh was baffled. "Blackmail her with what, pictures of bad hair days?"

"No." Ari tittered. "Some monsters use external weapons to help enhance their bents."

Rayleigh tightened his hold around his lumicand.

"She hasn't left this vessel this past month and a half, and she's too scared to send her guard far in case my family comes for me. She is strongest in water, even without her comb."

"She hasn't left the ship in a month and a half?" Bogey had been missing for close to the same amount of time. "You're sure?"

Ari nodded. "As far as I know, stealing me away was the last thing she did. Catch the thief, and D'Leau will give you whatever, who-ever, you want. As for the second debt, when you decide what you need, contact me with this." She unclasped a string of pearls from around her neck and dropped it in Rayleigh's hand. "Toss it in any body of water deeper than two meters, and I'll appear. Until then—"

"Wait, how will you get back without your gills if D'Leau has your talisman?"

"I'll be fine in the channel. Besides, when Mama D'Leau notices I'm missing, I'm sure she'll send my talisman over with many, many apologies. My queen doesn't take kindly to blackmail any more than the river witch. Best of luck in your search, and thank you again." She dived overboard, landing in the channel with a muted splash.

Pocketing the necklace, Rayleigh legged it back inside the ship. It was imperative he find the Terrors and relay everything he'd learned about D'Leau now that it was near undeniable she was working with the Illustrious Society. An army, a stolen comb that kept her boat-bound and unwilling to part with her guard but desperate enough, perhaps, for another means of power that she'd commission Slydus to steal the key. That had to be it!

He didn't quite know who would take her comb, but Marley said she was officious when it came to the channel. Maybe she tried to boss around the wrong person, and they stole it in revenge. Whatever. All that mattered was, she didn't have it. And for that reason, she wanted the Supreme's Key.

Thelonious was wrong about her, which meant the Terrors were in trouble.

Trainers squeaking in the puddles made by Ari's wet footsteps, Rayleigh ran to the banquet suites. When he couldn't find any of the Terrors in the dense crowd, he headed upstairs to the ballroom. He flung its doors open to find the decadent space empty of all guests save Mama D'Leau and the Terrors—who were encircled by a ring of hybrid monsters with the lower bodies of men and torsos that shimmered like plates of armor. They were like knights, but coated in large shell-shaped fish scales—even their faces bore scales, like they'd been gilded in the stuff.

"Ah," the river witch crooned from her glass. "And Rayleigh Mann makes five. You see, Thelonious?" Her accent was as musical as Nana's, but up close, her beautiful face was hard, and there was no looking past the serpent lower half of her body twisting in the martini glass. "I told you no harm had come to Bogey's son—and would not, aboard my vessel." Her locks stirred on her shoulders—not hair, snakes. Thin, snapping snakes that curled around her head. "The way you charged in here, virga ablaze, Terrors behind you, with the most impertinent questions coming out of your mouth, it was almost as if you were accusing me of moving against the Confederation. Surely I'm mistaken in thinking that's what your actions meant?"

Thelonious accused her?

"Forgive me, Mama D'Leau." Thelonious bowed his head. "I didn't mean to insult you."

"And yet," she said, "you have."

The doors opened across the ballroom. Music drifted in, a reminder there was still a party taking place outside. One of the scaled knights approached the river witch. His boots clicked across the wooden floor ominously. Rayleigh tried to catch his uncle's attention, any of the Terrors, but they were all watching the exchange before them—until they weren't. D'Leau turned to Rayleigh. The crew shifted his way too. Thelonious took a protective step before him.

"You released the finfrail?" D'Leau sent Rayleigh's way. "You have no idea what you've done."

Thelonious raised a placatory hand. "With all due respect, my nephew wouldn't trouble anything that didn't belong to him. Would you, Nephew-mine?"

Lying was out of the question. Not when the truth was on Rayleigh's side.

"She said you stole her away," he addressed D'Leau, ready to show the Terrors she wasn't who they thought she was. "She said that she was one step in your grand plan to take over the Confederation."

One of the Terrors, most likely Shade, inhaled with disbelief.

"Stop, Nephew-mine," Thelonious warned.

"You need to hear this. All of you. She said—" Rayleigh continued, despite his beating heart, the menacing quiet of the fish knights and their tridents, the hissing of Mama D'Leau's snakes (hair?). "She told me you lost your comb, and might be in need of an upgrade in the shape of my dad's key."

D'Leau recoiled in her seat. "How *dare* you."

Her guards shifted without warning. Weapons were raised and thrust outward at the Terrors—at Rayleigh. His bones grew heavy in response; lumicand forgotten on his hip, he raised his hands, ready.

"D'Leau, please." Thelonious stepped between the guards and Rayleigh. "He doesn't know what he's saying. He doesn't know customs."

"Then perhaps," the river witch hissed, along with her snakes, "he should. I will not stand for disrespect on my waterways, Thelonious. And I certainly will not endure accusations regarding my loyalty to this Cabinet—to our Supreme!" The boat rocked, seesawing in a reminder that D'Leau commanded the channel it sat atop.

"He's confused." Thelonious waved a hand behind his back.

One of the Terrors reached forward and yanked Rayleigh back.

"He's overwhelmed," Thelonious continued. "He's a good kid. He saw your prisoner and obviously felt for the finfrail. Please, don't think anything of it. We'll leave. Now. With your blessing."

D'Leau looked beyond him, seeking out Rayleigh with a hard contempt. "What you saw in the hull of my ship, child, were rescues. Creatures who struggle amidst the pollution in the channel. Don't you know your stories? Cha! And that beastly finfrail you freed? She is even worse than the monsters who dump their toxic waste in the Undersea. She was the true traitor. A spy sent from her underwater realm to seize an opportunity to infiltrate our Supreme-less city."

"A spy?" Rayleigh called. A large green hand landed on his shoulder and drew him further back. "She was barely older than me." He scrabbled to plug the holes in his theory.

"And a great deal smarter, to be sure." The river witch drew herself up in her glass perch. Her tail was thicker than Rayleigh's entire body. "You look to me—in possession of my comb, celebrating another year of life—and accuse me of treason—"

"You have the comb?"

"Of course I have the comb!"

"But—"

"But nothing. Not when you may very well be the reason the Confederation comes under attack by the Queen of the Undersea."

Rayleigh blanched. A queen? That finfrail was working for a queen who wanted to make a move on Below-London? His head spun. He hadn't felt like Ari was a liar. And now—now he couldn't feel anything beyond his own crippling doubt. Had he been so wrong about everything? Was D'Leau speaking the truth, or Ari?

"D'Leau, forgive us, please." Thelonious seemed to believe the river witch, given his next offer. "We can track this finfrail. We can undo this damage."

"You'd better hope so. And you can start tonight. *Now.* Because I want you off my boat."

"Forgive us" were Thelonious's parting words before the Terrors fled the ship.

It was a fitful journey back to Terror Tower for Rayleigh, who spent the entire glide anticipating the full version of the rant his uncle occasionally burst into, startling Kedara as she wove around great monoliths of earth and stone arching over the city.

Just when he didn't think anything could worsen, the very air around them began to fill with drizzle. It wasn't the cold and the wet alone, how they seeped through clothing to make home in the flesh and bone underneath; it was the way the city distorted through the rain's lens. For even the typical cozy warmth of the clubhouse couldn't escape the gray wash; it pressed against its windows in a physical reminder of the total washout back on the boat.

Or in solidarity with the spittle-flecked telling off Rayleigh received once seated on the sofa in the clubhouse.

"Next time I say go to Gasp. You. Go. To. GASP!" Thelonious roared, though he was losing steam, so Rayleigh's ears didn't ring quite so badly as they first had.

Gasp came through from the kitchen with a tray of drinks. He passed Thelonious a bottle and then gave Rayleigh a cup of tea, with a sympathetic look on the side.

"I'm sorry," Rayleigh said in a rush. "We talked about her as a suspect, and then I saw all the creatures in her hull and I thought—I trusted my gut, Thelonious. That finfrail didn't seem like a liar, I swear."

"Those with bad intentions rarely wear them on their sleeves, Nephew-mine." Thelonious sighed. "Never mind that now. What's done is done."

Mary and Shade didn't say anything. Were it not for the ticking of a clock somewhere, and the occasional sips Gasp took of his tea, the silence would have been maddening.

"What's next?" Rayleigh asked softly, needing to disrupt the quiet. "Will D'Leau still help us find my dad?"

"I have no idea, Nephew-mine."

"The only place she wanted to help us," Mary said, "was off that boat. I didn't get time to speak with Octavia. But there will be other opportunities."

"Not sure we'll receive another party invite soon." Shade kicked his feet up on the coffee table. "That's one boon to come out of this awful night. I do so hate leaving this house."

No one laughed.

Rayleigh's face was hot with another emotion. It made him blink rapidly, wish the Terrors good night, and after another apology, hurry out of the clubhouse to his room. Thelonious called after him, Gasp too, but Rayleigh wanted to be alone.

"Dance all night long, did you?" Winsome said, when he blew into his room.

"Not now." Rayleigh ripped off his coat, kicked off his trainers.

"Little Mann?"

"I said not now. Please, Winsome."

He'd burned two leads tonight, in D'Leau and Octavia. Not to mention any other Inductions, Welcomes, and Warnings office members who could have been in attendance. His dad was out there somewhere, and the likelihood of meeting him, of helping to return him to the world he'd served for years, had never felt further away.

That was the other downside to rain.

It showed the truth, and with everything out in the open, there was no denying that matters in Terror Tower were rather bleak.

TWENTY-FOUR

SHOCK AND AWE

The morning after the Worst Party Ever, window pockets in the lid widened to filter in a moody sunrise. An early visit from Thelonious led to Rayleigh mucking out the Bad Omens' cage with his uncle on the warehouse roof. While ramming a shovel into the avian creatures' hay piles was satisfying, he'd have preferred to stay in bed. Under the covers. At least the entire sleeping province was cast in shadow—Rayleigh hadn't quite been able to escape the feeling he alone was dogged by a persistent dark cloud, post chaotic confrontation with D'Leau.

It had been so disastrous, in fact, Rayleigh hadn't mentioned his significant screwup to Marley. She'd taken to calling near enough on the hour every hour, last night. Win had threatened to blow up the comms, as a former pyrotechnic. He'd thought about letting her.

"That's about the tenth time you've sighed." Thelonious picked through Kedara's feathers, checking for any injuries with care. "Last night's still eating you, hey?"

Rayleigh fidgeted in his trainers. He'd apologized so many times already, his uncle had to be sick of it. And yet, what was another try?

"I really thought D'Leau was the one working with the Illustrious Society after I saw the hull, the finfrail."

"I know, Nephew-mine. You had a feeling, and you ran with it." Thelonious shoved his hands in the pockets of his vest coat. "You don't need to apologize any more than you already have. So let's move on, okay?"

Rayleigh shrugged.

"There's not long left until the Citizenship Ceremony. I didn't want to push, but I'll be needing your decision about whether or not you'll stay."

"Do you still want me to?" Rayleigh half joked.

"Of course. You have made Terror Tower a joy. You could have been with us always. I wish your old man were here to see it. I'd hoped to have reunited the two of you by now."

A few moments of silence passed between them.

"Now we can't ask D'Leau for help, what if we don't get Dad back?"

Thelonious scooped bird feed into a giant trough as the omens glided around the rooftop, calling a song as tempestuous as the lid. "I'm still going to ask D'Leau for help."

"What?" Rayleigh gaped at his uncle.

"With Gasp. You and Miss Liu are going to complete your third trial right here, under Mary and Shade's supervision. Last night— maybe I shouldn't have brought you along to the party." It was Thelonious's turn to sigh. And it was a big one. "I said we'd move on, and I meant it. Know that I'm not mad at you. I'm mad at myself. When I think what could have happened—what a monster as prideful as D'Leau could have done to you if she found you without me. If her guard did. If she didn't know who you are—"

Thelonious cut himself off. "I'm going to make this right, because it was my mistake. You will complete your third trial, and then we can talk about what comes next, irrespective of whether we meet the Quorum's time limit to bring Bogey back. I hope you'll stay. But I understand that, without your father, there might not be enough to keep you here."

"Do you think we'll find him with D'Leau's help?"

Thelonious hesitated. "I think our time to look is up in a matter of days, Nephew-mine, but I'm going to try." His unsaid words lingered like the morning fog. He'd try to prevent the Cabinet coming clean to the Confederation: their Bogey Mann was missing. What would that mean for Above and Below? A new Supreme? A confirmation of the rumor that the role was cursed? An expedited Dimming, courtesy of the Illustrious Society?

Rayleigh was stiff with the cold, with his own disappointment. He had, again, caused more problems than solutions in a bid to help. He thought he'd found his place in Below-London. Far from causing the right kind of trouble, he was still doing the wrong thing.

Maybe it would be better for the Terrors if he returned home. While his lightning had caused a spark, he was the one who kept starting fires others had to put out.

"Come, Nephew-mine. I have work to do, and you'd better get ready for the trial." Thelonious whistled for the omens. It was sharp and piercing—a warning to them, and Rayleigh. If this was the outcome when he tried, he should stop.

He should return to Above-London.

"You absolutely cannot return to Above-London!" Marley's projection from the comms might have been small, but her volume was not. "Mary is already on her way to pick me up!"

Rayleigh cringed back into his pillows on his bed.

"Our third trial is TODAY, Rayleigh. The last one!" Marley's tails stood tall and bushy around her, as though they too were outraged with his decision. "The one we were almost beaten up for in Despair! The one we endured that ogre's vomit for! Come. On. So what if you insulted the most powerful river witch in Below-London."

"You weren't there," he said, miserable. "It was . . . the worst." Clearly he hadn't impressed just how truly awful it had been when he filled her in moments before.

"Well, you said your uncle is taking care of it, right? Right?"

"Right," Rayleigh muttered. "Yeah."

"Okay, then. Let him help you, because I need you to help me, like you need me to help you." Marley blinked at him with sad eyes. "We're a team, Rayleigh. You can't quit the team because things have gone a little wrong along the way. I screw up all the time. I also thought D'Leau was your dad's enemy. Screwing up doesn't mean we quit, Rayleigh. It means we start again, and we start smarter. We think longer. We ask more questions. We have this saying, curiosity kills—"

"The cat, yeah," Rayleigh cut in.

"No. Gross. Our saying—yours too now, because you belong here—is curiosity kills nothing. *Nothing*. If we don't look, how can we expect to find? And if we find something bad, it doesn't matter. We look elsewhere until we find something good. We don't stop," she implored.

Rayleigh considered her words.

He'd been ready to go, after Thelonious said his goodbyes earlier.

He'd marched right into his room and started shifting things into his backpack in the bathroom, so Winsome wouldn't see it when she woke. And when she woke, he moved her bulb into the bathroom across the hall, so he could call Marley in peace. A call that was meant to be a goodbye. He had the Vol-trix token his mum included in the pack that contained his first invitation. He could chuck it in a hamper and be back Above before lunch. There'd be no mind wiping. He wouldn't forget the life he'd lived. It would be both a gift and a curse, but one that felt a happy medium, given the mistakes he'd made. But Marley was right. Leaving before the third trial wasn't fair to her. Even though her fight for him to stay surprised him.

"I thought you didn't want to go to school," he said. "I thought you wanted to get out there and work with your mum."

She glanced down. "I didn't think I'd like the Induction. I didn't think I'd want to be down here studying, while monsters are at risk in the Above world. My ma always said she had it covered. That I should have fun, be a kid. I hadn't, really, before the Induction." When she looked up at him, her jaw was set with determination. "Now I want to stay. I want to start school. And I want you with me."

"I don't know if I can, Marley. Your speech was great, though."

"Really? I didn't practice or anything."

"So, rubbish at knots, semi successful at motivation."

"Idiot." She sniffed, as though fighting tears.

"Is that any way to speak to your partner for the third and final trial?"

Her disappointment was gutting. "You won't stay beyond that? What about your dad?"

If Cabinet workers did end up traveling Above to wipe his mind after he snuck off, it wouldn't make him forget his dad. He'd merely forget he was Supreme Scarer. The upside, however cowardly, was that he'd forget what he was missing. Life Above would resume as normal. He'd have no idea what could have been Below, who he'd met.

"You won't change my mind, Marley."

"Oh, yeah? Wait until I'm there in person. Any minute now. I think I can hear Mary chatting with my mum."

A muffled thump was followed by a cry outside Rayleigh's room.

"I better go. Sounds like Winsome is trying to make an escape."

"Make sure she's the only one," Marley warned. "I'll see you soon."

They signed off; Rayleigh ninja-rolled across his mattress to open his door. He ventured across the hall to check on the fairy light. She'd never tried moving the bulb before. But when Rayleigh opened the door across the hall, there was no Winsome. There was no nest of towels he'd left her bulb resting in. Huh. Maybe she *was* capable of mobility in the bulb. Like a hamster in one of those hollow balls. But where had she gone? Rayleigh inspected the other side of the claw-footed tub, behind the basket that sat beneath the sink. She wasn't wedged by the toilet either.

In the hall beyond the bathroom, a thud rocked Terror Tower's walls.

Pushing up from his crouch, Rayleigh darted out into his hall.

"Mary? Shade?" he called, running past the gallery. "Winsome?" Rayleigh skidded into the empty kitchen and kept the momentum through the double doors into the clubhouse.

The living room was also empty.

"Mary? Shade?" he shouted now. "Winsome!"

An answering thud echoed up the stairs, from the hallway.

Pivoting in his socks, Rayleigh ran for the landing outside the clubhouse. The angled nature of the stairs meant he couldn't see down them until he reached the second landing—he made it in one bounding jump. The entry hall was shadowed, save for tall shafts of light that cut through the stained-glass window above the bright red front doors. Rayleigh ran down the stairs, knees high, feet heavy. For caught in one beam of light, splayed like the etching of a body in a crime scene, was Gasp.

The troll lifted his head and squinted up at Rayleigh. His face was a mask of pure, unfiltered pain. He outstretched a thick arm and wheezed a weak "*Help*."

Fear seized Rayleigh by the heart. He skipped the final few stairs to jump again; he leapt and landed by Gasp's body. "What happened? Where does it—are you hurt?" He'd left with Thelonious earlier. Which meant—"My uncle, is he okay?"

"Help" was all Gasp uttered before his head and neck slumped onto the runner.

"MARY! SHADE! WINSOME!" Rayleigh bellowed. Helpless, he touched Gasp's forehead, as Mama, Nana did with his when he was sick.

They also gave him medicine—which they typically kept in a kitchen cabinet.

Rayleigh surged to his feet, prepared to run for a first aid kit. Gasp groaned; his chest rose and fell with stutters, as though he couldn't draw enough air. To leave him didn't feel right. But the stairs—looking at their height, how far up the hall they were, and back at Gasp, Rayleigh swallowed and rolled up his hoodie sleeves. No one else was coming. No one had called back. He had to help

Gasp. Rayleigh assessed the hallway. Dragging his frightfather might cause him more pain. He was lying on top of the runner—which, a quick check revealed, wasn't stuck to the floor. Spotting Thelonious's fluffy slippers beneath the bench by the coat stand by the door, Rayleigh ran for them to help provide some grip to his socks.

He'd need more than grip, though, to move Gasp.

His frightfather was a solid unit. Heavier even than Rayleigh had experienced during their training, when Gasp had been so careful not to crush him. But, as Gasp released a whimper—one that cut straight through Rayleigh—he seized the end of the runner with a steely determination. Gasp was folded inside as Rayleigh drew the material over, to connect with the top of the carpet, which sat just by the stairs.

Having watched Mama braid her hair his entire life, Rayleigh mimicked her finger movements to connect the tasseled ends of the rug. He tested their strength with sharp tugs. When they held, he looped one arm through the makeshift sling and another around the left post of the staircase.

"Mary, Shade," he tried, but even to his own ears, he sounded without hope that they'd respond. "Winsome. If any of you can hear me, Gasp is in trouble. Thelonious might be in trouble too. We need your help!"

He waited. His breathing filled the hallway. Compared to Gasp's, it was steady.

No replies came.

That was it, then. Rayleigh would have to save Gasp by himself. He had to lift the biggest person he'd ever seen in his life—no. That was wrong. The ogre from the first trial had been heavier. Rayleigh huffed a small, hysterical laugh. And then he began to pull.

No time at all passed before the stair post began to creak. Its wood bit into Rayleigh's arm, despite the tailor's protective clothing. Gasp didn't shift. Gritting his teeth, Rayleigh tugged with all his might. His slippered feet desperately sought purchase on the wooden floor, and the post—it splintered. Panting, Rayleigh looked back at it. A crack had formed in the wood. The solid wood. He tightened his arm and gave a third almighty tug.

Two things happened.

The post, as old as Terror Tower, maybe—older than Rayleigh, for sure; taller than him too—split. It splintered with a sickening crunch between his forearm and biceps. Rayleigh turned his face from the spray of wood. Sharp pieces bounced away from his neck, his cheek. Without its leverage, his arm slipped. His legs quivered for a moment, thighs singing. For a fraught second, he was sure his feet would slip and he would go down.

Then his muscles tightened. His legs withstood.

Rayleigh placed his second hand over the top of his first, closing it around the rug. It folded like paper in his grip. Marveling at his own endurance, he drew the rug and Gasp toward him with a grunt. They glided toward him like the wooden floor was slick with polish. Gasp settled by his feet. Rayleigh's mouth popped open. He was . . . strong. Stronger than he'd ever been. Strong enough—he checked the distance he'd pulled Gasp again, the shattered staircase post—to do all that.

What else was he capable of?

As it turned out, maybe whatever he wanted. When he squatted to take hold of Gasp's forearm, he found it as light as a large dinner plate. He hooked Gasp's arm over his shoulder before, not quite able to believe himself, standing up. He stood with Gasp's entire weight over his shoulder (one shoulder!) and took the stairs. First at a slow walk, in case reality set in and they both fell. When that didn't happen, he increased his speed, building toward a light jog to the first landing outside the clubhouse.

Rayleigh paused; his legs were steadfast. Gasp felt no heavier than a jumbo bag of rice he'd dragged inside for Mama once. It was world upending, to hold something so giant across his shoulders. Mentally cheering for himself, with relief for Gasp, Rayleigh hurried them both into the kitchen. Gasp he settled on his side on the table.

"I'll be right back," Rayleigh told him. On legs so strong and capable he couldn't help staring down at them in wonder, he ran to the wall and hit Shade's and Mary's intercoms. "If any of you are out there, I need help! Gasp is hurt, we're in the kitchen." He turned to check on his frightfather. "And I—"

Rayleigh's fingers slipped off the intercoms.

Gasp was still atop the table; around him the walls and windows dripped downward, as though melting. Sluicing away, they didn't reveal the province outside the tower walls. There was only darkness. Rayleigh turned back to the intercoms, panicked, to find they were half melted too. It was as if the kitchen had been made of wax—only, the melted parts did not sink to the floor, congealing in an oozing pile; they disappeared. He jumped black spots on the floor to clamber atop the table beside Gasp. A boy amidst a black sea, it was all he had as the kitchen around him was overcome with an all-consuming nothingness.

Growing warier by the second, Rayleigh reached for his lumicand.

But of course he hadn't brought it with him when he left his room to check on Winsome.

A heavy weight settled on his waist.

Rayleigh, grateful for Terror Tower, unclipped the weapon that had appeared at his summons.

A spark appeared across the counter; he recoiled, lumicand at the ready. It hissed and popped before fading. An envelope was left in its wake. Knowing came fast and sure, even as reality disappeared around him. He didn't need to open it to understand what was happening. His third and final Induction trial was afoot.

"STOP!" a voice bellowed.

Not Rayleigh.

Not Gasp.

Mary.

The melting walls ceased their dripping and simply faded away—but not to the nothing behind them. The tower brightened, as though a light had been switched on. For a moment, Rayleigh remained crouched on the table beside Gasp, envelope in hand. He watched as the tower melted into itself, stunned.

"Rayleigh—" Mary burst through the kitchen doors, followed by Shade and Marley. "I'm sorry," she said. She clambered atop the table and took Gasp's head into her lap. A black bag appeared on the table; from inside she withdrew several tiny vials, which she emptied into Gasp's mouth. "This was meant to be your trial's beginning," Mary breathed. "But I didn't realize at first—couldn't tell that it was *real*, not the Tower's magic."

"That's not your fault," Shade said.

Beside him, Marley cried silent tears.

Rayleigh didn't feel right, crouched atop the table. He eased himself down, awkward and concerned. "What's happening?"

Mary glanced up at him. "I need you and Marley to wait in your room until I come for you."

"No." Rayleigh looked from her to Shade and back again. "No. This—this is a trick. It's my third trial. I have the invitation right here."

"It's not a trick." Marley sniffed. "Rayleigh. It's Thelonious too. Mary heard from a fairy light. Gasp and your uncle, they were attacked."

Rayleigh's breathing shallowed.

"She's right," Shade confirmed. "They were attacked. Gasp escaped, but Thelonious—he's been taken."

TWENTY-FIVE

THE TRIAL OF TERROR TOWER

Having paced himself tired enough to sprawl across his bed, Rayleigh glanced across at his open trial invitation for the umpteenth time that evening.

The Monsters Cabinet
Bureau of Monster Regulation

Master Rayleigh Mann,
The time has come for your third and final trial.
In the first you accepted yourself. In the second, the city accepted you. Now it is time to embrace the full scope of what it means to be monstrous.
Never forget, you cannot have light without darkness.
Should your Trial of Terror Tower be a success, we look forward to swearing you in as a bona fide citizen of the Confederation of Light-less Places, at the Monsters Cabinet, Parliament Square, Wednesday, November 16.

It was scarily prescient, the line about no light without darkness. He rolled onto his back; Winsome sat watching him from her bulb, as she had since he'd arrived, alone, some hours earlier. Marley had been forced to take a Vol-way home, given the rocky waters the Terrors sailed through as Mary treated Gasp. His concussion had been bad enough that Terror Tower had let him break through the magic it used on the trial.

Watching from afar, neither Mary nor Shade had known he wasn't one of the tower's creations until Winsome came running with news from a fellow fairy who'd seen the entire ambush. The fight that left Gasp wounded and Thelonious missing. Taken. Just like Bogey. And it seemed likely D'Leau was behind it. Who else knew they were on their way to see her?

Every (mis)step Rayleigh had taken led to Gasp's attack and Thelonious's capture. D'Leau had turned on them because of Rayleigh. In fact, he was waiting in his room for Mary and Shade to reach the same conclusion. To deem him too much trouble. To agree that he should go home. But when Mary called him into the clubhouse, what he received was something quite different.

"I owe you a life's debt, Rayleigh," said Gasp. Seated in one of the wingback armchairs, he wore spotty pajamas and was wrapped in a bright pink blanket. He typically wore his bright colors well; this evening, as pale and weary as he looked, they were wearing him. Mary stood at his side, her black bag resting on a side table. Shade lounged on the zebra chaise.

"You don't owe me anything," Rayleigh said, stunned. "You're okay?"

"Thanks to your quick thinking and super strength, my dear boy. Along with Mary's bag of potions."

Shade cleared his throat.

"Oh, I'm sorry," Mary said, her voice dripping with sarcasm. "What did you do?"

"I gave moral support to all involved."

She rolled her eyes.

"What happened?" Rayleigh asked; he hurried to sit in a chair beside Gasp. "Was it D'Leau?"

"I don't know." Gasp shook his head and winced.

"Easy," Mary warned.

"It could have been," Gasp continued, slower. "She was expecting us. But it wasn't her men who attacked us. They bore no armor."

"And," Mary added, "thanks to you, Rayleigh, we know that whoever took Bogey, ransacked our flat, and came after you wants the Supreme's Key. It stands to reason that they jumped Thelonious and Gasp to acquire it."

"The Illustrious Society member," he said. Which D'Leau had cleared herself of being. Mostly. Given the timing of the ambush, Rayleigh wasn't so sure he could exclude her. "But why would they think you guys had it?"

Gasp averted his gaze. "Because Thelonious allowed some rather unsavory feddies to overhear him telling me that he had it. Not to mention Octavia Brand."

Rayleigh shot to his feet.

"He wanted to keep you safe," Gasp added weakly.

Words failed Rayleigh. His uncle told him he would handle

matters. Rayleigh hadn't realized he meant he'd put himself in harm's way.

"Now then, don't be upset," Gasp soothed. "If anyone can handle themselves, it's your uncle. He's the reason I made it back here. He held those thugs off."

"You know what that means, don't you?" Mary looked down at Rayleigh with a stern expression. "You have to make his sacrifice count for something. You have to stay safe. Here."

But what was safety without an anchor?

Thelonious was the weight that kept Rayleigh steady when he felt liable to be washed away. With his uncle gone, *missing* just like his dad, and all for a key Bogey's enemies first believed Rayleigh had, he felt far from safe.

He felt responsible.

A night's sleep did little to soothe Rayleigh's conscience.

The moment he woke, he ran straight to the kitchen to argue in favor of looking for his uncle. While Shade and Mary thought they should hit the pavement in search of Thelonious, Gasp, chief in his absence, told them he'd want the team to gather evidence on the Illustrious Society.

"He's a big monster," Gasp had breezed, his cavalier tone contradicted somewhat by the tap, tap, tapping of his foot; his skin was still a sickly green too. "He's probably already on his way back to us."

But it wasn't Thelonious who arrived, minutes later. It was a flyer. Terror Tower spat it right onto Rayleigh's plate of toast and eggs at breakfast.

"Is that the post?" Shade asked, from across the kitchen island.

"I'm expecting something, and you're in my usual seat. Pass it over."

Rayleigh, grimacing, peeled the paper away from one jammy slice. He couldn't help but glance at it. Six words were scrawled across a cartoon of a broad-shouldered bull with horns, blowing steam through its nose. *COME WITH THE KEY, OR ELSE.*

"I don't think this is for you," he said through a bite of toast; it had lost all flavor in his mouth. "I think it's about Thelonious."

Chairs screeched against the tile underfoot as the three Terrors rushed to crowd around Rayleigh and read the entire flyer.

HORNED HEAT
Despair's annual race for all horned creatures
(wings excluded) returns once again!
Come along, November 16.
Be sure to pick up tickets early to secure the best views.
(Audience members risk maiming, gouging,
spearing, and bludgeoning.)
WE HOPE TO SEE YOU THERE!

"Why would they enter him in this?" Rayleigh was confused. Was this how adults handled conflict? Unnecessary invitations rather than a quick scuffle?

"He has horns." Mary was the first to return to her seat. "They needed a trap."

"A public trap," Shade added.

"Which is why we cannot go." Gasp rounded the island to lean back against one of the cabinets. "They're likely trying to lure us out of hiding, and kill—" He glanced at Rayleigh. "Ensure we don't live to see another day. Thelonious isn't the biggest member of the monstrous world in possession of horns. Either we're caught, or we're trampled. He wouldn't want that."

"But we could get him back," Rayleigh pushed. He was good at thinking of elaborate schemes. He could find a way to rescue Thelonious.

"It's too risky." Mary sighed. "Instead of one current Terror, and a highly influential former in Bogey, our enemies could have us all. And then who will watch you, Rayleigh?"

"I can take care of myself."

"I don't doubt it," Gasp said. "But your care is my responsibility—our responsibility." His voice softened. "We have to think about life after. The Citizenship Ceremony is a couple of days away. You need to think about your future. Cleaning up this mess is our job. Run along now. Why don't you call the old bird?"

Rayleigh couldn't bear the thought of Nana's disappointment, her worry, when he was heavy with both himself.

"Why are you scowling?" Winsome asked when he trudged into his bedroom.

The walls of his room were a stormy gray, as they were every day until they turned dark with nightfall. How ironic that the fairy was the light amidst the dark.

"I'm not."

"That was convincing."

Rayleigh abandoned his plate of toast on his bedside cloud. Dropping onto his bed, he closed his eyes. Silence was his preferred companion.

"I don't care for the horned one myself," Winsome continued, unfazed by his lack of response. "The eyes are the windows to the soul, and with his concealed behind those gaudy sunglasses all the time, I was beginning to believe he was entirely without one. But *you* clearly feel something different toward him. Though one would never know it from the way you're lying there feeling sorry for yourself."

Rayleigh rolled his eyes to where she stood in her bulb, arms folded. "He was taken because of me. Because of something I wish I knew how to find."

"You're hardly in a position where you can't do anything to fix it, are you? The Terrors don't have to lose two chiefs."

He'd been trying to fix things since he arrived in Below-London. Only it turned out that he wasn't so deft at putting things back together, only breaking them apart.

Two chiefs, Winsome had said.

"Don't think your silence will deter me," she sniped.

Two chiefs.

Both taken for a token neither had in their possession, and by the same monster.

Rayleigh bolted upright on the bed.

"Movement! Be still my heart. I was beginning to think you'd desiccated. What is it, then? An irritated bowel or the end of your solo pity party?"

"The second one."

"Mercies bestowed. I'll take that *thank-you* right now, as I have the time."

Rayleigh slid off his bed, dragged the chair beneath the bulb, and climbed atop it so he was face-to-face with Winsome. He had to conceive the best plan of his life, and he didn't need her sharing it with the Terrors when she next took one of her little walks.

"How about you take a trip instead?" And with that, he unscrewed the fairy from the ceiling, leaving her spitting insults from atop a pile of towels in the bathroom across the hall. Firmly closing his bedroom door behind him, Rayleigh snatched up the comms device.

If whoever took his dad and Thelonious wanted the Supreme's Key, why didn't he give it to them? Or, rather, pretend to.

"I need your help," he said, before Marley's head and shoulders finished rising up from the screen.

"You heard that Verena and Victor passed their third trial, and you want to make sure we're not attending the same school as them in January?"

"What? No—but, hang on, the third trial's over?"

"Happened the same day ours was meant to. And yes, they really did pass."

"I wasn't calling about them. But"—Rayleigh paused to consider Marley's earlier plan—"we will talk about the school thing later. There's no way that's happening."

"So if you didn't call to tell me the Terrors covered for us, since we didn't take our third trial, then this is about your uncle."

"Uh-huh."

"The Terrors won't let you help."

"Right."

Marley nodded. "What's the plan?"

Relieved to have a friend who understood him without delay, Rayleigh told her about the flyer, the race, and the dare. "I'm going. I'm going to the race. Whoever took Dad and Thelonious will think they've caught me. That I'm going to give them the key—"

"Because they've always thought you had it."

"Right."

"But you don't—and don't say *right* again."

"Okay. Yeah. They'll think I have it, but really I'll have a pocket filled with trackers. We have them, Above. You keep them in your wallet or your suitcase, and you can find something if it's lost by activating them. Do you have anything similar down here?"

"Ma uses them on infant monsters. The rare ones that some feddies try to capture to sell. I can get some for sure. And you'll trick whoever took your dad and Thelonious into taking you too so you can lead the other Terrors to them?"

"Yep. Two chiefs, one stone." Rayleigh exhaled. "You don't think my plan is stupid?"

"Oh, it is, very. But—" Marley sighed. "Family is about the only excuse for stupidity, I think. If I could have helped my dad, I would have come up with a dumb plan too." She drew a deep breath, and then another. "He was hunted by bovers in the Above world. Killed by them." Marley's voice thickened. "That's why I never wanted to transform. To tell you the truth, monsters scared me for a long time. Becoming one, I didn't want that. And I look at what's happening to your dad and your uncle, and I don't want it all over again." She sniffed. "But what happened to my family made me choose to keep monsters safe. I never wanted anyone else to hurt like my dad did, like I did—" She broke off, her words choked by tears. "My allergies are really bad today."

"High pollen count." Rayleigh covered for her, his friend. "I heard it on the news."

"Yeah." She wiped a hand across her face. "So, your plan is stupid.

But it's the only one we've got. And I'll have your back through it all."

"We make a good team," Rayleigh said. "I mean, we did avoid getting brained by Slydus and his henchmen—"

"And we survived Terror Tower. Twice."

"Exactly," Rayleigh agreed. "Things have never looked better from where I'm standing."

"Then you need glasses, not trackers." Marley laughed. "So, we're going back to Despair. I suppose we can grab your uncle once the race starts. We'll just need to get his attention somehow. Wave a flag or something, a red one."

"From up high," muttered Rayleigh, ideas already percolating.

"I was joking."

"Were you? Shame. It wasn't a half-bad idea. Whatever we decide, this is going to be our most dangerous outing yet," Rayleigh felt the need to say.

"I'm counting on it." Marley turned her nose up. "I'd like to see my ma stop me becoming a hunter after all is said and done. Reckon we can get your dad on the ten o'clock news?"

"That's the spirit. I'll call you once things are sorted on my end."

Marley's image pixelated before retracting back into the comms, but the glint of her incisors was unmissable. Rayleigh exhaled. He was without her enthusiasm at present.

What he needed was a map.

Rayleigh crept down to the office. He listened for a moment before inching the door open bit by bit. To his relief, no one was inside.

On the mezzanine level, he woke the map with typed instructions.

The Province of Despair bloomed from its surface. Rayleigh walked the table, studying the 3D depiction as he'd studied the instructions to make the catapult, as he'd studied his science teacher to determine when his back would be turned so he could spill the glue on his chair.

He went to bed, later that day, with the map on his brain. When he woke and returned to the office, his final day to clarify his plan, the Despair's docklands looked the most open space to pluck Thelonious from the air using a Bad Omen—the red flag he'd glide above the racing monsters to lead his uncle to safety.

And put himself in the eye of the kidnapper's storm.

Though there was one thing he couldn't work out. The Horned Heat would take place the next day. That gave him no time to practice gliding Kedara. He wasn't sure he could glide to Despair himself. And he didn't want to travel without Marley on the chance that Seamus or Parcter intercepted him before he made it to the race.

There was nothing for it; he needed more help.

TWENTY-SIX

RUNNING WITH FOOLS

A hand in his suit trousers pocket, Rayleigh looked out across Below-London for what might very well be his final time. Tonight, the city was steeped in gold beneath a glowing sunset, but darkness waited in the wings.

Illuminated by garlands of globe-sized fairy lights, the Monsters Cabinet terrace was slightly lower than the dome where he'd celebrated his first successful trial. Then, he'd been in the thick of things. Tonight, he stood by one of the cocktail tables furthest from the door, Gasp and Mary to either side of him. Shade was positioned somewhere providing clandestine surveillance.

"Anyone fancy a drink?" Gasp did his best to sound excited, unburdened; but his worry for Thelonious was present in the wringing of his hands; there were dark stains in the armpits of his white suit jacket too.

"I'm okay," Rayleigh said. His stomach was in knots; his throat tight with worry.

"And I'm thinking we get two," Mary suggested; she looped her arm through Gasp's. "Shade is close by, Rayleigh. And we'll be right back."

Nodding, Rayleigh pushed his glasses up his nose.

"They're still working," Mary assured him. They were her gift, a potion-imbued pair of square spectacles that changed his face, depending on who looked at him, so none of the inductees or their families could place him as the son of the Bogey Mann. "Stop touching them. You'll rub the coating away. We'll return momentarily."

The duo wove through the crowd gathered to celebrate the Citizenship Ceremony for the successful inductees who'd completed their trials. Rayleigh didn't recognize any of his peers who smiled and celebrated with their families. It was no easier now that their vast number had been whittled down to a couple hundred. He'd only seen a small percentage of the thousand Thelonious said would pass through the trials; they'd looked human then. Now nearly everyone was monstrous. One of their number had grown into a troll who could have been related to Gasp. She was the size of a large truck and very pleased about it, by the look of things. As were her family; human in appearance, they looked undeterred by the fact that one rogue hand wave, and their daughter could knock them across the room. Several boys and girls wore black pointed hats. Rayleigh guessed they were witches, warlocks, or sorcerers, maybe. While he wasn't part of their conversations, their words drifted his way on the evening wind. Many inductees were discussing the schools they wanted to attend—the next step. Part of him ached with jealousy. Enough that he couldn't help imagining, for just one second, what could have been Below: Marley, the Terrors, and Terror Tower. He touched the lumicand on his hip, the vessel with which he could direct his lightning. He'd miss it when he returned home. After he fixed his mistakes.

Including shining a spotlight on the kidnapper.

It was why he'd agreed to attend the Citizenship Ceremony in the first place. Whoever took his family, wrote the note summoning him to the race, they'd had access to him in his first and second trials. D'Leau was still a strong suspect, even more so given the location he had to meet the kidnapper, but she wasn't in attendance at this party.

Octavia Brand was, though.

Rayleigh sought out the Cabinet worker amidst the party guests. Studious, in her suit jacket, she rolled around the party looking entirely at ease. Like a monster who might expect to receive the Supreme's Key before the night was over. A neon sign overhead would have come in handy. *I did it, I'm the villain.*

A monster pulled away from the crowd and approached Rayleigh; he straightened, checked the glasses on his face.

"They still work," the Undersecretary murmured, when he was close enough to do so. "Gasp told me where you were. Thought I'd come over." His face was open with kindness, despite its harsh angles. "I understand Thelonious is sick. You'll tell him he was missed?"

"Oh, yeah. It's some weird flu going around that he picked up from Above-London. Didn't want to infect anyone."

"Kind of him." Undersecretary Duplicious glanced up. "And Shade is somewhere in the vicinity?"

"Yeah. Yes, sir."

"Good. I'm so sorry we haven't been able to locate who was behind the events of your second trial."

Rayleigh rocked on his feet. "I have a feeling we'll know soon enough."

Duplicious rested his glass on the table, and leaned in close to Rayleigh. "The Terrors have leads?"

"They don't tell me anything." Not a lie. "I just have a feeling. It's probably my bent."

"Oh, really? Thelonious mentioned something about that. How's it all been going?"

"Slowly. But there's time before school." Also not a lie. He just wouldn't be attending school Below-London.

"Of course, of course. Do you—have you any sorcerer abilities, like your father?"

Taken aback, Rayleigh looked up at the Undersecretary. It was an invasive question; he felt that as surely as he did Above, when people would ask where he was from. Over Duplicious's shoulder, a bulky monster shifted. Parcter. The pale green monster stood stiffly; his ruffled shirt was tight around his neck and under his chin. Seamus had to be somewhere close. He was the last thing Rayleigh needed.

"Mr. Mann?" The Undersecretary's features became tight with concern. "Are you quite all right?"

"That monster—" Rayleigh nodded at Parcter. "He's Seamus's man, my uncle said. That means he's somewhere near. We don't get along."

"I wouldn't worry. The Captain doesn't attend gatherings where I'm in attendance. I'm sure Thelonious told you we don't get on either."

Ah yes, Rayleigh remembered. "He wouldn't say anything of the sort."

Duplicious laughed.

"What's the joke?" Marley asked, joining them. "Good evening, Undersecretary Duplicious. Rayleigh."

The two touched fists beneath the table; Rayleigh's shoulder lowered from his ears.

"Ah, Miss Liu. Is your mother here?"

"I'm afraid she's running late. Last-minute callout for a monster caught in a snare somewhere in Derbyshire."

The Undersecretary's face shifted to concerned. "Bovers. They are the biggest monsters of all, at times. You'll thank your mother for me, won't you? If I don't see her myself later."

"I will."

"Well—" Duplicious took up his drink. "I'll leave you young ones to your celebration. Mr. Mann, should you need anything, I'm always willing to be a listening ear."

"Thank you, sir."

With a smile for Rayleigh and Marley, the Undersecretary rejoined the throng.

"Cool suit," Marley said, looking Rayleigh over.

"Your dress is nice."

Rolling her eyes, Marley flicked the poufy yellow fabric. Her tails bristled with annoyance. "Not the easiest thing to move around in, but at least my ma let me keep my boots on." She glanced around before leaning in. "We still good?" she whispered.

"Yeah, Shade's around somewhere," Rayleigh said, letting her know they weren't alone.

"Oh, right. That's cool." Marley glanced out across the terrace and pulled a face. "Someone else is here too."

Rayleigh followed her line of sight and grimaced. Victor and Verena were making their way toward them.

"I brought more rope," Marley muttered. "How'd you feel about abseiling over the side of this building?"

Rayleigh didn't manage to answer before the twins sidled up to their table.

"Wow," the former said. "You actually passed the third trial, Marley? Didn't think you finished the second." He turned to Rayleigh. "And who's this?"

A quick glance ascertained that they weren't in danger of being overheard by the guests celebrating; Rayleigh took off his glasses.

Verena's eyebrows shot up to her dark hair. It was drawn away from her pale face with a blood-red Alice band. "You made it too? How is that possible?"

Marley's hand edged toward her fanny pack.

"What do you mean?" Rayleigh asked sharply. "Because you set us up during the second trial?"

"Because you didn't *finish* the second trial, and we didn't see you at the third," they said in unison. "Your parents got you in, right?"

Marley edged forward; Rayleigh spoke before she had a chance to reach inside her fanny pack.

"Why are you like this?"

"Like what?" The twins blinked.

"Why are you coming over here with negative energy?" Perhaps it was nerves about what was ahead of him, but Rayleigh didn't have the patience to pretend with Verena and Victor. "If you don't like us, fine. You can not like us from over there." He jutted his chin across the terrace pavilion.

"You're the ones who don't like us," Victor insisted.

"We offered to team up," Verena said.

"And you didn't want to," they said together.

Marley laughed. "That didn't mean we don't like you! It meant we wanted to stick with just us. Logistically, larger parties tend to be harder to control than smaller ones. Look at what happened to us. We all made it."

"Oh." The twins looked sheepish.

"Yeah," Rayleigh added. "But after everything you've done, I have to say, I don't think I like you very much."

"We're used to kids hating on us because of our dad," Verena admitted. "We thought you two would get it. And when you said no, we thought—"

"You were like everyone else," Victor finished.

The siblings exchanged an awkward look.

Rayleigh shrugged. "We should move on and be cool." He wanted that for Marley.

"Absolutely," the twins were quick to say; their faces relaxed from sneers to expressions that were rather pleasant. "Our dad thinks the world of you, Rayleigh. And he has nothing but compliments about your mum, Marley, what she does."

Rayleigh sighed. At this point, he had to ask. "Who is your dad?"

"Hello, everyone," the Undersecretary called via a microphone from the small platform before the portico of French doors leading into the banquet room. "I'm sorry to interrupt, but we're moving inside to the tables."

"He is," Victor and Verena said.

"The Undersecretary?" Rayleigh confirmed.

"Yes. Let's talk more after!" The duo, brighter than they were when they first skulked over, hurried to join their dad.

"I kind of like them more now I know they're not related to Seamus," Rayleigh mused.

"Right? Though, telling them their dad is the reason we passed trials we didn't finish, or complete, might ruin things again."

"I'd say so," Rayleigh agreed.

"Hey." Marley elbowed him. "I need the restroom before we're called up there."

Rayleigh, who hadn't drunk a drop all evening, pulled a contemplative face for Shade. "You know what, I need to go too. Um, Shade?"

There was no response from wherever the penumbra had secreted himself.

"We're going to the restroom. If you're coming along—see you inside."

"I'll watch from the doorway," came his disembodied voice. He was close enough to whisper, but remained unseen.

Part one of the plan was a go. Rayleigh hadn't accounted for Shade's secret appearance at the party, but he'd known getting away from the Terrors would always be difficult. It would call for the most daring and inventive thinking yet. Unfortunately, Marley had talked him out of his wilder idea. She preferred a simpler method of egress. Pulling a fire alarm.

The one she mentioned was in a camera blind spot near the women's restroom. It would guarantee that no one would know they—well, Marley—were behind it. Also, in the chaotic exodus of the two-hundred-plus attendees, not to mention any government officials working late, no one would worry about them. They'd get a good head start to Despair.

A rousing success, Marley and Rayleigh were among the first to leave the Monsters Cabinet the moment the sirens began to peal through the stately halls.

While Marley flagged down a pony and trap across the street, Rayleigh looked back at the flood of monsters running down the white-stone steps. He crossed the fingers on his left hand for Shade, Mary, and Gasp. The crossed fingers on his right hand were for himself, Marley, his dad, and his uncle. Either he was a genius or he was about to land himself and Marley in deep, deep waters. While there were no sharks below the surface, there was one formidable river witch.

An agonizing half hour later, the pony and trap rattled to a stop at the end of a long line of traffic attempting to make its way into Despair for the Horned Heat.

"Let's hop out here," said Rayleigh.

He and Marley thanked their driver and took off into the crowd, squeezing and elbowing a brutal path. The province, still and eerie their first visit, was rammed with monsters eager to witness the night race. Creatures placed bets with bookies about victors, tugged tiny monsterlings alongside, and jostled for the best position behind the shimmering barrier that would keep them safe during the race.

The duo sped through Despair's dim alleyways, the roar of the crowd at their heels; it wasn't long until they skidded to a stop before a fire escape clinging to the side of a residential building. Rayleigh went first, taking the metal steps two at a time until he hitched a leg over the lip of the roof and felt an elation the likes of which he never would have imagined feeling when he saw the monsters waiting for him there.

"Right on time," Rayleigh said.

The twin in the leather jacket stepped forward. "You're wrong. As am I."

"I'm Right," said the second Bigfoot.

Bypassing them both, Rayleigh stroked Kedara's beak, murmuring apologies for subjecting her to those idiots. The Bad Omen nipped him with affection, her dark eyes jewel bright.

"Did you hear us, little Mann? We said—"

"Give it up," said Marley, joining them. "He knows your real names are Andrew, not Right, and James, not Wrong."

The twins shouted in outrage.

"You told on us, little sis?" they said in unison.

"I *apologized* for you. You're not in some poor bover kid's bedroom after dark, confusing them with your double act now. You're helping us stop the Illustrious Society."

"Actually, they've helped," said Rayleigh. He couldn't have got Kedara to Despair were it not for them, their experience with rescuing monsters like Bad Omens. And while he'd argued they'd be a bigger risk, Marley had vouched for them. "Thanks for that. You can go now."

"Make sure you tell the Terrors, all right?" Andrew scratched the back of his neck. "We don't want any hard feelings after the little incident at your flat."

Those had been their terms. Rayleigh nodded, and the twins took their leave.

A veil of fog now hung low over the streets; tongues of gray licked buildings and rooftops alike. The crowd was eating the drama right up, given the din. There was a frenzy to their cries. Rayleigh rocked on his feet, wrung his hands. "Are the trackers still working?" he asked.

Marley pulled a slim tablet from her fanny pack. "Yep."

"And you'll—"

"Go to the Terrors with the tracking monitor as soon as you run for the dock. I know." Her vulpine nose, the whiskers on either side of it, twitched. "Rayleigh . . . be careful. This was a stupid plan from the start. But now—"

"It's the only plan."

She exhaled. "Remember, let the omen gather height first. It's important to build speed before zooming down."

Though her brothers had given him extensive tuition over the comms in how to glide yesterday, the thought of zooming anywhere with Kedara on his own made Rayleigh's stomach jolt.

Across Despair, a horn blasted.

The race had begun.

"You should go," he told Marley. "Thanks for everything so far."

Though it looked like she had more to say, she smiled. "I'll see you soon," she said.

Both pretended it was convincing.

From this distance, Rayleigh couldn't see any of the running horned creatures, but buildings trembled beneath the pounding of their hooves and claws. Trying to ignore the acrid bubble in his throat, he shook out his legs and hands. They felt as unyielding as stone, as heavy.

But he could do this—he had to do this.

With a fervent wish on his breath and a silver spoon in hand to catch Kedara's eye, he took off across the roof; seconds later, her forked feet closed around his middle and he was airborne in a rush of nerves. She rocketed upward with a speed that blew Rayleigh's cheeks back, made him squint in the chilly night air.

Right's next instructions ran through his thoughts.

"Seize the steering feathers once you've caught a wind."

He felt the telltale tug of a current, an invisible lead drawing them into the arms of a gale. Kedara's hard work was over. It was his turn. He unstuck his arms from where they'd been hugged to his chest and reached for the gliding feathers—to no avail.

He couldn't reach.

Kedara was too big; his arms weren't long enough.

Fear carved a place in the bottom of his stomach. And speaking of bottoms . . . Despair was a speck beneath him. Wind rushed in his ears. If he fell—Kedara turned her head and squawked at him.

Rayleigh gave up using both arms and waved the one. He shifted in the omen's grip, his stomach plummeting to his feet, to grab hold of the feather. She turned her head and tucked the wing in. Without its balance, they dipped in the sky. Rayleigh's heart pounded, deafening him, but with a little more stretching . . . he did it! He reached the feather.

"Got it!"

Kedara squawked again. There was no way he'd catch the left feather, but according to the directions Wrong had given him, he wouldn't have to: "Circle around the province" is what he said. Rayleigh could do that.

With one tug, the omen leaned to the right and put them back on track. Rayleigh shook; a muscle spasmed in his back and right shoulder. What was it with near-death experiences in Despair?

As the docklands neared, its waters black beneath the dark sky, Rayleigh drew back on the feather to slow Kedara, eyes on the streets in search of Thelonious. He spotted a distinctive pair of gray horns. Was that—

"Argh!"

With a screech, the omen jerked violently to the left. Rayleigh lost his grip on the steering feather as she flapped her wings. He peered through cloud and fog. Some of the spectators were pointing—no, not pointing.

They were aiming lumicands. At Kedara.

"Get around them!" yelled Rayleigh, his hands waving uselessly. "Get around them, Kedara!"

The omen cried out as bolts slammed into her feet, her wings. The stink of singed feathers stung Rayleigh's senses, but she rallied. Catching another wind, she tilted to the left and right to avoid more bolts streaking through the air. Spectators yelled below them. Rayleigh couldn't tell if it was in support or disappointment that the omen hadn't been brought down yet. He hadn't considered that anyone would care if he glided her. A folly. Rayleigh didn't know all the rules, and he'd charged in regardless. Again. Guilty, he shouted encouragement to Kedara, who feinted valiantly, but couldn't evade every pulse of light. One caught her wing for a second time. They went down.

Rayleigh was cocooned behind a barrier of feathers as Kedara held him close. Wind screamed as they plunged toward the ground but he preferred it to the painful friction of feather against gravel as Kedara hit the road and skidded to a stop. Thrown from her protective hold, he hit the ground and rolled. He was on his feet without delay to rush back to the omen's side.

Breathing slowly, the omen watched him through eyes squinted in pain. She keened in her throat, smoking wing clutched to her chest. Rayleigh felt an anger the likes of which he'd never felt before. It swelled inside him until his fingers tingled with unspent energy. With his bent.

"I think you'll find," a familiar brogue trilled, "that illegal flight is up."

In one maneuver, Rayleigh freed his lumicand and turned to face the poltergeist.

"You hurt my omen."

"An unfortunate necessity," Seamus said. "You shouldn't have been gliding. You've got yourself in a world of trouble, boy. Can't you see that you're surrounded?"

The Cabinet's Guard encircled him in a white cyclone. Behind them, even more spirits filled the lid with their swirling faceless figures.

Kedara mewled. Rayleigh sent his weight to the balls of his feet, and raised his lumicand higher. "You don't understand what's happening here."

"No, you don't understand. You are a *child*. You have no business gliding above an event as dangerous as this. It is foolish of you to argue, but then I expect no less." Seamus clicked thin fingers. Behind the spirit guard, monsters with lumicands gathered around Rayleigh too. "I don't suppose the *Terribles* would have told you about the Cabinet's Spookers, hmm? They police Below, and they're just as unhappy with you as I am."

Those who weren't armed with lumicands bared fangs, dragged hooves, or flashed talons that might put Ms. Modiste's clothing to the test—if Rayleigh somehow avoided being fried by all the lumi-cands.

"Like me, they take their job protecting Below-London's citizens seriously." Seamus drew his unsightly coat together, buttoning it in place with his puffed-up self-importance. "And you, Mr. Mann, are jeopardizing them with this display. Not to mention endangering yourself and that omen. I have no jurisdiction outside the Cabinet, but the Chancellor will vouch for me if I am the one to bring you in. Now, will you come quietly?"

Rayleigh eyed the long crocodile mouth of a Spooker nearby. Teeth scissored along their jaw. It was . . . unsettling to say the least. But if he gave up and went along, Nana would never forgive him. Mama too always wanted him to try his best. He hit the shield button on his lumicand's base, and a violet sunburst of his energy spun into existence before him. He thought that a clear enough response.

"I see I must say it again. If I don't take you in, the Spookers will. Any attempt to resist is futile, Mr. Mann."

"Actually, gov," another voice called. Rayleigh's heart soared to hear it. "I find one should always resist. Especially when they're told not to by a garden tool like you."

Seamus and his Spookers parted in the road, revealing Thelo-nious.

Though his lip was cut, his clothes were torn and filthy, and blood ran from a wound on his arm, he'd retained his sunglasses; somehow his horns seemed even bigger, thicker, before the backdrop of fog. With a smile, he nodded at Rayleigh.

"Wotcher, Nephew-mine. Thought that was you and my omen

those Spookers will regret shooting down. Do me a favor will you, and get out of here."

Rayleigh stood his ground. "I don't think you're in a position to be handing out orders."

Seamus looked between uncle and nephew. "Neither of you are going anywhere! I'm trying to help."

"You've done brilliantly, kid," Thelonious said, not taking his attention away from Rayleigh. "Go on, now. Let me take it from here."

"Enough!" shouted the Spooker with the crocodile mouth. "Captain Scáthach, we've given you time," he continued, in his low gravelly voice. "The runners will be upon us soon. We need to clear the road. Spookers, move in!"

"I wouldn't, if I were you," said Thelonious. Though his tone bore a casual edge, it was far sharper than any anatomy or weapon carried by the Cabinet operatives. "I've already memorized your faces. Squbbible, Vindictus." He nodded at two of the Spookers. They lowered their lumicands, concern on their faces—their ordinary faces. Maybe they had a capacity to transform. Or maybe, when confronted by a monster such as Thelonious, with his gall and his horns, no transformation was sufficient to stand against him. "You've worked with me. You know how thorough I am when I'm after someone."

"You have no power over Cabinet officers, Ick," Seamus spat.

"Not everyone is a megalomaniac turncoat like you, Captain. These good monsters respect the authority of their Bogey Mann. An authority I report to. And speaking of coats, old boy, who hates you enough at home to let you leave the house in that?"

The poltergeist didn't blush, most likely couldn't, but his

otherworldly hue darkened. It was like a bank of clouds drifted across the window pockets and dimmed him with shadow.

He spoke through gritted teeth. "Spookers. Do as you will."

"Move in," their long-jawed commander cried.

Vindictus and Squbbible raised their weapons once more. They didn't take more than a few steps before tendrils of shadow snaked between their ankles and tripped them up.

Shade stepped from the night beside Rayleigh, his top hat tilted at a jaunty angle.

Rayleigh couldn't help but smile. The twins weren't the only ones he'd been banking on.

Looked like Gasp found the note he'd left in the bathroom at the Cabinet.

A crack from the road silenced onlookers. The pavement itself was splitting wide open. Seamus and the Spookers pulled back, mouths agape as, like a lit stick of dynamite, the fissure splintered until the ground resembled a chaotic spider's web. A deep groan ballooned through the gaps. It was like the awakening of something ancient. Or its death.

Instead it was Gasp. The troll emerged from beneath the wide fissure, elevated upward on a platform of earth. His kerchief and tie were the color of pitch, and a similar thunder was emblazoned on his brow.

"Old friend." Thelonious nodded Gasp's way. "Shade. And here I was hoping to win best entrance."

A cackle echoed through the night. "Good luck with that."

The Spookers turned this way and that, their lumicands before them as they tried to determine where it came from. Finally, they beheld Bloody Mary, who'd appeared beside Thelonious in her military jacket, black boots, and high ponytail. She gave a little wave, sparks dancing between her elegant fingers.

"You said she wouldn't be here," said Vindictus, suddenly antsy.

"*She* has a name. You'll wake screaming it after tonight." Mary launched her sparks at the Spookers.

Then the Terrors launched themselves.

TWENTY-SEVEN

BOO! THERE IT IS

The legendary crew were a sight to behold.

Rayleigh should have run for the Undersea Channel the moment the Terrors arrived. Instead he couldn't help but linger. Sparks flew from Mary's fingertips like fizzing darts; Spookers screamed as their long coats burned beneath her silver flame. But there was no sympathy to be found when Bloody Mary, Wandless Witch and Bane of London, struck—she was an unrelenting storm of palms, elbows, and roundhouse kicks.

Not one to be outdone, Shade stood with both palms aloft; from his left, a symphony of shadows played a song of chaos. Bolts and orbs from Spookers' lumicands crashed into their swirling midst, only to be swallowed by the maw of darkness. From his right, shadowed nets blustered toward Seamus, eager to ensnare. But, softening to smoke, the poltergeist phased through them again and again. Irritation colored his ghostly cheeks, but he was otherwise unharmed—not even Thelonious's stolen lumicand could make an impact.

The Terrors' chief shouted taunts at the Captain over the roaring audience. The latter now seemed more invested in the fight than the race. Spurred on by their cries of encouragement, Thelonious alternated between swiping the weapon at Seamus's ankles and circling it in a cyclone of energy at any Spooker foolish enough to venture too close.

With another baleful groan, the ground quaked.

Blazer ripped, kerchief lost, and curls in a state of complete disarray, Gasp raised stalagmites from the road like springs; beneath them, Spookers took to the sky like jack-in-the-box clowns. It all laid a terrible weight on Rayleigh's shoulders.

If his plan failed, he would, once again, leave them in an untenable situation: protecting him. Again.

With a click, his shield rescinded into the lumicand. "Watch Kedara!" Rayleigh commanded Shade, before he turned and bolted into Despair's narrow streets.

Someone hollered from behind—the penumbra?

Slowing at a corner, Rayleigh looked back. Yes. A trio of Spookers had managed to slip past Shade's shadows. They gave chase. Including the one with the crocodile maw. He'd dropped onto all fours. Limbs that had been human bent at unsightly angles to accommodate. There was no way Rayleigh, a lumicand novice, could take him.

Not when his yellow eyes, glowing like lamps in the near-dark, narrowed in on Rayleigh.

Not when four sets of claws were clicking across stone toward him.

Whipping around, he put his head down and took off. He ran flat out through the alleys that twisted through Despair like arteries. Dim, their only benefit was the abruptness of their turns. When his pursuer's breath puffed close at his heels, Rayleigh pivoted sharply around a corner. Four legs would scramble, slow.

The same couldn't be said for the two-legged Spookers.

An orb whistled past his left cheek. Rayleigh ducked. Skidding around a bend, he aimed his lumicand over his shoulder and fired a battery of bolts. A single cry told him he'd hit something. Wind rushed past his ears; heat tore through muscles tight with fear as he bore down on a fork. He couldn't remember which way to go.

Panting breaths filled the side street. Claws tore against stone behind him. He couldn't outrun the monster. There was nothing for it.

He stopped, turned around.

His hands shook so violently in the face of the Spooker hurtling toward him, it took several tries to hit the correct switch on his lumicand; the virga crackled out of the cylinder, a thin shard of violet strength. His bent. Him. Rayleigh sank back, an arm tucked behind him for balance, and dropped the tip of his weapon. Just as Thelonious taught him.

One breath. Two breaths.

Yellow eyes lit with a cruel delight as the Spooker sprang forward. Rayleigh flicked his sword up and, rather unfortunately, closed his eyes. There was a yelp of pain, but no weight on the tip of his weapon.

He squinted one eye open.

The side street was empty.

Fog drifted through the alley, and something scuttled in the dirt piled against either wall.

All three Spookers may have been gone, but Rayleigh didn't feel he was alone.

"Left," he murmured, backing away, virga angled before him. "Left at the fork."

He spun and ran. Alley sludge was exchanged for cobblestones; the temperature declined as a chill blew in from the docks. The water was as dark as a starless night. Dark as the warehouses' windows encroaching on the wharf. He'd made it. Where was the kidnapper?

D'Leau, who might rise up from the water.

Or Octavia.

Footsteps echoed from the alley behind Rayleigh. The shuffling gait of something heavy. He gripped his lumicand, waited. A shadow slanted across the cobblestones, the distorted frame of something large. Rising onto the balls of his feet, he slipped his right before his left, sank down a little, and raised his weapon.

Then his body sort of . . . levitated.

Stunned, Rayleigh could only look on as he was lifted into the air, stilled, like a living doll.

"It's rare that the authority of my position is ignored, Mr. Mann," an all too familiar voice said. "And I have to resort to using my bent."

Rayleigh wrestled for control. He looked at the lumicand in his grip and willed his finger, so close to the virga button, to press it. Nothing happened.

Captain Scáthach clicked his way out of the alley. He was followed by a plodding Parcter.

"I did say resistance was futile." There was something indecent about the joy on Seamus's face. "Hold him."

Parcter strode stiffly across to take Rayleigh in his arms. He looked up, up, into the hideous face of Seamus's lackey from the hearing, the Citizenship Ceremony. Rayleigh's limbs softened as the invisible hold on him lifted. But there'd be no fighting himself free. With one of those unnerving twitches, Parcter began marching him away from the water.

An all too familiar congested feeling burgeoned in Rayleigh's body. This time it centered in his chest, like his entire middle crackled with lightning waiting for the right moment to be spent.

"You don't get it," Rayleigh said. "I found my dad." He forced his voice to remain measured as he spoke to Seamus. Adults never listened when kids shouted. "If you let me go, you can come with me to bust the monster holding him hostage."

"That won't be possible." The poltergeist shook his head as he knocked a bin lid off. He tossed a token inside. A Vol-way spun the garbage into oblivion.

"Do you hate him that much?"

"No." Seamus paused. "Actually, yes. I do. But I meant letting you go won't be possible." He clicked at Parcter, and the silent monster plodded toward the bin.

Rayleigh slammed his hands and feet against the monster. "You're a fool!" He launched at Seamus. "You can't see that you're aiding a worse enemy? And what's more—" He shared a few of the more colorful insults pinballing around his head, where pressure was mounting. "Look, it's Mama D'Leau, okay? Or Octavia Brand. One of them has my dad. Or they have him together."

The Captain laughed. "D'Leau? Brand? Oh, Mr. Mann, there is much to teach you about the way of this world. Of my world. I told you once before that I don't take kindly to those attempting to disrupt order."

"I'm not trying to disrupt order!" Rayleigh roared. "I'm trying to put a stop to it."

"By finding your father? There truly is no need. I know exactly where he is. You see—" Seamus drew himself taller; the half-frantic, half-pinched expression he always wore when Rayleigh saw him changed. In fact, it hadn't appeared at all since Rayleigh first noticed him in the road, where the Terrors still fought. Seamus's entire face pulled taut; a wiped screen, it became cold. A sneer drew his thin lips up in the corners. The Captain, meek, afraid of Thelonious, had become an arrogant stranger. "I know exactly where your father is."

Weight filled Rayleigh's bones in a rush. Energy tingled in his fingertips. He couldn't press any buttons on his lumicand, but it didn't matter.

Violet lightning exploded from Rayleigh.

It zigzagged from his chest, his arms—*he* was the lightning, a living boy-shaped current that launched a shock bright enough to light the world.

Parcter's arms were flung from him. Seamus was catapulted away in a tangle of fabric; he hit the wall with a sickening crunch. Rayleigh, sparking like an exposed wire, took only a moment to notice that he wasn't pulling from the atmosphere at all. His lumicand wasn't active either, without touching the glyphs. The lightning was in *him*. He was creating it. Rayleigh curled his hands into fists, raised his chin. Surrounded by a corona of purple tendrils of his bent, he felt like more than a monster. He felt like a Mann. And he would not be afraid of Seamus. The Captain groaned, dazed. A slim contraption slipped out of his pocket and lay beside him. A remote of some sort.

"Ray-ray?"

A chill engulfed Rayleigh. That was his childhood nickname. Nana was the only one who used it now, but that hadn't been her voice. He turned to where Parcter was pushing himself onto his feet.

"Ray-ray?" Seamus's lackey repeated; he shook his head, as though dazed.

Seamus had said he knew where Rayleigh's father was.

Parcter looked nothing like Bogey, yet Rayleigh's inexplicable knowing brushed against the logical part of his brain. The side of him that was instructing him to run, loudly, quieted. It encouraged him to take a chance, to walk with courage.

"Dad?" Parcter, large and bulbous, nothing at all like the painting of Bogey in Terror Tower's hall, looked at him with muddy eyes that had never been clearer, and nodded. Their color was wrong, but they blazed with the heat of a thousand golden sunrises.

Across the wharf, Seamus groaned. Both Rayleigh and his dad whipped around to look at where he lay. The poltergeist phased in and out, solid one moment and incorporeal the next.

"Run," Parcter said.

Rayleigh glanced toward the bin where the Vol-way's shadows still churned.

"Not Terror Tower." Parcter's words came slowly, like he'd forgotten how to speak. "Ray-ray, go somewhere else."

"What about you?"

"Wrong question." Seamus materialized before Rayleigh, translucent and incorporeal.

Rayleigh started back with a shout; Parcter charged toward the Captain. Seamus raised a single hand; Parcter took to the sky before smashing into the same wall Rayleigh had sent Seamus into.

"Hey!" he cried. "Don't hurt my dad!"

"So you figured it out," Seamus spat, in a voice quite unlike any he'd used before. There was something ancient about it. Something more monstrous than anything Rayleigh had seen in Below-London. "You should have figured out what will happen to you now, Mr. Mann." He jabbed a bony finger at Rayleigh's chest.

There was no physical contact, yet it landed like the swing of a bat. It was as though Seamus had more power in that single digit than Rayleigh had in his entire body. His bent fizzled out, abandoned him. Rendered breathless, Rayleigh flew backward into the black depths of the Vol-way, helpless to stop himself from falling into its shadows.

TWENTY-EIGHT

THE SCHEMES OF MONSTERS AND MANN

The fall was short.

Rayleigh's trainers brushed against a checkerboard floor in a soft landing. He managed to maintain his balance, which was handy, given the company he had.

The Sphere of Doors, bustling during the first day of the Induction, was even busier with feddies. Their chatter was muted. Rayleigh shook his head, like he did after swimming to clear water from his ears. It didn't improve the sound any. A pale gray creature with antlers strode toward him; a briefcase swung in one hand, and they clutched a clipboard in another.

"Excuse me." Rayleigh stepped into their path. "I need to see the Quorum, it's—"

He recoiled, for the monster was faceless. But he was not quick enough; the creature passed clean through him, as though he wasn't there.

With a gasp, Rayleigh clutched at his chest. He hadn't felt them exactly; they hadn't been cold, but they'd been there somehow. A watery memory that filled his lungs, making it hard to breathe. A cluster of monsters, long coats billowing behind them, charged toward Rayleigh.

Like the first, they were faceless.

And like the first, they didn't slow either.

Rayleigh jumped back to avoid them. Perhaps the movement shook something loose in his head, a past conversation, because his confusion, an amorphous cloud that filled his thoughts, cleared.

"I didn't really want to lock you in the holding cells." Seamus's voice carried with ease within the cavernous surroundings.

Rayleigh gripped his lumicand and sought the Captain out in the crowd, more stone effigy than boy in his stillness. Monsters passed through the doors along the curve of the wall; they traveled up and down the halls spearing off the main atrium. Soft blue sconces, as pale as the ghosts, flickered on the walls.

"From the moment I saw you in the hearing," Seamus went on, from wherever he was, "I knew you needed to be secreted away in harsher climes. But the Quorum wouldn't make the ruling. Here we are all the same, in a prison of my own design."

A passage from one of the books Rayleigh studied to prepare for his second trial came to mind. Tempus and spatia liminaria always had tells. For the former, it was an absence of color. The past was a lifeless place.

Soundlessly, Rayleigh turned on his heel—straight into a pair of ghostly monsters. They passed right through him without breaking their conversation. Like he wasn't there. Because he wasn't, not really. These, his surroundings, were an example of time magic—a spell.

Seamus had trapped Rayleigh in a past version of the Monsters Cabinet.

"You've probably figured out by now that you won't be leaving here. Something that surprises me to no end. Your capacity for successful thought." It was reflected in Seamus's voice, his wariness. "I expected failure during your first trial. You should have been physically stunted after your time in the Above world, harmless. And yet you proved me wrong."

Rayleigh wasn't so sure he'd do that again. He tried to summon his bent, as he had done before. It was there, he could feel it waking at his call, but it would not come out. No matter how he strained, begged, shook himself like a bottle of pop. It would not come.

"And yet," Seamus called, still from an indiscernible location in the tempus sphere, "you have caused me no end of difficulties. You passed the first trial. My leaks to the media did nothing to provide me with your location. You managed to evade those idiots Slydus and Poltroon in that garage."

So, if it was Seamus who had Bogey and Seamus who hired the imp, that meant one thing. It wasn't an officer from Inductions, Welcomes, and Warnings who'd been after Rayleigh.

The poltergeist was working with the Illustrious Society.

"Worse still," Seamus said. "Your delightful uncle managed to convince Octavia to allow you to sit your next trial at the Terror's secret HQ. How was I meant to take the key from you, if I didn't know where you were?"

Willing himself to breathe quietly, Rayleigh dodged the memory versions of Cabinet workers, visitors. He had no idea how to get out, never having found that answer while he studied. But if he stood still, Seamus would only find him faster. He couldn't count on Marley, their trackers. Not when he didn't know how the magic around him may affect them.

"And then," the Captain called. "When I next see you, you're gliding across the lid in the talons of an ancient creature. For a monsterling, you were proving almost formidable."

No noise sounded beyond the drone of Seamus's story. His boots didn't click; he didn't breathe, which shouldn't have come as a great surprise given that he was dead. Inside and otherwise.

"It has only confirmed what I suspected the moment you revealed yourself during the hearing. All those trips Bogey took to the Above world, the ones concentrated around a particular estate, they were to see you. Brutely, I believe it's called. A terrible place, filled with terrible people. It was the perfect hiding place for the Supreme's Key. I trust you have it with you now."

Sweat dripped down Rayleigh's back. He had no exit plan, and Seamus's tale appeared to be reaching its end.

"Come now, Mr. Mann. Surely you see what is happening here. Either you will give me what I seek—" One of the past monsters turned to Rayleigh, stopping him dead: translucent, mercifully dulling the vibrancy of his hideous coat, Seamus was the ghostliest he'd seen him. "Or I will take it."

Rayleigh gripped his lumicand. "Where's my dad?"

Seamus smirked. "No good to me any longer."

"If you hurt him—"

"You'll what?" Seamus's body seemed to solidify to something more corporeal before softening into smoke once more. "I think you'll find yourself too busy to issue threats."

Nails scraped against stone in a threatening whine.

They were followed by the scuttle of insect legs—many legs;

pincers tick-tocking in a deadly countdown across stone. A wailing shriek from the dome launched Rayleigh's focus, and his hand holding the lumicand, upward. He looked on in horror. The paintings of monsters in the dome overhead, the ones he'd admired during his first visit, were pulling themselves free with relish. Unlike the lower sphere, where he and Seamus were, they were as vibrantly coloured as the real painting in the present-day Cabinet. Hope flared. If they weren't grey, they weren't part of the spell. They weren't in the past.

"I told you to come quietly," Seamus said. "You did not. I warned you that if you would not give me what I asked for, I would take it."

"I don't have the key," Rayleigh breathed. One touch of the lumicand, and his virga erupted from its core. "And even if I did, I'd never give it to someone working for the Illustrious Society."

"Maybe you aren't as quick as I've given you credit for."

"You're not working for the Illustrious Society?"

Seamus tilted his chin upward to look down his sharp nose at Rayleigh. "I do not work for the society. I can be reasonable, Mr. Mann. When you have lived as long as I, patience is nothing. A fight is nothing." The Captain considered Rayleigh with curiosity. "You can't take all the painted beasts on." It sounded like a question. "And they won't listen to anyone but me."

"I don't need to take them all on," Rayleigh said.

Gripping his lumicand between both hands, he flexed his fingers. "I don't even need to take you on. I just have to be myself."

"Aren't you an inspiration," Seamus drawled.

"Most people tend to go with 'massive pain.' 'Trouble maker.' 'Destroyer of trousers and windows.' That last one might be my favorite. I do enjoying destroying things." Rayleigh plunged his virga's tip into the marble floor of the Sphere of Doors—a place he hoped existed, beneath the time magic. He hadn't been sure if it would work, but his bent snaked toward Seamus. The poltergeist took one look at the current traveling toward him and ran. Hunched over his lumicand, Rayleigh looked out and up as his bent spiraled up the walls. Violet veins of magic blew out glass bulbs, cracked the doors on the walls. When it reached the painted monsters— the swarm making their way down the dome—they exploded. Paint flecks clouded the air like ash. Seamus shouted, ducked as they rained down.

"Hey!" Rayleigh shouted at Seamus. His uncle had told him lumicands were weapons of honor. He didn't feel good about shooting a bolt into Seamus's back. So when the Captain glanced back over his shoulder, Rayleigh wrenched his lumicand free from the ground, aimed, and fired. The purple baton crackled and popped, like a firework, a living missile. Seamus dived aside; it caught his hideous coat. Tore a hole straight through.

"Few monsters can touch me with bent or hand." He gaped at Rayleigh. "What *are* you?"

"No clue." Rayleigh switched back to his virga. Placing his left foot behind his right, he sank into defensive position. "But I'll tell you what I'm not, and that's someone who would ever agree to come quietly." Thelonious would have been proud of that line, he thought.

Seamus patted his smoking coat. "You think I fear you because you can touch me?"

"I think you should fear me because you don't know why I can touch you. That, and—" Rayleigh jutted his chin upward, as though he wasn't completely stunned at his own bent. For the gray Sphere melted around them, dripping down the walls to reveal, as he suspected, the real Sphere in all its glorious, rich color.

With a snarl, Seamus took a step toward Rayleigh.

"I wouldn't, if I were you." He waved his lumicand, the hissing might of his luminous virga. "I've heard this hurts."

A sparking doorway split the time magic at Seamus's back, creating a silver sparking tear in the disintegrating spell; Marley strode out of it.

"I have a feeling these guys are going to make things hurt a whole lot more." She jerked a thumb over her shoulder as more spitting silver tears weakened the integrity of the magic, through which Bloody Mary, Shade, Gasp, and finally, Thelonious entered the fading tempus Cabinet. His father trailed behind them, hands bound before him with cuffs made of the same magic eating away at the spell. Mary's bent. The witch wore her monstrous face, wrinkles, sharp angles, anger, and all.

"This time," Thelonious said, unleashing a whip from his lumicand with a snap, "how about you try not to run, Captain? I think little enough of you as it is."

"And I don't think of you at all."

"That's a lie," Rayleigh chipped in. "All he's been doing is thinking about us. Turns out the Captain is the one working for the Illustrious Society."

"Is that right? Scáthach, you sly old dog."

Seamus merely sneered.

"Can't say world domination looks good on you there, gov. It's done something unpleasant to your face."

Shade and Gasp fanned out, blocking the poltergeist's escape from each compass point. Mary remained by the holes her bent had torn in the spell. Hands aloft, she knitted them back together, reversing the silver sparks so they shifted inward, like a closing mouth. Marley stood beside her, one hand on her fanny pack, another held before her.

"Where's my brother, windbag?" Thelonious asked.

Seamus, focus bouncing between their growing audience, each Terror, and Rayleigh, flickered between corporeal and ghostly. "Where's the Supreme's Key?"

Thelonious's whip lanced through the air. Mini tongues of light flickered along its sizzling length. But it passed through Seamus without doing any harm. Rayleigh stepped forward, lumicand ready; his bent would affect the Captain. Something he was aware of, given the dark look he cast Rayleigh's way.

"I'll take this to mean we're at an impasse," he said. "A shame I can't stick around to resolve matters. But the numbers don't seem to be in my favor." His eyes sliced Rayleigh, from head to toe. "I'll be seeing you soon, Mr. Mann. I can't abide unfinished business. Ick, I trust you'll pass along my resignation to the Quorum. I don't think our ideals align any longer." And then, like an ice cream left out in the sun, he melted into the floor and out of sight.

"Mary?"

She glanced over her shoulder at Thelonious; her face relaxed into the one she wore most often. "I'm doing my best, but we don't have long until the spell collapses entirely. By which time—"

"We need to be gone," Thelonious finished. He started for Rayleigh, and swept him up in a hug. "You're all right?"

"Fine, yes." Rayleigh wiggled free. "Why don't we let the spell fade? We can tell everyone who Seamus is. It's been him, Thelonious. He's been behind everything."

"We can't say anything, let the spell fall, for multiple reasons, Nephew-mine. The primary one being, we don't have Bogey to prove everything."

"We can beat it out of this guy?" Shade suggested, turning to grab Parcter.

"No—wait!" Rayleigh ran to separate his dad and the penumbra. "This *is* the Bogey Mann."

The Terrors and Marley stared at him.

"Scáthach must have cracked the boy's head," muttered Shade.

"I swear," Rayleigh insisted. "He knew me. I think Seamus had him under some sort of control."

Gasp waved a slim contraption. "Maybe with this? I found it with Parcter."

Cries rang from the real Cabinet beyond the spell; Rayleigh looked up at the ceiling; the painted monsters his bent hadn't disintegrated were beginning to advance.

"We have another situation." He pointed upward, at the hundreds of creatures Seamus had warned would listen to none but him.

"That spineless—" Thelonious swore. "He activated the Siege Protocol while you were alone with him?"

"I was handling it."

"I don't doubt it." Thelonious cupped Rayleigh's cheek in his spare hand. "I couldn't be prouder of you if you were my own son."

Rayleigh's heart fluttered, like it grew wings.

"We're going to get matters sorted," Thelonious told him. "Don't you worry."

"At the tower." Mary spoke through gritted teeth. "We have to go! The Cabinet officials can take care of the guard dogs in the dome.

There's a mirror in my pocket, Miss Liu, please take it out."

The Terrors and Rayleigh crowded around Marley and Mary.

"The Province of Dreamers," the latter said, clear and sure, and within seconds, they were all absorbed into its surface, leaving the tempus spell to die in their wake.

The Terrors moved fast, once their party appeared in Terror Tower's clubhouse.

Mary took Bogey/Parcter straight to the infirmary off the clubhouse. Clinical in its whiteness, it was equipped with an array of beds and machines. Kedara was already there, atop a bed. Her wings were fanned open and coated in a salve. Thelonious checked on her. So did Rayleigh and Marley.

"Hey—" Rayleigh nudged his friend. "Thanks for coming."

Marley pulled him into a hug. "I can't believe you fought a poltergeist and won. What happened with Seamus?"

"He can tell you later," Thelonious interrupted. "I need to have a chat with him first. Mind staying with Kedara, Miss Liu?"

Marley blinked at him. "I'd consider it an honor."

"She's my favorite, so take good care of her. Come on, Nephewmine."

Rayleigh hurried after his uncle. Thelonious opened a cupboard hitherto unnoticed in the clubhouse. It was filled with coats.

"I'm going to wake the Quorum, the Chancellor, and the Undersecretary," he explained, removing a long leather coat. "They need to look for Seamus, because if I find him—" He slammed the cupboard door. "There's also the Cabinet's Guard to look in on. Seamus had friends whose loyalties will need to be ascertained and—the key."

Thelonious bent to take Rayleigh by the shoulders. "Did you figure out where it is too?"

"No. Do you know where it is?"

"The location of *The Book of Night Things*?"

Confused a moment, Rayleigh had to think. "I—I left it in my room."

Thelonious stilled. "Not with the fairy light."

"Yes, but—"

His uncle took off running; Rayleigh sped after him. The pair burst into Rayleigh's room. Winsome startled, but it was Rayleigh who shouted, for the fairy—the tiny fairy small enough to sit in his palm, if he'd ever removed her from the bulb—lounged on his bed. It wasn't just that she no longer inhabited her bulb. She was tall— taller than him. She wasn't a dainty fairy, she was a lithe monster who rivaled Thelonious for ceiling space. Horns and all.

"Where's the book?" Thelonious shifted in front of Rayleigh. His lumicand was out, his virga bright in the darkness of the room.

Winsome rolled her violet eyes. Her wings—the width of Rayleigh's vast bed—wafted lazily. "Am I meant to understand that?"

"You're big," Rayleigh said, stunned. He hadn't blinked. Hadn't been able to since they'd entered his room. "And—And you're out of the bulb. Thelonious, you knew?"

"Never mind that now, Nephew-mine."

"He knew." Winsome sat up to smirk at Thelonious. "It's why he didn't want me in here. Like I'd ever do anything to betray B's trust in me." Her focus shifted to Rayleigh. Something softened in her sharp face. "And I wouldn't hurt you. Of all the Terrors, you're, like, my third favorite."

Rayleigh was taken aback. "Third?"

"Nephew-mine." Thelonious didn't shift his lumicand away. "Where did you put *The Book of Night Things*?"

"It's in his bag behind the toilet across the landing," Winsome answered. "Whoops. Am I not meant to know that?"

Thelonious backed across the landing, a fistful of Rayleigh's coat in hand.

"You know I could have done anything I wanted to in the weeks he slept beneath me, right?" Winsome called out. "I can also leave this room and join him in the clubhouse."

"I dare you to do just that," Thelonious snarled.

Rayleigh, dazed by all that had happened, allowed his uncle to tug him out of the bathroom and down the hall to the kitchen.

"She's big," he kept saying, dazed. "She's bigger than you."

"Yeah. We can talk about her later." Thelonious bustled about the counters, adding water to the kettle, and switching on the hob to heat the water. "Right now I need you to tell me everything that happened with Seamus and—" Thelonious held up the book. "Everything about this."

Rayleigh covered the book first. Nana gave it to him before he left Above-London, and said it came from his dad. As for the events with Seamus, it was clear they'd all been wrong about who was behind matters with Bogey.

"Will my dad be all right?"

The kettle whistled. Thelonious took it off the hob. "Mary will take care of him. Magic is her speciality. Not sure when it became Seamus's, with that tempus sorcery, but I will be by the end of the night."

"And *The Book of Night Things* will help with that?"

"It will." Thelonious added tea bags and milk to two mugs. "You know when it hit me that you had the Supreme's Key, that Bogey had entrusted it to you to keep safe?"

Rayleigh held his hands out. "Wait, I actually had it?"

"Yes. And I realized when I saw you standing before the Captain, the Spookers, this evening." Thelonious shook his head and slid a cup of tea to Rayleigh. "You looked like the hero he knew would be capable of defeating an Illustrious acolyte. All you were missing was some armor."

Rayleigh's tea sat untouched. "What does that mean?"

"Drink that tea. The sugar will combat any residual adrenaline."

"If I drink this, will you finally give me a straight answer?"

"I—yes."

Rayleigh sat at the kitchen island and blew on the steaming mug of tea. "Go."

"I suspect your old man left you the book because he knew you were coming here. The one place no stranger has ever infiltrated. And managed to leave. We do have those lost wanderers in here somewhere still. I think he knew someone was after him, the key, and he stashed it with the old bird, with you, right before they took him."

Rayleigh filled in the rest of the blanks. "Seamus said he didn't know about me, at the hearing. He must have been lying. He knew my dad visited me, and that's why he came after me. He thought I had the key, and I did."

"You did." Thelonious's voice softened. "Bogey knows more than anyone what it means to be a Mann. He would have seen that in you, Above."

"Oh, yeah?" Rayleigh snorted. "That's why I messed up with D'Leau and didn't see Seamus coming."

"None of us did." Thelonious rested his elbows on the kitchen island. "So don't beat yourself up for it. I know that's why you attended the race, which you should never have been at. Even though I'm awfully flattered you were."

"Hey, I wrote a note."

Thelonious laughed. "Thank goodness for that." He checked his watch. "I need to alert the Quorum and the Spookers. The rest of the Shadow Guild. And, most importantly, I need to get this key out of the book."

"You think Dad hid it in there?"

"He's done things like this before, when we were younger. It's the only proof we have that your dad is your dad, since he doesn't look like himself."

"Why is that?"

"No clue, Nephew-mine. Not yet. It's going to be a busy night."

For Rayleigh too.

There was a decision to be made about his tenure in Below-London. He'd managed to avoid the Citizenship Ceremony, but that wouldn't matter once the smoke settled. The Cabinet would need his answer. He thought leaving was the best thing he could do for his Below family. But the threat against the Above world, his family there, hadn't passed.

"If I returned Above," he broached, setting his tea down, "what would happen with my bent?"

"You'd pass through the Creator, and it would mute it in you once again. You'd be accepting a human version of yourself. Is that what you want?" Thelonious's brows drew together. "If it helps—" His voice lowered. "I'd miss you something terrible, if you left."

Rayleigh took up his tea, sipped. "Just as well I'm staying, then."

There was a beat; Rayleigh braced for a bone-crushing hug from his uncle. Instead he heard sniveling. When he looked up, Thelonious was rubbing his eyes under his sunglasses.

"Are you crying?"

"Might be." Thelonious sniffed. "Nothing wrong with a little eye leakage every now and then. Especially when you're happy. Which I am. Which I want to be for a little while longer, before I have to go and shout at some idiots. I'm very glad you're staying, Nephew-mine."

Rayleigh laughed, happy himself. "You changed my life, Thelonious."

"Nah, kid. You're the one who agreed to come Below. You changed your own life. And I can't wait to see what you choose to do next."

TWENTY-NINE

ILLUSTRIOUS REVELATIONS

L owering his sunglasses, Rayleigh peered up at the lofty silhouettes of palm trees splayed against a cloudless sky. Whoever thought being pooed on was good luck had clearly never mistaken a dollop of it for sun cream. Rayleigh had rubbed a good deal on his stomach before he realized something was very, very wrong.

Why Thelonious would allow birds to ruin the tranquility of his floor, Rayleigh did not know. It was modeled after Negril Beach, in Jamaica. A favorite place of Thelonious's youth before he'd moved Below. It was an oasis of white sand beaches that shimmered like crushed diamonds, a blue sky striated with only the faintest hint of clouds, and the clearest water Rayleigh'd ever seen outside a bath without suds. Marley had been jealous when she and Rayleigh caught up via their comms earlier. With Seamus on the run and capable of phasing through solid objects like locked walls and doors, Marley's ma wanted her home where she could keep an eye on her. There were plans for both families to meet soon—something Rayleigh couldn't wait for. As much as he loved his beachy reward from Thelonious—for his successful trials and imminent citizenship certificate, not to mention his daring rescue, creative genius, and pigheaded determination—it would be great to have his best friend back.

For one thing, he hadn't told her about the Supreme's Key. Thelonious didn't think it wise to talk about such a thing on a device that could have other listeners. Because, as it transpired, *The Book of Night Things* had indeed been concealing the Supreme's Key. A witch friend of Thelonious's who specialized in that sort of thing had used magic to draw it out.

"Like a rabbit," Rayleigh had said.

"That was my comment exactly" had been Thelonious's reply. "Which is why I have a headache. Don't poke fun at any witches, Nephew-mine."

Nana hadn't known anything beyond the book's importance to Bogey, when they'd also caught up. And Rayleigh hadn't known anything beyond its importance to his family, but his uncle was pleased with his guardianship of the book all the same. Respect for oneself was easy, Thelonious had said, as he held an icepack to the back of his head; respect for another was the true mark of character. According to him, Rayleigh's care of *The Book of Night Things* might very well have saved the Confederation from the Illustrious Society.

Rayleigh didn't tell his uncle he'd used the book as a coaster, several times.

Beyond the key, many discussions had been had about the villains' plans, but the Terrors, Rayleigh included, had yet to settle on any one thing so far. And then there were Undersecretary Duplicious and the Chancellor. Thelonious had messengered them over a statement Rayleigh wrote, rather than let them interview Rayleigh at the Cabinet or Terror Tower. Even Marley was made to forget the address of the tower, thanks to a little tincture Mary gave her—after seeking permission from Mrs. Liu. From the wink Marley gave Rayleigh before she jumped into the Vol-way that would take her home, after their rescue of Bogey and Thelonious, he wasn't sure it had worked. Knowing her, she had something in that fanny pack to combat whatever Mary gave her. He hadn't said anything to the Terrors. They were worried enough.

It was clear the Society Seamus served had their sights set on the old Barney Rubble, but what they'd hoped to achieve with Bogey was still a mystery. After Mary was successful in removing the collar from around the Supreme's neck, his appearance was restored to all his golden-eyed Mann glory. Another spell Seamus had commissioned. But, according to Mary, who had sedated Bogey to give his mind time to heal, he had no memory of anything Seamus had him doing while under the collar's influence.

A door shut at Rayleigh's back. He turned to see his uncle coming through the beach hut entrance to his floor. He was a good distance away. Thelonious raised a hand in greeting.

"Let's put you hearing me down to your continued transformation, and not what Shade said about someone of my stature being incapable of creeping." Thelonious sank into the empty lounger beside Rayleigh and clasped his hands across his legs. His shorts were a dark blue, like his nephew's. "Have you moved at all since I saw you for breakfast?"

"Didn't you see the hut's door?"

Rayleigh'd pulled it clean off its hinges earlier.

"The tower likes a challenge. It's already replaced the door with steel instead of wood. I don't think it expects you to defeat it twice. That alone should make you want to try."

Rayleigh slid his sunglasses down his nose to peer at his uncle. "You have a bet going with the others, don't you?"

"Shade might have mentioned a wager regarding your physical transformation. . . ."

"Oh, yeah?" He sat up, interested, and asked a question he'd never have thought himself capable of. "What does Shade think?"

"That your appearance won't change much more than it already has. No surprises there from our eternal optimist. I, on the other hand, believe there's a little more still to come." Thelonious took up a coconut from the base of a neighboring palm tree and punctured it with one of his horns. "You know what that means, don't you?"

"Yeah, yeah. Training, school."

"I was going to say puberty." Thelonious shuddered. "I think I like yours better."

For a moment the sound of waves lapping against the sand filled the silence, but Thelonious had something else to say; the anticipation of it made Rayleigh's skin itch.

"What is it?"

Overhead, a flock of birds left the fronds. The palm's long trunk swayed in their wake.

"Your old man's up, and he wants to see you."

Rayleigh felt light and heavy at the same time. He'd thought a lot about what he wanted to say, of course, and yet he had no idea what to say.

"I don't know where to start."

"Maybe you listen first, and then take it from there?"

Rayleigh picked up the thud of heavier feet against the sand.

"I'll be around afterward, Nephew-mine." Thelonious clasped his shoulder in farewell.

Heart pounding at what would be, quite possibly, the most significant conversation he'd ever had in his life, Rayleigh twisted back around and remained focused on the view as his father sat in the vacated lounger.

He was hit by a sudden, inappropriate desire to laugh.

"You saved me," Bogey finally said in a smoky rumble. "I don't know how to thank you, son. I haven't the words, and I know I owe you more than that. . . . Thelonious tells me you're aware that I can't remember much about my time with Seamus, or what I was doing before he captured me."

Rayleigh nodded. Mary suspected it was the charge of Volence injected into his spinal cord each time Seamus used the remote. It needed to travel into his brain to dull his thoughts. They could return, but it was likelier that they'd never find out the entire truth.

"I do know that I missed picking you up on your twelfth All Hallows' Eve, and for that, I am sorrier than you know."

For the first time, Rayleigh twisted to look at his dad. He thought it would have been easier before, when he looked nothing like his portrait—muddy eyes instead of golden ones, and the unfortunate mug of the monster he was inhabiting. But there was something comforting about their matching features. And he wore shorts. It was hard to be intimidating with your knees and ankles out.

"You couldn't help it. And now, you know, we have time."

Bogey nodded; relief flashed across his face. "I'm looking forward to nothing but time with you." After a moment's hesitation, he sank back in his lounger; for a time, father and son lay side by side, that chasm not gaping as much as it initially had.

"Did Thelonious tell you about your key?"

"Oh, yes. Thank you for keeping it safe for me. I knew you would."

"How?"

"Well—" Bogey turned onto his side; Rayleigh did too, so that they were facing one another. "Sometimes, when Mama would read to you, I'd be there."

"Where? In the flat?"

"Yes. I suppose you know now that my bent is sorcery. A little enchantment, and I can go where I please without being identified. My favorite place was your front room when Mama read to you. I saw how you reacted to the stories, how they fascinated you. More than that, I saw how close you were with your nana. The book I knew you would keep safe, Below, because it was a part of you. Of you and Nana, your mama, and even me. Though, you didn't know it yet. Our history as a family is in those pages. I trusted you to respect that. It doesn't surprise me to learn you did."

Rayleigh's warmth had nothing to do with the tropical conditions on the floor. Thelonious had said as much, but it was another thing entirely to have it confirmed by his dad.

"Here I worried you would come Below, and our family name would garner attention for you. But I see you'll get enough of that on your own."

"Oh, because of the race?" *The Vulture Culture* had reported Rayleigh's flight over the Province of Despair, his fall, and the standoff with the Captain of the Cabinet's Guard—until news of a disturbance in the Cabinet itself drew the attention away from him. They had yet to place him there too, for which he was relieved.

"Which race?" Bogey asked.

Before Rayleigh could answer (he had a feeling they were referencing different things), the ocean ahead arched into a small hill. Thelonious stood beneath it. His eyes bounced from Bogey to Rayleigh, who nodded that all was well.

"There's something you both need to see."

Rayleigh accepted a hoodie from his uncle as he passed by, trailing sand into the snug. He nodded his hellos to the other Terrors. They all looked as grim faced as Thelonious. He perched on the arm of one of the red cinema seats beside Mary. Bogey took up a place behind his son. Winsome, leaning against the back wall by the door, waved two fingers Rayleigh's way. He nodded back, still not yet used to the supersized fairy walking free in Terror Tower, now that the secret was out of the bulb.

The Seer's Eye was on the news channel again. The reporter was issuing a statement with a dire stiffness of expression.

"For those tuning in after the weather, we can now confirm that the body of Captain Seamus Scáthach has been found inside his townhouse, located in the Province of—"

"He's dead?" Bogey remarked.

All the warmth Rayleigh'd amassed during his time on his uncle's floor melted away.

"Wait for it," Thelonious said.

"Be warned," continued the reporter. "The next details are graphic. Poltergeists, as a rule, do not decompose like the majority of the Confederation residents. Largely due to the fact that they're already dead. But a consultant necromancer has stated, with confidence, that the Captain has been dead for some time."

"Hang on a minute—" Rayleigh began.

"Wait for it, Nephew-mine."

"Which begs the question—" A still of Rayleigh and the Captain facing off in Despair during the Horned Heat appeared beside the reporter. "Who is this monster with the son of the Bogey Mann?"

Bogey shifted closer to the projection. "That's not Seamus?"

"Thanks to a source inside the Cabinet, we can confidently report that our Bogey Mann has returned from his time away. But the reappearance of the Supreme Scarer cannot distract us from the showdown between this monster, who looks like the Captain, and Rayleigh Mann, the Supreme's son. Especially when it was reported that another disturbance took place in the Cabinet. We here at *The Vulture Culture* demand answers. We demand the truth." The still of Rayleigh, captured by some sort of drone perhaps, expanded until Seamus was cut out entirely. As was the reporter. Rayleigh was the sole focus of the image, in his long coat, lumicand in hand, and a righteous anger on his face. He swallowed as the reporter issued his final statement. "We demand Rayleigh Mann come forward as a suspect in the death of Seamus Scáthach and collusion with an impostor."

Bogey shifted. "Ridiculous."

"A suspect?" Rayleigh surged to his feet, alarmed.

Gasp touched the Eye, and the white cloud withdrew back into the orb.

"It won't stick, kid," Thelonious said. "I understand you're upset, but, as usual, the news is burying the lede."

Bogey moved to stand by his son. "What could be more important than Rayleigh's safety?"

"Nothing." Thelonious looked up at his brother, sunglasses flashing. "This danger has Rayleigh very much at the center. Seamus is dead, Bogey. He has been for a long time. How, then, was another

Seamus dragging you all over the city for several weeks? How was he maintaining not one, but two disguises?"

"I told you I can't remember anything."

"Oh, I'm sorry. That question was hypothetical. We know the answer."

Charged, the atmosphere between the two brothers tightened to a breaking point.

"We thought he was using a witch," Mary intervened. "But identity concealment for you and himself, possible murder, and then the combination of time and space magic he used on Rayleigh leads us to think he isn't. That's too much for a witch. Even a spell caster."

"But easy enough for a sorcerer," Rayleigh stated. "Right?" World builders, Winsome had said. He looked over at her, picking her nails in the corner as though she'd rather be anywhere else. "You think Seamus is a sorcerer. The impostor."

"Oh, far worse," Thelonious sighed. "His interest in the key gave him away. His interest in you, big brother."

"I don't understand." Bogey looked from Rayleigh to the Terrors. "He's a sorcerer, so what? I am too. I can find the impostor and—"

"End up trapped again?" Thelonious shook his head. "Seamus isn't just a sorcerer, can't you see? He's strong. Without scruples. He ran circles around you, Bogey, which suggests he is an extremely learned and scholarly magic practitioner. That comes with time, education."

"Patience," Rayleigh added, remembering what Seamus said to him in the ghostly Cabinet.

"For goodness' sake," Winsome cut in. "Can't you just say you think he's one of the Illustrious Three and get on with it?"

Rayleigh glanced around the room at the Terrors; only his dad looked stunned.

"No." Bogey shook his head. "They're imprisoned."

"Checked in on them lately, have you?" Shade drawled. "No disrespect meant, Supreme. I can't tell you the last time I've heard of *anyone* looking in on them."

"In that case, I think our best bet would be to—" Bogey broke off when he noticed that all present were looking to his younger brother for answers.

Thelonious took his time, scratching a horn absentmindedly.

"Do you know where the Illustrious Three are imprisoned?" Rayleigh asked.

"I don't have the foggiest, Nephew-mine," Thelonious said. "That was the point, you see. No one would know everything about their internment, so no one would be able to free them. But someone might have figured it out, if they spoke with enough people. If they looked hard enough, hunted." He rose to stand. His shorts, knees, and ankles did not affect his commanding manner. Not when his horns glinted beneath the lights in the ceiling. And not when his sunglasses flashed with menace. "And we, Terrors, need to learn how. If Seamus, the impostor Seamus that is, is one of the Illustrious Three, we know exactly what he plans on doing next."

That would be locating the other two, Rayleigh understood.

Because while the best things came in threes, Below, so did the worst.

EPILOGUE

A GHOSTLY TALE

Atop a craggy, windswept hill in an inconsequential town at the back end of a place few had heard of, and even fewer cared about, the ruins of a manor perched on the edge of an old fort.

The monster who had stolen the identity of Seamus Scáthach still bore his face and body. More ghost than corporeal man, sorcerer, he drifted through the crumbling rooms. They were gutted and graffitied by local tearaways. Despise bovers though he did, he couldn't hold them entirely accountable. Monsters from the Confederation had found the Illustrious Society HQ first. They were the ones who'd burned it back to its studs.

Each visit Seamus made, his mouth still soured with the bitter taste of ash and dashed hopes. He remembered when dappled light from chandeliers danced across the decadent furnishings and he was a member of an exclusive club of monsters set to extinguish the candle that lit the world. Dimming it, as it longed to be.

From the outlook of one of the upper rooms, gaping and forlorn, Seamus took in the unfettered dark of the countryside. Starless and without streetlights, the Above world had never looked riper for the picking.

A rich wind blustered behind him, carrying the unmistakable sweet tang of magic.

"You're late," he drawled, not turning to face his visitor.

"If we delay this reading for the purpose of your ego, you'll be the late one, boy."

Seamus started at the impertinence, rounding with his full authority. He soon thought better of the tirade at the tip of his tongue, however, when he beheld his appointment.

A wizened dark-skinned witch sat across from him behind a table bedecked in all manner of curious objects. White whorls of flaking paint covered her bare shoulders and neck in an intricate dance of patterns and symbols; in the center of her forehead, a finely drawn white eye stared down at him—it matched the two alabaster orbs in her face.

She was a Seer. And one from a Caribbean Below city, at that.

"My apologies." Seamus's coat caught around his ankles in his haste to bow low. To anger a Seer almost guaranteed that his future would be altered for the worse. Magic was magic, whichever continent it came from. "I wasn't aware I'd be in such fine company."

"My bottom's just fine without you plastering your lips to it."

His mouth curled in disgust. "I was told you had information of interest."

Her foggy eyes dipped to the animal-skin cloth before her. A wooden bowl rested atop it, filled with shells, white stones, and a long dark feather tipped with gold. "I can show you your future, should you be ready for answers to your questions."

Seamus closed the space between them, seized the bowl, and tossed the contents onto the cloth. "Tell me what stands between the Illustrious Society and complete power."

A golden coin the size of a goose egg illuminated on a chain around the Seer's neck as she hummed, gnarled fingers running across the items.

"Power is a door, and only one has its key."

"Who?"

"One who could use it to unite the four realms."

"Who?"

The Seer held up a hand to silence him.

"One with a choice to make."

Seamus breathed through his nose, fighting for patience. "Yes. Who?" he ground out.

"How am I supposed to know? They haven't cast the bowl, you have. I can only see that they're someone you've already met and been thwarted by. Without caution, you'll find yourself hitting that brick wall once again. And let me tell you, I will be the first one to laugh."

Seamus's body chilled; the skin it looked as though he didn't have, in his current disguise, pimpled into gooseflesh.

Someone you've already met and been thwarted by.

Could the insufferable witch be referring to Rayleigh Mann? He'd been able to think of little else since their showdown in the Monsters Cabinet . . . since he was forced to reveal his allegiances. Seamus, the Captain, had been an easy role to play. Not simply because he was overlooked. There were few monsters who could get away with touching a poltergeist without its permission. Even the faked one his magic allowed him to imitate. For the boy to play a greater role in ruining his plans than he already had was a problem.

He paced to the edge of the ruined room to stare down into the shadowed garden, as if he could see through all the layers of rock and dirt to where Rayleigh Mann lived with the Terrors somewhere Below-London. He was so preoccupied with compiling plans and schemes, he didn't notice the small smile on the Seer's face.

Only one face flooded his thoughts, and one goal—capturing Rayleigh Mann, silencing him, before all the Illustrious Society's plans came to naught.

He never could stand the impertinence of children.

Acknowledgments

Rayleigh Mann's story is a dream fulfilled, and a story that wouldn't have been possible without the village I'm fortunate enough to have in my life:

Thank you, firstly, to my family, who have championed Rayleigh from the very beginning. Particularly my mum, who knows, above all else, what his character, his world, means to me. And for those of you who haven't read it (Christopher and Calvin Smart, I'm looking at you), your excitement is appreciated—but your expressions will be better, dear brothers, once you've read these acknowledgments.

While this story encapsulates much of what *I* love about magical worlds, this adventure is also for my littlest monsters, Marley and Raphael Smart. You were far tinier when I envisioned writing a story in which the two of you could see yourselves as heroes, but I hope you carry the message of this book with you always. Being your Cool Aunt is my pride and joy. Love you, little monsters. And to my big monsters, Diaz and Neveah—I haven't forgotten about you. Rayleigh Mann has more stories to come.

In this weird publishing biz, I am grateful to have a formidable agency team to don their armor and ride into battle with and for me. To my agent, Suzie Townsend, Rayleigh came to you with a home already, but you have supported him, as you support me in all things. Thank you for being the sword and shield I need, always. And Sophia Ramos, thank you for being the axis upon which we all turn, for the DM lols, and for caringly hacking away at this book in the final hour. I'm so grateful to be part of Team NewLeaf. Thank you, too, to Taylor Haggerty and Root Literary, who championed Rayleigh in the beginning.

And speaking of teams, this is my third book with both my US and UK publishing houses. It feels apt that a story in which the number three plays such a pivotal role takes bronze. Huge thank-you to my Harper editor, Alice Jerman. Your love for this story is second only to your patience as my right hand in all things fantastical. Thank you for believing in Rayleigh, and me, as you do; for humoring every joke like a true Brit; and for accompanying me on every hairbrained scheme I have, whether it be witches or monsters. Thank you, Clare Vaughn, for your support and your passion, felt in everything you do. To the amazing design team, Chris Kwon and Alison Donalty, who spoiled me yet again with a brilliant cover, thank you. As for the cover illustrations: Raymond Sebastien, you have brought Rayleigh to life like no other. Thank you for the added afro pick, which encapsulates the care and understanding you took with my cast and world. I can't wait to see your designs for book two! To managing editorial, who came back for more after editing my last book—which, while not solely about monsters, was monstrous in size—thank you, Jessica Berg, Gwen Morton, Ana Deboo, and Dan Janeck for the attention and meticulous edits. Mary Ann Seagren, with a name like that I have to thank you for catching all that slipped through the net in the final hour. To production, Sean Cavanagh and Vanessa Nuttry, thank you for all you have done for Rayleigh.

As mentioned, this is my third book with my UK home, but my first with Ella Whiddet and Picadilly Press—something that doesn't feel quite true since, Ella, working with you has been a dream from the moment we were introduced. Thank you for welcoming my characters and me as warmly as you have; for the support and wisdom you have offered, and the excitement for Rayleigh. I'm so grateful to have you on my side, along with familiar talented faces such as Isobel Taylor and Tia Albert, from my Hot Key Family. Many of whom are working on this book, as you have my others. Thank you for being such a steadfast team, not to mention a pleasure to work with.

Developing Rayleigh wouldn't have been possible without early readers such as the hilarious and talented Kylie Schachte and Harps Aujla. Thank you both for your feedback, your support, and your enthusiasm so early on. Equally, thank you to Dhonielle Clayton for your endless support in all things I write. The fact that you're not tired of me yet is nothing short of surprising. I am happy to know you, and better still, to call you a friend. And thank you to Kwame Mbalia, another author whom I admire, who took the time to read Rayleigh—and liked him. Even better. To Charlotte Reynolds, I can't believe that in a few years, Beau will be able to read Rayleigh. Something that excites me to no end; I'm grateful to know you, and to have your friendship. Encouraging your son to be a little naughty in life, through Rayleigh, feels like a fair trade off. Deborah Falaye-Savoy, can you believe we're here? Meeting you and having your support has been life-changing. Just as well I don't plan on letting you go anywhere. To my UK YA author friends, and US YA author friends, as well as those around the world, thank you for all the DMs, commiserations, and congratulations.

And lastly, to you, Dearest Reader I hope I hope this story gives the different among you, the shelved, a chance to been seen as you deserve: the hero of your story.

Always remember to Walk With Courage.